W9-AVR-992

# THE LAKE CHAMPLAIN MYSTERIES

# CRIMSON SNOW

## WILLIAM KRITLOW

WITHDRAWN

SOMERSET COUNTY LIBRARY
6022 GLADES PIKE, SUITE 120
SOMERSET, PA 15501-4300
(814) 445-5907

Publishers Since 1798

**THOMAS NELSON PUBLISHERS**
Nashville • Atlanta • London • Vancouver

*Dedication*
*Like everything I do,*
*this book is dedicated to my Lord first,*
*my wife second,*
*my shrink third.*

DEC 1 2000

Copyright © 1995 by William Kritlow

All rights reserved. Written permission must be secured from the publisher to use or reproduce any part of this book, except for brief quotations in critical reviews or articles.

Published in Nashville, Tennessee, by Thomas Nelson, Inc., Publishers, and distributed in Canada by Word Communications, Ltd., Richmond, British Columbia, and in the United Kingdom by Word (UK), Ltd., Milton Keynes, England.

Scripture quotations are taken from the HOLY BIBLE, NEW INTERNATIONAL VERSION ®. Copyright © 1973, 1978, 1984 by International Bible Society. Used by permission of Zondervan Bible Publishing House. All rights reserved.

The "NIV" and "New International Version" trademarks are registered in the United States Patent and Trademark Office by International Bible Society. Use of either trademark requires the permission of International Bible Society.

Library of Congress Cataloging-in-Publication Data
Kritlow, William.
Crimson snow : a novel / William Kritlow.
    p.    cm. —(Lake Champlain mysteries ; bk. 1)
ISBN 0-7852-8098-7
    1. Clergy—New England—Fiction. I. Title. II. Series: Kritlow, William. Lake Champlain mysteries ; bk. 1.
PS3561.R567C75  1995
813'.54—dc20                                        94-25844
                                                            CIP

Printed in the United States of America
1 2 3 4 5 6 7 - 01 00 99 98 97 96 95

Chapter 1

Brandon Harp had been Martin Sorrell's chauffeur for three months, and he knew, beyond any doubt, that this Saturday night would be his last night employed. Harp was drunk. Had he been driving his weather-beaten Chevy, he wouldn't have cared—but he wasn't. He'd taken Sorrell's limousine, a leather-lined stretch Lincoln, without permission. His goal had been to get his date into the sprawling backseat—but he hadn't. Drowning his disappointment in half the booze in Burlington, Vermont, he still thought he might get away with having "stolen" the limo had the weather held—but it didn't. As he warmed his favorite bar stool, the roads disappeared beneath fresh mountains of white.

At 2 A.M. the curtain of flakes thinning, the plows through only an hour before, driving was treacherous when sober, death-defying when drunk. But he'd made it through the network of streets in Burlington and safely onto a deserted Highway 7. A breath of confidence returned.

Finally on Highway 2, his tension dribbled away. This two-lane road meandered north up the Grand Isles, a string of irregular pearls that hung down the middle of Lake Champlain from Canada. Perpetually in a vacation laze, the islands would be snoring peacefully at 2 A.M., and driving past the houses speckled with Christmas lights would be a piece of cake. Even his employer would be asleep, and Harp could traverse the broad meadow surrounding Sorrell's inn undetected.

A few hundred yards later, just before a stand of snow-laden trees, he glanced in his rearview mirror. Off the road, back near Sugar Steeple Church, a set of headlights flicked on. Without regard for the danger heaped all around, they pulsed and jarred erratically toward the highway. Accelerating when they hit it, they overswung recklessly, then swung back—now moving toward Harp. Within seconds they were gaining on him.

Astonished at the driver's death wish, Harp kept blurred eyes on the mirror—too long. His right fender scraped a freshly plowed wall of snow. He recovered quickly and saw the other car pull up and plow around him. For an incomprehensible instant the glare of mud-sprayed paint came alongside and cut in front of him—too close.

Harp pulled the car to the right. A shock of white and the limousine burst through the hood-high drift and pounded through the meadow. Adrenalin swept away alcohol as Harp slammed the brake pedal to the floor.

Too hard.

Bumper-deep snow flared, then piled up on the passenger side as the limo's extended rear swung uncontrollably. For a moment Harp thought the car might still escape any real damage. But that dream lasted only until he heard the scream of tearing metal. The rear of the car slammed into the one tree in the meadow. Harp sat for a moment, eyes blurred by the wet windshield, watching his job and two crimson taillights fade to black.

"So this is how he repays me." Pastor J. Sanders "Worlly" Worlton groaned. Worlly's groans boiled up more frequently these days, all in response to the antics of Dan Bryce, his young assistant. He stood beside his chief trustee, Charlie Briggs, who fidgeted with a set of keys. Worlly eyed the keys irritatingly then fished out his gold pocket watch. He flipped the engraved cover and stared at the Roman numerals in anger. After snapping it shut with a flourish, he raised impatient eyes. "Five minutes and we're on." He sighed. "And I've done so much for him." He added, steel eyes on the rattling keys, "Do you have to do that?"

"Yes," Briggs replied, continuing the symphony unchecked.

Worlly's flushed round cheeks and thick, puffy brows added

at least a little color and character to his six-foot, predominantly marshmallowy, physique. Briggs, on the other hand, looked like a living nail—thin, driven, and iron hard. The two very different men stood in the waiting room separated from the sanctuary by a thick oak door.

Worlly loved this room. At times, even during the week, he'd just sit in it. Four soft white fluorescent tubes, one on each wall, each hidden near the ceiling by an ornately carved ledge, formed an ethereal halo for him, their glow restful—heavenly. When taken with its white walls and the comfortable aroma of thick, ancient enamel, the room soothed Worlly. The world outside and its tension died away—there was suddenly no God, no responsibility, and certainly no congregation. That's why, even though in the past few months Dan Bryce had caused him no end of trouble, Worlly hated him more now than ever before. His tardiness had disturbed the peace of Worlly's white sanctuary. Even more than Briggs's jingling keys.

"The collection plate will be lighter 'cause of this," Briggs said, the weight of his words causing the slight stoop in his shoulders to become even more pronounced.

"I have a backup sermon," Worlly affirmed. Then he added, "The keys . . ."

Briggs grunted but slipped the keys into his suit coat pocket. The silence grew thick. Briggs broke it. "It'll look like a mistake—like we don't know what we're about. Maybe people won't give as much." Then he added with wagging head, "Why in heaven's name did you give your pulpit away on the Sunday before Christmas?"

"A weak moment," Worlly admitted darkly. "My relationship with Bryce has deteriorated so much lately that when he asked I thought it might help."

"*This* won't help," Charlie grumbled, running a bony hand through thin, iron gray hair. "And I liked him at first."

A subdued knock rattled the hallway door.

A single step, and Charlie opened it.

Maggie Selkirk stood there, her apologetic expression

framed by mousy brown hair, her befuddled eyes peering up at Charlie from beneath a pronounced cliff of it. She waited to be acknowledged, afraid she might be interrupting. Maggie never interrupted, not out of respect or courtesy, but because Maggie simply never interrupted.

"Find him?" Charlie asked.

"He's not at his apartment," she said in her small, intimidated voice. "I called. Maybe he's caught in the snow."

"It's not snowing," Charlie stated as if speaking to a fool.

Maggie caught her breath, "I know, but maybe . . ."

"Well, if he is stuck, I hope he's got blankets," Worlly said flatly.

Sugar Steeple, Vermont, on Lake Champlain's Grand Isles, knew harsh winters: deep, arctic snow, severe winds that swept angrily off the water driving icy spikes into the bones, and air so cold that nostrils froze shut at a single breath. But not this winter. Although there had been great piles of snow, the winds had been unusually subdued, at times even warm. Lake Champlain had failed to freeze over only a handful of times in its known history, and this year was one of those times. More snow had fallen last night. Large, wet flakes started early. Although plows appeared quickly to clear the roads, traps lurked everywhere, covered by packed snow, hidden in embankments, all made even more dangerous by the penetrating cold.

"He's not a Vermonter," Maggie said with a touch of defiance—all she could muster. "He's from Florida—maybe we ought to go looking . . ."

"Nonsense," Charlie said firmly, "we've got a service."

Maggie swallowed hard. As head deacon, her job was caring about people. Danny was very special—at least to her. "We should look for him," Maggie said, eyes on her shoes. She raised them, pleading. "It's Christmas and it's near zero outside."

"Christmas or not," Worlly pronounced, inflating himself importantly—an attitude he struck when determined to avoid either discomfort or work. "Flatlanders must learn. Especially this one." He turned cool, haughty eyes toward Charlie. "We'll go on."

Defeated, worried, more lost than usual, Maggie watched the door close in her face. After studying the white enamel in front of her nose for a long moment, she finally turned her back to it and faced another door. Hope sparked. The door across the hall led to a familiar place for her and Danny. She crossed quickly to it.

In the front of the church, families, couples, and an occasional single person stomped snow-laden boots on their way up the six broad, wooden steps. Reaching the cement landing, they gave them a final shake before continuing onto the lobby's richly surfaced oak floor. Some shed coats and boots and deposited them in the cloakroom while others, still chilled, kept coats on and let metal boot buckles slap raucously on their way down the aisle.

Bill Simms slid into the same pew he'd been sliding into all his life. Sugar Steeple Community Church, built in the mid-1880s, had been his family's church from the beginning. In his early thirties, Bill's coal black hair and gray eyes gave highlight to the forest green Pendleton and charcoal slacks he wore. He looked good. He liked looking good, and he liked this invigorating cold morning. He also liked the role he played in the church and felt a pride when the pews were filled as they probably would be this morning. He looked around satisfied.

On cue, Worlly and Briggs stepped in from the pulpit side entrance. Bill laughed to himself—both looked like ravens: Worlly in a flowing black robe, a yellow velvet stripe about the collar for accent, Briggs in a black double-breasted suit. The only things missing were green eyeshades.

*No Bryce—strange*, Bill thought. He'd heard that Bryce had asked Worlly for permission to preach and that he had been working on his message all week. He had also heard that Charlie had been against it. Maybe he'd prevailed at the last minute.

An imposing personage invaded the corner of Bill's eye. Draped in violet, her massive chest adorned with strand upon strand of pearls, Roz Swift swaggered in. Rooted deeply in her mid-forties, Roz viewed the world through dark, hawkish eyes—instinctively predatory, they darted here and there taking in everything. Satisfied that all was as it should be, she sat where she always sat, behind Bill—a habit that made Bill nervous.

Bill heard Roz's pew groan under her weight, a signal for him to glance back with a stiff smile of welcome. "Ready for Bryce's exposé?" she asked wickedly.

"What are you talking about?" he asked. Over her shoulder he saw Sandy Sweet in the doorway. Delectably beautiful in her simple cream sweater and blouse and brown skirt, she was framed there for an instant—as lovely and delicate as any painting. *She's alone*, Bill mused, his lips pursed in gratified appraisal. *Peter must have opened their candy store instead of coming to church. If only I weren't already involved* . . .

Moon-eyed, he felt Roz's imposing glare and realized he was staring. He reestablished his stiff smile, nodded congenially at Roz, and turned around, eyes forward.

Although most older regulars wintered in Florida, it being Christmas, their numbers were replaced by the less-than-regular, so the pews were filled when the service began. As always, it started with the first three verses of a traditional hymn followed by the congregation reading a prayer of confession. The sins they confessed were always the same: not loving enough and gossiping. But then something altered the routine. In the middle of the second hymn the organ seemed to emit a curiously harsh, unusually penetrating sound. Yet it wasn't the organ. When the music died the high-pitched wail continued—pulsing and frantic. Heads turned toward the back of the sanctuary.

Bill cocked his head and identified the sound. It was a scream—visceral, terrified, supported by every sinew the frightened screamer possessed. Though muted by century-old wood, the very persistence of it unnerved him. At first the congregation sat stunned. Then a guy in the back pew scrambled past an elderly woman who was between him and the aisle and darted outside. The moment he cleared the sanctuary door, the rest of the congregation followed. Bill now became part of the anxious crowd, surging into the aisles toward the rear doors. As they went, heads asked other heads what was going on and still other heads replied they didn't know, but for all their ignorance, they chattered and bantered nervously back and forth, herding themselves out.

When Bill made it to the steps he called out, "What's going on?"

"She's up there." Someone pointed.

All eyes followed. To the side of the church stood an old bell tower. The bells had been silenced for a decade, but the tower remained. A woman now stood at the single, small, upper-story window, her arm pointing toward the ground, her screams exploding in quick gasps.

"It's Maggie. What in heaven's name?"

"What you screamin' at, Maggie?"

But she didn't answer. She only pointed and screamed.

Someone near the base of the tower cried, "There's someone back here, in the snow."

Maggie kept screaming. She couldn't help herself. She knew how silly she must sound. But rivers of electricity surged through her, and although she desperately wanted to stop it seemed that screaming was the only way to keep from exploding. Knots of people began to gather around the horror she'd seen.

In the snow was a man-shaped depression like the imprint of a grotesque cookie cutter in white dough, an image of arms, legs, head, and body. Someone lay in that depression, a few hours' snowfall as his or her blanket.

The instant others knew what Maggie knew, she felt able to catch her breath. Her screams died to a desperate whimper. Although there was no way she could see who lay there, she knew who it was. Dear Danny lay cold beneath the snow. Dear, dear Danny . . .

# Chapter 2

**D**etective Bray Sanderson peered through the ice-etched windshield with battle-weary eyes. Before getting into the car, he'd carefully wrapped his thickly lined London Fog around him, and it kept at least some of the chill at bay. His fur-lined gloves eased the freezing steering wheel around as he parked his black Scirocco near the church's front steps. However, not even the fur cap could keep his newly emerging patch of bald warm. Age was getting the better of him, and he didn't have the energy to fight back. In all his life he'd never been so grateful for a working heater. It blew hot air at him full blast, and he hated to leave it.

The blue shirts and coroner were already there. Ninety-odd members of the police department and most of them seemed to be here—ants—crawling over everything, messing it up. Their cars, white Chevy Caprices with blue and green stripes down the side, both cut by huge 911s branded there, were stacked everywhere. The bubbles on top flashed a red and blue that danced with mock cheer across a stage of piled white.

The moment Bray's boots crunched against the snow, weariness became irritation. This crime was causing a glitch in his world. Sanderson grew up on logic. After studying math at the University of Vermont for a while, he chose police work. He found it exciting to see clues uncovered and interpreted and lead like logical footprints to an arrest.

But a murder in a church wasn't logical. It was insane.

Cold attacked his skin like a cheese grater. That morning, the instant his feet hit a frozen hardwood floor, he'd made the decision he made every Christmas. Florida. There had to be at least one constable's job down there, perhaps a nice easy one in a senior citizen community. Herding old folks around can't be all bad.

Before Bray could move far from his car, Officer Ginger Glasgow stepped up. Ginger was tall, with angular, Scandinavian features, and a puff of blonde hair escaping from the back of her fur hat. To everyone else she was beautiful. To Sanderson she was just a blue shirt who sometimes did her job and sometimes nearly did it. Just like the weapon she wore, a Glock 9mm. He wore a Smith & Wesson .357 Magnum. You knew when you shot a Magnum. "Glasgow," Bray greeted flatly. They didn't shake hands. "That eight-year-old son of yours still a handful?"

"He's ten and yes."

Sanderson nodded with an emotionless grunt. "Now, who died?"

"Daniel Bryce—the assistant pastor."

"Bad sermon?"

"Broken neck, we think."

"A fall?"

Ginger shrugged. "That's why you're here."

It was indeed. Sanderson was from homicide. "One of God's finest do it?" he asked with heavy sarcasm, a critical eye on the ragged congregation huddled behind the yellow police ribbon. He turned his attention to the ambulance attendants placing the frozen body on a gurney. "What about photos?"

"The photographer did a thorough job," Ginger said.

"You saw the pictures?"

"Some of them—he's around back now."

"Are those body jockeys messing anything up?" Sanderson dared her to tell him they were.

"No. The pictures were complete." Then she added, "There wasn't much to see anyway."

"There doesn't need to be," Sanderson said pointedly. "I want to see them."

"I'll get what he's taken so far." Glasgow hurried away.

Sanderson hated churches—hated everything they stood for:

superstition, oppression, surrender. Sanderson eyed the on-lookers again. The congregation, ragtag at best, looked more cold than caring. Some stood bundled in coats and boots, while others, the hearty or the foolish, huddled stiffly in shirt-sleeves and dresses. Others milled inside at the windows, their warm breath fogging the glass. White palms wiped them frequently. "Shouldn't they be praying or somethin'?" he muttered to a blue shirt who happened by. "They pray for everything—a long putt, a parking space for cryin' out loud. Somebody's dead here; shouldn't they be praying?"

The blue shirt shrugged disinterestedly as Sanderson turned his attention to the church structure itself. Like most rural New England churches, it was white and boxy with a steep roof piled high with undisturbed snow, and a steeple on the side that topped a three-story tower. Below the tower the body had lain.

Glasgow crunched up. "Here are the pictures." She handed him a fistful of Polaroids.

The photographer, someone whose name he never could pronounce, knew his business. He'd taken pictures of the twisted remains from every conceivable angle and distance. First as a depression in the snow, with a thin layer of snow covering it. Then as a body, cold and still, emerging from the white. Some showed Bryce's face. In this case it was neither peaceful nor violent, it neared disinterest as if death had come mid-thought. Sanderson came to a long shot. "Whose foot-prints are these?"

"Don't know," Ginger answered stiffly.

Sanderson turned and addressed the crowd. "Which one of you approached the body before we got here?"

Worly stepped forward and stood at the yellow police ribbon. He tried to appear rock solid, but failed. "I checked to see if he was still alive."

Sanderson took a couple of steps toward Worly. "Who are you?"

"Pastor Worlton."

"You run this place?"

"I'm the pastor here, yes."

Sanderson nodded vacantly. "What did you find?"

"He was dead." Worlly replied, glancing to where the body had been.

"Did you disturb anything—footprints maybe?"

"No. Nothing."

Glasgow reaffirmed, "No footprints."

Sanderson nodded as if assimilating the information then turned back toward the church. Worlly returned unthanked to his disheveled flock.

Sanderson said to Glasgow, "He either flew there on the wings of angels—or he fell." Sanderson looked to the roof. No snow appeared to be disturbed there. Then he turned to the tower. "That's a pretty small window up there. But I suppose . . ."

"One of the congregation," Ginger consulted a notepad, "Mrs. Maggie Selkirk spotted him from up there."

"Selkirk Ford?" Sanderson didn't wait for an answer, but instantly turned a critical eye on Ginger. "Why was she up there?"

"I don't know," Ginger answered, a sheepishness entering her voice. Instantly she regretted it. As a woman in a predominantly male profession she worked at sounding strong. Now she sounded weak, but she couldn't help it.

"Didn't you ask?"

"No," she replied, now thoroughly pushed down.

"You told me once you wanted to be a detective. Detectives ask the right questions." The brief lecture over, Sanderson glanced at the tower again. "What reason would she have to be up there on a morning like this one?"

Ginger said nothing.

"I'm going up," Sanderson stated. "Find her and send her up."

Just inside the tower door, Sanderson peered up the vertical corridor. A thick post provided center support for the stairs that wound steeply to the ceiling high above. Cold, void of air, the place smelled of age and crumbling wood. To keep from ruining any fingerprints, Sanderson took a pen and flipped a cheap plastic light switch just inside the door. A bare bulb, perched high on the wall, lighted. Though it gave little light now, when the stairwell was midnight black it was probably adequate. Wood creaking beneath his weight, Sanderson ascended. The stairs finally reached a small landing and a door.

The door opened with a tortured squeal onto a small square room. Perhaps ten feet on a side, it reminded him of the attic in the small farmhouse where he'd grown up. It was dark, musty, void of furniture. Home to cobwebs, bare studs, and damp chills. And wood. Ancient wood, worn smooth in the well-traveled places, agonizingly rough in the others. His footsteps were hollow echoes as he crossed to the window. From it he could see, quite distinctly, what was left of the impression the body had made in the snow.

He looked up. Two bells hung only a few feet over his head. They looked in good condition, but the rope was piled on a crossbeam high out of reach, and the belfry openings from which the sound would reach out to the countryside were boarded up. These bells would disturb no more Sunday mornings.

The door squealed again, and a slight woman with mousy brown hair stood there. She shivered beneath a heavy coat and waited for him to speak.

"Who are you?" Sanderson asked coldly.

"Maggie Selkirk," she offered, her lower lip quivering, probably more nervous than cold.

"You the wife of the guy who owns the Ford dealership?"

"John Selkirk, yes," she said as if she found the question repulsive.

"Are you the one who first saw the body?"

She nodded.

"That must have been a shock."

"Yes," she said, eyes slightly away from him.

"Please look me in the eye when you answer."

Like soldiers coming to attention, her eyes shifted just enough to obey.

"Why were you up here?"

Surprised by the question, she hesitated as if trying to figure it out herself. Sanderson saw the hesitation as having all the earmarks of a lie in the making.

"I'm the head deacon and Danny was missing. He wasn't at home so I thought he might be up here. He'd come here sometimes to be alone. Sometimes I talked with him here. Sometimes he'd lose track of time. He was a little disorganized, and this was an important day for him."

If a lie, she told it well.

"Why talk here? Why not his office?"

"This was more private."

"Why privacy?"

"People were always barging into his office, and if at the wrong time they could hear things they weren't supposed to."

"Like what?"

"Things. Things you tell your pastor or your deacon—money things, counseling needs."

"Real private stuff."

"He's a pastor. People have problems."

"Did *you* have problems?"

"Me?" A hesitation—a dart of the eyes. "No. No problems."

A lie. Bray could hardly contain himself. Was hers a problem severe enough to kill for? He studied her face for a moment but saw nothing there. Turning back to the window he surveyed the scene below. Glasgow was dutifully taking names and addresses. If someone didn't jump forward and confess it would be a long investigation—if Bryce was really murdered.

"What problem do you have?" he asked, turning back to her.

"I told you—no problem."

"Did you love Bryce?" Now he turned. "Did your husband find out about it?"

"What?" Maggie showed the first sign of real life. But it disappeared as quickly as it came. "It wouldn't matter to him anyway—but, no, there was nothing between Danny and me. He was just a very nice guy. Very nice." She rubbed her shoulders as if to ward off a sudden chill.

Bray turned back to the window. "What about all of them down there? Anyone else have problems?"

"Everybody has problems," she pointed out, her eyes still away from him.

"Bad ones?"

Taking the sense of his question, she shook her head. "They didn't like him much, at least some of them, but . . ." her voice trailed away in a thought.

"You said this was a special day for him. Why?"

"His first sermon. He'd been here nine months or so, and this was his first time in the pulpit."

"What was he going to talk about?"

"I don't know—I'm not sure anyone did."

Sanderson nodded vaguely then asked, "Does this room look like it did this morning? Has anything been disturbed?"

"Here? There's never been anything up here but dust. We'd sit on the floor while we talked." Her eyes drifted rather dreamily to a corner to the right of the window. But they snapped back abruptly. "It'd make a great storage room, but no one wants to carry anything up the stairs. It's always empty."

"I think he might have been killed up here."

That idea caught her unawares. Eyes suddenly wide, she stepped back and glanced furtively around as if the killer might still be there—maybe tangled in the cobwebs. "Here? Really?"

Her reaction looked genuine. But then the mousy ones usually were good actresses. A survival tactic. Of course, the lie had been obvious. "What makes you think so?" she asked.

Sanderson stepped to the window. He pushed it open, and when he did he saw a torn piece of cloth caught on the rough edge of the sill. There were only a few threads; they quivered in the blast of cold air. He removed his gloves and quickly rummaged through his overcoat pocket, found a pair of tweezers and an envelope, and gently pulled the threads loose. After carefully inserting them in the envelope, he turned and said, "I think someone nailed him in here and pushed him out that window."

The moment he said it he realized that the hypothesis probably eliminated this woman. She was so slight she'd never be able to get a 180-pound man out a small opening like this. The window was at least four feet off the floor.

"Poor Dan. Why would anyone push him out the window?" she muttered.

"Did many people come up here?"

Again she hesitated, eyes flickering (another lie?). "No one—except me and Danny, I guess. I don't know. It's not locked. If the church is open, the door to the tower is open."

"There's no other way in here?"

"No."

"Is the church always locked?"

"Yes."

"So who ever did it had a key to the church?"

"Yes."

"Who had keys?"

"Just about everyone—and if they didn't have one they could get one easily enough. All the leadership has one, and I guess even people who have been part of the leadership in the past. We never collect the keys."

"Why not?"

"I guess a better question is why we lock the place at all. There's nothing here to steal—a few books maybe. But I suppose now that we have a murderer . . . Oh my. Did you hear what I said? I just realized what I'd said . . . one of us . . . oh my." Her hand covered her mouth.

"Assuming the killer didn't dump him out the window in daylight, who, besides you, would he have met up here late last night?"

She shrugged. "No one is here on Saturday nights. His office would have been good enough." Then she added, "Unless the person wanted to meet him here—I mean made a point of asking him to meet here. These past few months he'd go anywhere."

"What's that mean?"

"He wanted to help. He'd go anywhere to help—anyone."

*Isn't he supposed to?* Bray thought.

"What about girlfriends?"

"No. No girlfriends."

"You're not planning on going anywhere in the next few days are you?"

"No. I never go anywhere."

"I may want to talk to you again. If you think of anything you've heard or seen, or anything that seems out of the ordinary, please contact me. You can go now."

She looked a little lost for an instant as if she had a question. But she'd been dismissed and that was that.

When her footsteps had died away down the stairs, Sanderson crossed to the window. Glasgow was talking to someone in an expensive mohair overcoat. Someone who leaned toward her, talking to her more as a beautiful woman than a police officer. Sanderson cursed softly. Mike Grogan. *Why is he here?*

Grogan was muscularly built with a broad, handsome, Irish face and coal black hair. He had three strikes against him in Sanderson's book. He was a good detective, he was recently hired from New York, and he was young. Four strikes, actually; Sanderson was next in line for chief detective, and Grogan wanted it.

After taking a moment to wish Grogan would disappear, he called down, "Glasgow. Send crime scene up here. Here's where it happened."

"Up there?" Glasgow called back. "They're working in the front trying to resurrect some tire tracks. I'll get them." She crunched away leaving Grogan to fend for himself.

He looked up and smiled warmly but revealed predator's teeth. "How's it going?" he called up, his New York twang unusually nasal.

"Why are you here?"

"Sounded interesting."

Sanderson gave him a vacant nod and pulled away from the window. Grogan rattled him sometimes and being rattled wouldn't help. Drawing upon a store of infrequently used mental discipline, he erased Grogan from his mind and refilled the empty slate with the room. Now that he was sure the man had died in it, it deserved detailed scrutiny.

He stepped outside on the landing and planted himself as firmly as he could in Bryce's shoes. After closing the door he reentered. Now he was Bryce, seeing what he had seen, thinking what he had thought.

Since the window was directly across the room from the door, he must have seen that first. Even in the dark. Dark. Next to the door was the same cheap plastic light switch. Taking the same pen, he flipped it. Another bare bulb in the corner opposite the window lit and washed the room in a pallid yellow. The light on, the window seen, Bryce would have scanned the rest of the room. That wouldn't take long. The killer. Where was he—or she? He couldn't sneak up the stairs behind Bryce. He would have heard the creaking. The killer was hidden in the room—behind the door.

Or had he hid?

If Bryce knew his murderer, he wouldn't have to hide.

But Bryce was probably nailed from behind. An attack from the front would have been too risky. The murderer hid behind the door.

Bray stepped quickly to the door and looked behind it. Nothing obvious. Crime scene would do their thing, and maybe something would pop out at them. He pushed the door back against the wall and turned again to the window.

What would keep Bryce from closing the door behind him as he entered? He might do so for any number of reasons:

privacy, habit, neatness. The killer had to make sure he didn't. He would have to keep Bryce's focus on the window.

Sanderson stepped to the window and pushed his nose a breath from the ancient wood. The room had been painted once, but age had eroded the paint to just a few scattered flecks in the deeper grain. After a few seconds, Bray found what he was looking for. A new pinhole, maybe large enough for a thumbtack. The killer had put something up, maybe a note or a sign, maybe something with Bryce's name on it, something that Bryce would examine closely.

Bray straightened and his eyes narrowed. He closed them, allowing himself to become part of this room last night. In his mind's eye, he could see Bryce bundled in a worn blue ski jacket, pushing the squealing door open. After climbing the steep stairs in the arctic cold, he caught his breath. Plumes of white billowed from his mouth as he idly scanned the room. He would think he had arrived first. It was cold and he hoped the person wouldn't be much longer. Then he saw the note. Was the guy telling him he couldn't make it? He stepped those last few steps, bent slightly to read it, then the shock at the base of his skull as the hammer came down.

Bray winced.

*The autopsy. I hope the cold doesn't mess it up too badly. The time of death always matters,* Sanderson thought.

He looked around for the thumbtack. It would have a wonderful print on it if it were somewhere around. It wasn't.

 Chapter 3

In September, at the beginning of the school year, the seminary students had demanded Nautilus equipment—as strongly as seminary students could demand anything of the dean. They'd quoted verse after verse that showed they should be training not only their minds but their bodies as well. Dean Joel Watkins hadn't needed Nautilus equipment growing up. He'd worked a Vermont dairy farm with his father—enough muscle-building activity for four normal human beings.

They couldn't do that, of course; this was Atlanta, the big city. So Dean Watkins gave in. He'd looted the library budget and put in the exercise room. Now, with March ending and spring brushing aside winter's cold, only one student still used it. And he wasn't really a student. He was a hanger-on. Winsome "Win" Brady. And he used it only at night—late at night. He'd wander down from his room cocooned in darkness when a pesky element of some complex biblical doctrine bothered him, and he'd work out. For hours. Sometime during the night, when sweat and gray-matter merged and the problem was either solved or a course of further study was defined, Win would return to bed. Win Brady had come there six years ago a wimp—now he was all muscle.

And brain.

Dean Watkins was a smallish man with a calm, understanding face that always seemed on the verge of a smile. A face at odds with his New England accent, a rarity in Atlanta. This morning its most important task was to welcome Win Brady's father to the dean's mahogany office.

Walter Brady had been in the office several times before. It was Walter's money that had built at least a third of the seminary and when he'd called that morning, even though the dean's calendar had been filled, time was made.

"It's always good," the dean said, pumping Walter Brady's hand.

"Always," Walter echoed, his accent gently Southern. A man in his early fifties, he sported a small tummy and jowls that were beginning to droop. Although he'd built his sporting goods company on hard work, the softer management life was taking its toll. He didn't wait to be shown to a chair; instead he crossed brusquely to the coffee nook in the corner: a sofa and overstuffed chair around a low, broad glass table. He took the chair and sank into it.

As the dean poured coffee into two delicate china cups, he said, "I didn't expect your call."

"Why would you? I'd already sent my check," Walter stated.

"And we've already spent it," the dean responded, as he always responded within this ritual. He handed Brady the steaming cup, which rattled slightly on the china saucer. "What can I do for you?"

Walter took a quick sip and sighed. What he'd come to say he'd rehearsed, but now the words didn't fit. Yet he had to say something—right words or not. "Win graduated, what—three years ago?"

"Three and a half."

"But he's still here."

"Still here," the dean repeated.

"When do you think he'll leave?"

Now it was the dean's turn to sigh. He'd asked himself that same question several times—more frequently lately. "I don't know. He's invaluable here. The professors love him. They don't have to pay him—you do—and he'll work on anything they give him. He's done some remarkable work—he knows Scripture—truly knows it. Incredible mind. And he's happy, terminally so."

"Do you think staying here is best for him?"

"I've asked myself that question too."

Walter Brady nodded again. "He's hiding here. I'm not paying him to hide."

"Succinctly put," the dean said, getting to his feet and taking his cup with him.

"It's time Win Brady left here," Walter Brady said flatly. "I didn't raise him to be buried in a library—and certainly not one of his own making."

"Have you talked to him about this?" Dean Watkins asked.

"He's sensitive about my injecting myself into his life. In fact, he hates it. He'll let me refill his checking account, but he won't take my advice.

"I want my son out of here. There's a church out there somewhere that needs what my son can offer. There's a pulpit out there that oversees a thousand faces every Sunday. There he can help thousands—not just a few professors. And that's where I want him."

Dean Watkins only nodded. At graduation ceremonies more than three years ago Walter had convinced one of the larger Nashville churches to install his son as an assistant pastor. They agreed but Win hadn't, deciding instead to continue his study through research at the seminary. Walter Brady had never recovered from that. Now he left no room for negotiation.

Dean Watkins spoke softly but firmly, "God opens and closes doors, not us."

"But sometimes we have to reach for the handle."

The dean nodded again. "I, too, think Win needs to move on. He's comfortable—worse than comfortable—he's settled in. And for someone his age and with his potential, that's not good."

A thought began to form—a news article the dean had read that morning at breakfast—a church not far from his roots that might be a combination classroom, proving ground, and crucible. "I'll talk to him," he said simply.

Walter Brady got to his feet. "Do more than talk. If he's still here next week, future checks from me won't be."

"You are a man of infinite clarity," said the dean. Then he added, "Walter, your son is a brilliant man, and I believe the Lord will use him. But," he went on, after remembering a certain goat in a certain professor's bathtub and a certain professor's wife being resuscitated on a certain bathroom floor, "he has some rough edges that need smoothing."

"Then smooth them out. But not here—in a church, with people, where my son can shine. Understood?"

"I remind you again of your clarity," the dean responded.

"And I remind you again of your budget."

"I'll do what's right, in spite of my budget," the dean stated firmly.

Walter Brady only nodded, then added, "Thank you for understanding reality. Have a pleasant day."

Dean Watkins stood to shake Walter Brady's hand and felt the firm grip of a man who expected to get what he wanted.


"What in heaven's name is that?" Dean Watkins eyed Win Brady with narrowly disapproving eyes.

"I don't know," Win said, standing in the doorway of the dean's office. "I found it in a box Professor Claris had me unpack—books willed to the seminary. Wanna try it?"

It was a small, barrel-shaped, brightly painted block of wood tied to a stick by a foot-long string. On the opposite end of the barrel from where the string was attached was a hole. "You swing the barrel-thing here so it spins, and you catch it with the stick in the hole." Win had just about mastered it. "I remember seeing one of these when I was about five." He flipped the barrel up, it spun midair, then came down— clack!—bouncing off the stick. "Don't worry, I'll get it." He tried it again.

"Were there any books we could use?"

"Don't know yet," Win said, preoccupied with the toy. Again—clack!—the barrel bounced off the stick. "I'll get to 'em later."

"Don't you think the books are more important than that?" Dean Watkins admonished.

"Won't know until we unpack the books. But considering who they're from I doubt it."

"Who?"

"Some old geezer who would play with one of these—he couldn't have been much of a theologian." The barrel spun and bounced off, then he tossed it up again.

"*You're* playing with it."

"Well, my point's made."

Dean Watkins didn't laugh. "I asked you in here because we need to talk, Win," he said soberly.

"I'll do the books—this'll keep my attention for only another hour or so tops."

"You haven't got another hour."

Clack! The barrel bounced off the stick and hung. "I don't?" Win said, his eyes wide. Win had thinning sandy hair, iron gray eyes, and a strong, cleft chin. His weight training had broadened his shoulders and thickened his biceps. He was a strong, thirty-year-old man—but now, with this new toy swinging back and forth, standing before his trusted mentor, he looked like a lost child.

"Win . . . " the dean began, then softened. "Son . . . " a deep sigh, "it's time for you to get some more settings."

"Huh?"

"Settings. I've been watching you for a while. The dial that controls who you are and what you do seems to have only two settings: Einstein and Goofy."

"Goofy?"

"You do brilliant work for the professors—brilliant. Your research on the Trinity, predestination, and the work of the Holy Spirit in the Old Testament are wonderful. You've found and explained types of Christ in the Old Testament that astounded all of us. Exciting, brilliant—the articles you've coauthored with the profs are respected by the best."

"Goofy?"

"But then there's the goat in Professor Winters's bathtub—"

"Just a prank—Mrs. Winters wasn't supposed to be back for a week."

"And the surgical glue on Professor Turner's telephone earpiece."

"I didn't know it would stick like that."

"Or the water balloons, or the frogs in the cafeteria food line, or . . ."

"I'm just having fun."

"Goofy. Two settings—and it's time for you to develop more. Win, it's time for you to leave the seminary." Dean Watkins said flatly, but not without compassion.

"Leave? Because of a few pranks?" Shocked, Win found himself holding up the stick, the barrel hanging like a man's head.

"No. Not for the pranks. That's not to say that the professors—and their wives—sometimes think you go too far. But, as I see it, the pranks liven things up around here, and heaven knows we need a little of that. Mrs. Winters didn't think so, but the goat gave some of us a chuckle. But it's not what we want or need, it's what's best for you and your development. We'll just have to get our comedic stimulation from *Nick at Nite* and *Mary Tyler Moore* reruns."

"But what I do here is important. Your words." He glanced at the toy. "Well, most things. The research is good." Win's brows screwed up inquisitively as he sank dumbfounded into the same chair his father had vacated only an hour before. Dean Watkins thought he looked so little like him.

"You are important," Dean Watkins said. "And it's time you became even more so. You need broadening, the kind only experience gives."

"Are you sure I can't stay? Maybe a counseling program would broaden me out enough." Win's eyes narrowed as a thought struck him. "My dad's in on this, isn't he?"

"Your father and I agree . . . "

"Of course . . . when things are going good, enter Dad."

"Win, be fair. You've been here over six years. There's more out there than the written word. If your dad hadn't suggested it, I would have concluded it myself—very soon."

"I've spent most of my life rubbing his boot marks off my butt." Win sighed.

"I want you to do something for me," Dean Watkins leaned forward and locked eyes with his protégé.

Feeling their intensity, Win leaned back, still cautious. "What?"

Watkins slid a newspaper across the coffee table. "Read the highlighted story."

Win eyed him again then reluctantly took the newspaper and read the paragraph. "A murder? In Vermont?"

"An assistant pastor."

"And?"

"I called this morning. The position's still open."

"I can imagine." Win's brows furled in disbelief. "But isn't that a little morbid? Looking for jobs in the obituaries?"

"I know that church. I grew up not far from there. There was a time when it was a real beacon on the Grand Isles. But no longer. People are hurting in that church."

"One of them isn't hurting anymore."

"I want you to work there for a while."

"Couldn't I just do a research project for a month or so?"

"Research is being outside looking in. I want you inside looking in deeper. I want you involved. God is there—find him," the dean told him, his eyes alive with instruction. "I have a niece who lives there. She'll show you the ropes. She's a policewoman." Dean Watkins took a folded sheet of paper from the inside pocket of his suit and handed it to Win.

"A policewoman? Great—I'll pull a practical joke and end up in jail." Win glanced at the folded sheet. It was a letter of introduction to a Ginger Glasgow with a yellow Post-it stuck to it. On the Post-it were neatly typed directions to her home. "You're sure about this?" Win asked in almost a whine.

"Positive. You love and want to know even more about Jesus. Doing what I suggest will accomplish that."

Almost without thinking, Win flipped the string and barrel into the air, it spun 180° and landed neatly on the stick. "Just when I get good at this. They'll never understand this in a church—never." He looked up at Dean Watkins. "I don't know," he said, still apprehensive. "I really need to think about this. Some people are born to hide behind thick walls and do their work. I may be just one of those people."

"You have an hour."

Win's face came up with consternation. "An hour?"

"I'm kicking you out of the nest, Win," Watkins said firmly. "It's either into Vermont with my help and blessing, or into the street. You're part of God's army, and the bus is moving up to the front lines."

"As a buck private." Win stared up at his mentor for several long seconds. Maybe Dean Watkins was doing this out of love. Maybe it wasn't just because his father threatened to cut the seminary off without a dime. Maybe there'd be fun in the foxhole. Maybe . . . Who was he kidding!

A few moments later, flipping the barrel perfectly onto the stick three out of four times, Win walked down the hall toward his room. With only him and the groundskeeper living on campus, accommodations were far from palatial. But they were comfortable. Everything was comfortable.

Years before, when Win had moved into his room it was little more than a cell that had been used for storage. The walls were filthy cinder blocks and the floor naked cement. In less than a week, Win had changed it all. With childlike energy, he scouted book, furniture, and art stores, local estate sales and, aided by his magic checkbook, the transformation began. When complete, bright, humorous posters brought two walls alive while warm, sensitive photographs and prints brought the other two heart. Plush rugs softened the floor. The furniture consisted of brightly colored beanbag chairs, a bed in the shape of a '57 Corvette, and lamps with cowboy lampstands.

When he was growing up his room was impeccably decorated in wood hues and sterile, sky blue walls. It was cleaned once a day by a housekeeper who scolded him for leaving out his toys. Although this room was reasonably clean, his toys were all over the place. Most were books, and the rest were Rubik's cubes, other puzzles, and a cylinder of pick-up sticks.

He lay on the '57 Corvette, propping himself against the pillows nestled below the half-opened convertible roof canopy.

He was being kicked out of the nest. And though he wanted to deny being a fledgling, he knew he was. Taking a moment to assess his years at the seminary he could see that he'd slowly, but deliberately, become a hermit. As he had progressed toward that state, he'd felt more at ease, more comfortable. He knew this world he lived in and was a king in it. King of Scripture, king of goofiness. Safe, above criticism—except for Mrs. Winters's near heart attack.

Now the safety would end. Win's heart throbbed in his chest. Fear, uncertainty—he'd felt neither in years. Would his wings work? Would it hurt if they didn't? Was God going to let him fall?

Win mentally kicked himself. God had placed him there. God wouldn't let him fall. Trust—why was it always the last thing he considered? Why was it never instinctive, always manufactured? What was happening now wasn't the result of a capricious fate, or some accident of human invention. It was God. Ephesians 1:11: ". . . predestined according to the plan of him who works out everything in conformity with the purpose of his will."

"But you call this a plan?" Win blurted out. "Taking the place of some murdered guy on some island in Vermont? That's a plan?" Win crossed arms defiantly on his chest and waited for the lightning. Not even a flash.

"You really want me to do this?" Win said to the Spirit he knew was in the room with him, in his heart. "Aren't I better off here? Can't I do more for you if I'm freed up to think?"

*For God did not give us a spirit of timidity, but a spirit of power, of love and of self-discipline.*

"Where'd that come from?" he muttered. He knew it came

from 2 Timothy 1:7, but the intrusion had been so strong he almost thought he'd heard a voice. "Timid? I'm scared. I admit it. Terrified. I've never done well out there. People I love die on me. Things I do turn out to be wrong or stupid. Here I'm a success. Even the goofy things work—most of them. If you wanted me out there, why did you make me a success in here?"

*I will go down to Egypt with you.*

Again a verse injected itself into his inner ear, and the fear that had washed over him in a huge wave began to subside. Dean Watkins's words came rumbling back—the war, God and his army against the powers of the dark world and their general, Satan.

"Couldn't I just be in personnel or run the chuck wagon or something?" Win muttered, rubbing frustrated fingers over burning eyes.

As his hands dropped to his side and his eyes closed, his spiritual vision cleared. He saw the battlefield, saw the author of ugliness and lies rising up, jaws wide seeking him to devour. He heard the blast of distant thunder, the whine of bullets, the cries of anguish. As the battle formed before him, a strong part of him wanted to charge in. It was time. Maybe researching it didn't matter as much as living it—maybe it was time he actually started living by faith.

Win swallowed hard. "This better be good, Lord," he muttered. "Where else would people actually let me put live frogs in a food line—or goats in bathtubs?"

There was silence in his inner ear. A silence that finally ended when he heaved a deep, resolute sigh. "Well, Lord, here we go."

🔔

The end of April found spring blooming on the Grand Isles. One day winter's icy shackles clung deep and confining, the next they melted and released their grip as a warm plume of air swept up from the south. Policewoman Ginger Glasgow would normally have reveled in having her day off simultaneously with spring's entrance. She might have planned to meet her son, Chad, at school for a lunchtime picnic. But not today. Spring's renewing spark went unnoticed.

Sitting at the kitchen table, the memory of hot coffee still igniting her tongue, she fumed. She read and reread the offending sentence in the morning newspaper. When the words didn't change, she stood and tossed the paper angrily to the table. After grabbing her coffee mug, she stepped into the garden.

Her home was little more than a cottage among a scattering of other cottages on the islands. It was her garden in the back that made it special. The mesh of the chain-link fence that surrounded it made a natural lattice upon which the yellow and red roses climbed, a backdrop for the camellias, crocuses, and tulips. All were piled expectantly with buds, promising the splash of summer colors. Ginger usually loved this time of the morning when Chad was at school. She loved stealing off to the corner of the garden to enjoy her mug of coffee while she visualized the spray of color she'd soon be seeing. The news story killed all that.

It had come through the wire service, a particularly pointed story questioning the assumptions that were at the foundation of a speech by a United States senator. The senator's thesis: We are requiring an ever-increasing level of morality from our elected public officials and at the same time ridiculing their religious beliefs, but it is religion that produces morality in the first place. The writer indicated, on the other hand, that there was nothing moral about religion. He went about proving his case by rehashing every problem every televangelist had ever had and by adding to the list the murder at Sugar Steeple Community Church.

> No longer content to merely financially rape their brothers and sisters in the faith, there is now an unsolved murder. Is it unsolved because there are too few clues or is there a cult of silence—a cover-up? Is there only one guilty, or are there many made guilty by their collusion?

"Hey." Ginger heard the voice come at her from the other side of the white picket fence.

"Betty," Ginger greeted absently. Betty Sherman was a tank of a woman in her late fifties with salt-and-pepper hair. She'd lived in the house next door to Ginger since Betty's husband had left her ten years before. There were times when Ginger thought he probably left out of self-defense. "Want some coffee?" Ginger offered.

"Naw. What's wrong with you?" Betty demanded. "You're stomping around like the last buffalo."

"A newspaper article."

"That one slamming Christians?" she asked. "Glanced at it."

Ginger had never made up her mind as to whether Betty knew the Lord or not. She seemed sympathetic at times . . . "That's the one."

"Wondered about that murder. Don't have many of 'em on the islands. A church murder gives ya something to wonder about."

"A non-Christian killed that man," Ginger said. "And Sanderson should have discovered who by now."

"So that's it. You don't care who killed 'im just so long as the killer was the wrong kind of people."

Ginger winced. "That's not entirely true," she protested.

"What is true?" Betty asked, the words a scalpel.

After a long moment, Ginger found herself laughing softly. "Who knows what's true?" she said. "When I got married, I thought it would be for life, and then Frank died leaving me to be both mother and father to a kid who really needs at least two of each. I've been a policewoman for six years, and instead of taking advantage of my talents—whatever they might be—I have to spend my time fighting for recognition and respect. And, not only am I a woman in a predominantly male occupation, but I'm a Christian woman—which brings its own set of pressures. Finding Dan Bryce's murderer—and showing that it was the world who killed him and not a Christian—would bring me a little justice."

"Then go find the guy," Betty said simply.

"I'm a cop—not Miss Marple," Ginger said and took another drink of coffee. "Finding the murderer is Sanderson's job."

"So, you want the joy of complaining without the work."

Ginger looked into Betty's face. No sympathy there. "Maybe complaining's just good for the soul right now."

After a long moment, Betty suddenly exploded with laughter. "*I* never complain," she said laughing. "Sure! About every third word I'm griping. I guess you're entitled to a complaint or two." She glanced at Ginger's coffee. "You look like you're about out. Maybe I *will* have a cup."

No one laughed like Betty. She put everything into it. And when everything got to bouncing with it, there was no way to remain serious. The tension broke—shattered.

But Betty never got her coffee. As Ginger was pouring them each a cup, the phone rang.

Ginger recognized the voice on the other end—Chad's principal's secretary. "Mr. Mann would like to see you. Your son assaulted Joanne Morton. I believe this is the second time."

Ginger sighed deeply. She wondered what his excuse would be this time. It was hard being both mother and father. Hard. "See you in a minute."

She found Chad sitting outside the principal's office as she had a couple of times before. Chad was built much like his father had been—pear-shaped with round, lively eyes, round face, rounder middle.

Henry Mann, the principal, greeted Ginger coolly and invited both of them into his office. Mann was normally congenial, fair, easy-mannered. But now he looked grimly weary.

"Well, we have another situation. One we've had before."

"Joanne Morton," Ginger stated flatly.

"Chad took a poke at her—again. She's in the nurse's office—scraped cheek, I believe."

Ginger looked down at her son who looked sheepishly back up at her. "Why?" she asked.

"It wasn't an accident—she called me 'Bubble Butt,'" he confessed. "I lost my temper."

Ginger nodded, then looked at Mr. Mann. "I'll take care of this."

"Ah. You've said that before," Mr. Mann reminded her, taking just a little pleasure in doing so.

"I know."

"You, of course, are the parent, and I believe firmly that parents should be the disciplinary agents. But, if there's another incident, we'll have to take action ourselves."

"I understand."

Mann smiled condescendingly. "That's it. He's suspended for the rest of the day," He extended a hand. "Thank you, Miss Glasgow."

"It's still Mrs.," she corrected.

In the Blazer in the parking lot she eyed her son. "Just for calling you Bubble Butt?"

"It wouldn't be so bad if it weren't true."

"It's not true—you're just built like your father. But you can't knock girls around for calling you names. You can't knock little girls around for any reason." She fired up the engine. "When we get home, you're going to have some repenting to do."

Chad was sent to his room for the rest of the day. Let out about dinnertime, he was asked if he understood what his responsibility was before the Lord, and he nodded. But it was a mechanical sort of nod. Then there were words of repentance that sounded less than sincere. Chad had a temper—he'd always had it. Even as a baby, his terrible twos had been particularly terrible, but it truly became a part of him when he was four—when his father died.

After dinner, while she and Chad did the dishes—she washing, he drying—the phone rang. Ginger grabbed it. "Hello . . . Uncle Joel. Are you in town?"

"No. Still in Atlanta," Dean Watkins said. "How's Chad doing?"

"*What* he's doing is more to the point," she replied with a hint of bitterness.

"I'm sorry to hear that," her uncle said, as if he meant more than just to commiserate.

"You sound funny. What's going on?"

"So he's really a handful, is he?"

"Both hands. You sound like I should be worried or something."

"Oh, no," Dean Watkins said, still sounding as if he were hiding something. "No. Nothing like that." He was about to blurt out, "How'd you like to be taking care of two kids?" but he didn't. Instead he told her, "I have a good friend who'll be in your area. I'm wondering if you could help him settle in."

"Sure. When will he get here?"

"In a couple of days, assuming all goes well. His name is Win Brady. Nice fellow. Put him in my mom's cottage." The dean changed subjects abruptly. "Chad's giving you a lot of trouble, is he?" His tone revealed that he was having second thoughts.

"You sound like you think I can't handle helping someone. How much trouble could this guy be?"

"Oh," her uncle said, musingly. "No trouble."

# Chapter 4

On Friday morning, Pastor Worlton sat behind his cherry wood desk, a critical eye on the man sitting before him. At thirty, he was a little older than what Worlly had expected when they first started advertising for the position. But only one other person had responded, a twenty-three year old who found out about the murder and left the next day. Now there was this older guy, and Worlly found he liked the idea. This Brady would have been around the block a few times—would have had his ideals tarnished and dented enough to make reasonable decisions. He probably understood the realities of life.

So, after fifteen minutes, Worlly was satisfied with his work habits, his ability to work with people (particularly youth), his willingness to work for peanuts, and his being able to put his pride in his back pocket. The applicant had answered all the questions correctly, nodded at the right times, and, more important, seemed to fit in.

He even looked distinguished. His hair was thinning just slightly, and his brows were slightly furrowed as if always in thought. His hands were large and his arms muscular, indicative of steadiness. And his name—actually it was his name that Worlly found most intriguing—Win Brady. There was strength in that name—Win. He liked it. Charlie Briggs would like it. Even Roz would.

"I'm still a little fuzzy on how you came to find out we were looking for someone." Worlly said, now ready to start asking the trivial.

Win Brady smiled. Though stiff, there was a world of warmth in it.

Worlly liked the smile. This boy would be no problem.

"A friend told me about the position."

Worlly liked his voice too—steady, but not arrogant, just a hint of intimidation—this applicant respected his authority. Even if he hadn't been the only applicant—who stayed—Worlly would have offered him the job.

"You'd be willing to start right away?" Worlly asked.

Win nodded stiffly, apprehensively. *At least you're right about one thing, Dean,* he thought. *During the whole interview, Jesus Christ was never mentioned.* "Right away," he said.

"How will we get in touch with you?"

"I'll find a motel for the night," Win explained, "then call you—when?"

Worlly thought for a moment—he thought about who might have an objection, who might just assent to his recommendation, and whose decision it was, anyway. And who would dare to suggest that he pass the guy up.

"I don't think that will be necessary," he finally said. "Why don't you make your permanent arrangements this weekend, take Monday to get settled in, and show up Tuesday morning?"

Win smiled, although not as broadly as he was capable. Up to that moment he could have just walked away. After all, Dean Watkins's faith in him was based on an external view. Win knew the truth about himself, and that truth produced doubts. All he had to do was nod and he'd be committed. Confident or not, he'd have to perform—or they'd fire him and he'd leave in disgrace. "So you're not as good as I thought. You couldn't even make it in some podunk little berg in an apostate little denomination," he could hear his father say. His frozen smile remained, then, "Great," Win managed. He swallowed hard. "What time Tuesday?"

"Nine A.M.—sharp, now."

"Sharp," Win repeated.

Worlly watched the young man stand and present a hesitant hand. *It's a pleasure to see such respect,* Worlly thought. After Worlly shook it he remained standing and watched his new assistant disappear out the door. He hadn't noticed the car Win had driven into the parking lot. But after a few minutes, through the office windows that faced the parking lot, he saw the U-haul pulling a vintage, two-tone blue '54 Chevy. *Good choice,* Worlly thought, *I had one of those when I was a kid. Solid choice.*

Within an hour he'd gotten the tentative approval of both Charlie Briggs and Rozalyn Swift. Though not enthusiastic— they would never be that—they said okay. They were the only ones who might have challenged him.

"Hello, is this Ginger Glasgow?" Win spoke from a phone booth not far from where the map indicated Ginger's cottage.

"Who's this?"

"Win Brady. Dean . . . "

"Oh, the inmate from Uncle Joel's. You lost?"

"Not completely. I just wanted to call first."

Ginger found a certain charm in his hesitant, self-conscious tone, and she smiled to herself. She'd not seen a lot of men with charm lately. "Come on over."

Win ground the sixteen-foot U-haul truck to a halt, his '54 Chevy on the car carrier behind, and rechecked the address on the letter. Satisfied, he slid to the ground and knocked on Ginger's front door. He was impressed when she answered. He was over six feet and towered over most women, but he stood eye to eye with Ginger. And they were such beautiful eyes— blue, deep as sky. He smiled a bit sheepishly. "Win Brady," he introduced himself haltingly and pushed out a hand.

Ginger smiled, thinking him just too shy for words. "Uncle Joel says you need a place to stay."

"For a while. I'm working at a church near here."

Ginger stepped back and cocked her head inquisitively. "Which?"

"Sugar Steeple. I'm the new assistant pastor there."

She took another step back, surprised that Joel had not mentioned Sugar Steeple. "That's not Uncle Joel's kind of church."

"Not mine either." A part of him wanted to explain everything. But another part hesitated. "It's sort of a project—seminary stuff."

She gave a vacant little nod and looked at him for a long moment. Although shy, she thought, he was definitely strong enough to take care of himself. Maybe while working there he could keep his eyes and ears open. That's just what Sanderson needed—an inside guy, though, of course, he didn't know that yet. Maybe Dan Bryce's killer would be brought to justice soon after all. "I was wondering," she began, gnawing her lower lip slightly. "While you're working on this project of yours—how would you like to earn a little extra credit?"

Win's brows dipped. "Extra credit? What kind?" Then it struck him what she meant. "You're a cop—uh—policewoman. Are you thinking I could help you find the murderer? You've got to be kidding."

On the drive up to Vermont he had indulged in long hours of fantasy planning. He'd thought about witnessing to each member of the church, one at a time, in all kinds of situations and under all kinds of pressures. He had fantasized about bringing his first convert to the Lord and thumbing his nose at Satan and his destructive plans for the church.

Only occasionally had he thought about the murderer—and then it was only in terms of staying on his good side.

"So you must think it was a member of the congregation?"

"Probably," Ginger answered.

"Boy, that's apostacy with a vengeance," Win exclaimed. "Are you *sure* it wasn't just a random thing—by a transient maybe?"

"Not the way it happened."

Win nodded appraisingly then shook his head firmly. "I'm really not here to sniff out killers. I'm here to . . . " That's when the words began to fail him. "Jumping out of a nest" didn't seem to fit. Nor did his loftier goals: start a revival, live his faith. Somehow they sounded fine when announced in the confines of a sixteen-foot U-haul. But they sounded silly and pretentious in front of this Scandinavian beauty.

"Well, what *are* you here for?" Ginger pressed when Win's voice trailed off.

Win hesitated again, then said, "Your uncle Joel thought I needed to get out more."

Dean Watkins's mother's cottage had a deep musty smell, and only after the front and back doors and the back window had been opened for several hours did it begin to dissipate. When Ginger first unlocked the front door and Win stepped in, he thought he'd stepped into another century—one of dim shafts of dusty light, creaky wooden floors, and ornately carved wooden cabinets and sills.

"Uncle Joel's mother owned this and rented it out before she died. I've been taking care of it. Well, I drive by now and again. Uncle Joel pays the gardener and uses it when he comes up. But he hasn't been here in a while. It's been empty all this time."

"Feels like it. But it'll be fine."

She nodded then pointed toward the lake. "There's a boat-house out back."

Win's eyes lighted and he took a few quick steps to the kitchen. Through a dirty window he spotted the grubby white shed at the water's edge. "I've always wanted my own boat in my own boathouse at my own place on the water," Win confided as a sleek, blue outboard burst from the left and skimmed the deep blue surface.

"You'll change your mind if you're still here in the winter. It's cold. Nostrils freeze shut."

"Sneezing must be lethal," he quipped. When she cocked her head inquisitively he explained, "People die from flying ice."

"Ah," she said, unimpressed. "Good one."

"Well, it doesn't matter. I'll probably be gone by winter."

"Ah," she said again. "How long is this project supposed to last?"

"Don't know," he shrugged.

He walked idly down the hall to the bedrooms in the back. One in the back corner was larger. A phone sat on the floor where a nightstand would probably go. He didn't have a night stand, but his '57 Corvette bed had fenders.

"I'll get the phone turned on."

"Thank you."

Ginger nodded and took a moment to let her eyes sink into his, trying earnestly to see beyond the veneer—beyond the shyness. For an instant, when the boat came by, she thought she'd seen the curtain part slightly and an excited child peek out. But now the curtain was closed again.

"I never asked if you'd had dinner—Chad, my ten-year old, and I ate—I got off early. We could talk more about the murder."

"Then you were serious."

"Very. I'm not working the case but I know who is. He needs help."

Win gave a knowing nod. "Then he doesn't need me. I have trouble finding my keys in the morning. I'd never find a murderer."

He turned and surveyed the cottage. Quaint, livable—he actually liked it—with the peaceful blue-gray lake lapping gently in the background. He'd dreamed of a refuge like this. Why did he have to find it when it was no refuge at all? "How much for rent?"

"If you're still here in a couple months we'll talk price. For now, just clean the place up a little. Are you sure you don't want to help find the guy?"

"Or gal," Win pointed out, his eyes still moving around the cottage. He turned to Ginger. "I've had a long drive. I'm really tired. I'll take a rain check on dinner. All I want to do is unload a few things and crash."

"Can I help?" Ginger asked with polite eagerness.

SOMERSET COUNTY LIBRARY
6022 GLADES PIKE, SUITE 120
SOMERSET, PA 15501-4300
(814) 445-5907

Why did his mind flash on the '57 Corvette bed? He loved that bed. Why did it suddenly seem so juvenile? "That's okay. It's mostly small stuff. I'll unload it. No problem. Maybe we could have lunch or something tomorrow. Bring your son— Chad is it?"

"Sure. Want me to bring anything?"

"Naw, I'll go out and do some shopping. Why don't you just be here about noon and I'll have lunch ready."

"Fair enough," she said, taking an awkward moment to look at him again. He was such a curious contradiction. Physically he looked like a Chippendale dancer, but emotionally he seemed like Winnie-the-Pooh. "Well, have a nice night. I'm only a few minutes away if you need anything."

"Right—thank you," he said and a few moments later watched her car disappear around the corner.

Although he'd slept erratically, Win woke at 6:00 A.M. as always. After his morning ritual—the next three chapters in Scripture then prayer beneath a steady warm shower—he donned a sweatshirt and jeans and finished unloading the U-haul. He stacked boxes in the guest bedroom and distributed the beanbag chairs, lamps, rugs, and wall hangings, then decided to leave the books for later.

Seminary mornings were always busy with people scurrying about, discussions at breakfast, last-minute study or paperwork. But here in a lakefront cabin smack in the middle of the great Northeast he was alone, and after the Bible and prayer there was little else but the sound of his own breathing.

He made coffee and drank a cup on the pier, but after a few minutes a wave of restlessness buffeted him. He had to do something. Last night the peace was almost thrilling. Now it seemed threatening—as if by taking part in it he was leaving something important undone. Even though it was still early, he decided to go food shopping.

At eight, the only market on the island that Win had seen was closed, so he took Highway 2 south to Burlington and found a supermarket. Next door was a small boat lot. The moment he saw the slightly rusted, red and blue sign and the long row of speed and pleasure boats he drifted in that direction. A chain was draped across the driveway, but after a moment, a plump fellow with a cherry red face stepped out of a trailer in the middle of the lot. "We open in a couple hours," he called to Win.

"Too bad," Win called back, slapping his magic checkbook challengingly across his palm.

On its third try, Win's brand-new five-horsepower Mercury outboard whined to life. The outboard rested on a wooden crosspiece that formed the bench back of a horseshoe-shaped rubber inner tube. Win revved it several times, then he eased the small, air-filled craft out of the boathouse, onto the lake.

It was all he hoped it would be. He found the drone of the engine electrifying, the response from the tiller exciting, and as he circled a ragged island not far offshore and headed south toward Sugar Steeple Community Church, adrenalin started pumping. Power. He had power. Not the walk-through-brick-walls kind of power, but the go-anywhere-do-anything kind he'd experienced so seldom in his lifetime. Out here with the watery world laid out before him, with no curbs or stop signs, with only a weak motor and a few islands to slow him down, the power took a name: *freedom*. His breathing quickened, his heart thundered, his muscles loosened. He was in control. What a feeling! Like a soaring eagle—"they will run and not grow weary, they will walk and not be faint"—Isaiah must have been cruising a lake when he wrote that.

Unable to contain himself, Win suddenly shouted. The sound surprised even himself and certainly the old fisherman in an equally old aluminum craft not far off. It was a yowl. A wild, liberating yowl. When the first one faded, he let out another.

"Are you nuts?" the fisherman cried across the water.

Win laughed. Win knew how crazy he must appear. But crazy or sane, he loved the exhilaration of it all.

He pushed the tiller hard left and the boat spun 180 degrees.

After straightening it out for a second, Win pushed the tiller hard left again. This time he just kept it there and the boat spun like a corkscrew.

"Good," the old fisherman shouted to him. "Maybe you'll screw yourself right to the bottom."

Win yowled louder and then in a sudden surge of total insanity, he leaped to his feet. The throttle automatically died and he nearly lost balance, but after struggling for a heartbeat, he sensed the arms of invincibility wrapping around him, and he stood erect—but only for a moment. Instantly unsteady, Win nearly plunged headlong into the still icy water. He immediately experienced what best could be described as a compensating burst of reason. Dropping back to the wooden seat, he regained his equilibrium, but only physically. Emotionally he just had to laugh again. "Whoooa! Now that was fun!" he cried, hardly able to keep from launching himself to his feet again.

"Only for some of us," the fisherman called back.

He saw the top of a white tower jutting above the rusty red cliffs—Sugar Steeple Church. Taller than the trees surrounding it, reflecting the sun, the cross at its pinnacle was a brilliant beacon. "Boy, what a difference we're going to make, eh Lord?" he cried to the gulls.

Suddenly everything changed. Exhilaration died; laughter ceased; his heart leadened; the boat slowed; the engine sputtered. For a moment he thought dizziness had brought him down, but he tested himself. No dizziness. He spun the boat around again, much slower this time, his shoulders slumping under an invisible weight. A moment ago his emotions soared, now they stumbled through a bleak, dark valley. "Lord?" he muttered confused. Pleading propelled the word.

Depression.

An old enemy had found him—even in the middle of this huge lake. "Was I having too much fun, Lord?" he groaned, his body deflating. The symptoms weren't new—self-doubt, the certainty that he was facing life alone, knowing the impossible was on the way and that he would have to struggle with it by himself. Yes, the components were all there. But he had never felt them quite so profoundly before. Usually a few strands of emotional muscle persisted and worked to reason him out of it—*God won't let you down, everybody has faults, you're a bright guy, you won't fail.*

But that voice of truth and reason remained silent this time. Maybe he'd fallen from such a great height that he was suffering from the emotional bends. Maybe his suspicions were true. Maybe he was incompetent, arrogant, foolish—maybe he really was alone. Maybe there really was no God and all the good things were merely luck and the bad things "just the way it goes sometimes." *No,* he argued, *DNA couldn't have evolved. God created that. Nor the human brain. Well Madonna's might have evolved.*

"Time to snap out of it, bonehead," he ordered himself. But he didn't snap out of it. His emotions remained shackled to a very black spirit.

Then he saw the tower again and the cross glistening above it.

"This isn't you, is it, Lord?" he muttered.

He spun the boat again. This time when it pointed toward the church, he slowed, his eyes riveted on the church steeple. Another prayer—a plea for joy, for trust, for all those things Christians need to buoy themselves, to lift themselves above the clouds into God's rich sunlight. No change. The black spirit seemed to have him by the vitals, its grasp unbreakable. Knowing deliverance lay in God's house, Win pointed the bow of the rubber horseshoe even more deliberately at the steeple and plowed toward it.

But if anything the depression intensified. His dead mother's face emerged from his gray cells . . . that desperate mask just before death whisked her away . . . the only person who had ever cared. His heart became granite, dragging the rest of him down. "Oh, no. Not this," he muttered and in an act that he saw as defeat, he pushed the rudder to the right and, as he pulled left, he removed his eyes and heart from the steeple.

"Okay—enough's enough," Win stated, taking control. He punched the throttle and steered a straight course toward home. After only a few yards, as if entering sunlight from deep shadows, the depression began to dissolve. Instantly, drooping muscles tightened, breathing returned to near normal, and relief rushed over him like a prayer. But he'd escaped by turning away from God's house. Was God saying something to him?

Relieved, he muttered, "I'll think about it later." As his heart regained confidence, he said, "At any rate, that's enough boating for one day."

Chad stormed Win's kitchen, saw an open lunchmeat package, and cried bleakly, "Bologna!"

"Well," Win greeted, standing at his counter, spreading white bread with mayonnaise. "Bologna to you too."

"Mom," Chad cried again, "he's fixing bologna. Yuck!"

"You're Chad, right?" Win asked, but the boy gave no answer before Ginger entered.

A little worse for her son's behavior, she stepped wearily into the kitchen. "Hush, Chad," she ordered, then turned to Win. "Just remember, you invited him." She, like Win, wore jeans, and though he wore a white T-shirt, she was draped beautifully in an oversized, blue sequined sweatshirt. With her Nordic blonde hair and sky blue eyes, Win found her a notch or two above drop-dead gorgeous.

Win smiled, "I gather bologna is not a staple at your house."

"Never gets through the door," Ginger said, mirroring just a bit of her son's culinary disdain.

Win tossed a finger toward the refrigerator. "How 'bout ham?"

"Ham's good," Ginger nodded. "A little mustard. I see tomatoes. They're good. I'm surprised you found any this time of year."

"I got up early—a supermarket in Burlington."

"Long way for tomatoes."

"Nothing open around here."

"I'll get the ham," she offered, opening the fridge while he sliced tomatoes.

Chad had already disappeared down the hall.

"Pringle potato chips okay? I had a taste for them."

"Pringles are fine."

Chad burst from the hallway. "Mom, come on. You gotta see this."

"Not now, Chad." She groaned. "Your stomach depends on my continuing here."

"Mom, no kidding, you gotta." Chad grabbed her hand and pulled her toward the back hallway.

Win stiffened.

A few seconds later she sauntered back. Striking a chiding pose, she said, "You sleep in a car bed."

Feeling "found out," Win didn't answer right away. "I wanted one as a kid," he said simply.

Ginger didn't respond to that; rather she nodded and added, "As a kid, I wanted to play cops and robbers with the boys. Maybe that's why I'm a cop now, who knows?"

Win looked at her appreciatively. "Who knows," he echoed as Chad flew out the back door.

Ginger peeled off slices of ham and stacked them generously on a couple of pieces of bread, then spread gobs of mustard on each. "We're a mustard family," she explained as she slapped the bread together.

"My mom liked Pringles—all kinds of junk food, really. It came back to me at the market—bologna sandwiches with mayo and tomatoes, Pringles. A lunch from heaven. She died when I was Chad's age."

"That's tough. Chad's dad died about six years ago. Chad was four. He was a house painter."

"Fall off a ladder?"

"No—a six-pack—maybe a whole case. We're not sure."

Win let that go, but added a moment later, "Losing a parent's tough on a kid."

"On the other parent too," she pointed out. She sounded as if her statement were just the tip of a very large iceberg.

Win didn't reply, but he stopped fumbling with the bologna for a moment and looked at her. She saw deep caring in his eyes and she appreciated it.

But she also felt strangely uncomfortable with it. "Killer white," she muttered, looking down at the bread.

"You're a wheat bread person."

"It's healthier."

"But there weren't any balloons on the wrapper. When I was in the supermarket I saw the balloons. Ah, 'Memories,'" he crooned badly.

"I bet you're going to tell me about them, aren't you?"

"I usually ate in the cafeteria at the seminary and at the student union in college, and before that Dad's cook prepared everything—"

"His cook?"

"Dad's knee deep in money," Win said blandly. "But on Saturdays, when the cook was off, my mom made bologna sandwiches for lunch. Dad hated her eating junk, but on Saturdays, when both he and cook were gone, she ate mounds of junk, and she let me eat it with her."

Chad suddenly burst into the room. "He's got a boat," he cried. "Can I take her out?"

Ginger turned an incredulous gaze on Win. "A boat? When did you get a boat?"

"Next to the supermarket there was this boat lot," Win explained.

"It's one of those long inner tube things with a motor," Chad said excitedly.

Ginger groaned. "You're kidding!"

"Can I take her out?"

"It's a boat," Win reaffirmed, ignoring Chad. "It's my first. Gimme a break."

Ginger wasn't so sure she wanted to. Even though buying a boat the first day on the lake seemed adventurous, buying a real boat might have been a sign that this guy who slept in a car bed and fawned over long lost memories of bologna sandwiches and balloons really was a man. But, alas, it wasn't a boat. It was a toy. "If you wanted a boat . . . "

"It's a starter kit," Win stated, with a hint of humor. "It'll serve its purpose."

"Which is?"

He looked out the kitchen window to the lake. "I'm free out there." But as soon as he mentioned freedom, he thought of the emotional shackles he'd also experienced on the lake.

"I just get sick," Ginger said dryly. She took the pile of sandwiches out to the white wrought iron table in the middle of the even shabbier backyard.

Win followed, his smile returning in the sunlight.

After Win said grace, which Ginger liked, they ate.

Eyes on the boathouse, Chad piped up. "Mom won't buy me one of those boats."

"You'd outfit it with torpedoes," Ginger replied.

"My dad wouldn't get me one, either," Win told him.

"My husband had boats from the time he was a boy," Ginger said.

"How'd he die?"

"Car accident—he'd been drinking."

"I was four," Chad said, suddenly immensely serious.

Win screwed his face up repentantly. "That's me, sensitivity plus."

Chad recovered quickly. "I won't take your boat far," he pleaded.

"You won't take it at all," Ginger said, firm eyes on him.

Only half finished with her sandwich, she took a long drink of diet Coke, set the can down, and eyed him tentatively. "Have you given helping me out any thought?" she asked. "Actually helping the whole Christian community."

"Killer catching?"

"I thought after you'd slept on it—driven the Corvette a few times around your bedroom—you might have changed your mind."

Win shook his head broadly. "If I find anything out, I'll tell you. But I'm no detective. I'm not sure what I am, but I know I'm no detective. I'd probably do more harm than good, and soon you'd be investigating two murders. No, I haven't changed my mind."

Suddenly they heard a muffled growl from the boathouse.

"Where's Chad?" Ginger spun around just in time to see the black rubber craft, powered by the Mercury outboard and guided by her son, emerge from the boathouse and glide lithely over the water. "Chad Glasgow, get back here!" she screamed.

Leaping to their feet, Win and Ginger scrambled to the shore. By the time they'd reached it Chad had covered at least thirty yards. Although he'd started on a straight course for the island, he'd wavered and spun around playfully a couple of times. "Hey," he called back. "This is great!"

"Get back here this instant!" Ginger called, angry hands on hips.

"I'm taking it around the island . . ."

"I'm not sure how much gas . . ." Win called out. But gas wasn't the problem. Suddenly the shadow blue speedboat that had thundered by yesterday returned. It exploded from the other side of the island and cut a broad swath, roaring past Chad. The wake slammed into the rubber craft and gave it several violent shocks. Chad's bravado vanished, and he clung desperately to the rubber sides, but there was nothing to cling to. The last wave struck more violently than the others, and he bounced like he was on a trampoline out of the boat and into the water.

Win stood at the end of the boathouse pier. Seeing Chad's predicament, he immediately jumped into the surf. Ginger glanced his way and marveled at the Olympic form but quickly looked back to Chad. He had recovered from the cold water's jolt and was making his way back to shore. Chad had always been a good swimmer and he proved that now.

One thing was puzzling, though. The boat didn't stop.

Although not a boat person, Ginger knew that the throttle mechanisms on outboards automatically throttled back when abandoned. This one must have stuck, because the black rubber boat continued on, skipping joyfully toward the island.

What about Win? Turning, she saw him standing in knee-deep water clutching his side, his face twisted in pain. "A little shallow, was it? You okay?" she called, taking a few slow steps his way while keeping an eye on Chad's progress. Chad had made it about halfway.

"Fine." Win groaned, straightening slightly and watching his boat plow unfettered toward a particularly wooded place on the island's edge. The instant it hit, there was a resounding pop and an audible hiss.

Ginger eyed him with a sheepish grin. "Oops!" she said.

The rest of the afternoon was a bit strained. Chad was unrepentant—after all, he had just taken it for a little ride; there wasn't anything wrong in that. No one had said he couldn't. Even after being reminded that everyone had said he couldn't, he said something about not hearing that. And, after all, it wasn't his fault the throttle stuck. Ginger took him in the house and reprimanded him anyway.

Win stood at the water's edge nursing his rock-bruised side and wondering how he was going to retrieve his boat, now a crumpled black mass caught in a jutting tree branch, the motor submerged.

The discipline as complete as it would ever be, Ginger came out and stood beside him for a minute or two before she spoke. "You okay?"

"I thought lakes were deeper than that."

"Not there." Then she looked out at the boat. "I work with a guy who can help," she said simply.

About an hour later Police Detective Mike Grogan growled up in a twenty-four-foot power cruiser. His white shorts and shirt were a sharp contrast to his already tanned, muscular arms and legs. *A tanning salon,* Win thought, although Grogan looked born to the outdoors and knew it. When he was within shouting distance he throttled back. "Is this where the damsel in distress is?" his New York accent icing every syllable.

"Mike," Ginger called. "This is a friend of my uncle's, Win Brady. Win, Mike Grogan."

Win hailed him from the end of the pier while Ginger stood at the edge of the rocky shore. She pointed toward the island. "Win's rubber boat got away from him."

Grogan turned and studied the island for a moment. "If I ever had a son I'd probably buy him one of those things." He looked at Win and smiled. "But you're a little old for it, don'tcha think?"

"Never found out," Win said.

Grogan laughed good-naturedly, but Win sensed an unmistakable mocking undertone. "I'll get it."

He did. Fifteen minutes later, the wounded, perhaps dead, rubber craft lay on the deck of the boathouse, its engine a garland of underwater plants. Chad stood curiously over the tangled rubber.

"Big hole," Grogan commented, standing on his deck, smiling down, pleased that this good-looking hunk had a problem. "If you'd only used your American Express card."

"I'm sorry, Win," Ginger said repentantly. Then she turned to Chad and said with clenched teeth, "Chad and I will discuss this again later."

Chad shrugged. "What did I do? It's not my fault that boat came by. I was in control 'til then."

Win was just as glad it wasn't his son that needed "training up." He didn't feel up to it just then. The idea of revenge was far more appealing. He looked at Grogan. "Join us for a Coke?"

"Coke? No," he declined as if he would have accepted had he been offered a beer or something harder. "Ginger owing me something is good enough." He leered. "I'll collect one day."

Win thought he saw a spark of admiration in Ginger's eyes. He didn't quite understand why. She was a Christian and he seemed to be a bozo.

"Well, thanks for your help," Win said.

"See you Monday?" Grogan said, ignoring Win.

"I've got traffic duty all day. But maybe I'll see you."

"You will," Grogan stated, with the same leer.

With a final wave, he gunned the cruiser and thundered off.

"I should be grateful, but I don't think he was helping me," Win finally said.

"He has his hopes," she said, still watching the cruiser with an admiring eye as it headed off around the point.

Win only pursed his lips with a grunt of muffled disgust then looked down at the lifeless rubber. "I guess a tire patch won't help."

# Chapter 5

Sugar Steeple Community Church glistened white in the center of an emerald meadow. The meadow, speckled with yellow and white dandelions, reached through a stand of budding maples to the summit of a worn and rugged cliff. Below, the lake lapped lazily at a confusion of rust-red boulders. A long drive reached to Highway 2, which strung the islands together. A parking area lay at the side of the church, the same side as the steeple from which Dan Bryce had been thrown.

After losing his rubber dream boat the day before and his conversation with Ginger about solving Bryce's murder, Win had had a long talk with himself about priorities and gifts, and wants and not-wants. His top priority was getting back to the seminary. That would happen only after Dean Watkins knew that he'd lived—that he'd met the enemy on the battlefield, smelled the spiritual napalm in the morning, witnessed to real people with real problems, and maybe won a few of them to Christ. That was it in a nutshell. And no pranks—none that would get back to the dean, anyway.

His gifts? He interpreted Scripture. Wrote a little. Sometimes said clever things. But he wasn't a detective. He wasn't devious, couldn't lie, couldn't pretend to be something or someone he wasn't. Couldn't worm his way into someone's confidence and use it to nail said someone—even a killer.

Wants? After seminary, he wanted his books. He wanted to read, write, and think great thoughts about his great God. And he didn't particularly want to think them on the shores of a lake that froze over most winters. There were plenty of warm lakes in warm places.

Not-wants? He didn't want to be what someone else

wanted him to be. He'd been doing that most of his life, and he didn't want to do it anymore. He didn't want to take on something just because someone else wanted him to. Particularly being a homicide detective. The truth was, he didn't care who killed Dan Bryce. God knew who the murderer was, and God could reveal him or her whenever God wanted. With or without Win's help.

So, when Sunday morning dawned clear and crisp, he made himself a good breakfast and ate it with a clear conscience. He ate at his kitchen table, the French doors to the backyard open, fresh lake air coming in earnest waves. Then he drove his '54 Chevy to church, eager to meet the congregation he'd soon be serving.

Although he preferred jeans and pullovers, his magic checkbook had produced a number of suits over the years—expensive ones because expensive ones looked and fit the best. He wore one this morning—a gray wool that hung elegantly accented by a light blue dress shirt and floral tie. Although clothes meant little to him, he often dressed as if they did.

Walking toward the entrance, he fell in line with others, some single, most couples and families with children, all chatting among themselves or calling to others. The women were experimenting with bright spring colors while the men seemed indecisively caught between drab winter wools and light shirts and slacks. He shook hands formally with one of the two greeters.

The interior, like the exterior of the church, was white, accented by dark hardwood floors and railings. After stepping through the outer lobby, he entered the main sanctuary. Also white with accents of dark wood, it was adorned with cheerful splashes of spring flowers, some in the front corners, and a large spray in the center of the altar behind an immense, open Bible. In front of the Bible stood a transparent plastic pulpit.

Feeling a little overwhelmed by the responsibility of ministering to the crowd now slowly filling the pews, Win shrank into himself a bit. He found a spot in one of the back pews near the exit and sat.

He immediately became aware of hawkish eyes boring through him. Looking up he found them deeply set in a cheerless granite face.

Roz Swift hovered there. "That's my place."

If Win was anything, he was nonconfrontational, particularly on unfamiliar ground and more particularly when the rock hard eyes reminded him of his father's. Win stiffened. "I beg your pardon."

"That's my place. I sit here every Sunday, and I intend to sit here now."

Win wondered if there was anything in Proverbs that would allow him to strangle this woman. But he knew that was impractical. He was now part of the church leadership and would have to behave graciously. "I'll just slide over here," he said and launched himself to the center of the pew.

Accepting Win's capitulation as her due, Roz sat. When she did, Bill Simms, who now sat in front of her, turned, eyed her, then gave his head a disappointed little shake. Bill slid closer to Win. "Bill Simms," he introduced himself as he turned. "I'm a trustee."

"A pleasure," Win said, shaking his outstretched hand.

"You're new," Bill offered. "A visitor?"

"Employee," Win said and caught Roz's hawkish eyes glancing his way. He saw her expression harden even further.

"You're the new Bryce?" Bill smiled. "I heard Worlly'd done something."

Win felt a warmth from Bill, and it almost made up for the glacier grinding toward him from Roz's side. "I'm Win Brady."

"Win? What kind of a name is that?"

"Short for Winsome—my folks were sixties flower people."

"At least they didn't name you 'Fruit Stand' or 'Zinnia.' No. I guess those are girls' names—maybe 'Tubers' or 'Root,'" he said thoughtfully. Win couldn't tell if he was kidding. Then Bill said, "Talk to you later." And he spun around and faced front just as Win saw Pastor Worlly and another fellow enter.

Win found the service a little dry: a lot of reading by the

congregation, music from a thirty-voice choir, and a few hymns sung halfheartedly by a congregation always searching for both words and music. Even J. Sanders Worlton's sermon didn't help much. Although it was delivered in a flamboyant manner befitting the pastor's name, there was scant substance projected in the booming voice and emphatic, broad sweeps of his billowing, raven sleeves. But, Win mused, at least he was entertaining and the jokes were good. Win never could tell a joke.

At the end of the service, Pastor Worlton stationed himself at the center doors leading out. The center aisle jammed, and naturally averse to crowds, Win inched toward the side aisle to make his escape.

Bill Simms stopped him. "Win," he called, "want some coffee?"

Win turned and smiled mechanically. His natural inclination was to make an excuse of some sort. He was feeling slightly claustrophobic among all these strangers. But he knew it would send the wrong message to refuse, particularly to a trustee. "Sure, that'd be nice. Thank you," he managed.

"Let's get a cup where we can get acquainted."

Bill and Win made it between the pews to the side aisle, but instead of turning toward the door with everyone else, Bill led him toward the front of the church and out a side exit to a long hallway that ran the length of the sanctuary and connected the church offices.

"Worlly always has coffee on in here," Bill said as he grabbed an ancient brass doorknob. The door creaked slightly as it opened. The room might at one time have been a kitchen. A counter ran along one wall, a sink about halfway, cupboards above it and circular patches here and there in the far wall and ceiling where pipes used to go. In the corner was a desk. In disuse, it was now pushed against the wall with various sized boxes stacked on top and beside and probably behind a tattered vinyl chair.

On the counter was a Mr. Coffee maker with a half-filled

pot. "It'll still be good." Bill quickly hunted up a couple of Styrofoam cups and poured Win and himself some.

Win took a grateful sip. "Thank you."

Bill nodded. "This'll probably be your office. It was the last guy's."

Win glanced at the desk and the boxes. One box was open—books. At first he felt nothing. It would be cramped quarters, but that was nothing new. But then an eerie mist broke over and entered his consciousness. The guy who had last sat at that desk, in that chair, was dead—murdered. Win suddenly pictured Dan Bryce there, maybe the day before it happened, maybe planning out his next week, maybe planning the rest of his life. *Short plan.* Win shuddered. Maybe, at that very moment, someone was planning to do away with him.

"I understand he was murdered," Win said as casually as the shudder would allow.

"Four months ago. Early Sunday morning, before his first sermon here," Bill answered, just as casually. "Where you from?"

"Atlanta."

"You here primarily to get the youth involved?"

"That's part of it."

Bill nodded as if running out of things to say. That's when a woman with a confused expression and oblique eyes stepped into the doorway. "Bill," she said, her voice small and unobtrusive.

"Maggie, meet the new Dan Bryce."

At the mention of Bryce's name, Maggie fired a disapproving glance at Bill. But it quickly faded, replaced by a wan little smile. She stepped forward and offered her hand. "Maggie Selkirk," she introduced.

"Win Brady." Win shook it gently.

Her eyes faltered beneath his. After a moment, she said, "Forgive me, but I need to speak with Bill for a second."

"No problem," Win managed cheerfulness. "I have my coffee; I'll just look around a little."

Maggie nodded and left the room. Bill followed. At the doorway, Win watched as they found another room and disappeared inside. The door closed.

Win glanced back at the desk again. It was just a desk, old, maybe walnut. A couple of pens lay between the boxes. Nothing out of the ordinary. *What's it like to die?* he wondered, *Or know that death's next?* Feel vicelike hands slowly and unwaveringly crushing the windpipe. Or watching the earth fly up at you and know that any moment you'll be splattered all over it. *I guess that's worse than finding a goat in your bathtub,* he mused, darkly.

*What did you feel, Danny boy? Did you know the guy? How does it feel to know someone you've trusted is about to snuff you out?* He remembered his dad leaving Win's dog at the pound. *Now that's not quite the same thing,* Win thought. But almost—he'd forgotten to feed the puppy twice in one week. *I had to learn.* He wondered who the lesson hurt most. *Me or the dog?*

Another memory—maybe more apropos. When he'd made the decision to stay at the seminary instead of going to a large, prosperous church in Nashville—the church to the country/western stars—his father gave him a look of profound disappointment. It rubbed like ground glass on Win's heart.

Coffee and rolls were served on a small patio at the side of the church, and it was there that everyone staying for Sunday school classes congregated. Win decided to join them. But as he walked along the hallway he noticed swarms of historical photos of the church and its activities on the walls. Since the church was more than a hundred years old, the wall was crammed—pictures of all sizes, some quite primitive, most in black and white. Each had a small explanation beneath it. Win decided that one day soon he'd have to spend some time reading them. As it was he glanced only at a few. Finding the patio, he slipped through the crowd to the large stainless steel coffee urn and levered himself a refill. He then moved a few feet away and stood quietly waiting for something to happen.

Nothing did.

He was on his second cup from the urn when the woman who'd forced him to move from her pew came up to the coffeepot, an arctic breeze blowing from her eyes as she did. Win had the distinct feeling that she wanted to make the same impression on him as the iceberg made on the Titanic. He acknowledged her with a smile.

"So you're the new hire," she said, her coal black eyes locking onto his.

"Win Brady," he said without presenting his hand.

"Roz Swift. We're an old and proud church. We want a hard worker who keeps his nose where it belongs."

"I'll help where I can," Win said, feeling slightly intimidated by this tank of a woman.

Watching her disappear inside the church, Win shook his head in disbelief and allowed the intimidation to vanish. After a moment he stepped away from the table to stand behind a couple of older ladies.

"Are you going to Maybell's funeral?" one of them asked the other.

Maybell Winowski had died. There'd been a quick mention of it during the service. No eulogy, just an emotionless invitation to the funeral.

"I doubt it. I only spoke to her once, and she's been away for so long—holed up in that cottage of hers. How long's it been—a year, maybe two? No. I don't like funerals and certainly won't go when I don't even know the casket's occupant."

The woman speaking suddenly noticed Win. He half expected a cold reception to his eavesdropping, but she winked. He nodded politely and stepped away.

A young boy's voice burst into angry sobs. "I want to go!" the choking voice insisted. "Daddy, I want to go!"

It took only an instant for Win to locate father and son near the door. The father was about Win's age, athletically handsome in a dark suit. The son was a tow-headed little guy with fat cheeks and his own dark suit and bow tie. He looked about five.

"Now, Jeremy, you can't go. We're going to Grandma's after church. Not today."

"You never let me go," the lad fired back in angry defiance, his little legs beginning to churn, a tantrum forming.

The father dropped to a crouch and laid a firm hand on his son's arm. "Son, now remember where you are."

"You never let me do anything," the boy raved, his lips twisted furiously. While legs pumped like pistons and eyes flashed, the boy clenched his fist and hit his father in the shoulder.

The father took a restraining breath, then did something Win found unorthodox. He wrapped loving arms around his son and held him to his chest and spoke softly to the boy. At first the boy squirmed violently like a threatened puppy, showing his anger in muffled cries and kicking at his father. But after a short while the boy calmed. He still pouted with his lower lip, and his eyes were stained with tears, but the eruption had subsided. When it had, the man released his son and eyed him with loving firmness. "You know that's unacceptable behavior, Jerr," he said, still at eye level with his son. "We'll deal with this later. For now, we'll just enjoy Sunday school, okay?"

The boy kept his lower lip poised, but he said obediently, "Okay, Daddy."

*Train a child in the way he should go, and when he is old he will not turn from it.* Win's reflexes brought the verse to mind. He also knew the truth of "Spare the rod, spoil the child." Win's father wouldn't have spared the rod—he wouldn't have spared it right there in front of God and everyone. And yet this father seemed to be setting a different priority, sending a different message. Maybe later there would be a rod. Who was right? His father or this boy's? Win wasn't sure.

Win found himself drifting, smiling casually at this person and that, sometimes receiving a smile in return, often not. When he finally came to rest, he stood for a moment and surveyed the room. Win soon overheard a conversation he found instantly arresting. It was between two men. One was a slight fellow with intense black eyes, thin, drawn lips, and receding black hair. The other was his opposite: casual, handsome, with a smile that went on forever. Win stood in such a way that he could hear clearly, but was only able to see them out of the corner of his eye.

"A note?" questioned the casual one who had been called Steve. "Let's see it."

There was the sound of paper unfolding.

Steve read: "Watch out—it's going to happen." He refolded the paper and gave it back. "Come on, Peter, this has to be a joke."

Peter grunted incongruously. "This is no joke." He took a sip of coffee and grunted knowingly a few more times before taking the cup from his lips. "I'm being stalked."

"Stalked? Movie stars are stalked. You and Sandy own a candy store, not a bank."

"The security service says it takes a real pro to do what this guy—or these guys—did—slip into my place at night without tripping the alarm just to leave a note. It was there when I came in yesterday. A real pro." Another sip of coffee. "Yesterday a note; tomorrow a bomb."

Steve sighed. It was obvious to Win that Steve didn't buy into all this paranoia. Win didn't buy it either. This church not only had its hardcases in Roz Whozits, it also had a first class neurotic in this guy.

"Peter, it's just a joke. Everyone knows you're a little high strung."

"High strung? What's that supposed to mean?"

"How many ways can I say it? I'm nearly comatose—you're strung tighter than a banjo. The note was probably left before you closed up and you just didn't see it until the morning."

"Not possible. It was on the cash register. And I'm not high strung." He fidgeted slightly. "I just know how vulnerable we all are."

"Sure we're vulnerable. But you can't go around worrying about it all the time."

"Did you ever stop to think that while you're on the golf course—two or three times a week, I might add—you might get hit by a golf ball? That guy did last year—detached retina." Even Peter must have heard how silly he sounded for Win saw his expression change from uptight to hang-dog. "Oh, you're probably right. I got it from my mom—inherited it . . ."

"Stress isn't part of the gene pool."

"She lived through the Battle of Britain. The buzz bombs and V2s. She wanted me to understand it all, and before bedtime she'd tell me stories—how she'd be lying in bed at night and suddenly hear the buzz and then silence. They'd wait—and then the explosion. Everyone praying it wouldn't be them. They'd wake up in the middle of the night to the sound of the sirens and the explosions. She lost her neighbors one night. Friends."

"Charming bedtime story."

Win found himself agreeing.

A woman stepped up to Peter—probably his wife, Sandy. The instant Win saw her, he could hardly help himself from staring. She was remarkably beautiful—softly innocent, hazel eyes, piles of cascading auburn hair, a perfect figure made even more perfect by a flowery spring dress and short rose jacket. At one time she must have been trained as a model, because she glided effortlessly everywhere. Now she glided up to her husband. "Can I get you more coffee, dear?" She kissed him gently on the cheek.

"Sure. Thanks."

She took his empty Styrofoam cup and glided away. Steve's eyes followed her. Finally he smiled and shook his head appreciatively. "A peach. Never let her go. Mine would no more get me coffee than dance naked on that table over there."

Peter smiled. "An image worth pondering," he muttered to himself.

"Not really." Steve laughed.

"Sandy's okay. Devoted. Works all day in the store and never complains. But too straight. I wish she'd loosen up. I wouldn't mind her suddenly dancing naked on that table."

Steve laughed and glanced at Sandy, who stood by the coffee. "Now *that's* an image to ponder."

Win was still envisioning that dancing naked thing when he heard Maggie Selkirk's soft, unassured voice. "Hello," it greeted. "I'm sorry I had to interrupt you and Bill a little while ago."

Win looked down and saw her large, soft eyes looking up. "That's okay. I'm doing fine," he told her.

"Good," she said, the ever-present apology knit into the fabric of her words.

"It's a nice little church," Win offered. "Has your family been attending long?"

"Well, my husband doesn't attend." Her eyes dropped. "John works Sundays. Works most days, actually. Have you found a place to stay yet?"

"A small lakefront cottage."

"Well, please call if you need anything."

"Just your support," Win said, a little surprised at how political it sounded.

"I'm head deacon," she pointed out. "Supporting you is my job."

"Then let me thank you in advance." So formal. Even slick. And yet her vulnerability seemed to require that kind of response.

Maggie smiled with a misty blush. "I'll look forward to doing it," she said and then, as if she'd caught herself in a faux pas, her expression became instantly befuddled and she fluttered slightly. "I mean, I'll help where I can."

"I guess I'll have the previous assistant pastor's office."

Maggie's eyes darted uncomfortably. "Probably."

"What should I do with all the books?"

"They're the church's. Danny bought them with church funds. Do what you like with them, I guess."

"What was Mr. Bryce like?" Win asked offhandedly.

"He was a bumbler and a busybody." Maggie Selkirk hadn't

said it. Pastor Worlly had as he stepped up, a firm hand outstretched.

Win took it and gave it a single firm pump—his father shook hands that way. "Pastor Worlton, good to see you." Win put on his formal face.

"And you," Worlly said. "What do you think of us so far?"

*Ah, to tell the truth,* Win thought. "I'm looking forward to working with you all," he said.

"Good," Worlly said with emphasis. "Well, I have to get ready to teach a class. Good to have you here. Get to know people."

"I will, thank you."

Worlly turned abruptly and walked away, leaving him with Maggie Selkirk, who now looked like a bomb had gone off nearby. Win turned to her. "Was he?"

"Who?"

"Mr. Bryce. Was he like that?"

Maggie glanced off to Worlly's memory. "We don't talk about him much."

"He was murdered?"

"Yes," she said putting many syllables into the word. "Most think by a transient."

Win nodded, sensing she wanted to say no more about Bryce. "I think I'll take a look at my new office and then get home and do some unpacking."

Maggie became anxious. "I didn't mean to sound harsh, or anything. Really. It's just a difficult thing for us. For me." Her eyes dropped as if she'd just decided she'd failed again.

"It must be very difficult, and I was insensitive to ask," Win said warmly.

She reacted to his tone with a warmth of her own and after placing a gentle hand on his, she excused herself and left.

A few moments later Win sat in his new office, with the old desk, the boxes of books, and the odor of burned coffee. He'd already flipped off the coffeepot and pulled the desk from the wall. Now he sat in an unusually comfortable forest green vinyl chair repaired with black vinyl tape. When he moved the chair, though, he dislodged a box of books.

Win lifted the box onto the desk and scooped up the books one at a time. A glance at one of the titles, then the author's name, and he froze. "Oh, no," he groaned as if his worst fears had been realized. He opened the cover, eyed the flyleaf—Dan Bryce had scrawled his name inside. His book. He'd bought it with his own money, and it looked like it had been read completely through. Folded corners marked Bryce's progress. "Lord, I'm not ready for this. You didn't prepare me . . . Isn't it at least good manners to prepare someone? . . . Isn't there some other poor sap you can throw to the wolves—or wolf?"

Win slapped the book lightly against his palm. Then he waited for God's response. It came. In the depths of his brain came the picture of Elijah, the prophet, facing Ahab, the most evil man in the Old Testament. Win sighed. "But the ravens won't bring *me* bread every morning—they'll probably bring hand grenades and drop them one at a time from a great height."

A half-hour later, his mind still reeling from what he'd just learned, Win walked to his car, slid behind the wheel, and cranked the engine. Then cranked it again. It didn't start. It always started. Even on its worst day. Out of gas? No. Plenty. He cranked it again. And again.

He slid out from behind the wheel, stood for a long moment while he weighed all his options. He only had one, and he avoided it as long as he could. Finally he lifted the hood.

He loved the car but hated working on it. He knew nothing about cars—the fact that they ran at all had never ceased to be a mystery to him. And now the longer he hovered over this enigmatic hunk of iron the more inadequate he felt.

"Problem?"

Bill Simms didn't wait for an answer. He pushed his nose into the engine. "Fifty-four, isn't it?"

"My dad bought it for me," Win said. It wasn't entirely true. But he wasn't prepared to tell anyone yet about his magic checkbook, the marvelous moneymaker that never ran low. He'd seen the car soon after graduation from seminary, the very day he decided to stay and officially become a hermit in fact. The guy who had originally owned it had restored it. Win thought it fitting somehow to drive such a car.

"Nice," Bill said appreciatively. Keeping his hands respectfully behind his back, his eyes pored over the straight 6 engine. "It's beautiful," he cooed, then he stood. "Not all that smog nonsense. Crank it over and I'll have a listen."

"You know cars?"

"Do bears know honey? Crank it."

Win turned it over.

Simms's ears perked. "No spark. This happen before?"

"Never," Win replied, slipping Simms's sports coat over his arm after Simms had wiggled out of it.

"Work time." Simms rubbed eager hands together and dove in. Soon those hands were all over the engine, his head deep inside.

"While you're working there, can I ask you a question?"

"Sure."

"Just so I don't make the same mistakes my predecessor did, I've heard two descriptions of him. One that he was a bumbling busybody, and the other called him a friend. Who's right?"

Bill emerged, his hands grease-smudged as was his light blue shirt, the corner of which was now untucked from his pants and used as a rag. "The coil wire was loose. Come by the shop and I'll fit you a new one."

"Shop?"

"I'm a mechanic at Selkirk Ford. Maggie Selkirk's husband owns it. Come by and I'll get a new coil wire for you. The metal plug is worn."

"Thank you," Win said with true sincerity. "Uh, about Dan Bryce."

"You won't let me avoid it, will you?"

Win furrowed a brow. "I can't ask these things?"

Bill smiled broadly, putting Win completely at ease. "It's

just not a popular subject here. But I'll tell you this much. We're private people—even when there's nothing to hide we sometimes behave as if there is. Our lives belong to us, and we don't give them out to just everyone we meet. Toward the end, Dan forgot that—or didn't care about it. People quickly forgot what a good guy he had been at first."

"The person who thought him a friend . . . ?"

"Maggie, right?" Bill smiled again still wiping his hands on his untucked shirttail. "The funny thing is that she's probably the most private person of all." Now the smile became a grin, one of finality. A newly wiped hand was extended. "Well, Win Brady, welcome to Sugar Steeple. We're expecting great things from you."

"I'll do my best," Win said, meaning every clichéd word of it.

Win's telephone hadn't yet been activated so he drove directly to Ginger's after church. As it turned out, Ginger and Chad were just getting out of the car when he pulled up. Both were dressed like they, too, were just returning from church. Well-dressed, or not, though, they were battling, and when Win slid from the car he was thrust right into the middle of it.

"How could you do that?"

"A spark of genius."

"How could you carry a worm in your pocket, and how could you put it down that girl's . . ." Ginger stopped. She saw Win standing there. "Oh, hi," she said unenthusiastically.

"I wanted to talk with you."

"Chad and I are having a little discussion."

"I noticed."

Chad's expression became very serious. "Mr. Brady, you were ten once, right?"

"For just about a year."

"Now, remembering back—if you found a nice fat worm, what would you do with it?"

Win laughed. He wasn't sure if he'd been ten or not at the

time, but he remembered finding such a worm in the back-yard—his mother had been gardening. He'd brought it to her, and they'd talked about it for a while. She'd leaped three feet into the air when he'd tossed it at her—but she came down laughing. Then she'd chased him down and stuffed the worm down *his* back. Was it wrong to be thirty and still miss your mother?

"Go fishing with it," Win lied.

"You fish?" The worm was suddenly forgotten.

"I tangle a lot of line." Another memory sprouted. His father had taken him fishing once. On his first cast, Win had tangled the line into a snarly mess. He'd been promptly returned to shore. He'd been eight or nine. It definitely had been before the worm.

"Will you take me fishing?"

"When you use the worms you find to go fishing with, then he might take you fishing," Ginger stated flatly. "Putting it down that girl's back . . . "

Win laughed inside but kept a neutral expression. "You two have lunch yet?" he asked.

Ginger looked a little worried. "If you're staying I need to go shopping."

"I was going to invite you out. Maybe a hamburger or something."

Now that was an idea that Chad could endorse. "They just opened a Burger King on North Hero."

"Burger King's fine," Ginger said.

"Great!" Chad jumped into the air.

"But the treat's mine," Ginger offered.

"No," Win protested gently. "I'm doing the inviting."

"I want my own fries," Chad announced as he climbed into the backseat.

Chad shared Ginger's fries and stole a few of Win's, and an hour later Win drove into Champlain Boat Sales. They parked between two rows of boats—boats that got bigger and more expensive the further down the row one walked.

"I thought you were going to get another inflatable," Ginger said as Win walked past those and strolled toward the longer, sleeker, fiberglass models.

"Just dreaming a little," Win said boyishly.

Chad had already dismissed the sixteen-footers that Win stood before and was climbing on a twenty-foot cabin cruiser.

"Get down from there," Ginger barked.

The balding, red-fringed salesman with cherry cheeks came up. "Oh, you again," he greeted, his smile huge and genuine. "We always appreciate our repeat customers. But usually they don't come back quite so soon. What can I do to help?"

"Just looking right now," Win said to him.

The salesman waved politely and said, "When you're ready."

Win stood before a blue striped Bayliner, a sixteen-footer. $6,995.

"Assistant pastors dream big," Ginger injected, standing next to him.

He ran a hand over the sleek fiberglass. Eyes never leaving the boat, he said, "Over cornflakes this morning I reviewed all the reasons why I'd be a fool to help you find Bryce's killer."

"And?" Ginger asked, staying a respectable distance from the boat.

"I have no gifts for it; I want to get back to the seminary."

"We've traveled that road." Ginger pointed out. "Your helping was just a thought. Albeit, a stupid one."

"Well," he said, eyes still on the boat, as if it were still the primary focus of his thoughts. "I changed my mind."

"You did?" Ginger's brows raised suspiciously. "Why?"

"A book I found that Bryce probably read," Win explained, facing Ginger. "Ever hear of O. Palmer Robertson?"

"Should I have?"

"He's a conservative Christian theologian. A non-Christian

would have a tough time reading his stuff—he'd get mad or bored or confused. He'd never make it to the end. Bryce did."

"So?" Ginger's brows coiled even tighter.

"Bryce may, and I emphasize, *may* have been a Christian?"

"And?"

"There's no denying the Lord's brought me here. He's given me this information. Dan Bryce may—probably was—my brother in Christ. I can't ignore that."

"Well," Ginger said, caught a little off guard, "okay—then you'll help." She shuffled her thoughts to bring everything in line again. "Maybe we ought to go back to my place, and I'll tell you everything I know about the case—and the guy running it."

"Talk while I look."

Although she started reluctantly (she didn't like talking about these things in the open air) when she got going, the story unfolded quickly. By the time she'd finished, he was asking pointed and, she had to admit, intelligent questions.

But it was the final question that was the most important. "How do we get started?"

"With Sanderson," she said. "You'll have to meet him in the morning." Her face twisted in sudden concern about that. "If you survive that meeting you're in."

"Sounds like he's got pretty big teeth."

Ginger laughed. "Wait till he starts chewing on you."

"Tomorrow's good—I don't start at the church until Tuesday."

Now Ginger hesitated. Maybe he wasn't the right guy. Even though he wanted to help, he slept in a car bed and knew nothing about being a detective. And yet, he did want to find the truth. And at least Win would seek it intelligently, honestly—and—she was suddenly beginning to believe—fearlessly. Finally she said, "Seven A.M. okay? I know where he is every morning at seven."

"Good," Win said with finality. He turned back to the boat and placed a loving hand on the fiberglass hull. If he'd felt free in the rubber boat, he wondered what he'd feel in this one. He motioned to the salesman, now stationed by the car. As he approached, Win reached into his back pocket and pulled out the magic checkbook. As he opened it, he muttered, "Dad's going to love this."

And, while Ginger's mouth dropped to her knees, he wrote the salesman a $7,000 check.

# Chapter Six

The Lake Bakery and Donut Shoppe would never be mistaken for a Burlington high spot. The torn black tile floor provided a dingy background for the scarred yellow Formica counters, and grease covered everything as thickly as it did the donuts. But Detective Bray Sanderson liked nothing more than their large cheese Danish. He'd missed having one only a handful of mornings in the past ten years. This Monday morning was no exception. But the Danish was only part of a larger ritual. At 7:00 A.M., accompanied by a cup of tar-black coffee and the comics section of the *Burlington Morning News,* Bray spent a half-hour reading, sipping, and eating.

The ritual was a touchstone for Bray. It centered him for a day that usually had no center. And this particular day needed all the centering it could get. Friday afternoon he'd been in his cubicle when Chief of Detectives Larin Breed, his boss, had called him into his office.

Located in the relatively new police building on South Winooski, Breed's office consisted of new walls enclosing ancient file cabinets, wooden chairs, and a mahogany desk that Bray was sure was the first one ever built. And Breed looked even older than the desk. Wrinkles gathered on him like ants on a cake. "Sit," he commanded, and Sanderson sat.

"How's the church murder going?"

"Murder investigations take time."

"Grogan says he could do better."

Mike Grogan was a shark, and Sanderson suddenly felt like a wounded swimmer trailing blood.

"It's my case."

"For now."

"What's that supposed to mean?"

"It means solve it. That's what it means."

Sanderson wasn't one to whimper, so he got up from the tired, sagging chair and left. Grogan stood in the hall outside, a glint of anticipated triumph in his eye. "What did the chief have to say?"

"Something about New Yorkers coming up here and driving property values into the toilet." He was disappointed with the jab, but it was all that came to mind. He stewed all weekend. Now he looked forward to his morning ritual. Performing it meant all was still right with the world. To have it altered in any way, particularly today, would throw him off balance and introduce an unpleasant, perhaps dangerous tension.

"What do you mean someone's paid for it? I pay. I always pay." Already his ritual was altered, and he became instantly angry.

Marge, the gum-chewing octogenarian behind the glass counter, shrugged. "Schwarzenegger over there paid already."

Bray turned. Win smiled broadly and gestured for Bray to join him. Bray scowled. He slipped his folded newspaper under his arm, grabbed the Danish and coffee, and stomped to the booth. "This better be good," he warned.

There was no denying Win was intimidated. With Bray, Win would have to perform, and Win always found a demand for performance intimidating. Win stood and forced an uneasy smile. Seeing Bray's full hands, he said, "No need to shake hands."

"I wasn't going to," he said flatly.

"I'm Win Brady."

"Why would I care?" he retorted. "Listen kid, crimes are reported at the new building on Winooski. If you want to sell me something, I'll have to kill you. Nobody—I mean nobody—interrupts my morning comics."

Win remained standing while Bray Sanderson set his coffee and Danish down then tossed his paper on the table and sat. Win studied his face—the thick brows, the chiseled cheeks and chin, all hard and as expressive as granite. "What's your choice—the new building or being killed?"

"I'm here to help you," Win said, realizing too late how lame he sounded. "I'm the new assistant pastor at Sugar Steeple." He waited for that to sink in, but he couldn't tell if it had.

Bray didn't reply. Rather, he took the lid off his coffee and took a cautious sip. When he set the cup down, he eyed Win critically. "So?"

"So, I can help."

"How can you help?"

"With information."

"Give me a for instance." Bray tore off a piece of Danish, stuffed it in his mouth, and chewed, his eyes drilling into Win.

"I haven't gathered anything yet," Win parried.

"Deal in categories. What type of information would I get?" Bray was enjoying this. Win hated it.

"What kind would you like?" Win felt himself reining in a growing anger.

Bray leaned back as a triumphant grin grew on his face. "I don't need amateurs," he said coldly.

"I said something wrong. What did I say wrong?"

Bray softened. Maybe because the test was over and Win had flunked. "The help part was okay. The rest stunk. Listen," he said, "I appreciate your wanting to find Dan Bryce's killer. I myself would love to hang me a hypocrite. But an operative—that's what you'd be—needs to bring it all back. Everything he can remember, and he remembers everything. He's not the guy who decides what's important and what isn't. I am. And he's smart enough to detect the stuff that doesn't fit, doesn't ring true—and remember it."

"Piece of cake."

Bray smiled and took another long drink of coffee. "You ain't smart."

"I'm smart—try me. Tell me something smart, and I'll tell you if I know it already. Go ahead, take your best shot."

"You ain't smart—you call interrupting my comics smart?"

"I'm smart enough to know what happens if you don't solve this."

Bray frowned. He didn't like the battle being taken into his own camp.

"You fail—you want to fail?"

"Who wants to fail?"

"Nobody," Win said empathetically. "But I understand you're under some pressure to find the killer."

"I'm always under pressure. This is a pressure job—stress is my middle name."

"You've got two strikes against you on this case."

"Just two?"

"First, you're on the outside breaking into a church family—very difficult—especially in Vermont, I hear. And second, you don't understand church people, what they say and what they mean. And there's a third thing . . . "

"Three strikes? You're not smart enough to count."

"You don't understand the spiritual war, and the combatants."

"Ah, ghosts."

"Right," Win smiled slyly. "Amateur or not, I'm better than what you got."

"In a way you're right, kid. Nothing's better'n what I got. And you're as close to nothing as I've seen so far today." He grabbed his paper and started fumbling for the comics. "Beat it."

"How many offers to go undercover do you get in a day?"

That rang a bell in Bray's head. His brows pitched up, his mouth tightened—a memory came alive. Vietnam. Bray had been an MP detective. An army sergeant had murdered a Vietnamese prostitute. He hadn't thought about that case in many moons, but he'd felt the same way about that one as he did about this one. No one would talk, neither the soldiers nor the prostitutes, and after poking around for only a day or two he felt locked out. And then the daughter of a Vietnamese friend went underground. The case came apart within a week.

He straightened after a long moment, and he leaned back. Then he said with a conciliatory tone, "I'm running out of questions, and the facts I do have lay on the table unconnected."

"How about a motive?" Win asked, pleased that he sounded like he knew what he was talking about.

"Motive? Bryce knew something," Sanderson stated flatly. "Maybe the kid was a blackmailer, or maybe he'd tried to convert the guy and spilled some beans the killer wanted back in the bag. Maybe the killer just *thought* he knew something." Bray took a sip of coffee. "The usual reasons are the usual reasons." He studied Win for a long moment, then said, "Tell me something."

"I'll take a shot."

Bray leaned forward. "One of their own's been murdered— right there in the church. One of 'em slammed their preacher in the head then stuffed him through this mouse hole of a window to fall thirty feet to a cement walk. Strange behavior even for church people. And yet they act like nothing happened. Why? I had a murder at the Elks Club a couple years back, and the moment I walked in the door they were telling me everything about everybody. The more bizarre the information the more people told. Not here. They can't all be covering up. Why the stone wall?"

Win wasn't sure where the words came from, but they were suddenly tumbling out. "They know the truth," Win began, "but to talk about it *makes* it true, and they don't want it to be true. If one of them could have done it, they all could have done it. And if they're capable of murder then they have to look inside themselves and clean house. But there's something else you need to know."

"And that is?" Bray challenged.

Win wasn't sure why he needed to tell Bray this. He wouldn't understand. But the words kept fighting their way out. "I realize I don't have all the facts yet, but I've thought a lot about what I do know," he began. "And the more I think the more I'm convinced that this is no ordinary crime."

"Murders never are."

"You know that better than me. But I believe when you've solved this thing we'll see that the motive is strongly spiritual."

"Ah—palm readers and entrails."

"No—God and Satan."

Bray nodded deeply, mocking him. "Aaaahhhh." He stuffed another piece of Danish in his mouth. "At the church—can you keep your mouth shut?"

"Sure."

"I mean really shut. A murderer on the loose is another murder waiting to happen. If he suspects anything you'll be next."

"So you'll give me a try?"

"And little more than that," Bray stated flatly.

Win filled his lungs with air. He had succeeded, yet part of him had hoped he'd fail, hoped he'd leave the meeting prevented from playing detective. "I tried, Lord," he would have said. "I gave it a shot." Now he was in. The Lord was opening doors whether Win wanted them opened or not. "When do I get to see what you have?" he asked Sanderson.

The detective stiffened. "You just get me information—that's your job. My job is to combine and correlate it with what we already have."

Win frowned. "I could be a target," he stated with a corresponding sense of urgency. "Correlating information before you see it could save my life. Either you trust me or you don't."

Sanderson thought for a moment, then nodded. "How much time you got?"

"All day."

"Then come on."

Passing gum-chewing Marge, they were about to go outside when they heard a muffled roar—an explosion somewhere in the neighborhood.

Bray charged out the door, Win right behind him.

Down the street where small shops stood like dominoes, a billow of dust and debris was still churning in front of one of them. A siren erupted and a moment later a fire truck sped around the corner.

"Gas main?" Win conjectured.

"Maybe," Bray said, eyes following the fire truck. "One thing's for sure, there's nothing down there worth bombing. Come on. We'll read about it in the papers."

Bray's cubicle wasn't much of an office. Walled by ancient wooden dividers, it was cluttered with folders and stacks of paper, and an occasional dusty figurine and a trophy or two. Plastered over every other available inch were comic strips, most of them "Broom Hilda" and "Duffy."

Bray indicated a wobbly wooden chair, and Win sat. After thumbing through the stack on his desk, Bray found a thick folder and handed it to Win, "It's all there."

"Where can I spread out?"

"The floor."

"Really?" Win had hoped for something a little more library-like. "Well, okay."

Win opened the folder and balanced it awkwardly on his lap. As he began to read the file, Bray noticed someone who looked familiar standing at the front desk. He was a slightly built fellow with black receding hair. His face was angular, and intense bead-black eyes darted over the blue shirts behind the desk. At first Bray couldn't remember exactly where he'd seen the guy before, but then he remembered. The church. The guy worked downtown, so Bray had interviewed him first. A long time ago.

Peter something.

Bray hung back as one of the desk blues turned bored eyes toward the visitor.

"I need some help," said Peter something.

"You and half the world."

"I'm Peter Sweet. I own the candy store downtown. Across from the explosion this morning."

"You gotta claim? The mayor's office."

"No. No claim. I have a note here. Right after the explosion I found it in my mail slot."

"What note?"

"This note." Peter Sweet produced a piece of folded bond paper.

The blue shirt grabbed it. After glancing at it, he exclaimed, "I been a cop for ten years, and I never seen one of these. Hey, guys, take a look at this!" The note was constructed from cut-out letters of varying newspaper fonts and sizes.

Another asked, "What's it say?"

When two other cops grabbed at the note, Sweet protested, "Fingerprints?"

"You think anyone taking the trouble to put this together would leave prints?"

The desk sergeant grabbed the note. "Well, let's see here. 'It could happen to you.'" He looked at Peter. "What could happen to you?"

"The explosion," Sweet said emphatically. "They're saying that the explosion could happen to me. I got another note Saturday morning."

"Two notes. You got a regular pen pal. What makes you think this is referring to the explosion?"

"What else would it refer to?"

"I really wouldn't know."

Bray decided to cut in. "What is it?"

"Guy here got a note after the blow this morning. Says it's his second."

Bray took the page and read it quickly. "What did the first one say?"

"Something about—'It's going to happen.' Something like that."

"You still have it?"

"In a fit of courage I tore it up. Threw it away."

"Well, in another fit of courage you'd better call the fire investigators. They ought to know about this. Who would do this to you?"

"I don't know." Peter sounded deeply befuddled. "But it shows how vulnerable you are—hey, you're the cop who's investigating Bryce's death, aren't you?"

The moment Sweet mentioned Bryce, Bray heard Grogan's chair squeak and felt the New Yorker's eyes on him.

Bray didn't miss a beat. "Yeah. Anything like this ever happen to you before?"

"I don't think so. They didn't even ask for money or anything. . . . "

"Do other people know you feel like this—kind of vulnerable?"

"You think I'm paranoid?"

Grogan was circling now. Easing himself up to the front desk, pretending to be there for something else—anything else.

"No, but someone's jabbing you where it hurts. When the store across the street blows they put this note together to shake you up. It could be a joke."

"Joke?" Sweet exclaimed. "This is no joke. It came through the mail slot only a few minutes after the explosion. There wasn't time to put it together after the explosion."

Bray gnawed his lower lip for a moment and cast a wary eye on Grogan. Grogan was near the coffeepot now. He'd left his cup behind and just stood there as if he were taking coffee in through his pores. Bray handed the paper back to the desk sergeant. "Contact the fire investigator. Maybe Mr. Sweet has a point."

Sweet raised a vindicated eyebrow as Bray turned. As he did, Grogan slithered toward the front desk. As Bray walked away, he called to the desk sergeant, "Grogan will want to read that."

The sergeant handed the paper to Grogan who took it and, after shining a bold smile Bray's way, read.

Back at his cubicle, Bray found that Win had spread the contents of the folder out all over the floor and was down on his hands and knees poring over them. He was currently buried in the coroner's report but looked up as Bray approached.

"He was still alive when he hit the ground. The fall killed him."

"The guy who threaded him through that window killed him."

"If I wanted to kill someone I'd make sure he was dead."

"He did. Dropping a guy headfirst from a thirty-foot tower takes some of the risk out of it." Bray sat at his desk, the chair heaving a tired squeak as he leaned back in it.

"I like the way time of death was determined."

"Brilliant," Bray said as if brilliance had nothing to do with it. Which, in his mind, it hadn't.

"Makes you almost think there is a God," Win took a dig.

"Well, if there are miracles, that was one." Bray said candidly. "Or just lucky. Sometimes we get lucky." His expression didn't change. "Lucky an amateur meteorologist was making a snowfall depth study; lucky that he knew how much snow fell and when; lucky the pictures of the body showed how much snow had piled up on the body since it hit the ground, and downright lucky when the coroner was stymied trying to find the time of death, this kid's mother, who just happened to work for the coroner's office, made the connection." Bray shook his head, "If you're a Bible thumper you call it miraculous. If you're an average Joe you call it luck. I choose to call it real good police work."

Win forced a smile. "Why do you think Bryce met someone in the church tower at two A.M.?"

"That's why they call it a mystery. We tried to believe it was a transient. Cases can go away easier if the perpetrator's gone away. But that didn't wash."

"The killer could have broken in. Maybe he was using the tower to get away from the cold."

"But why was Bryce there? Why would someone leave a warm apartment to go out in the cold, especially that late? We thought maybe he'd stayed late to work. If he had he would have heard the intruder, but more likely the intruder would have seen his light and gone somewhere else. No. He was lured there."

Bray kept his eyes on Win while he studied the interview notes. "One of Sugar Steeple's finest was just in here."

Win looked up. "Really? Why?"

"He feels vulnerable. People are leaving him notes, things are blowing up around him. Aren't you Bible thumpers supposed to trust the big guy upstairs?"

The question triggered guilty memories in Win. "We fail sometimes. Was he involved in that explosion this morning?"

"He got a note threatening him with the same."

"There was a guy who got a note at his candy store a day or so ago threatening him. I overheard it at church yesterday morning."

"He said that. And this one came a minute or two after the blast."

"Then the explosion was set."

"Could be. Find anything besides the obvious?"

"Probably what you did. Three months before his death something happened to get him moving." Win found that fact particularly interesting. Maybe he'd been saved about then. "He made appointments with everyone in the church, and some outside the church. He even took flowers to several of them a couple times a week."

"Nobody ever got flowers," Bray said.

"Somebody got flowers."

"Nobody I found." ·

"Did you find the florist shop?"

"There's only one on the island, and Bryce was in there only twice in nine months."

Win flipped through the pages again. "There's at least two entries a week. Maybe it's a person."

"There were only three Flowers in the phone book, and none of them had heard of Bryce."

Win nodded absently. "When he saw the people he didn't talk about anything earthshaking. Just normal pastoral visits?"

"He must have found something on one of those visits and it cost him. The people interviewed wouldn't tell us anyway.

'Sure, he came by,'" Bray mimicked, "'and we talked about my cat, the new transmission in the car, my lesbian lover—and please don't use the bathroom, her body's still in pieces in the bathtub.' We don't usually get interviews like that. We look for contradictions, innuendoes, lies—we love lies. But we sure didn't find them here."

Win had been leaning low over the pages. "They found him strange—awkward, one said. What he was doing was new to him—he probably kept it simple." He leaned back.

"Something he heard cost him."

"He did make an impression on Maggie Selkirk. She was sympathetic." The image of Maggie's large lost eyes flashed in his brain. "I met her Sunday. Mousy, small, intimidated." Saying it brought a sudden empathy for her. "It had to be tough on her. But your comments indicate you think there was something between them."

"She's hiding something. They met in that tower. Only a couple times, she says. But it could have been more. If it had been just a couple of times why'd she go up there to check? Maybe Bryce took her out, and her husband decided to make him pay. Maybe Bryce felt guilty and was going to come clean, and she nailed him. There's more to that lady than on the surface, and your first job should be finding out what."

Spy on Maggie. Interesting thought. Win gathered up the pages, straightened them, and slipped them into the folder. He handed the folder back to Bray. "I start tomorrow morning. I think I'll use the rest of the day to get settled." He eyed the thick folder. "It's time to see what the Lord has in mind."

"Okay. Tomorrow." Bray watched Win get to his feet. Then halted him, "Wait a second."

Win stopped short.

The detective's brows twisted, and he rubbed the side of his nose. "Don't you think it's just a bit coincidental that we have both Bryce's murder and what looks like first-rate extortion going on with that candy man in the same congregation? It's not a big congregation, either. Is that normal for the churches you frequent?"

Win took a moment to think. "Not so far."

"Think these two crimes might be related?"

It was a logical question, and had Win been the unsaved detective he might have come to the same conclusion. But after reading the evidence and combining it with what he already knew, Win was beginning to color a picture. Somehow, the bombing at Peter Sweet's fell outside the lines. "They might be, but I'm not sure."

Questions lurked behind Bray's deadpan. Finally he said, "I guess we'll see."

"God bless, Bray. See you later."

"Later," said Bray, then he added, "Watch your back."

# Chapter 7

Peter Sweet loved the smell of the candy shop. He'd never succumbed to snacking, but he loved to breathe the rich sweetness in the air. Every Monday morning was the same. Arriving before eight, he'd open the back door and immediately the aroma of sugar and caramel and chocolate and popcorn seduced him, and he'd fall in love with what he was doing all over again.

But not this Monday. Not after the explosion and the cool reception at the police station.

Rather than going directly back into the store, he walked over to the location of the blast. It was a deserted storefront—a T-shirt store that hadn't survived last summer. Peter could easily see the commotion inside, firemen in black hats and yellow rubber jackets roamed around bumping into uniformed inspectors. A yellow ribbon laced between orange traffic cones, just like the one the police constructed at the church, cordoned the area off. Whoever set the blast had picked the right spot to send him a message. Nothing important seemed damaged. And the right time—no one was hurt.

It was so close.

But why would someone try to scare him? He was hardly rich. He worked hard for a living and owned little more than his house, and even that was mortgaged heavily, the money planted deeply in a two-bit candy store. Why would anyone want that?

He finally entered the store through the alley, and as he put a key into his security system and turned it to "off," the usual luscious smells washed over him, but he didn't notice. Someone was trying to frighten him by doing violent things. One of those violent things might be waiting for him inside.

The storage area was four walls of boxes, molds, and tools. If a bomb was hidden in there he'd never find it. If the person just wanted to frighten him again, he'd put it out front. After giving the store a quick once-over, Peter stepped through the swinging half door, threaded his way between the glass cases, and stood like a lighthouse in the middle of the customer area.

He turned completely around scanning everything. Nothing was out of place. He went around again. Now he gave each item individual attention. In the popper area he scanned the glass popper and hamper, the canisters of caramel corn, cheese and other flavors, the stainless steel counter where he not only worked the popcorn but also made and displayed caramel and candied apples. He scanned the glass cases, the two shelves crammed with trays of chocolates. Then the ice cream in the back counter. He looked over the top of the cases and the boxes of commercial candies. Then he examined the shelves on the wall opposite the cases, the figurines, the product displays. Nothing.

Although he should have felt a sense of relief, he didn't. What if the bomber had changed his demented mind and wasn't going to just scare him? There still could be a bomb in there.

"Honey." Peter's wife, Sandy, entered through the back. She was returning from the grocery store. "All they had were dinner napkins."

"Those are no good," Peter snapped, his eyes scanning the store for a third time.

"I'm sure they'll be all right." She smiled. She knew her husband was troubled and she determined to keep a soothing tone. She stood behind the counter now and, although she looked beautiful in a colorful spring blouse and slacks, he didn't notice.

"No, they won't." He finally eyed her with a steel malice. "Go to Howard's. They have what we need. They'll be open by the time you get there."

"I'm sure these will . . . "

"Don't argue."

"Okay, I'll be right back." Although her voice was strained, she did her best to force love into it. Peter had been brooding all weekend, first about the note he'd found Saturday morning and now about the blast across the street and the second note. The notes were probably just a cruel joke and Peter was only worrying again. But that didn't matter. He was her husband, and she didn't want to add to his torment.

Howard's was a restaurant supply store that catered to a gourmet clientele and was located a block beyond the police station. Having walked about halfway, Sandy felt a sudden chill as a crisp breeze blew off the lake. As she massaged her upper arms briskly to bring back the warmth, she had no idea she was being watched.

"Did they have what we needed?" Peter's mood hadn't sweetened since she left.

"They were expensive, so I only bought a couple packages. I'll stop at the Shuler's on the way home." Shuler's was their regular supplier. Things were definitely cheaper there.

Peter grunted. He'd been busy. The popcorn was popping, the aroma wonderfully thick. All the wax paper covers were off the candy on the shelves, and a small vat of caramel was warming for caramel corn.

"Are you okay?" Sandy asked when he nearly burned himself on the warming vat. Sandy slipped next to him and wrapped her arms around his neck.

"Not now," he snapped, grabbing her wrist and roughly pushing her away.

But her husband needed her more than ever, and even though her wrist burned a bit, she said soothingly, "Peter, I know you're worried. But the Lord'll take care of us." She slid warm arms up his chest to his shoulders.

"I'm not worried," he insisted defensively—a sure sign that he was.

She eyed him with exaggerated suspicion and smiled. "We're in this together. The Lord will take care of both of us." And she kissed him lightly on his nose.

A kiss on the nose always worked. It was his smile button. He couldn't help himself.

After a swarm of them, though, he sobered. "You really believe all that."

She nodded and kissed his nose again. "Uh-huh, the Lord *will* take care of us. And there's another thing I believe. I believe I love you."

Peter found his hands resting on her hips. They were so slender, so smooth. He rubbed them gently. "I *am* worried. All we have is in this place. . . . "

"No," she spoke in that wonderfully airy voice that she used when they were about to make love. "All we have is each other—and Christ. It's just money we have in this place, and we can always get more of that."

Peter smiled. All her talk of God sounded good, yet he knew it was all wishful thinking. If there was a God, why would he care about a silly little candy store?

"I'll be fine," he murmured. "I'm sorry I got upset."

He was about to kiss her when they heard a sharp rapping at the front door. Peter turned while Sandy peered over his shoulder. Through the blinds he made out three people. One stood in back with a large professional-looking video camera hoisted on his shoulder.

"Is it ten?" Peter asked Sandy.

"Close."

Peter hesitated a moment. Something wasn't right. But with no reason to remain closed, he stepped to the door and unlatched it. The three pushed in. Two were women. One had a round face, an uncomplimentary bowl cut, and covered a huge girth with a tent-sized overdress. The other was attractive, in a business suit—uncomfortably overdressed for a trip to the candy store. The third was a long-haired guy with a weeping cold sore who held the video camera on his shoulder at the ready.

Before Peter could take a breath, he found a microphone shoved in his face.

"Mr. Peter Sweet—owner of this candy store?" The woman asked the question as if accusing him.

"Yeah." Too surprised to do much else, Peter recoiled and knit his brows tightly.

"Do you recognize this lady?"

Peter eyed the fat woman. She looked like a woman who really enjoyed her candy. "Not particularly. What's this all about?"

The microphone was shoved into the fat woman's face, and the guy with the cold sore aimed the video camera at her.

"Please, tell Mr. Sweet what you found."

A sudden wave of dread broke over him. Disaster was about to strike. "Hey—what's . . . "

"Mr. Sweet, I found ground glass in your caramel corn—long slivers of it. I bit into one and drove it into my gums. Thank God I didn't swallow it. If I had . . . "

"What are you talking about?" Peter became instantly agitated. Sensing that Peter's volcano was about to blow, Sandy placed soothing hands on his shoulder. But her tenderness did no good; his rage fomented beneath a thin surface.

The female suit spoke into the microphone. "I'm Sheryl Dumbrowski, consumer editor for the eight o'clock news. What is your reaction to what Miss Hollingsworth has said?"

"Reaction? Are you nuts? You come barging in here and accuse me of having ground glass . . . You're nuts! I've been . . . "

The woman took the offensive. "There was ground glass in that popcorn. I have the doctor bills to prove it. I'm going to sue you for every penny you have. I'll close you down." She shook her fist at Peter.

Sandy spoke with forced calm. "Please, please. You've gotten your reaction. Peter's worked hard and built a business producing a good product and by treating people fairly. Even if true this is not a fair way to . . . "

"Thank you, Mrs. Sweet," the suit cut her off.

"I'll see you in court," the fat woman screamed.

"Get out of here. Get out!" Peter threw an open hand at them. Although he had no intention of striking anyone, he knew instantly that the threatening gesture would be misunderstood. But he was too upset to care. All he wanted was a gun—just one little gun to finish them all off. One gun and three bullets.

Of course, they didn't give him the chance. They spun in unison and scrambled into the street.

Peter chased them and stood outside the door shaking a fist. "Get out! Go ahead, take me to court. I'll take everything you've got—" and as they walked unceremoniously away, his voice died to a whisper. "Or you'll take everything I've got."

Sandy stood next to him. "I don't believe it," she soothed.

Too agitated to be soothed, he pushed Sandy away, stormed inside, and slammed the door behind him.

After facing the closed door for a moment, Sandy sighed and followed him.

Had she waited a few minutes and watched the three people walk up the street, she probably would have noticed a car pull out from around the corner and park on the opposite side of the street. She would have seen the three of them cross the street and talk to the person in the car.

Because the person in the car was clever, she wouldn't have seen three envelopes pass to the three people. And she never would have known that each envelope contained $500. But she would have seen the car leave after the driver took the recording and the three accusers had scattered.

After a tense day that saw Peter blow up at a customer, one of his suppliers, and even at Sandy, he got a phone call. It was from a man who identified himself as Grant Edwards, station manager for WBTN television. He called to let Peter know that they'd decided not to use the film. They were going to keep it in their library in case more glass was found and they felt it their duty to air it.

Though relieved, Peter felt like the survivor of a bombing raid now watching enemy planes disappear over the horizon. He knew there were more planes out there and that they would return one day unannounced, at the worst possible moment, their bomb bays full.

# Chapter 8

About noon, after a leisurely attempt at emptying all the moving boxes and putting things away, Win made himself a bologna and tomato sandwich, and sat out in the little garden and ate. As he finished he heard the throbbing sound of an inboard closing in on his boathouse. His boat! To his surprise, he'd forgotten it was going to be delivered. He ran to the boathouse pier and found the blue and white sixteen-footer moving calmly through the water toward him, the rosy-faced salesman at the helm. Dressed in whites and a skipper's cap, he cut a jaunty figure. "Ahoy," he called, as if ready to dock a three-masted schooner.

"Mr. Rosewood," Win called out, a name that seemed to fit.

"Hi, lad," he called back. "She's a beaut, ain't she?"

"Can you pull her into the boathouse?"

"No problem."

As it turned out, it was. Mr. Rosewood was not a helmsman, but he did finally manage to bump and badger the boat into the boathouse dock, and he did so without losing his cheerful bluster. "There," he said and finally grinned.

"She *is* beautiful." Win said, in awe of what he'd done. He'd never abused the magic checkbook like this before, and it felt good.

"When you get her out in the middle of the lake, open her up. You'll love it," Mr. Rosewood gushed.

Win suddenly remembered—was it only two days ago? The rush he had felt—and that boat was so slow in comparison to this one. What would the rush be like now? *My heart'll explode.* "You need a ride back?" he asked.

"If you could."

"Sure. Nothing can't wait here. I'll take her for a real spin after work."

After dropping Rosewood off, he decided he wanted to show Ginger his new toy. Making a mind-map to Ginger's cottage, he headed in that direction.

Soon he was gliding sweetly over the lake's surface, reacting gently to the afternoon swells. Still a little timid, he kept it between five and ten knots as he rounded a point and saw the outline of Ginger's cottage exactly where he thought it should be.

Opening the throttle just a bit more, he closed in on Ginger's pier, but quickly veered off. Tall and beautiful in jeans and a colorful sweater, Ginger stood by her own boathouse. But she wasn't alone. Mike Grogan's powerful cruiser was moored at the pier, and the two of them stood on the bridge embracing.

Even though Grogan had helped Win out the other day, he had no use for the police detective. To Win, he represented everything bad about authority. He was arrogant, sarcastic, quick to play his advantage, and now he had his arms around beautiful Ginger. A shudder rifled up his spine.

But that was her business, not his. He had wanted to show off the boat, but he'd also just wanted to talk for a while. Disappointed, he headed back home.

The afternoon went slowly. Not only was Win nearly finished unpacking, but he kept thinking about what he'd seen at Ginger's. It bothered him more than he thought it should.

The phone rang. It was the phone company letting him know service had been turned on.

Not long after that, about 2:30, the phone rang again.

"Win? Great, you're reachable now." Ginger—her voice uniquely sweet and strong. It was a voice he could become used to. However, after seeing her with Grogan, he answered coolly. "How'd your meeting with Sanderson go?"

"Fine. I saw the files this morning."

"I'm impressed." There was a congratulatory smile in the voice.

"He needs the help."

"I've been on the traffic detail all day so I haven't seen him. There was a blast downtown this morning that's kept me busy."

He'd seen how busy she was at lunchtime and he *wasn't* impressed. When reminded of the explosion, he was about to tell her about Peter Sweet and his threatening notes but thought better of it. "I heard it as we came out of the donut shop. Pretty loud."

"Gas main."

A thought occurred to him. "I'm sure Sanderson wanted to keep my working with him quiet. He doesn't even know you're involved. And I'd like it that way too."

There was silence for a heartbeat or two. Maybe she was offended that he would think she might tell someone, or maybe she already had and she was formulating a reply. "I'll keep that in mind," she finally said.

"If it gets out, my life would be in danger."

"If it gets out," she said.

*She has told Grogan,* he thought.

"Well," she said with finality, "I guess I'll talk to you soon."

"I appreciate your help the past couple days," he said, more to end the conversation on a positive note than for any other reason.

"That's okay," she said, the distance between them further than the telephone line. "Later," she said and he heard the receiver click.

A curious wave of loneliness crashed on his shore. Why? Nothing had really changed since he'd seen the two of them.

He thought for a moment about going to visit Peter Sweet to see how he was doing, but Peter would wonder how Win knew about the notes. So he decided to take the boat out, and spent time winding around the islands until dusk. Later, as he was sitting by the fire, Win prayed. He prayed mostly about his new jobs—his work at Sugar Steeple and his work for Bray. When he finally curled up in the Corvette, he was still apprehensive about both.

In order to keep the tension generated by his apprehension

to a minimum, Win kept his first day at church as uneventful as he could. He arrived just before nine and found Pastor Worlly on the phone talking to someone about interest rates, municipal bonds, and mutual funds. Only mildly interested in Win's arrival, Worlly waved a casual hello without missing a word on the phone.

A little disappointed that there had been no band to welcome him, Win strolled idly back toward his office. After only a step or two he encountered the wall of pictures. He decided to slow down and learn a little bit. Dean Watkins had said there was pain here, but Win couldn't tell it by the pictures. Everyone smiled and seemed content with their lives and the work they were doing.

One picture in particular caught his eye. A building project of some kind. Someone in the distance was standing on a tall ladder leaning against the tower. He was hammering slats onto the belfry openings. Below him, facing the camera, stood two men shaking hands. According to the caption, Worlly was one of the men shaking hands, Charlie Briggs was in the crowd in back of Worlly, and John Selkirk, Maggie's husband, was the guy on the ladder. Except for the guy on the ladder it looked like the meeting of the continental railroads, the driving of the *Golden Spike*. The inscription painstakingly written in ornate calligraphy: The Bell Ceremony.

Toward the end the pictures were drawings or reproductions of ancient photographs, several of the church being built: one with only the studs, one with the siding half on, one with the tower being built, and finally one with a bell being raised with rope and pulley. *Another bell ceremony,* Win mused.

The pictures ended, as did the hallway. Win stood by the last door across from the sanctuary waiting room. On the door was a large padlock. He knew it immediately. He'd seen a layout of the church in Bray's folder. Circled in red had been the tower door; the next door beyond his office. This was it. Either the padlock was there to keep the curious out, or the church had learned a lesson.

One thing about Worlly, he liked good coffee. The rich aroma seduced Win the moment he crossed the threshold. As he filled a Styrofoam cup, he decided he needed his own cup—a mug—maybe one that reflected his personality. Win chuckled softly to himself. He never thought of himself as having a personality. Maybe he did have only two settings. He chuckled again. He'd have to get a mug shaped with the head of Einstein and a Goofy nose.

Planting himself in the vinyl chair he leaned back. It was his own office—his first. He'd never had one at the seminary. He leaned further back and tried to put his feet up on the desk, but his legs were too long and the wall too close. When he finally managed to get them up there the back of his knees were up there too. "Here comes Goofy again," he muttered and pulled them off. He pulled out the lower righthand drawer and planted his heels there. *Yeah, that works.*

He looked around the room. The blank walls he mentally filled with graphics and paintings—evangelistic graphics and spiritually evocative paintings; he envisioned comfortable chairs for visitors—two for couples; bookshelves—a whole wall of Spirit-filled books that would shake these people up and point them to Christ. This office was going to mean something to the church. Wow! What a difference he and Jesus would make.

Some of the exhilaration he'd felt in the rubber boat returned, and he all but leaped to his feet.

Grabbing the desk's corners, he immediately repositioned it. But the moment he pulled it around to face the coffee counter, all his lofty thoughts vanished.

The door to the office was to his left side, and since he was righthanded, he tended to position himself to the right when working or studying. But doing so caused him to lose sight of the door. Someone—a disgruntled murderer for one—would be able to enter unseen. That instant, Bray's admonition to "watch your back" became frighteningly real.

He immediately swung the desk around to face the door. No surprises now. Satisfied, he took on the next task. The books. When he saw the boxes yesterday, he thought he'd be moving them to a closet somewhere. But after finding Robertson's book, he'd changed his mind. How many books had Bryce bought that proclaimed a deeper, more thorough message of Jesus Christ? One book does not salvation make—curiosity maybe, but . . .

About 10:30 he was summoned to Pastor Worlly's office. Worlly was apologetic for all but ignoring Win when he'd arrived. But Win had the feeling that was Worlly's way of doing things. Worlly went about greasing squeaky wheels, and this morning his finances were squeaking far louder than the assistant pastor. But he gave Win his attention now, albeit briefly.

"Youth," Worlly stated with a flair in response to Win's first question concerning his priorities. He tossed Win a thin, blue photocopied church phone directory. "Look through that and find the families with kids, then propose appropriate programs for them. If they really are appropriate we'll get going on them. Sound good?"

It did, and Win was just about to leave and get to work when Worlly added, "There's a deacon meeting this evening—seven o'clock. I can't attend. Represent me. It'll give you a chance to meet some of the people and see how we operate."

Win said he would attend, then quickly made it back in his office. He scanned the phone directory, in which he discovered about one hundred families, sixty-three with little M's by their names indicating membership.

"I've gone here all my life, and I still don't know everyone listed in there," a small voice drifted in from the doorway.

Win had been wrong. Someone *could* sneak up undetected. In this case, that someone was light on her feet and carried no gun. Maggie Selkirk stood framed in the doorway looking far more formal than needed for a weekday church visit. She wore a white dress splashed generously with pink and purple flowers, white high heels, and white fur wrap.

But it wasn't her dress that intrigued Win. He found her remarkable in her shyness. Not only did her hair betray her inability to cope—mousy brown, disheveled, looking like she'd just dragged herself out of bed—but her eyes did too. They peered at the world as if completely subjugated by whatever surrounded her, frightened that if she were to make a mistake or in some way fail to please, the very walls would collapse on her and the floor would swallow her up. Since there were times when Win felt precisely the same way, he empathized and found those frightened, misty green eyes, those eyes that looked so lost and tentative, quite appealing. "Well, I'm sure I'll have trouble meeting them too."

"No," Maggie said, her eyes dancing to the right and left. "I'm just awkward. Terribly so."

"Not to me," he said, suppressing a sympathetic smile for fear that it would make her feel even more ill at ease.

"Really? You don't think so?" she asked, a light dawning expectantly in her eyes. Win could see that the answer he gave would mean a great deal to her.

"I find you charming," he said. She *was* delicately charming, butterfly charming.

She smiled sheepishly and took two steps toward him, her eyes locked on his. Then she glanced around the office. "You've settled in," she said.

"I moved a few things around," he offered. "The walls get theirs tomorrow."

"I'll look forward to seeing what you do," she said. "I've kind of an artistic flair—I mean I'm not really artistic—I do a few things. But I've seen something at a gallery—can I get it for you?"

"I've got some things at the cottage . . . "

"Please?" A kittenlike pleading in her voice. "I'd really like to."

Strangely enough, Win knew how she felt. He'd made her feel safe, and she longed to be good to someone she trusted to appreciate her generosity. He'd bought Dean Watkins a tie one Father's Day for the same reason—a wonderful thing the color and shape of a northern pike.

"Okay, but something simple," he allowed.

She grinned with childlike excitement.

She returned about an hour later with the wall hanging—a poster. The instant Win saw it his eyes grew moist and his hands wanted to reach out to it. Black and white with secret grays, it was a woman about Win's age, hauntingly beautiful with cascading black hair. She looked down on a boy of about ten who sat with her on the floor. The boy, in turn, looked down on a puppy who played in his lap. Mother and son had love in their eyes. The mother's was a deep, wondrous love, a love she wanted to communicate but couldn't. The boy looked with love on the puppy, the wondrous love of discovery and joy.

It wasn't the first time Win had seen this particular work—he'd longed for it years ago, and he was grateful—more than grateful—for it now.

"Do you like it?" Maggie asked when he didn't say anything. Then she noticed a tear roll down the big man's cheek.

"About a week before my mother died, she and I went walking," Win began. "We came to a shop with this picture in the window. Both my mother and I were touched by it, and she said that she ought to buy it for me because it would be the only way she'd be able to buy me a puppy. I wanted it because of the look in the woman's eyes. I'd seen that look in my mom's eyes before. Anyway, when she died—it took about a month, but I finally worked up courage to ask my dad to buy it for me. He scoffed a little, but not much; he actually agreed rather quickly for him. But when we finally found the shop . . . "

"It was gone?"

Win finally turned her way, his tears overflowing down his cheeks. "Not anymore," he said. "Thank you."

Now it was Maggie whose eyes filled with tears and while smiling joyously said, "I saw it yesterday afternoon, and I thought of you. I don't know why. I guess it touched me too."

Win gave her his handkerchief, and she dabbed her tears taking care not to smear her mascara. He wiped his on his sleeve, and they looked at each other, each knowing that there was more to say. Win's heart was so full that its contents begged to be shared with someone. But like the mother in the picture, there were no words.

Maggie, however, could talk, and right now it was her face that arrested him. Her eyes were huge, round pools that ran deep. He could feel himself falling in, getting lost in them—moving closer. The love within him, kindled by the memory of his mother, enlivened by these eyes, longed to sweep Maggie up in its arms. But he knew he couldn't do that. He pulled back slightly and took a deep breath of resolve. Her eyes pulled away, disappointed.

He looked at the picture again, trying to pretend that he'd never seen those eyes, never longed for this woman. "I really appreciate this."

She looked at him all smiles. "I really have to go. I've a luncheon—John likes me active in civic things."

"You said he doesn't attend here?"

Her expression soured. "He did when we first met, but no more."

"Do you really have to go?" he asked, suddenly not wanting her to leave. "There's coffee on. Have some and tell me about the church."

Maggie shook her head and took a step backward. "You'll find out about the church tonight. Worlly says you're coming to the deacon meeting. He'd send a stray dog in his place if he could train him to sit fast enough." The magic had gone from the moment, and Maggie seemed to have come back to reality with a crash. "I'm the chairperson," she laughed awkwardly. "So I'll make sure you learn a lot."

"Are you okay?" Win asked, wanting to take care of her.

"Sometimes I wonder," she said bleakly.

From the back of his mind came Dean Watkins's voice, *There are people in pain there.* Win was now looking at one of them. The next thing he said seemed to come from outside himself, came without thinking. "You know there is Someone who can help," he said seriously and with honest caring.

The words hung there, suspended between them like a charm. Maggie swallowed hard as if battling an emotion. Her eyes became a little harder, and her mouth tightened. "I really do have to go," she said quickly, taking several tentative steps toward the door.

She looked as if there were a world of things yet to say, but she turned, gave him a frightened little wave, and left.

Only after several minutes did the vision of her eyes begin to fade. He missed them already. And that scared him. "She's married, dodo," he said out loud, "Careful, Win. That would definitely be tough to explain to the dean."

The afternoon went slowly. Pastor Worlly left soon after Win returned from lunch. Continuing to work, Win counted the families with children. There were only twenty-two, and it was hard to tell the kids' ages. He figured someone at the meeting that night could tell which kids were prospects for youth programs. Then there was nothing to do. He dallied with Robertson's book, thumbing through the pages, quickly, but he didn't want to read. He really wanted to get back out on the lake with the boat. But he was being paid to work, not play, even if there were very little work to do.

Eventually, he headed home and, after slipping out of his clothes and getting into a pair of jeans and a sweatshirt, he took his boat out.

After winding up the island coast for a while, spinning around a couple of islands, and opening it up only half-throttle, he headed home. He was too preoccupied about Ginger and Maggie, and youth groups, and a certain picture that now hung by his door and the mother it reminded him of for him to enjoy his freedom.

To Win's surprise, Bray Sanderson was sitting at the end of his boat dock when Win returned. Bray had taken one of the wrought iron lawn chairs and planted it and himself there to wait, an occasional puff of smoke rising from his pipe. He didn't look happy.

"I told you to keep your mouth shut," Bray said, the accusation slapping Win the moment the Bayliner cradled itself in the mooring.

"This about Grogan?" Win said.

"You told Grogan?"

"Who are you talking about?"

"No one, but it worked."

Win just shook his head realizing he'd been tricked. Of course, he planned on spilling that particular bag of beans soon anyway, but it was embarrassing to be caught.

"How do you know Grogan?" Bray went on.

"Ginger Glasgow does. She may have told him."

"You told Glasgow? You *are* having a good time."

"Ginger is the one who led me to you. I think she told Grogan."

"You *think* so?"

Win tied the mooring lines and stood before Bray, whose pipe now puffed like a locomotive. "Give me a second, and I'll tell you the whole story."

A few minutes later Bray knew everything. More than he wanted to. Particularly about Ginger and Grogan. "And I liked her," Bray groaned.

"I don't know for sure whether Grogan knows."

"I'll find that out," Bray offered darkly. "At least neither one of us trusts him. Shows we're both smart." They were inside the cottage now. "Got a beer in there?"

"A Coke?"

"Not interested. What did you find out today?"

"Not much. They want me to handle the youth program, and there are only a few youth. Maggie Selkirk stopped by for a while. She seems like a very unhappy lady. Her husband used to go to the church but doesn't now."

"How long ago?"

"Don't know. A long time, I think. She doesn't like answering questions."

Bray got to his feet. "I need a drink. Call me every day. Then I'll know you're still alive."

"A goal worth fighting for."

"Don't forget—that guy you're up against fights with a blunt instrument," Bray said in a perfect Bogart.

He saw those misty green pools again in his mind's eye about an hour later. The sun was making its way toward the western horizon, burning its edges, preparing for a big exit. Spring breezes grew long, chilly spikes. Soon he'd have to return to the church for the deacon meeting. But that wouldn't be for a while yet. There was still time to think.

He finished a ham sandwich, sipped a diet Coke, and stared into his empty plate. As he sat idly cleaning up the last few crumbs he thought about the picture Maggie had bought him. He was thirty, and he did miss his mother—she would have fixed him more than a ham sandwich for dinner. She would have sat and talked with him. She would have kept him company and asked about his day and marveled at the clever things he did. And she would have gotten involved. There was no one who got involved now—well, maybe Dean Watkins, but that was long-distance—and there was Maggie. Buying that picture was certainly getting involved.

But why didn't he now see his mother's eyes? He saw Maggie's and her tentative, fearful little smile, a smile longing to have someone smile back. He saw her fear that he wouldn't return that smile, that her longing for someone to reach out to her would be rebuffed.

*Good grief, I'm thirty. I'm thinking like a kid.*

He reminded himself that all he really needed was a little more discipline and that he certainly didn't need to get involved with the owner of those eyes, or anyone else up here in this woodsy, watery little berg. Soon he'd be making his way back to the seminary and the safety of his books and practical jokes.

But as he stared into his plate, the misty green eyes seemed to stare back up at him. They were magnets, working on his soul as if it were only a pile of metal shavings.

By the time he left for the deacon meeting, the shavings were in a neat little pile, waiting for her to shake them up again.

 Chapter 9

Churches need people in order to be churches. They need noise, commotion, talking and laughter, the murmur of expectant prayers and even a few sour words to be alive. At night, when bathed in forlorn shadows from a few dim invasions of light, when footfalls are hollow on the hardwood and the only sound is one's own breathing, they feel abandoned—lifeless.

As Win stood at the sanctuary door, he knew, of course, that Sugar Steeple was only asleep. The slightest mention within its walls of a problem or longing or need, the softest whisper of the name Jesus, and the church would awaken.

Looking up at the rich oak cross that hung above the large opened Bible, Win whispered, "Jesus." It was a plea, the sound of royal respect laced with frustration and fear. "I'm here to do your will." How clichéd it sounded. He wasn't sure why he was there. This morning he thought he knew. But not now. He wanted love and acceptance, he wanted respect, he wanted his opinion to be asked and his answer to be heard. He'd gotten that at the seminary, but the Lord had moved him away from there.

Maggie's voice echoed from the far end of the sanctuary, near the hallway, "Who's there?"

His heart leaped. "It's me—for the deacons' meeting." He couldn't help the self-conscious tone in his voice, and he cleared his throat as if by doing so he'd dislodge and swallow all the unwanted emotions she evoked.

"Win," she called cheerfully, and when she saw his shadow turning to find her. "Over here—in back."

"In the conference room?" he asked.

"See you there," she called back with a hint of excitement in her voice.

Her shadow turned and disappeared toward the hall. Win quickly followed, but the moment he entered the still dark hallway, he realized the rush he felt. *Easy, boy,* he told himself. *She's not right.* Then he stopped and leaned against the wall. *You lead-head. You're acting like a ten year old. Wake up and smell the coffee.*

To his surprise, the talk seemed to work, and a rush of self-confidence pumped through his veins. Straightening to his full six feet, he walked down the hall toward the wash of light that came from the conference room. When he reached it he found Maggie and Bill Simms.

"Oh, hi, Bill."

Bill only nodded. Though usually animated, he appeared subdued. He wore Reeboks, jeans, and a light jacket. His hands were etched in black grease. Maggie, on the other hand, was wrapped elegantly in a pearl silk blouse and long, forest green skirt. Even her hair was done, brushed back on one side exposing a dainty ear and a lavish diamond earring that sparkled nearly to her shoulder. Looking at her, Win wondered if he was underdressed for the meeting.

"Hello," Maggie backhanded Win's cheerfulness with a detached coolness. If she had been excited to see him earlier that excitement had vanished.

Bill finally reached out a hand, grabbed Win's, and gave it a single pump. "How's that car running?" he asked.

"Fine," Win smiled. "Not even a hiccup."

"You need that wire replaced, or it'll hiccup at the wrong time."

"I'll come in soon," Win replied definitely. He added, "I didn't expect to see a trustee here tonight."

"Maggie and I needed to cover a few things before her meeting."

"You're early," Maggie said to Win accusingly.

"I'll wait outside," he said, trying to hide a sudden, unexpected hurt.

"Probably a good idea, Win." A roll of Bill's eyes told Win he needed time to pacify Maggie.

But Maggie was noticeably upset, and Win had the feeling that no amount of consoling would help.

"I'll wait in the sanctuary," Win volunteered.

"Thank you." Maggie was ice.

The moment he returned to the hallway, the door closed behind him and he was plunged into darkness. He headed toward his office and with every step he began to chant: *You're a jerk; you're a jerk; let me count; the ways you're a jerk.* He was actually hurt that a woman he should be avoiding wasn't paying attention to him. The prayer he'd started in the sanctuary definitely needed finishing behind the closed doors of his office. But the moment he entered it and flipped on the lights, he heard a voice behind him. "You're the new guy?"

Win turned and saw a tall, lanky fellow. "I'm Win Brady," Win introduced himself, taking a few steps forward. "Pastor Worlton wanted me to attend the deacon meeting on his behalf."

"He never attends deacon meetings so he *has no* behalf," the fellow said, Win recognized him from Sunday's service—he'd been talking to Peter Sweet, the candy store owner. His name was Steve something, he played golf, and he would rather see Sandy Sweet dancing naked on a table than his wife.

"You're Steve something," Win acknowledged, proffering a hand.

"Taylor." Steve stepped toward Win and shook the hand. Steve wore a baggy shirt and trousers and his sandy hair was in windy disarray.

They stepped into the hallway in time to see Simms leaving the room. Maggie, still tense but not as hostile, nodded to them as they entered.

"I guess it's just us tonight," she began.

"With our new assistant pastor we're up by thirty-three percent," Steve quipped.

Maggie nodded and said to Win, as if she owed him an explanation. "We used to have other deacons, but Steve and I did most of the work anyway. So now it's just the two of us. So Steve and I would like to officially welcome you, Win Brady, on behalf of the deacons, as our new assistant pastor."

Win nodded and gave each an official smile.

Taking an agenda from her purse, she tossed each of them a copy. First item: weeds need pulling. Steve suggested a spring gardening day. Few people showed up for the last one, but at least they would have made the effort. Then they discussed the boy who cut the grass weekly. He was forgetting to come now and again. They talked about getting someone else, but hiring took time and no one had time. They decided just to call him and give him a lecture on diligence.

In the next hour they dealt halfheartedly with a number of maintenance issues. Even though Steve discussed things at times vigorously, Win noticed that when the "to dos" were handed out, Maggie ended up with all of them.

"Now—Maybell Winowski," she said.

"What about her?" Steve asked. "She's dead."

Maggie nodded. "She hadn't attended in more than two years. Dan visited her several times before he died." Maggie stumbled almost imperceptibly on Dan Bryce's name. "We need to send flowers, and one of us should be at the funeral. Worly's presiding tomorrow."

Steve just shook his head. "I can't go. The hardware store." Then he eyed Maggie again. "I guess as a housewife with a rich husband you're it again."

Maggie groaned under the weight.

Win piped up, "I'd be happy to attend for you."

Maggie, unaccustomed to having anyone do anything for her, beamed. Turning those eyes on him, she gushed, "Thank you, Win." The vote was unanimous.

"It's at ten A.M. tomorrow—at the Celestial Shuttle Mortuary on Temple Road."

Win nodded, and Maggie placed an exaggerated check mark next to Maybell's name. "Well, that's it," she said.

"Good meeting," Steve said and got to his feet. "See you folks Sunday."

"Can I help you with anything?" Win asked Maggie after Steve left, a restless part of him hoping she'd have something to keep him there.

"No," she said, eyes remaining on her notes. "I just need to formalize the minutes. Worly's a stickler for formality when he doesn't have to do anything."

"Are you sure?"

"I'm sure," she reaffirmed, her tone more abrupt than he would have expected.

"Well, then . . . uh . . . I'll see you when I see you." He got haltingly to his feet.

"Thanks again for going to the funeral tomorrow."

"No problem," he said, smiling warmly then stepping reluctantly out into the hall. "Well," Win muttered to himself as he walked toward the front of the church, his footsteps hollow echoes on the old wood, "looks like Dean Watkins was wrong, you don't have two settings, you have three: Einstein, Goofy, and *Goofier*. And you're heading toward a fourth—*Jerk*."

But when he reached the front steps, the church door closing behind him, something stopped him. Donning his detective hat for a moment, he remembered Maggie's abruptness—a sure sign of anxiety—when she'd said good-bye. And why was she sitting alone in a drafty old church to finish up some minutes that could be easily done comfortably at home? Something was wrong. Plus, Bray had stressed that Win's first job was to find out why Maggie had lied to him in the interview. *Those eyes couldn't lie . . . Or are they all lies?*

Win decided to stick around for a few minutes. To punctuate his leaving he reopened the front door quietly and then slammed it. He stepped loudly down the wooden steps, walked across the grass to his car, and slammed the door deliberately. Easing onto the two-lane, he drove north for a few hundred yards, found a companion road, and headed back. When reasonably close to the church he parked in the trees, doused his lights, and waited. Maggie's Ford Taurus was parked near the front door, and a light still burned inside the conference room. From where he sat, at a steep angle from the window, he could see nothing inside.

He didn't have to.

A moment later a car rolled up next to the Taurus and turned off its lights. A man with a familiar build got out, took the front stairs two at a time, then disappeared into the church. After a moment Win heard muffled footsteps echoing off the hardwood floor heading down the hall to where Maggie sat.

A moment later the conference room light went out.

With thumb and forefinger, Win pinched his lower lip. "Good grief," he groaned, "is she really doing this?" Of course, any number of reasons could account for the room going black—the bulb or fuse could have blown, for example—but, as a reluctant detective, he had to make sure. He gingerly slid from the Chevy and went to the visitor's car—a sleek, two-year-old Ford Probe. He found it locked.

With nothing but moonlight, and very little of that, he could see nothing inside that revealed the identity of the owner. Giving up, Win moved cautiously around to the back of the church and huddled in the shrubs beneath the open meeting room window.

He heard sounds. "Oh, no," he whispered. "I'm not up to this."

The sound of a table creaking rhythmically, deep guttural breathing, urgent sighs and groans—Maggie and the visitor were making love.

Leaning against the siding, Win took a huge breath and tried to pretend the sounds didn't matter, that they were just sounds. But they weren't—two people, one with eyes as deep as the universe, were making love just a few feet away from him. His face caught fire.

He made a move to leave—the reluctant detective had learned all there was to learn—but he couldn't move. The bush he was hiding in had attached itself to him with insistent claws. He pulled, but the bush rattled loudly. He'd have to stay. Escape meant detection.

"It's no big deal," he muttered to himself. "It's like a modern TV sitcom in the next room. It's just no big deal." But it was a big deal. Win had never made love. At times he was proud of the fact, but there were other times when the reason for his virginity haunted him. Even in seminary he'd been an oddity. For the other guys it was either marriage or pre-Jesus wild oats. Win had never sowed wild oats—he'd been too afraid. What if his father had found out? Or he'd gotten a disease? What if she'd yawned?

There'd been only a few women in his life—girls really. Leaning against the church, his mind racing, trying to ignore what could never be ignored, he thought of Trudy Spreg. The summer after high school at camp—Trudy Spreg, a Midwestern girl, had fallen hard for him. She went to church and said churchy things, but she knew her way around a late-night bonfire. He shuddered and melted simultaneously at the memory. It had almost happened one night—and surely would have the next. But her father was suddenly called back to Little Rock on business and she wasn't there. "I guess you knew I'd overcome all this shyness," Win said to the Lord.

What would it be like? Not the sex—that was only a physical sensation. What would love be like? Would it come with big liquid eyes, eyes he could swim in, belong to someone who cried out that what he was and said were important? What was marrying and growing old with someone like?

A longing raged over him. Something he wanted so much, yet God had never fulfilled—never brought the right one.

Then he brought those eyes.

His heart suddenly reached out to Maggie. Lost in a marriage that had soured on her. Frightened, like him—without Jesus, unlike him. What should he do? He should do something. Matthew 18 said to intervene, and if she doesn't repent, take another with him next time. Yet that didn't seem right in this case. And it certainly wasn't right for his detective job. As detective, operative, and snitch . . . he'd have to tell Bray. He suddenly felt dirty for having to do it.

But he wasn't the dirty one. She was committing adultery in

the church—couldn't they go out on the beach or something, in the weeds where behavior like that belongs? But the anger was only a miniature wave lapping on the shore—it struck, then receded. And as it did, his heart built a bridge to her again.

"Maybe I could just strangle the guy."

He suddenly realized that the room had fallen silent. *Maybe they heard my heart thundering.*

Voices beyond the wooden wall—subdued whispers. No words, just punctuated hums and buzzing. The volume rose, an angry intensity for an instant, still more echo than words. Then silence again. A single set of receding footsteps. Was the guy leaving?

As a detective Win had to know who the Probe belonged to. His own sense of justice and, he had to admit, a sprouting seed of jealousy, required it. But with Maggie still in the room, scrambling to the front of the church meant noise and discovery.

So he just listened.

Silence. Thick, not even breathing. Maybe they'd both gone to the front. He decided to chance it.

Gingerly, he tried to extricate himself from the bush, it still held him fast. Sighing frustratedly, thwarted by both heaven and shrubs, he fell back against the wall—trapped.

He heard a car door close, and he realized that his window of opportunity was shutting rapidly. Still concerned that Maggie was in the room, he cautiously unzipped his jacket, crawled out of it, and let the branch ease down under its weight. He'd return for the jacket later.

But he'd taken too long. As he rounded the corner, he saw the silhouette of Maggie's lover settling behind the wheel and closing the car door. Immediately the Probe's ignition fired up, the lights flared, and the tires threw fists of grass in their rush to the highway.

The license!

He should have looked at the license. Sanderson will explode. But he wasn't thinking about license plates. He was kicking himself for not wiggling out of his jacket sooner. Now he had that *and* the license place to kick himself about. Why did he ever leave quiet Atlanta, the cloistered library, his room with his books? But he was here now, in the middle of the night spying on people with his jacket held prisoner by a bush. "You getting a good laugh out of this one?" he asked, his eyes cast upward.

He moved to the front of the church and realized that Maggie was still inside. He stepped loudly up the stairs, then reached for the door handle. But the door opened before he touched it.

Maggie's eyes popped with surprise. "Oh, you!" she exclaimed. "Why are you here?"

Also surprised, Win babbled, "My car stopped . . . uh . . . somewhere back there." He saw the redness in her eyes and when she sensed his concern, she dropped her eyes and gripped the papers in her arms to her breast. "You okay?" he asked.

She pushed by him. "I'm fine," she said stiffly, leaving him on the landing to watch her back.

"I can help if you . . . "

"You can't even keep your car going," she said bitterly, opening her Taurus door. In the sudden burst of interior light he saw that she was still crying, her mascara and nose both running. She brushed her nose with her sleeve. "The walk'll do you good," she said, facing him, angry at all men—particularly nice ones.

A few moments later her taillights faded to black as she headed north.

Not only had he fumbled his detective thing, he'd failed as a pastor. She was in pain and he'd said nothing meaningful. He'd only been a dog to kick. *I can help you? I sounded like I was in real estate—or hair transplants.*

He sauntered back to his jacket, lifted it easily out of the bush, and slipped it on. Poking a thumb at his own chest Win grumbled, "Well, Lord, this fish is certainly flopping out of water." Finding his car he slid behind the wheel and slammed the door—thunk!

The noise caused him to stiffen.

While he had huddled under the window, prisoner of the bush, he had heard a car door shut. Somewhere out in the darkness. Before Maggie's lover had shut his. Long before Maggie had shut hers. Someone else . . .

Win threw open his door and all but fell out of the Chevy. He spun on his heels, peering frantically into the darkness. He saw nothing. He had not heard a car start up, but he had heard a door close. The car could have easily been driven away while he was in front on the church. Had someone else been spying on Maggie? Had someone else seen *him*? Was that someone still out there? He spun around again and suddenly felt as if a gun sight were trained on him.

"More likely it was just some kids," Sanderson said when Win called him from a gas station phone booth not far from the church. "Kids love to make out along those cliffs. It's dark—no one patrols."

"Think so?" Win asked hopefully. He still felt the gun sight drilling into the base of his skull.

"Sure," he assured. "I'll run a check on who at the church owns a Probe. We'll know who's thumping her tomorrow."

"Maybe I don't want to know," Win muttered.

"Sure you do," Bray fired back as if to say "detectives want to know everything." Then he added, "By the way, aren't you a little embarrassed?"

"Embarrassed?" Win replied, stalling. "About what?" he asked thinly.

Bray laughed. "About what? We're talking about a church here. Murderers walking around, maybe Bryce was a black-mailer, some guy's worried about his candy store being blown up—maybe by someone sitting in the next pew. And now you have the mouse lady having an out-of-wedlock thump—by some guy who's probably sitting in the pew next to *her*."

Win swallowed hard. He *was* embarrassed. He knew that this was a church on the edge of apostasy, but how do you explain that to someone like Bray Sanderson, king cynic? How could he possibly tell people how different a life with Christ is if what they saw coming from his people, or from those who appeared to be his people, was just more of the same? To Bray, church was church.

Win put on his seminary hat. "Well, the Lord's in control. It may not look like it sometimes, but when the fat lady sings she'll be singing God's praises."

Bray chuckled sarcastically. "Believe what you want, but the place sounds more like that Elks Lodge than a church."

Win's stomach tightened. He hated witnessing. "Christians are sinners, Bray," he said, his voice tense. "But, particularly in this case, not everyone who goes to church is a Christian."

"Why else would they go? There are easier ways to get Sunday morning coffee and donuts." Sounding more conciliatory he continued, "I know you think this church is some great battleground between good and evil, but every place is—the local pizza parlor, out there on the lake. I've seen the good guys and the bad guys battle it out everywhere. Whether you like it or not, all you've done tonight is confirm my theory. The kid found something out, and someone nailed him for it."

"Does seem that way," Win said, resigned to being several points behind.

"You did good—now I know what was going through Selkirk's head when I questioned her. But instead of shortening the suspect list, you've lengthened it—now there's Selkirk, the lover, Selkirk's husband the Ford king, and maybe some religious fanatic who's dead set agin' church thumping. Your next step is to shorten it."

"Wherever the Lord leads," Win said feebly. He was silent for a moment, and then he heard himself add, "God already knows who the killer is, Bray. He's ordained how all this will end up. And he has his reasons for the steps we'll take."

Bray's reply crackled abrasively. "If I'm not stepping toward the killer I'm stepping backward. You signed on to do the same. Make sure you're stepping in that direction tomorrow. We understand each other?"

"Perfectly," Win replied.

Sanderson paused, maybe to soften the moment. Then he

said, "Bugs—gnats everywhere. Spring can be the pits sometimes. I think I'm going to trade them in for a scotch at Archie's." Archie's was a back room bar off of a hole-in-the-wall restaurant that overlooked a nondescript pile of rocks on the edge of the lake not far from Bray's house.

"I'll call you tomorrow night," Win said, feeling down.

"Bombs, adultery—quite a day. You got a criminal smorgasbord over there. Wonder what'll be on your tray next."

"I can hardly wait."

# Chapter 10

**S**andy Sweet woke early to a harsh scratching at her window—the tree limb outside. When she and Peter had gone to bed, even though Peter was upset, the night outside had been calm. Now, as she slid from the bed and headed for the bathroom, the restless limb signaled an approaching storm. Peter lay on his back, eyes open, as if awaiting an anxious death.

"This can't be happening!" He groaned, the sound rising as if from a grave. He knew he'd be in one soon. His head ached, his eyes burned. He'd been up most of the night. Now it was 7 A.M., time for another day—and he wanted no part of it.

"I'll get you coffee," Sandy said, coming from the bathroom in her flowery flannel nightgown.

He rubbed his eyes, felt the ache of invading age in his joints, and hated everything. "Coffee? Great," he grumbled sarcastically, pushing himself into a sitting position. "Now I can face the day wide awake. Not miss a minute of it."

Sandy stood behind him and slipped gentle hands on his shoulders. "This has all been very upsetting to you, and you need coffee, a nice breakfast, and a hug." She wrapped arms around him and ran her hands warmly down his chest. "What say you get the hug first."

"Huh?" his brows dipped incredulously. "Someone's trying to put me out of business. Ground glass in the popcorn—what's next, AIDS from the chocolate? Everything we have . . ."

"AIDS can't travel in chocolate."

"It's an example," he whined. "Do you know what'll happen if it gets out? And the evening news has it all on video."

Eyes filled with understanding, Sandy knelt on the edge of the bed behind him. She hugged him gently as he stared off somewhere, his skin clammy from sweat. Peter always sweated when agitated. "God'll take care of us."

Peter groaned, "This isn't a fairy tale. Reality is unfolding— page by miserable page. Someone out there wants to send us down the toilet."

"Jesus won't let that happen."

"Jesus? He's already let some fat-nik . . ."

Sandy moved around and put her face in his. "Darling, please realize that this could all just be a badly conceived joke. Do you know for sure it was a television news crew? Did you recognize . . . "

"You know TV news depresses me."

"Well, why don't you call—what station was it?"

"WBTN. Grant something."

"Call them. Find out if this Grant person really works there."

His haggard face suddenly brightened hopefully. "Good idea," he said as he grabbed a phone book from the nightstand drawer, looked up the station, and telephoned. A benign voice answered. Peter asked quickly, "I need to talk to Grant someone. He's with the news department."

"Grant Edwards. I'll connect you."

His hope vanished as he put a hand over the receiver. "He exists."

"Anyone could use his name. Talk to him."

"Grant Edwards." The voice had a detached dryness to it, but it didn't sound like last night's caller.

"Mr. Edwards, my name is Peter Sweet. Did you send a film crew to my candy store yesterday?"

There was a pause. "Candy store? Didn't they pay for something?"

"No, a video crew, complete with newscaster came to my candy store yesterday. They claimed to be from your station. They sort of did an unflattering piece . . . "

"From here? Why in heaven's . . . what did they do?"

Peter suddenly realized how "ground glass in the popcorn" was going to sound. "Nothing. Nothing. . . . Thank you for your time."

"Wait a minute, if someone's going around . . ."

Peter hung up. Collapsing on the bed, he turned to Sandy. "It was a hoax." He felt all the tension leave his body. Then, just as quickly, it returned. "Someone *is* really out to get me." They hired people . . . Why would they hire people to impersonate . . ."

"I think you should tell the police."

"Like it did any good last time."

"It might this time. It's the right thing to do. Maybe someone's pulled this somewhere else. Maybe they'll know who . . ."

Peter brightened just a little. "Think so?"

She rubbed his shoulders again and found them as clammy as before. Her poor husband. If he'd only believe.

Ten o'clock came, and Win drove up to the Celestial Shuttle Mortuary for Maybell's funeral. The morning had opened for him like a deep freeze. It was winter all over again. Dismal gray clouds swept down from Canada on the back of a driving wind. The lake reared up to fight, but retreated and returned, slamming the rocks and beaches contemptuously with great white fists. Although there was no rain, the heavy driving mist felt just like it.

As it turned out, the funeral was a lonely affair. The only visitor, besides Win, was Maybell's next-door neighbor. She was fortyish with auburn hair and efficient brown eyes. Pastor J. Sanders Worlton said a few words, a very few—none of them interesting—then left, telling Win that he had an appointment in Burlington and wouldn't be in his office until late afternoon, if at all. On the way out, Win took a moment to speak to the neighbor, Pamela Wisdom. She remembered Dan Bryce. He'd only visited Maybell for a few months before he died, but it must have been enough. She had spoken quite highly of him.

"He'd fix her lunch after reading to her for a while," Pamela Wisdom told him. "Mornings are my busiest time—I teach porcelain doll classes. I'd glance out the window about eleven when he arrived and again at twelve-thirty when he left. He'd come at least a couple times a week."

"Sounds like a good guy," Win said.

"You go to Sugar Steeple too?"

"I took Dan's place."

"That must be spooky." She smiled hauntingly.

"Not yet—maybe later."

They stood at the back of the chapel now, and as the light filtered through a stained-glass window and caught her auburn hair just so, Win thought she looked rather pretty.

"Well, I have to go," she told him. "My busy time. Say hi to Maggie Selkirk for me."

Win's brows twisted slightly. "You know Maggie?"

"I taught her how to make dolls. Now she pours and fires her own—or at least she used to. Sometimes she'll buy greenware from me."

"Greenware?"

"The molded doll clay—you smooth it, fire it, paint it. The greenware comes out of the plaster molds."

"Maggie does that? Pretty delicate work I would guess."

"Very—well, time to go. I've got a firing to get done before my classes start."

A few minutes later, Win climbed into his Chevy and headed for the church.

The weather had worsened. Now the lake slammed billowing white fists against the bridges that strung the islands together. It made driving treacherous. After a huge sigh of relief he closed the church's door behind him and shut the storm outside.

Stomping the wet from his Reeboks he pushed his hood off and slid out of his jacket. Even as warm as the church was, he felt a chill as he headed back to his office for a hot cup of coffee. The telephone in Worlly's office rang, and after a quick dash down the hallway Win answered it.

"Oh, hi," came Maggie's voice. It perked the instant she recognized Win. "I'm on my car phone. The storm's delaying me."

Win suddenly remembered the narrow patches of highway between the islands—the waves hammering the pavement, her car swerving to avoid them. "Worlly's not here anyway."

"You there for a while?"

"'Til lunch."

"I'll be there before then."

"Don't you want to wait out this weather?"

"I'll see you before noon," she said and the line died.

She sounded strong on the car phone.

He hung up and turned to leave the office when the phone rang again.

"Hello," Win answered again.

"You're not Worlly," the female voice stated abrasively.

"I'm Win Brady."

"The new boy," she said. "This is Roz Swift. Tell Worlly something for me."

"Anything, Miss Swift."

"Tell him Sorrell's going to be at the trustee's meeting tonight."

"Sorrell, yes—got it." He wrote the message on a pad near the phone.

"Don't screw it up."

"Yeah, right," he said doubtfully. The phone clicked and buzzed. As he hung up he wondered if there were any normal women at the church—or even on the islands. He suddenly thought of Ginger. So beautiful, so Christian, so blind about Grogan.

The sound of the wind had taken on an unearthly quality. It whined and whistled—a high-pitched moan like a wounded animal slithering among the eaves high overhead. He looked up toward the tower. The paint was beginning to peel on the ceiling, where a roof leak had once left a rusty stain. But he saw none of that—he saw what lay beyond.

How did the police report describe it? About ten-by-ten, exposed studs, the single small window. With the storm billowing outside the words all seemed sterile, void of the tragedy that had occurred in it. What did it really look like? What did it *feel* like?

He rose from the chair as if drawn. A moment later he stood before the tower door and the huge lock that hung there.

After holding the lock in his hand for a heartbeat or two, he made his way quickly to Worlly's desk, found a small fist of keys in the top drawer, then returned. He slid an appropriate looking one into the lock. Not that one. But two keys later, the lock swiveled open.

Standing in the gloom at the foot of the stairs, the wind moaning remorselessly above, he felt an eerie shudder crawl like a scorpion, its stinger poised, up his spine. These stairs had known a killer's footsteps, footsteps Win believed were on a spiritual mission—Satan's mission.

*Why do I think like this? I should learn to keep my mind shut—leave well enough alone.* But after a moment he flipped on the naked yellow bulb that hung three stories above, and began climbing. A couple of steps later, though, the seed of reluctance planted at the base of the stairs came to full bloom.

*I really shouldn't be doing this—I found* The Love Bug *too violent.*

Each step became an event, and each took him closer to the night Dan Bryce died. Had he been saved? Had the Lord reached into this dying church and plucked him out, a soul he'd planned to save from the foundation of the world? Or had Satan snuffed out that life for himself?

The first landing behind him, the stairs steepened, the whine of the wind increased mournfully. When he passed the second landing, he sensed it—someone watching, unseen eyes following him.

He spun. Looked up, then down. Nothing. A chill electrified the back of his neck.

He began climbing again. He suddenly envisioned red, burning, malevolent eyes, laced together with thick, hateful brows—something that could only have been the result of a collaborative effort between Steven Spielberg and Steven King. It watched him, its pupils rising like a predator's as he climbed each step. An evil force lived in those eyes, one daring him to keep climbing.

The wind growled angrily. Something shuddered, and he heard a steady, nervous slapping. The window? Loose siding? His breathing became shallow, erratic. But his feet didn't stop. "Fear not, I will be with you to the end of the earth." "...neither height nor depth...more than conquerors..." "All things work together for good ..." The verses ran through his mind and rolled off his lips. With each step they became more necessary.

He was afraid. When had he last been truly afraid? How old was he? Eleven? Maybe six months after his mother's death, his father was late getting home, as usual, and the sitter had left early. Win had gotten into bed to eat ice cream and watch television. He liked to watch it in the dark so he doused all the lights. Bathed in television's eerie glow he sat and ate for about a half-hour when he heard something outside his bedroom window—something in the bushes. He thought it was a cat until a white beam from a flashlight tunneled through the darkness into his room. Someone was breaking in! Terrified, he grabbed the covers, pulled them up to his eyes, and waited to die. Nothing happened. A car came by and probably scared off the intruder because the flashlight beam went black, the bush fell silent. But until his father came home, there was a chance the intruder might return—every moment felt like his last.

He was feeling that same terror now. He began to mutter nearly imperceptibly, "Jesus, Jesus, Jesus ... "

*And a garlic necklace, I knew I forgot something.*

The fear didn't subside, but his feet never stopped and soon he stood before the door to the room. Unlocked, it squealed as mournfully as the wind when he pushed it open. He stepped inside. The dismal gray room, although empty, was shrouded in clouds of cobwebs that hung in dusty gray drapes. Whipped by wind that leaked through cracks, they gave the room a deceptive aura of life. But there was no life here—from desolate corner to desolate corner, the room lay steeped in death. Oppressed with it.

*So it happened here.* His heart instantly leadened; his breathing strained; the muscles in his chest tightened. He looked behind the door. *The killer stood here, then when Bryce entered . . .* He pushed the door back and it slapped the wall. The window. He placed a hand on the glass. Cold, the wind beating against it. *It's hardly wide enough for his shoulders. There had to be something more than just wanting to drop him. Down the stairs would do more damage and be easier. There had to be more to it.*

Suddenly he felt someone behind him. He spun. No—it was an empty room, empty doorway, a howl of wind.

He looked up, half expecting death to be hovering above him like a black vulture with a bloody red head. But instead he saw two large bells hanging there side by side—silent, moving only slightly in the angry wind, their clappers uselessly at their center, its rope wrapped and piled out of reach on one of the crossbeams. It was a tall belfry with four arched windows. The bells looked like they'd once rung proudly, signaling to a hungry world that the Lord Jesus could be found here, that he was at work gathering his people to himself here. But the four arched windows had been meticulously boarded up. Win's heart caught. Would they ever ring again?

Then his brows furrowed. The impossible—someone stood beside him. He could sense it, sense breathing, sense the displaced air, sensed the sound, the smell. Yet when he turned he found no one. As if death were a person . . . "If it's not you," Win muttered, eyes glancing off the walls, then the ceiling, "it's one who belongs to you."

He studied the window, then compared it to his shoulder width. "Are you already planning how you're going to get *me* through it?" He examined it more closely. He even ran a finger over the sill, disturbing the thick layer of dust that the wind caught and blew into his eyes. Recoiling, he clapped the dust from his hands, and mused, *Just a couple more banana splits and I'm home free.* Having survived this long, he began to feel cocky. He walked the perimeter of the room with surer steps and said to the room, "Pardon me if I don't wish you the best. Would it be ungracious of me to tell you to go back to hell?"

Caught by the fist of wind, the window suddenly flew open and slammed against the outside wall. Glass shattered. Then it slammed closed, then open again. A remaining pane exploded against the siding—a sound packed with rage, violent and vengeful.

Some decisions are quick. His bluster swept away, Win fled. Before he realized it, he spun heels on the second landing heading toward the first. He decided further investigation could wait. The police report would do.

He pulled the door mercifully closed. Slapping the padlock in place, he snapped it shut. Whatever had chased him down wouldn't be stopped by a door or a lock, but they would keep Win from any silly notions about going back up.

"What were you doing up there?"

The voice, the question, the fact he'd been caught—all of it jolted him. He straightened to see Maggie standing not two feet away, her face a huge question mark. "Curiosity," he said, making it sound as casual as he could.

"We locked the murder away up there," she said, placing a furtive hand on the lock. "That way we don't have to think about it." Her eyes came tentatively to his. "It's horrible outside. Have any coffee made?"

"Just did," he said, moving toward his office door. "You take it . . ."

"Sugar and cream, like candy," she smiled, eyes lifted coyly to his.

He prepared it and handed it to her after pouring one for himself.

Taking a sip, she smiled appreciatively. "Perfect," she said.

"You okay today?" he asked.

"Better. You got your car going."

"Car? Oh, yeah. That wire Bill fixed. It came loose. I remembered how to fix it," he lied. It shocked him how easily the lie came.

She nodded acceptingly. "There are times when it just suddenly hits me and I get upset."

"What hits you?"

"Things," she said. Her eyes were fixed intently on his. He sipped his coffee more in defense than from thirst. She went on, "I thought I'd stop by and apologize for being disagreeable to you last night. You cared, and I didn't let you. You were nice. I'm not used to that."

"You're nice to be nice to." *There I go again—good grief, I'm flirting.*

"Really?"

"No apology needed—sometimes life can be hard." He felt the overwhelming need to say something spiritual. "The Lord sees you through, though."

"You talk like him," she said.

"Bryce?" he asked pointedly.

"He tried so hard to talk me into it," she said distantly.

"Salvation?"

"So hard," she again said, even more distantly. "I need to get going. John involves me in civic things—beautification projects, things like that. I hate civic things, but John is John and Maggie is Maggie."

Win felt a surge of panic. She was leaving. "Can you believe that storm out there?" he tossed out like a lifeline.

"Storms come up quickly. We used to live on the shore in John's uncle's old house, but once a storm came up—broke windows and ruined some pretty expensive things. The fire ruined everything else."

"Fire?"

"I was away but it was a close call for John." Win thought he heard her mutter, "Not close enough." Then she went on. "We're on a hill now. John likes the hill. He can look out over everything and pretend it's all his . . . he's sure it will be one day."

"John owns the Ford dealership?"

She nodded. "He inherited it from his uncle. There were some lean years, but now it's doing well. Ford's come back." She felt comfortable again.

"How long have you been married?"

"Eleven years now—no, twelve years." Her eyes drifted to the top of his desk. "What's this?" She fingered a yellow pad he'd been using. "Oh, your youth group work. That's how John and I met."

"Teaching a youth group?"

"Being in one. Here at Sugar Steeple. I never really fit in, but John did. We dated some in high school."

"Dating around the lake—sounds romantic."

"It was. Walks, moonlight. If only I'd known. He gave me up while he went to U of V. But in his senior year he found me again. We got married after he graduated. He stopped going to church a couple of years later—then took over the dealership when his uncle died." The romance out of her voice, she leaned toward Win. He could smell her lush shampoo. Her eyes came up, and they were only inches from one another. For an instant their eyes locked, and Win felt the warmth of her breath.

She asked, "What about you?" her eyes ranging from eyes to lips and back to his eyes.

"I'm just out of seminary," he said softly and simply—remaining close, drinking from the misty green wells. Her shampoo smelled wonderfully of jasmine.

"But you're so mature," Maggie whispered in a tone that said she valued his maturity—not many people ever had.

"I'm a late bloomer." He smiled and felt the urge to move even closer. He did. Imperceptibly. When he saw that she'd moved closer still and realized that the next move was his—a move he wanted to make more than anything—a restraining hand suddenly tightened around his heart. Awkwardly, his lips mumbling something apologetic, his eyes darting in lost fits and starts, he straightened. "I can't do this. I really can't."

"Sure you can," Maggie purred, and she closed the gap that he'd opened between them.

"No, Maggie," he said, his head shaking in sweeps from side to side, his throat raw. "I truly can't."

Maggie frowned and pulled back. Even the slightest rejection was immense to her, and this was more than slight. She grew instantly cold and hard. "You're not a late bloomer. You're a no bloomer. I've got to get going."

Win cleared his throat and tried to reestablish a certain formality. But he still didn't want her to leave. "You're a very attractive woman, and I've not been around attractive women very much. I lost my head. I'm sorry." He sat on the edge of his desk.

"Attractive? No. I'm a thirty-year-old frump." She planted herself beside him

"No one can be a frump in New England. All the history, the romance," he said, and suddenly he saw himself with Maggie on one of the island beaches—a picnic. *A picnic? She wants romance, and you want cold chicken and potato salad.* Her lips were so full and moist. *Oh, Lord, what am I thinking?*

"Danny thought New England romantic too," she injected offhandedly. Almost too offhandedly.

"I wish I'd met him. What was he like?"

She didn't answer. Still looking slightly miffed, she stepped around him toward the coffee. Almost to punish him, she brushed against him. Her nearness had its effect, the faint jasmine, the grip of his heart, the tug at his breathing.

"At first, Danny was a gold-plated jerk," she said, facing Win and leaning against the counter. "But then he turned nice. He cared. I found him, you know. From up there," she announced, cocking her head in the general direction of the tower. "Did you enjoy your visit up there?"

The question was an accusation, as if his "curiosity" had revealed a terrible character flaw. *She suspects something.*

"That must have been hard," he said, avoiding the question.

"Very," she said with a shudder—all pretexts gone. "Sometimes I wake up reliving it." A cast settled on her eyes as if she might be reliving it just then. "He cared about me."

"That's no trick," Win heard himself say—and instantly kicked himself squarely in the shin. *Flirting again!* Yet he couldn't help but relish the warm smile she returned to him.

She leaned close to him.

The hint of jasmine. *Why couldn't it be roses or gardenias or one of those ant-spray smells I hate? Why jasmine, Lord? Isn't the knot you've tied me in tight enough already, you want to give the rope a couple more good yanks?*

"I've done all I can do," she said, remaining close, the fullness of her lips stirring his.

"I believe that," he finally said, blood rushing to his face, leaving his heart empty—it was his hollow heart that brought reality. He pulled away. "You don't know how much I want . . ."

"Me, too . . . me, too."

"But it's wrong . . . very wrong."

"Haven't you ever done anything wrong before?" she asked, moving toward him again.

"Not with a married woman," he said, his tone pleading.

He must have said the magic words, for she frowned again, then stood stiffly. "I need to get going," she stated flatly, her irritation taking root. Gathering up her purse she added, "There's a trustee meeting tonight. You going?"

"I guess so."

She stepped brusquely toward the door. "Maybe I'll stop by tomorrow and find out what was said. No one tells me."

"I'd . . . uh . . . like that. I'll be here," he said, remaining by the desk.

"See you then," she said, wearing her anger prominently as she disappeared into the hallway. The sound of her footsteps was rapid-fire and deliberate. He glanced at the painting she'd bought him. It was hanging a little crookedly so he straightened it. "I made *her* day."

He fell into Dan Bryce's deep vinyl chair. He leaned back

until it hit the wall and pulled out the bottom drawer and planted his feet on it. There he sat—staring at the door. The storm was dying outside, the wind no more than a beleaguered whine, the rain a feeble grind against the windows. *You'd be proud of me, wouldn't you, Dean? A man of iron, that's what I am. Fling those temptations aside one by one, piling 'em up on either side of me like cordwood. What a guy. The John Wayne of Christians.*

That's when he felt his hand pressing against the place on his chest where she'd brushed against him. Savoring the sensation, the press of the hand reminding him of the press of her. He pulled the hand away as if from a hot burner.

*Lord, look at me. This is just flesh—why? She's no prize . . . all I have to do is be cool. Yet those eyes—hypnotic. No, I'm going willingly. You know that—you know everything. You know why you're doing this to me. Why? Let me in on it, so I can have a good laugh too.*

The phone rang. He made it to Worlly's office by the fourth ring.

"Good morning—oops, afternoon. This is Win Brady."

"It's Ginger." Her voice was warm enough.

"Hi. How you doing?"

"Fine. Sanderson nailed me today. Did you tell him I'd told someone about you?"

"What'd he say?"

"To keep my mouth shut. But the way he said it sounded like you'd accused me of not keeping it shut. Did you?"

"He tricked me into telling him about you. He might have done the same with you."

A long, cool pause followed while she considered this, then she said, "He told me to tell you that the Ford Probe belongs to Bill Simms. What's that mean?"

Simms? He suddenly hated him. It was a burst of hate—instinctive—hot and filled with rage. Calling upon all the self-control he had available, he dampened it. "It's just information."

"How's the investigation going?"

"It's going," he managed. "You want some lunch?" he suddenly asked. He hadn't planned on asking, but for all of what Ginger was, she was normal. He needed normal.

"Sure," she answered. "Why not? You know where Judy's is?"

"I don't know where anything is."

"Drive north on Two. You'll find it about two miles up from the church."

That's exactly where he found it. Judy's was a converted house with the dining and living rooms transformed into a restaurant. He got there fifteen minutes before Ginger. The rain a gentle mist, he waited in the car with his thoughts—thoughts that troubled him, thoughts he couldn't divert with a quip or smart remark. Ginger rolled up in her white patrol car. She looked powerfully official in her blue uniform, eight-point saucer cap, leather belt and holster with the Glock 9mm pistol, and yet remarkably feminine with her angular Nordic features, deep blue eyes, and the puff of golden hair at the back of her hat.

Judy greeted them warmly as they entered. A dwarf, she wasn't more than a yard tall, maybe less. "Well, Officer Glasgow, I haven't seen you in almost a month."

"At least."

"It's good to see you now. This way, please," Judy said and walked in her wonderful waddle to a table near the window. If Win craned his neck, he could see the lake and the mainland beyond.

Ginger ordered iced tea, Win, a diet Coke, then they wordlessly reviewed the menus. Win decided on a chicken salad, refolded the menu and waited for Ginger. When finished, she refolded hers, and the two of them stared at each other for a long, eventually uncomfortable minute.

"How's your boat?" she asked, jump-starting the conversation.

"Good. Fun," he said. The iced tea and Coke came and they ordered.

"Come over with it," Ginger invited.

"I did but you had company," he said, trying to sound unaffected.

"Come again. Chad likes you," she said, as if he were the only one in the house who did.

"I suppose I could take him fishing. We could tangle lines together."

"Or catch something."

"Maybe a cold."

"Well, now," she said, stirring her iced tea with the straw. "We are down this afternoon. It been a tough couple of days, has it?"

"Seems like a year."

"Is Pooh Bear homesick?"

He didn't like the mocking tone. But he had no defense against it. She was right. *Rejoice, I say it again, rejoice.* He didn't feel like rejoicing. And suddenly he didn't feel like being there.

"Maybe," he said resigned to the truth. "I'm good at book stuff—theories, doctrine, verses. It's all a giant puzzle just waiting to be put together and explained. People stuff's the pits."

"How many people do you have to deal with?" she fired off condescendingly. "It's a small church. Nothing goes on in small churches."

"Someone got killed in this one," he stated flatly.

Their orders came. Ginger waded into her burger, and Win picked at his salad.

When half of the burger was gone, she took a break from chewing. "What people stuff?"

"Just stuff." He stabbed a tomato and beat a cucumber with it. "Stuff that's getting a bit overwhelming."

Maybe it was what he said or the hint of defeat in his voice, but she dropped her haughtiness and eyed him caringly. "You okay?"

"I don't know," he said, frustration boiling over. "Maybe I just need to pull something on somebody."

"Pull something?"

"Yeah." Win came alive. "When I got a little down at the seminary I'd pull something on one of the profs—a goat in the bathtub, live frogs in the chow line. Fun things like that."

"Sounds juvenile."

"So what's your point? It gave me purpose and a few laughs, got me up again."

"And you want to do that around here."

"Well, yeah."

"Pull something on Sanderson and he'd shoot you. Pull something on me and I'd make you spend a day with Chad; pull something on someone from the church and they'd ring those bells with your head."

Win didn't respond right away. "I saw those bells today," he finally said.

"In the tower?"

"It's a spooky place."

"I went up only once during the investigation."

"When were they silenced?" he asked.

Ginger shrugged and then, remembering, her face brightened. "The year I graduated from high school. Before that they rang every Sunday morning—eight o'clock sharp—since the church was built over a hundred years ago. After all that time, neighbors started complaining. The church caved in and boarded the bells up. They even made a ceremony out of it."

Win remembered the picture in the hallway—"The Bell Ceremony."

"Uncle Joel was attending at the time, off and on, when he was in town, and he was heartbroken. He knew that a church sometimes needs to accommodate, but they did it as if the neighbors were right, that they ought to curb their outreach activities, not bother the neighbors." She eyed the plate thoughtfully. "I'm surprised I remember all that so clearly." Ginger set the half-eaten burger down and leaned back. "It'd be fun to ring 'em again someday."

"It's weird up there."

"In what way?"

Win shrugged. He wasn't ready to describe what may have been the result of an overactive imagination and was certainly not prepared to tell her about running down the tower steps, a ghost after him. "Just weird," he finally said.

"Come on, Pooh Bear, talk . . ."

Win stiffened. "I really don't need this Pooh Bear stuff."

"Okay, I'm sorry. You just remind me of Pooh Bear—well, not entirely—on one hand Schwarzenegger and on the other Pooh Bear."

"Your uncle said I was either Einstein or Goofy. That's me, a guy of extremes with a vast wasteland in the middle."

"Taking all this a bit seriously, aren't you?"

"If I can't handle this podunk church . . ." He let the rest trail away.

Ginger looked at him, her eyes glazed with concern. "You don't 'handle' a church—God does that."

Win just sighed, showing no enthusiasm for a fight. "Yeah, right," he said, wadding his napkin. "Listen, this lunch idea was a bad one." He tossed a credit card on the table. "Use this, and I'll pick it up later."

Ginger watched him leave. After a long moment, she ordered a cup of coffee and finished it slowly.


Once Bray and Larin Breed had been the best of friends. That was before Breed had made chief. Over the years their friendship had deteriorated to toleration and had remained at that level for years.

Now in Breed's office it was on a downward spiral again—since Grogan had arrived. It was about to gain toboggan speeds.

"You wanted me?" Bray asked.

Breed sat on the edge of his desk.

Grogan was sitting down, a smile on his thin, bloodless lips.

"We got a lead for you," Breed said.

"We?"

"That candy store owner from that church came in. Someone's squeezing him."

"I talked to him," Grogan injected.

"You did?" Bray said, rage coming to a boil. But he kept the lid on it.

"Here's my report." Grogan handed Bray a couple of pages stapled together. Grogan could touch-type, and the report swarmed with verbatim conversations. Bray typed with only one finger on each hand. His agonizing slowness kept his word count way down. He hated people who could type.

"We think the kid found out that someone was squeezing the candy man and died for it. Find your squeezer and you find your killer."

"A good thing I was here to make the connection," Grogan said, eyes twinkling victoriously.

Bray hated this. Grogan's conclusion would have been his. It was the obvious conclusion. But because Grogan had come to it first, it now belonged to Grogan. To agree with it would put Bray in a place he dreaded—on Grogan's side.

"This is a complicated case," Bray's voice betrayed a deep, restrained anger. "This is one lead but there are others." He was on the defensive, and he didn't like it. He wanted the offense. He wanted to skewer them both.

"This is the only lead you got and you know it." Breed's implication was crystal clear: The killer stands behind this door—leave it closed and fail to find him elsewhere and it'll be your head.

"Can we talk, Chief—alone?"

Grogan, dripping with magnanimity, stood. "I'm sure you have things to talk about." He spoke directly to Bray, "I'll be around if you need me again."

"I'm sure." Sanderson felt strangled by restraint.

When alone, Breed immediately took the offensive, "He's a good man. Makes things happen. It's cops like him that'll bring the twentieth century to this place. To start with, he's doing what you're not—he's thinking."

"This is my case." Bray took the offensive back. "I've been working this case for four months . . . "

"... and time's running out. Take Grogan's information and find your man."

"It's not information. I've already thought of it."

"Whatever. Just find your killer."

Bray stood there fuming. Then he collapsed inside and left.


After his talk with Breed, Bray called Win at the church. He'd hoped the junior Sherlock had come up with something he could use to fight Grogan, but he hadn't. Nothing new, no new twist, just some of the same. Maggie's husband had gone to the church during high school but had quit—whoopie! Maggie seemed to have had a fight with Simms—double whoop! There had been an interesting new name: "Sorrell?" Bray mulled it over. "Probably Martin Sorrell. Mr. Megabucks. Owns an inn on Bugle Bay. Lots of grass—ten acres in front, the lake in back. The grass is his mote."

"Money?"

"Inherited it. Throws it around at election time. Got anything else?" he asked.

Win wondered if he should tell him about Maggie's eyes, how he was drawn to those eyes yet kicked himself for it. Maybe later. "No. Nothing."

"Well, something's brewing here," Bray said reluctantly. Having gotten nothing from Win, he had no choice but to follow Grogan's lead. "That candy store owner ... "

"Peter Sweet," Win remembered the name.

"Looks like he's going to lead us to our killer."

"Another bomb?"

"More subtle. Someone's shaking him down and with ingenuity. He came into the station again. A television news crew barged into his store yesterday and accused him of serving ground glass with his popcorn."

"You're kidding," Win was impressed. "Blood pressure city."

"This morning he checked it out and discovered it was all a hoax. He comes in and asks for help. Bryce was probably set up too—for whatever reason. After refusing to be pushed, or maybe confronting the extortionist, he was killed. Find the extortionist, find the killer."

Win wasn't in the mood to fight him, nor to expound theories on the spiritual aspects of Dan Bryce's death. "Think so?" he said.

"There's nothing else to think. For now I'm putting a twenty-four-hour tail on our candy man. I'll do most of it personally . . . "

"Your boss agree?"

"More than you'll ever know."

"I'll keep looking around here," Win said as if he didn't have the energy to make good on his plan. "Maybe our paths will merge. Who knows?"

"I'll talk to you later," Bray said flatly. "Next time over Danish. At least something good will come of it."

"I almost forgot—you wanted to know everything, and I just remembered something. Maggie Selkirk makes porcelain dolls."

A hesitation. "She take classes on the island?"

"From a Pamela something—Wisdom."

Another hesitation.

"You know her?" Win asked, curious about the pause. Bray actually seemed at a loss, though it was hard to verify over the phone.

"Doesn't matter," Bray responded after a moment. "But I appreciate your leaving nothing out."

"Later," said Win and hung up.

He didn't want to go to the trustee meeting. He'd rather go out on the boat, maybe head north to St. Albans, maybe over to an island to have a bonfire on a beach. He was living where everyone came to escape, and he wanted to escape *from* it. Escape from those eyes and the guilt that accompanied them.

But he had to go. She'd want a report tomorrow, and for all his guilt, he couldn't let her down.

# Chapter 11

Charlie Briggs slammed a rich cherry wood gavel and the trustee meeting opened. The slap startled Win who'd been watching people, and he jumped slightly. Briggs chuckled. "Trustee meeting a little too much for you, Brady?"

"So far," Win said with a chuckle of his own.

Pastor Worlly, at the far end of the table, looked up from his notebook and laughed. "Another slap and he'll want combat pay."

While the others laughed Win suddenly hardened. Bill Simms stepped in.

"What'd I miss?" he asked, already laughing with the group.

"Win's facing death right here at the table." Briggs spun the gavel head.

"I hope he did better than the other guy," Bill quipped.

The room fell silent.

"Bad taste, eh?" Bill admitted.

"Very," Worlly agreed.

"Sorry," Bill said, subdued.

Through the banter a third trustee, Jim Marks, a man Win hadn't met before, sat next to Simms and said nothing.

"We have a full calendar, so we'd better get going." Charlie picked up a thick binder, opened it, and thumbed to the right page. "The take Sunday was down ten percent, but we're running even for the month. We'll be all right. We're starting to dig ourselves out of the hole the Bryce murder buried us in." He sounded like it was Bryce's fault. "Of course, Maybell Whats-er-face's dying will cost us about $100 a month. She was a persistent patron." Briggs eyed Worlly. "How was the funeral?"

"Poor turnout."

"I don't like funerals," Charlie stated flatly.

Simms shrugged. "Had to work. Wanted to go but . . ."

Jim didn't answer.

Before Charlie could begin again, Roz entered.

Win had a hard time keeping a straight face. To him Roz was little more than a caricature—an overdone resident of Toontown. She strolled with exaggerated steps, her lavender dress a drape, her shoulders wrapped in a fox fur stole made of heads, bodies, and tails. Eying everyone like a hawk scanning for weakness, she moved catlike around to the far side of the table. Seeing Win she frowned.

A man followed not far behind her. A male version of Maggie Selkirk, he appeared withdrawn, self-conscious, with darting, fearful eyes. He was tall and should have gained confidence on the basketball court, but he obviously hadn't. Upon entering he sat unobtrusively on a folding chair near the door.

*Sorrell,* Win thought.

"Good evening, Roz," Charlie greeted with caution.

Roz nodded stiffly and chose a chair near Worlly.

After a few minutes of verbal jostling the meeting settled down to business. It lasted an hour, then broke up with that same slam of the gavel.

Win followed the others out and kept an eye on Bill. Bill joked around with Charlie, verbally jabbing at the older man, enjoying the rise he got out of him. *Maggie's lover.* He didn't know Win knew—or that the police knew. For some perverse reason, Win enjoyed the power the knowledge gave him. It was a childish enjoyment—a game, a manipulative game, and he decided to enjoy it a while longer.

In the parking lot, Win strolled up to Simms. "I owe you something for helping me Sunday. Can I buy you a cup of coffee?"

Simms brightened. "Now there's a thought." Then, "A quick phone call and I'm yours."

He disappeared inside the church. Was he calling Maggie? *It's no goat in the bathtub—but this could be fun.*

After a moment Simms returned. "I've got an hour. That enough time to show your gratitude?"

"A year wouldn't be enough," Win said smoothly. "But an hour will have to do."

A few minutes later they drove up to The Broken Spigot a couple of blocks away. A ramshackle little place that rented a few boats on the weekends and acted as a diner during the week.

A moment later they sat at a table in a corner booth, two coffees in front of them.

Simms sipped his coffee and looked at Win. "Why this?" he asked.

"A thank you for fixing my car on Sunday," Win said.

"There are a million ways to thank me," he said suspiciously.

Win smiled congenially. *Thank-yous must be rare at Sugar Steeple.* "Maybe we have something in common." *More than you know, Simms.*

"Okay. You fish?" Bill asked.

"I tangle lines," Win admitted. "On a grand scale."

"What about sports? Basketball, football, golf?"

"Some weightlifting—but not since coming here."

"Hunt?"

"Not really into guns."

Bill took another sip. "Now it's your turn to suggest something."

Win smiled. He felt devilish as he thought, *Maggie, you bozo—you slightly more'n me. Why did I think you were such a good guy?* "We both work for the church," Win offered.

"But you get paid." Simms smiled wryly.

"Only, as you say, until someone bumps me off."

"I said that?"

"Sort of," Win said, then asked pointedly, "How'd the

church react to Bryce's death? Maggie Selkirk found him, didn't she?" Win coolly watched his eyes for a reaction to Maggie's name. Nothing.

"Something to see," he exclaimed, "her in the tower screaming and pointing. His outline in the snow down below. The wind chill doubled." Bill shuddered and finished his coffee.

"How'd it affect her?" Even more pointedly.

"Maggie?" Bill's eyes went distant. There must have been a longer answer than the one he finally gave. "She liked him. It went hard with her."

"What about you, did you like him?"

Simms's eyes came up a little surprised at the implication. "He was okay—less so toward the end."

Win took a drink and had a hard time smiling. "So the killer's still out there somewhere."

"Somewhere."

"Here?"

Bill leaned back and with a half smile glued to his face he eyed the new assistant pastor as if dying to ask, "What's got into you?" But he didn't, he merely said, "Maybe."

"How does Maggie take that? To think Bryce's murderer is still . . . " Win let the words trail away as he took another sip.

"Why the interest?" Bill volleyed, brows knit suspiciously.

"I've got his job," Win answered simply, the knife edge still on his voice.

"And you could be next?" he said with mock drama.

"Maybe."

Bill smiled. "You know, it takes real arrogance to think someone could be so passionately interested in you to kill you."

Win laughed softly. "If it means being prepared."

"Sandbagging your office? Placing a machine gun line item in the next budget?" Bill chided. "Suspect everybody? Even me?"

"The police suspect people—I just want to stay alive." *You are a suspect*, Win thought.

Bill saw the spark of concern in Win's eyes and laughed, "Don't worry. I never kill people I might earn money from. And that Chevy's going to need work—real soon."

"But, if not you . . . "

"Then someone else?"

"A member of the family."

"Ah," he let the sound ease out. "Our little church family?" Bill took a long drink. "Well, if it is, he's still here. No one's left since."

"You didn't speculate about who?"

"We hardly talked about it at all."

"Really? About a murder?"

"Officially, from the top, a transient did it," Bill said. His brows dipped doubtfully. "It's okay for the cops to say that theory doesn't wash. But if one of the family did they'd be calling another member of the family a murderer—or saying all of us could be." Bill stared into his cup, then looked up, a wan smile on his face. "And we're sensitive about that—all of us wanted to more or less kill him once or twice."

"Maggie?"

"What's this preoccupation with Maggie?"

Win knew his preoccupation. A kid's game that seemed to be changing—and he did enjoy the power. A kid's power. Win had even done it as a kid—laughed inside when he knew something some other kid didn't. Power. Over Bill. For some reason, Win needed that tonight. "She was the only one who liked him," Win said convincingly. "I just wondered if maybe . . . "

"You're a cop." Bill leaned forward, eyes narrow with deep questions.

Win laughed softly. "No. No cop." *Careful, Lead Head, lighten up.* "I did some thinking."

"Dangerous practice."

Win smiled. "I realized that the murderer is probably still around, and if he killed Bryce, he might kill me. Maybe he'd think I'd learn what Bryce learned. When I thought about that . . ."

*Be anxious for nothing . . . I am with you to the ends of the earth.* The verses leaped to mind—a spiritual reflex. And although technically he was leading Bill on, he suddenly flashed on his visit to the tower and knew he wasn't leading Bill on at all. Everything he was saying was true.

Bill became conciliatory. "I know where you're at," he said. "It's strange. Our pastor was killed, probably by one of us, the police ask questions, then leave. All the information they gathered went into a black hole. We had a murder in the family, as you put it, committed by a member of the family, and we were left to find out for ourselves who of us did it."

"Did you?"

"You don't see nobody hanging from the bell tower, do you?" He remained sober. "The killer had to be someone in the church. No way it was a transient. Bryce would have called a place in Burlington that takes transients. That was the rule, and Bryce followed rules. And he wasn't stupid. Transients can be dangerous. No, one of us did it. And that's the puzzle. Afterward no one changed."

"Changed?"

"We're church people with reasonable moral character. You'd think if one of us committed a murder there'd be a change. Someone would act a little different, maybe more on edge, maybe more relaxed, maybe more paranoid. But no one's changed. The nervous are still nervous, the relaxed are still relaxed, and the paranoid are still as paranoid as ever."

"You need a key to the church to get in the tower—and the killer had to have been there first. Maggie said there were keys everywhere. That true?" Win knew he'd gotten that information from the police files. He hoped Bill wouldn't cross check with Maggie.

"Not completely true," Simms said. "I did a key count about a month ago. Worlly asked for it—no reason given. The only people with keys were the deacons, the trustees, Worlly, and the cleaning people. A couple belonged to people who'd retired years ago to Florida—one's dead that we know of."

Win wrote the names in his gray cells: Maggie, Steve Taylor,

Charlie Briggs, Bill Simms, Jim Marks, Worlly. "Jim Marks seems pretty quiet."

"Quiet? Like a deaf mute," Bill said. "He was Sorrell's nominee. Sorrell's too busy to do the menial. Jim just sits, listens, and votes the way he thinks Sorrell would vote." Then Bill shook his head. "Not Jim. He doesn't bat bugs away on a hot night. 'Harmless' is too violent a description of ol' Jim." Then he added, "On land, that is. Get him on the water and he's a different guy. Knows boats. But that's Jim on the lake. Bryce, of course, was killed on land."

"Spouses?"

"I feel like I'm back with the cops—Briggs, Marks, and I are spouseless. John Selkirk—well, he's all but unapproachable, a real piece of work."

"In what way? Maggie seems a little down on him."

Bill took a long sip on a fresh cup. Win enjoyed watching Bill choose his words. "Down?" he laughed, his head shaking in disbelief. But he said no more about that. Rather: "He's my boss. I have to watch what I say, but John Selkirk's a nonperson around the church. The thought that he'd come back and murder someone is too remote a possibility."

John Selkirk. Maggie had little use for him and because she didn't, Win didn't either. But . . . ? "Tell me about him," Win asked.

Simms peered into the dark fluid, and Win saw rage in his eyes, maybe hate. Whatever the tangle of emotions, Win sensed Bill trying to suppress them.

"Well, now—something about John Selkirk . . . how might one describe the good John Selkirk? I got it. There's one story that describes him to a tee. It happened a while back—around Christmas."

"Before or after the murder?"

Bill thought, then shrugged. "Doesn't pertain anyway. Sorrell's chauffeur banged up Sorrell's limo one night. He took it out without permission and piled it up against a tree. Tree bark embedded everywhere. Sorrell woke up to find his car in the front of the inn and the chauffeur gone. Sorrell brought the car into Selkirk's body shop. He wanted to trade it in on another stretch Lincoln. Big bucks. He didn't have to go through getting the body done. The sales guys would have just knocked the trade-in allowance down, but Sorrell wanted everything neat and tidy.

"I was taking a quick break by the Coke machine, so I heard John and Sorrell talking. Sorrell's rich. Rich means important and John's into both. He was pretty nice at first, a real charmer—the more money, the more charm. But then he excused himself—the phone or something. When he returned, no more charm." Bill sipped the coffee and gathered up more words. "John comes back and Sorrell tells him how he wants to equip the new car. John explodes. I felt sorry for Sorrell—not normal for me when somebody's got his kind of money. But Sorrell wouldn't hurt a fly . . . he just likes to buy things. God knows it's his only fun in life, living alone in the middle of that pasture. He just wanted to equip the car the way he wanted it—and he wanted it with everything.

"You'd think John would see dollar signs with every option Sorrell added. But he didn't. He starts yelling, 'This car's the only thing you have in life—power windows? You oughta just seal 'em up. And a bar? Why don't you go to a real bar? There won't be any chicks at this one.' He says things like that.

"But it came to a head when Sorrell asked him about an electronic chess set. When that came up John really blew up. Sorrell was shocked. His face went red, like the top of his head was going to blow off. When John kept at him he deflated. John nailed him for having all that money and playing a stupid game like chess. He criticized him for being afraid of people, for hiding behind all that grass surrounding his land, for not just taking what he wanted. He yelled loud enough for everyone to hear, 'If I had your money I'd own New England . . . I'd be buying fifty stretch Lincolns. And what I couldn't buy I'd take.'"

Bill took a breath. "That sums up ol' John. He's the center. He's the reason the world exists. What he can't buy he takes. And people he can't own he hurts—destroys."

"Bryce?"

Bill gave a tense laugh, "He has to want to destroy someone. He couldn't care less about the church. He was the one who boarded up the bells—and was proud of that. He just didn't care about Bryce."

"Maggie liked Bryce—"

"Jealousy? John for Maggie?"

"John's a powerful guy. His pride might make him do things. Maggie's his possession. People, especially assistant pastors, don't steal from people like that."

"Pride?" Bill chewed on that one for a moment. Win saw a flash of concern in Bill's eyes. He relished it—at that moment Bill was like a puppet and Win had just yanked an important string.

"John just doesn't care," Bill said, his voice betraying a current of anxiety. "Pride's got nothing to do with it." He downed the coffee in a single gulp. "He doesn't care."

"He sounds like a violent guy. Sounds like if a person doesn't have money John could do that person some harm. He wouldn't be gentle with someone who's stolen his wife. No matter what he thought about that wife."

Bill didn't look up. He spun the empty cup on its base, then caught it between his palms. "He'd do worse than hurt 'em," he said to the cup. "But it wasn't that way between Maggie and Bryce. Not that way at all."

"Well, let's hope so," Win said, deeply serious. John *did* sound like a violent guy, and he wouldn't treat someone who'd stolen his wife gently.

In the secret recesses of his gray matter Win heard that car door slam back at the church—had John been spying on Maggie last night? Had John seen Win lurking in the bushes? Were John's sights already fixed on him? Win cringed inside. He was scaring himself.

About the time Win was walking into the Broken Spigot with Bill Simms, Bray Sanderson was stepping up to a cottage door he'd not stepped up to for more than three years. Before knocking, he hesitated uncomfortably. This had seemed a good idea while he sat eating a sandwich for dinner, but now, standing before this oak door, it didn't have the same allure.

As it turned out, though, he didn't have to knock.

"Is somebody there?" came the woman's voice from the direction of the side garage.

Bray turned. It was still dusk, and he saw the woman standing in the driveway near where the sidewalk met it. "It's me, Pam," Bray said, as if there would be no doubt that she'd recognize him.

Pamela Wisdom did. "Bray Sanderson? I'll be."

Bray saw her eyes widen happily, and she smiled excitedly. "I heard your name today, and I wanted to stop by and see how you're doing."

"I'm fine—more than fine—wonderful. And you've made me even better. Come on back. I'm pouring and can't leave the molds for very long. We'll talk while I work."

He followed her into the garage, and she indicated a worn folding chair. He brushed the porcelain dust off, then sat. She hadn't changed much in three years, the same solid figure, the same strong, fresh features. Maybe there were a few more strands of gray, but somehow they only made her more appealing.

"You want a tour?" She asked him as she stood beside several large plaster porcelain doll molds.

"Diane used to give 'em to me."

Pamela's expression became sympathetic, but only for a moment. There was no time for sympathy. A timer dinged, and she quickly grabbed one of the larger molds, one at least a foot on a side, picked it up easily and poured the liquid porcelain inside it into a nearby bucket. "This one's a twenty-four-inch doll—big molds," she explained. After shaking the last drop, she set it, opening down, on a draining table—a rack of wood dowelings placed over a blue plastic tub. Then she did the same with four more molds. When she had only one left, Bray grabbed the mold and hefted it. Twenty pounds, easy.

"No wonder Diane had muscles like a carpenter."

Pam laughed softly as she finished the last one. "Before I

stopped drinking I used to arm wrestle for shooters." Then she stepped from behind her workbench, "If you got a minute, I've got coffee on inside—maybe some iced tea?"

"Coffee'd be nice. Decaf—gettin' old."

"Not you—never," and she let appreciative, smiling eyes rest on him for a moment.

Bray returned the smile self-consciously.

Pam had a simple kitchen since she spent most of her time in her workshop. But it was clean and functional—no nonsense—like her. Bray sat at her handcrafted wooden table, and she poured him a cup. "So, what really brings you out here?"

"I heard your name today. And I hadn't seen you since Diane died. . . . I used to enjoy watching the two of you work. Tossing those molds around, doing that delicate painting—eyebrows, lips. I wanted to see you again."

Pam cocked her head inquisitively. "You recovered yet?" she asked.

He hadn't recovered. He didn't think he'd ever recover—maybe he didn't want to. He'd never been a good husband, never paid Diane enough attention, never loved her as much as she deserved, never made love to her enough. But it didn't seem to matter to Diane. She was always there for him, never complained about the erratic hours, the nights when he never came home at all. The danger got to her a little, and there were moments when she'd explode. But those moments were only because she was frightened she might lose him. She'd been the only one who'd ever been frightened about that.

Now there wasn't anyone. They used to laugh. He missed laughing. It took a special kind of woman to laugh with. A woman he trusted. He'd trusted Diane and he never wanted to get over trusting her.

But he mentioned none of that. He just shrugged. "We were married over twenty years. She put up with a lot. Making dolls was her only outlet. I still have 'em all over the house. Looking at them hurts sometimes."

He felt an empathetic hand on his arm, and he was about

to pull away when he realized how good it felt. He allowed the hand to remain.

"She was a good friend," Pam said, her eyes on her hand on his arm.

"You still giving classes?" Bray asked.

"More than ever," she told him, and with fluttering brows for emphasis, she added, "And some to the very rich. I'm actually making money with the classes and selling a few dolls. That twenty-four-incher out there is a special order—$500. Should be twice that—and it will be someday."

"I hear one of your students is Maggie Selkirk."

"Ah," she suddenly looked very disappointed. "You're here as a cop."

"I could have just called."

She smiled and recovered a little. "She took classes for a while, then she bought a kiln and a bunch of molds. I see her only occasionally now."

"Big molds?"

"They're all big—some are just bigger than others."

Bray sipped his coffee then set the mug down. "The lake's nice tonight," he said.

"I've got about fifteen minutes before I need to break open those molds. Want to take a walk?"

Bray felt his heart tighten, but it was a good tightening, a pleasant anticipation. He looked at Pam—a little more gray hair and her face shining like a sunflower. *A walk would be nice,* he thought. "Maybe just a short one," he said.

# Chapter 12

**W**in sat in the same booth as always at the Lake Bakery and Donut Shoppe and took the first sip of his second cup of coffee. Although he'd gotten some good information from Bill Simms the night before, his sadistic effort to scare Bill had only resulted in Win's scaring himself. As a result he'd had a poor night's sleep, had awakened early to burning eyes and a headache, and now was nagged by the thought that he would probably be gunned down on his way out of the donut shop. *I'm not in the mood for this.*

Bray didn't notice Win's state. He studied the comics spread before him. He never smiled. He couldn't. His mouth was crammed with Danish, his cup poised for the precise moment he'd need more coffee.

They'd said little to each other since meeting more than twenty minutes ago. Win reached into the barrel to find just a little more patience and came up empty. "How's your stakeout at Sweet's candy shop going?" he asked, hoping to get something going.

"Nothing," Bray grunted, not looking up.

A smoker lit a cigarette nearby, and Win sighed impatiently. "What say we take this outside and walk down the wharf?" he suggested curtly.

"What say you respect a man's life?" Bray growled through the crumbs.

Win was irritating to Bray. The others were just royal pains. But Win had an annoying habit of being childlike, from his aggravating smile to his perfect muscles. Youth was bad enough, childlike was beyond endurance.

"You've got something besides those comics on your mind," Win said as he stood. "A walk might jar it loose."

"How metaphoric of you. I don't walk—I sit and eat and read."

"Well, maybe it's time to live on the edge. There's a warm sun and a crisp breeze, and maybe you'll feel like talking out there. I need to tell you a few things, too, and we can have some privacy outside."

Bray finally looked up, frowned and, with weary resolution, refolded the paper. Stuffing it unceremoniously into his jacket pocket, he eased painfully to his feet and grabbed the remaining half Danish and coffee.

The Burlington marina was in the final throes of waking up. There was a small commotion around the New York Ferry's entrance, a red-bearded guy in a skipper's cap hosed off his portion of the walkway while a golden retriever puppy and his owner jogged, the dog yipping at his owner's heels. Win was beginning to love the lake early in the morning—fresh coffee on the end of his boathouse dock, the sun breaking golden on the eastern horizon. All was new, invigorating, the water possessing a distinct freshness as it slapped impetuously at the pilings. But not this morning. He didn't like anything this morning. Patience was gone.

"What's bothering you?" Win asked pointedly when they'd walked only a few yards.

"You're bothering me," Bray fired back. "If you expect a conversation, expect it from someone else. I don't walk, talk, and drink coffee at the same time. I don't walk and do much of anything at the same time." As if to solve the problem, Bray reached a bench not far from where they'd started and sat. "Walk's over. What have you got?"

Gulls squawked overhead while others camped statuelike on pilings and piers. Win leaned against a white barrier.

He took a deep breath. "I met Sorrell at the trustee meeting last night."

"Martin Sorrell's got about fifty million bucks," Bray began. "All secure. Muni bonds, things like that. And a real clothes horse. He wears 'em 'til they fall off. He comes from the New York Sorrells—real estate, stocks, a savings bank or two. Anyway, he held a few positions in the family businesses and messed up everything he touched. He was an embarrassment, maybe a little retarded, maybe inhibited by the power around him—maybe abused. Who knows? But his father gave him the money, forced him to manage it through one of their financial planning businesses and exiled him to Grand Isle. Now he goes through life a recluse. The inn's a hobby."

Win watched a scattering of gulls pitch and ride the wind. "Whatever his background, he's no suspect."

"That's my call," Bray reaffirmed gruffly, waving a morsel of Danish at him. "I've seen big money breed big passions—a feeling of being above the law. Sorrell's the opposite. He feels below everything. Life's got him down. Murder would be too risky for him."

Win only nodded. "On the other end of the spectrum is John Selkirk."

"You saw him?"

"Just heard some things. His wife's not fond of him."

"You expected something different?"

"No one else seems to be, either. He and Maggie met at Sugar Steeple when they were in high school. Then he stopped going. Now he has nothing to do with the church."

Bray nodded. "He took over the Ford dealership from his uncle about ten years ago. He always wanted it—trained all his life to take it over. Then, like clockwork, the uncle willed it to him when he died. John's quadrupled the business in ten years. Specializes in fleet sales and gets topnotch used cars. He's a good businessman—buys low, sells high, and does it often."

"I was trying to find out about his personal life," Win told him.

"What personal life? He works continually. If there's an affair or criminal activity in there somewhere, I couldn't find it."

"Where was he the night of the murder?"

"Like everyone else at two A.M.—sleeping."

"Do he and Maggie share a room?" Win asked, feeling a curious twinge of jealousy in the question.

"No. But you read the interview."

"Maybe not well enough."

Bray frowned. "Neither knows if the other is telling the truth. They both say they were sleeping—but sleeping alone."

"It would be a little tough for Maggie to push Bryce through that window," Win pointed out.

"Small people can have big muscles," Bray said. "She makes porcelain dolls—you told me that."

"And?"

"And the molds are heavy. She does a lot of weightlifting."

Win nodded, and his heart sank to somewhere deep in his stomach. He'd have to think about that later.

After a gulp of air, Win told him about the keys, and Bill's comments about the congregation.

"Nobody's changed?" Bray said, repeating Bill's words. "Some folks kill other folks and feel nothing—no conscience, ice in their veins. Scary people—and there seems to be more of 'em around lately." He paused. "He's right. You'd think church people wouldn't be that way. Interesting," Bray mentally chewed on the thought for a while, then shook his head. After a long moment, "But it's the key list that's important."

"But no one on it looks like a murderer."

"You want a sign? Maybe blinking neon. When I catch Sweet's extortionist, he'll be on that list."

A gull suddenly swooped out of the wind and grabbed the remainder of the Danish out of Bray's fingers. It happened so quickly, Bray was left sputtering confusedly. "Did you see that?" he flared, leaping to his feet. Instinct took over, and he pulled his Magnum and took aim. For a moment, Bray truly thought about blowing the miserable feathered demon out of the sky. He pictured the .357 tearing through the gull's body, bloody feathers exploding everywhere.

But he didn't.

He knew the frustration's origin. Although he was aiming

at the gull, he was actually aiming at Grogan and Breed—and at his own age, his aching muscles, the loneliness since Diane died, and the growing feeling that he'd outlived his usefulness. The feeling had been even more acute after seeing Pam last night. If there'd been a dog around he'd have kicked it. But there was only Win. "This is your fault," he exploded, "'Let's take a walk,' you say. I've had coffee in that shop for nearly ten years, and I've never had a bird fly off with my Danish before. Never!"

Win's expression remained unchanged, but he truly wanted to laugh. "Impressive bird."

Bray pointed his gun at the bird again, keeping the rascal just above the barrel. After he tracked the gull for a long minute, he said, "Bang!" then blew off the end of the barrel and slid the pistol back in its holster.

"Get him?" Win asked.

"He'll never sit down comfortably again."

Win found that very funny and laughed. To his surprise he detected a smile from Bray.

"You're a sadistic old man," Win finally managed.

"Keep that in mind," Bray replied, taking a long, deep breath. "And keep the information coming. I think I'm on the right track with Sweet, so all your work might be for nothing—but, then again, I have been wrong before."

Win nodded. Their conversation over, there were still several things he wanted to talk about—but he couldn't. He couldn't ask Bray just how strong he thought Maggie was. Could she really stuff a two hundred-pound guy through a window four feet off the ground? Were doll molds that heavy? Could John Selkirk really be a killer after his wife's lovers—or potential lovers?

Of course, lying in the '57 Corvette in the cavelike darkness the night before he'd decided that no matter how alluring Maggie's eyes, or how unconditionally accepting they were, Jesus was far more important. Win Brady was not one of Maggie Selkirk's potential lovers. He wasn't sure how to let John know that. And he doubted that Bray would have any good suggestions. So he only said, "Talk to you tonight or in the morning."

Win walked quickly to his car. It was nearly eight. Maggie would be at church sometime that morning, and he wanted to be there when she arrived.

The closer Win got to church, the stronger Maggie's pull on him. *You let Bert Larkin, that buck-toothed kid at seminary with a wonky eye, sow a whole field of wild oats—acres, for crying out loud, fields of wild oats waving golden in the breeze, whole counties of 'em. Why can't I just sow one lousy oat? Fair's fair, Lord. One, only one—promise!*

After unlocking the church, he headed to his office, flipping lights on as he went. He quickly put the coffee on and as the rich fragrance bloomed, he slipped behind his desk and waited for Maggie—his heart pounding, and his pulse thundering in his throat.

This wasn't the first time. He was suddenly twelve again. Waiting like today—for Gail Andrews—blonde, ponytail, eyes that beguiled and searched him out. They'd both pretended to be sick and stayed home from school, and she was to meet him at Myrtle Beach. The winter had been stormy, rain, icy sleet, they'd even been lashed by the tail of a hurricane, but spring was budding, and with it love—or as close to it as he'd ever come before. He longed to share that feeling with the object of those affections—with Gail.

They'd arranged to meet on the ocean side of a large boulder that rested a little back from shore. Win had gotten there fifteen minutes early, and he'd wedged himself in the sand at the base of the rock and waited, his heart pounding like the relentless surf.

But his wait was cut short. After only five minutes he suddenly looked up to see his father's angry face. "Before you lie to me again you'd better learn to cover your footprints," his father had said. There'd been nearly a week of silence. It had always been like that growing up—he could never get away with anything. Never. Of course he knew why. God knew what he was doing all the time, and God wasn't going to let him get away with anything. But God always seemed to cut the other guys a little slack. . . .

His Bible. It lay in the middle of his desk. He hadn't read it this morning. He read it every morning—three chapters—but not this morning. He wanted to blame it on his burning eyes, but he'd felt so distant this morning. He'd already decided that Maggie was off-limits—why hadn't he read it?

He heard a car door slam outside. A few minutes later he heard high heels in the hall outside, and then Maggie appeared at the doorway.

She wore an ivory silk blouse, a blue skirt with a gold-flecked angora scarf. But what she wore was secondary to the way she looked—comely, alluring, her hair swept back elegantly behind one ear and her misty green eyes fetchingly large. She was everything Win dreaded. "Hi," she said innocently, her head cast slightly down, her eyes slightly up.

"You look lovely," he heard himself saying.

"Really?" she asked, drinking in even the smallest compliment.

"Really."

"I hoped you'd like it. I got it yesterday. John says all my taste is in my mouth, so I don't shop very often. I took a chance."

"You won," Win said definitely.

She smiled coyly, running a finger idly over the top of the desk. A moment later she sipped from the coffee he'd poured her, beaming because he'd remembered her cream and sugar. "How was the meeting last night?"

"My notes," he offered, sliding a blank pad of paper in her direction.

"That's more than I figured they'd do," she replied, eyes watching him over her cup as she took another sip.

"Well, you've got what you came for . . ."

"No—not yet," she said, her eyes all over him.

Win sat on the edge of his desk so that he wasn't quite so

tall. "I know I'm really naive about these things—but are you trying to seduce me?"

"Is that what you think?" she asked, moving closer, her eyes peering up at him—deep, liquid pools. In those eyes he again saw everything he'd ever hoped to see in a woman's eyes: acceptance, reverence, awe. In those eyes he was a man.

"Yes, I really do believe you're trying to seduce me."

"And what reason have I given you to believe that?"

"Reasons—you mean, like clues?"

She slid a hand close to his. She didn't touch him, but she was close enough for him to feel its warmth, feel the pulse pounding within it. "Have I done anything to make you think such a thing?"

The tip of a finger touched a tip of his. His heart knotted. *Just one stinking oat, Lord? Just one?* "You keep moving closer, and you keep looking at me like you want to do terrible things to me."

"Things like what?" she asked, her hand on top of his now, her eyes searching his, her lips close enough for him to feel her breath.

His heart thundered, his pulse tiny detonations, his face hot.

"I really don't want to know," he said, but his voice was little more than a forced whisper, hoarse, uncontrolled.

"Let's not talk about me," she whispered back. "Let's talk about you. What would you like to do to me?"

*Oh, Lord—please. This can't be happening.*

He brought a hand up to her shoulder and gripped her. For an instant he held her there, taking his turn to drink in her eyes, her face, her lips, all of her. Then he pulled her toward him, and she came willingly, her eyes closing, her lips parting, her hands reaching for him, and finding and rubbing his chest. He thought of Gail Andrews. A month or so after they hadn't met on the beach they met at the same rock and shared a kiss, gentle, searching, innocent—the world became just Gail and him—a wonderful kiss. It was their only kiss, for she'd fallen for a baseball player a few days later.

He heard words—rising up from Maggie's lips like a vapor. He looked down and saw them moving gently, never closing. "Love me," she whispered hoarsely, the sound little more than breathing. "Love me. Love me." A chant filled with longing, laced with desperation.

He could feel the presence of her lips against his. In a heartbeat he would be pressing them with his own—in a moment, in the flicker of a dream, he'd be experiencing a woman who found him a man. He could hardly breathe.

And, of course, that's when it happened. He knew it would. It wasn't exactly what he expected, but it had the expected result. He'd expected lightning or maybe to look up and see Worlly standing there, or worse yet, John Selkirk with a bloody machete. But there was no lightning and the doorway remained empty. What he saw was only in his mind, but it was vivid enough—Jesus' bloody palm. "Love *me*," he said.


The Mercury outboard throbbed and he sat at the wheel trancelike. If someone asked him what he was doing, Win would have had no answer. All he knew was he was on the lake and in his boat. He was traveling slowly, almost idling. To go faster would take energy, and he was sapped.

He'd left Maggie in his office. He'd neither apologized nor told her where he was going. He just released her shoulder and left.

And now he was on the lake, dazed, tooling slowly along—going nowhere.

Somehow he surfaced near Ginger's house. It was only ten in the morning, but as he approached her dock, he saw the tail of her white patrol car in front of her house. "That's good," he said measuredly. "Ginger might understand."

He pulled the Bayliner up to the dock, killed the engine, leaped out, and tied it off. While it bobbed in the gentle surf, he walked toward the back of the house. Only a few feet from the French doors, he was about to call her name when he saw something that two days ago had spun him in his tracks and sent him back to his boat.

In the shadows, lighted partially by the sun streaming through the back windows, stood Ginger and Mike Grogan, she in her patrolman blues, he in Joe-Friday slacks and sport coat. They were embracing, but more than that, they were kissing—hungrily and passionately.

Win would never be able to explain completely why he did what he did. Even years later when things were much clearer. He acted because the turmoil inside demanded that he act—a pressure valve, long shut tight, was being released.

Watching the two of them, his breathing became deeply erratic, the rush of oxygen pumped energy into his veins. He grabbed the back door handle, wrenched it open, and in a single stride confronted them in the kitchen.

Their embrace interrupted, they faced him, still arm in arm. At first both registered surprise, but Grogan's face quickly flushed with rage.

Ginger never got beyond shock. "Win?! Why . . . ?"

"You did it now," Grogan growled with a sound bigger than his five feet, seven inches.

"It's time you left," Win told him, his arm up, a finger pointing toward the front door.

A cocky smile spread across Grogan's face as he released Ginger and took a threatening step toward Win. "There are so few things I really enjoy." He smiled like a shark. "Thanks for providing one."

Win felt an immense charge surge through him. He was about to be attacked. He'd never been physically attacked before—except when his father was punishing him. He should have shrunk from it. Grogan was smaller, but he was a pro—confident, capable. But Win stood his ground, just as confident though not quite so capable. When Grogan threw a jab at Win's chin, Win caught the fist like a fastball, and held it, then squeezed it.

It was a curious feeling. Adrenalin ricocheted off his inside walls, channeling all his strength to his right hand. Not only did Win sense the bones in Grogan's fist fuse as Win squeezed powerfully, he also felt his iron fingertips fold Grogan's hand backward. The pain must have been excruciating, for Grogan's face knotted, then his knees buckled as he began to melt like hot wax. Win squeezed even harder.

But Grogan was a pro. He had his own adrenalin, and he called upon it now. He overcame the fire in his hand, and threw a desperate jab to Win's solar plexus with the other hand.

Win took the first punch, but the second and third took a heavy toll. With lungs void of air, his insides bruised, Win couldn't help but let go of Grogan's hand. When he did he received two more quick jabs, one to his chin driving his head back and one to his throat. Knowing summary execution was only a heartbeat away, but unable to prevent it, he fell back. Now on the floor, he finally managed a breath, but his eyes opened to a black, steel hole only inches from his right eye. Grogan stood over his gun with a gleeful, nearly maniacal grin.

"Mike," Ginger cried. "No. Please, no!"

As if he'd suddenly become aware that he and Win were not the only ones in the room, Grogan glanced toward Ginger. He finally slipped the gun inside his jacket. "What's going down is too big," he mused darkly. He took a step toward Ginger, rubbing the hand Win had mashed. "It might've been fun," he said and headed for the front door.

Ginger's jaw dropped. "It might've been fun! What's that mean? It might've been . . . come back here. Come back here!" She stamped an angry foot. "What's that mean?"

Grogan didn't come back. After the latch clicked behind him the room was silent for a moment. A moment when Win lay still on the floor and Ginger stood facing the front door.

But it was only a moment.

Eyes ablaze, Ginger turned on Win. "You creep! What have you done?" she exploded. She grabbed a rolled newspaper from the table and battered Win's head with it. "How dare you just break in here and . . . "

"Me?!" Win slapped her weapon away. "Cool it, woman," he heard himself say.

"Cool it?" she screamed, slamming him on the neck, then right across the nose. "I'll cool it—I'll put you on ice."

When the newspaper bounced off his nose, Win grabbed it and held it at bay. The beating suspended, he dragged himself to his feet. But even at his full height he didn't intimidate Ginger. She straightened to hers and moved in on him.

"Let that go or I'll . . . "

"What? Shoot me? Like that boyfriend of yours wanted to? Such a fine, Christian gentleman." The vicious sarcasm felt wonderful.

"How dare you judge me!" she recoiled.

"That's called rebuking—Christians rebuke." He tore the newspaper from her grip and threw it away.

"Rebuking? Then it's my turn." She made her windup. "You just *think* you're a man!"

"Well, aren't we mature!"

"At least I don't sleep in a 1957 Corvette car-bed."

"No, you just chase jerks."

Ginger gulped and her arm came up. "Get out . . . get out . . . *get out!*"

She pushed him toward the double French doors. "Out!"

Win fired up the outboard, yanked the boat away from the dock, and threw the throttle to full. The engine strained and the Bayliner slapped forward, the wake peeling away white. But after only fifty yards Win pulled the boat around, killed the engine when it approached the dock, leaped out, tied it off, and all but ran back to Ginger's house. Throwing open the doors he cried to Ginger who hadn't moved more than an inch. "You wouldn't know a man if one jumped up and bit you."

"One did—and he's no jerk!" Ginger shouted back. "Mike's a real man—which he sure showed you."

"Boy, you got that right. It takes a real man to run out on you—the other one had to get drunk to stay."

"That's a horrible thing to say."

"Ah, a nerve is struck."

"Yeah. Are you proud? Takes a real man to hurt a woman's feelings."

"I call 'em as I see 'em."

"Well, see 'em somewhere else," she cried. "Come back and I'll shoot you for trespassing. Understood?"

"Sure I understand. And Grogan'll back you up—that's another thing you can do together."

"Don't ever come back."

After a single beat where he actually thought about staying, he spun on his heels, took the back steps in a bound, jumped into his Bayliner, and ignited the engine. Less than a minute later, the nose high, the wake peeling away, he plowed away from Ginger's. But when the minute ticked its last, he spun the boat around and headed back in. This time he didn't bother to dock it, he aimed the nose toward the grassy beach and just before the bump and grind, he killed the engine.

This time when he threw open the doors, he faced the business end of Ginger's Glock 9mm. Unceremoniously, Win grabbed it, jerked it out of her hand, and tossed it on the table. "Me showing up was the best thing that ever happened to you."

"Oh, it's you again."

"You heard him. He'd have gotten what he wanted, tied your insides in knots . . . then bailed. Why would a beautiful woman like you . . . ?"

"Because he was the only *man* who came along!" she screamed. "The only one—ever."

Pushing a chin into her face he said, "Then you should have waited."

"You self-righteous . . . " her voice grew to a shriek. "I did wait. I waited six years. Six long, God-forsaken years."

"You call that a wait?"

"A very long wait. Do you have any idea what it's like to raise a son by yourself? Do you? Mister self-righteous . . . being father and mother . . . I throw a baseball all wonky and he laughs. And the questions—one more about penises and I'll croak. I waited. Boy, did I wait. Don't you dare think I didn't."

"Six years is nothing. I've waited since puberty—and I'm still waiting."

"And if you're relying on charm to get it you'll be waiting a whole lot longer."

"What do you know?"

"I know a baby when I see one."

"A baby?"

"You haven't been waiting since puberty—emotionally you haven't *reached* puberty. Puberty . . . that's a laugh. Next for you is toilet training."

"I'd be in there visiting your mind."

"What's that supposed to mean?"

"You forget, I saw the kiss. You weren't unequally yoked—you were unequally fused."

"You're pompous, self-righteous—and you use your virginity like a club."

"You probably haven't used it at all since you were ten."

"Where's my gun?" She lunged for the table, and he ran for the double French doors.

Expecting a bullet to slam into his back any second, he ran like the wind to the shore. Leaning into the Bayliner, he pushed it from the grassy beach. The moment the lake cradled it, he leaped in. Just before he cranked the engine, he heard Ginger yell from the back doors, "I hope your next pastoral visit goes as well."

The engine roared alive, but Win didn't even turn the key. He strode boldly back toward the house. With the gun still raised, Ginger knew she had only two choices—kill him or listen to him. The rest of her life in jail or five more minutes of Win's ranting. It was a tough choice—she vacillated back and forth. She finally decided to kill him.

But he got there the moment she decided and pushed the gun away. "Being a pastor wouldn't be so bad if it weren't for women."

She fought his vise grip and tried to bring the gun up. "Let go—killing you's the least I can do for humanity."

"All you women do is complain, or lord it over us. You lead us on."

"I don't want to lead you on. I want to kill you. Let go of my gun hand, you creep!"

"Women run hot then cold, sweet then sour. You lure us to our dooms."

"Lure? I'll send you there."

"You make us want you then slam the door in our faces." He pushed his face a hair from hers. "And if we love you, you die on us . . . "

"She probably died in self-defense." She fought harder than ever, and this time she brought talons into play. With a well placed swipe of her other hand, she ripped two neatly spaced scratches on his cheek.

Seeing his own blood on his fingers, Win hesitated. "All you ever want to do is hurt us—don't you?"

Ginger screamed into his face, "Bingo!!"

"Hey, kids—hey! Stop for just a second." The woman's voice came from behind Win.

He turned and a saw a large woman in her late fifties standing in the doorway.

Ginger cleared her throat to recapture at least a little dignity—difficult with Win still holding her gun hand. "Betty," she said weakly. "How nice to see you."

"Now, Ginger, put your gun away and you," she looked at Win, "let go of her."

Win obeyed, allowing Ginger to drop the gun, and the two of them sheepishly faced Betty Sherman.

"I was just going," Win finally said and took a step to squeeze past Betty, but Betty's hand came up.

"No. Not yet. You're gonna listen to me for a second. Then you can do anything you want. I don't butt into people's business unless it happens within fifty feet of my house."

"Betty," Ginger started, eyes riveted on Win, the anger returning. "We were just having a little disagreement . . ."

"You wanted to kill me!"

"And he didn't want me to. See," she turned to Betty, "a disagreement."

"Now I'm not particularly religious, but while I was listening—actually trying to keep my drapes from being blown off my windows—it seemed to me that you guys weren't so mad at each other as you were mad at God."

"It wasn't God who came bursting into my house," Ginger retorted.

Betty continued, "And aren't you two supposed to be liking one another—isn't it the other guy who causes fights between religious people? Isn't that what you believe?"

Ginger cocked her head inquisitively. "The other guy?"

"The guy with the pointy tail," Betty said.

And Win understood—understood it all.

"Satan," he whispered and his eyes immediately turned in the direction of the church and the tower that rose above it. Understanding brought calm. "I think we'll be all right now," he said with a conciliatory tone. "And you're right," he said.

"I thought so. You two going to survive the day?"

"We will," Ginger said stiffly, "because he's leaving."

Win didn't reply but eyed her with an unusual intensity. Then he glanced at Betty and smiled. "I'm Win Brady. Thanks for taking an interest." He patted her lovingly on the shoulder.

Saying no more to Ginger, Win leaped into his boat and fired it up. He had someone to visit. A few minutes later he was bumping and slapping across the lake toward the church, then, with only a brief detour for the keys, to the tower.

The moment the lock fell open, the sense of dread took root at his core and with each step up the shadowy stairs, it intensified and grew. By the time he reached the first landing, his heart was tightening, and by the time he'd reached the second it felt like granite.

The window pane had not been replaced, and it let in a dusty shaft of light. But even for the light, the room was a grave of shadows and lifeless cobwebs. As a show of defiance, Win closed the door behind him and then turned toward the center of the room.

"I'm on to you," Win said, his voice a thread of sound. "Did you try to stop Bryce's ministry too?"

Outside a breeze kicked up and rattled a loose board above him. He looked up. The bells hung still.

"He wouldn't scare so you killed him."

He felt a chill. He swore he felt a chill—an icy spike to the aorta.

"Who'd you have do it? Whose hands did you use? Maggie's? Whose?"

Nothing. Although the dread remained, his heart remained stone. It was as if he were being ignored.

"I'm here because God wants me here. I'll win because God wins."

From behind came a eerie creaking—the door opened an inch or two. The breeze again? It was as if he were being asked to leave.

"I'll be back," Win said to the room, and he walked calmly down the stairs.

# Chapter 13

**B**ray must have conducted a thousand stakeouts. Most cops found them boring—sitting, watching, monitoring electronics for hours on end. For most it got old in minutes.

But not for Bray. An ardent people watcher, he had a lot of Peeping Tom in him, and stakeouts gave it a legitimate release.

This one was like most. He sat behind the wheel in his battered Scirocco, a large bag of peanuts next to him. Like his routine of a Danish in the morning, it would be impossible for him to stake out anything without a large bag of roasted peanuts. As the hours passed, shells piled up on the floor. Later he'd run the Dust Buster. Although it picked up most of the mess, over the years the inside of his car had become blanketed in dusty beige. At times, tired of shelling, he'd pop shell and all into his mouth. Although a little chewier, it didn't matter. The salt and the rich flavor of roasted nut was enough.

He also chose his spot, if possible, near a Coke machine. Peanuts needed Coke. This time the Coke machine was in the only video game parlor in town, and he'd parked right in front of it.

Content, he chewed his peanuts, sipped a Coke, and kept an eye on the candy store.

Two P.M. He'd been at it for nearly four hours since the candy store opened.

People watching hadn't lived up to expectations. A couple of kids, maybe age ten or twelve, had decided to be street musicians. One played a trumpet, the other a flute, both badly. After about a half hour, their dream of a fortune was as empty as the trumpet case between them. They repacked their instruments, barked a few angry words at each other, and left.

A few minutes later a bag lady hobbled from trash can to trash can. Reaching one, she'd attacked it like a frenzied mole, the contents flying furiously. When she reached the bottom, she'd straighten, her hand clutching a bit of treasure, and casually walk to the next one.

Several students walked here and there, some entering the candy store and leaving a few minutes later chewing something good.

A beautiful woman stepped outside the candy store now and again. Each time she'd look around, stretch, let the cool air revive her, and then go back inside.

She was lovely. Innocently so.

Sweet's wife.

Like her, Bray also felt the need for the same now and then. Periodically he got out of the car and stretched like a cat, then got back inside.

About 2:30 he bought another Coke, opened another bag of peanuts, and settled in for another hour or so.

"Excuse me."

"Huh?" Bray looked up into large, haunting hazel eyes. His eyes rested on them for an instant, then dropped to the cavern of cleavage below. A beautiful woman was leaning at his window, her eyes roaming all over him.

"Can you tell me how to get to seven north?"

"Seven north?"

"Yes." All of her smiled now. "May I have a peanut?"

"Peanut?"

"In the bag there. My goodness, you have lots of peanuts."

He presented the bag to her.

She took one and delicately split the shell with long, painted nails and popped the nuts onto her pink, expectant tongue. She tossed the shells back into his car. "Highway seven north?"

He thought seriously about breaking away from those eyes to give her directions when a car streaked around a near corner and passed quickly behind the woman. From behind her came a squeal of tires and brakes and an explosion of glass and wrenching steel.

"Oh, my!" The woman gasped but didn't move. Bray, heart pounding with unsatisfied curiosity, pushed her out of the way as he opened the door. He saw the car's nose buried into the front of the store next to Peter Sweet's. Splintered glass lay everywhere, while the car, an ancient Chevy now twisted and folded, held the driver prisoner inside. As Bray got out of his own car, the man struggled to the passenger side to try to get out of his.

Peter Sweet shot from the store, his face a mask of disbelief. "What the . . . ?"

His wife appeared next to him, her soothing hand on his shoulder. He pulled away. The threat of the near miss must have been too much for him. He boiled with anger.

Bray didn't bother with Sweet. He crossed the pavement quickly and met the man as he struggled from the car window.

"Police," he announced, flashing his badge in the guy's face. He was forty-five or so and shaken; blood streamed from a gash in his forehead.

Someone ran up and announced that he'd called an ambulance.

"What happened?" Bray asked, helping the man to his feet on the sidewalk.

Suddenly Sweet was on him. "Who put you up to this?" he blared in the man's face, his own red with rage.

"Huh?" The driver was beyond reply. "Something ran in front . . ."

Bray imposed himself between Sweet and the man, "Mr. Sweet, back off."

"This is no accident. This can't be an accident! Someone's . . ."

"Honey." Sandy was next to him, hands massaging his shoulders. "Come on, sweetie."

"Get away from me." Sweet broke free of Sandy again and pushed a finger toward the man's bleeding nose. "Who are you working for?"

"Please, officer," the man pleaded, and Bray quickly bellied Sweet away from the man.

"Relax, Sweet," Bray ordered as he pushed his face into Sweet's. Eyes clashed with eyes, and finally, still exclaiming violent protests, Sweet pushed Bray away, stormed past Sandy, and disappeared into his shop.

A moment later a siren whined around the corner, and an ambulance roared up. Two white patrol cars also arrived, and four blues got out and joined the confusion. Seconds later the driver was being helped, and the blues were questioning people. Mrs. Sweet finally followed her husband into the shop. Bray stood for a moment watching the circus. He found a peanut in his hand and stuffed it, shell and all, into his mouth and chewed the fibrous mass intently.

Bray stepped back across the street and from there he studied the scene again. The car had slammed into a small clothing store, and the shock had shattered the display windows and thrown clothes onto the car. A couple of the employees stood near the front door. The woman who'd asked directions was across the street surveying the car curiously. A paramedic treated the wound above the driver's eye.

Bray popped another peanut in his mouth. The stakeout was over for today.

Bray looked up and found Chief Breed looking down. "My office, please."

"Why?"

"My office."

Bray was confused. There were no fanny-chewings due.

His confusion lessened when he saw Grogan sitting in the corner chair.

Breed took his seat behind the desk and made a steeple with his hands. He looked over the fingertips as if aiming a sight at Bray.

"You were on a stakeout this afternoon."

"Sweet's shop."

"What did you see?"

"Get to the point. I wouldn't be in here unless I missed something. What did I miss?"

Breed glanced toward Grogan. "Tell him."

Grogan gave a quick, pretentious smile, then began. "I decided to spend a few minutes watching Sweet's place too. I saw the accident, I saw the woman block your view, I saw Sweet explode, and then I saw something else. I saw the woman look at the driver and the driver look at her, and they smiled at one another. Not a 'how are you' smile. A smile of recognition. They know one another."

"Why didn't you come to me with this?" Bray's eyes narrowed with the challenge.

"I didn't want to bother you until I was certain."

"That was something easily missed. You should have come to me with it. Why didn't you?" Bray's pulse raced. He was going to be snookered again, and he hated it.

Grogan ignored him. Finally Breed asked, "Are you certain, now?"

Grogan said nothing but took a palm-sized notebook from his inside jacket pocket, flipped the cover, and referred to his notes. "The man is Carl Bedlock, the woman, Nellie Stall. I ran them through the computer and found no priors. Carl had a couple parking tickets. Nellie was clean as a whistle. Since we—"

"We?" Bray hissed.

"—were dealing with what appears to be extortion, I checked the banks. I found Carl's account at First Vermont." Grogan's eyes came up. "Two days ago he deposited $10,000. He's self-employed; owns a bookstore. His nightly deposits average a couple thousand; recently deposits have dropped. But, what the hey. He could have had a good day, right? Then I find Nel's bank—Bank on the Lake. Two days ago—you guessed it—$10,000."

"What's their connection?" Bray asked, still fuming but curious.

"Nel works at Carl's store. I haven't been able to check on

a personal relationship. But there's an old saying 'Those who extort together contort together.'"

Breed burst into laughter, a good-natured finger poking the air toward Grogan.

Grogan acknowledged the laughter with a wry smile and tore the pages from the notebook and handed them to Bray. Bray took them, his insides tight.

"I hope I can do the same for you one day," he said, his voice tremored, acknowledging his restraint.

Through a residue of laughter, Breed acknowledged his star, "Good work."

"Can I talk with you alone?" Bray asked Breed. This time Grogan remained seated.

"No, I don't think so. You've got some follow-up to do. You need to know who paid those people. Getting that information will show you the would-be extortionist and a killer."

"I want to talk to you alone."

"Later," said Breed, eyes cold.

Bray gave Breed an angry stare and left.

🔔

Sandy Sweet flipped the open/closed sign to "closed" and locked the door. Peter didn't protest. Peter didn't do much of anything. He sat in the corner of the shop on a stool they usually used to rest on and stared blankly toward the opposite corner.

Although Peter had left the accident scene boiling with rage, threateningly animated, when he entered the store something had happened. Sandy didn't know what. But when she entered a few minutes later she'd found him sitting, staring blankly, his hands folded tightly in his lap, so tightly his skin was a snow-white halo around his fingertips. He remained mute. She heard the distant growl of a plane overhead. As it grew nearer, she noticed Peter's eyes widen, look up, then flinch. The sound grew faint and finally disappeared.

Sandy laid a gentle arm on his shoulder. "You okay?"

No answer. Eyes fixed ahead.

"The Lord will take care of us," she whispered to him and laid her chin against his temple.

He moved. At first she just felt his temple throb against her chin, but then she felt his head move. She stood to see two fiercely angry eyes staring up at her. They pulsed with fire.

"There is no God. There's no one but us taking care of us, and someone out there's trying to kill me." His voice a bullhorn, his body coiled, he sprang to his feet and pushed her away. She fell hard against the far counter.

That's when it happened—she couldn't believe her eyes.

Frantic, emotions uncontrollable, he turned to the glass countertop. "They're getting closer, and there's nothing I can do. Nothing!" The moment the last word flared from his lips, he brought his fist down on the glass. Although tempered, it shattered from the blow.

Blood gushed from Peter's wrist.

🔔

Nellie Stall had worn a wig when she'd asked Bray for directions to divert his attention at the moment of impact. Everything else was real. She answered her door, saw Bray standing there, and immediately knew the jig was up. Though she didn't confess at first, Bray knew she'd crack. It took three questions: "You and the driver know each other, don't you?" "Where'd the ten thousand dollars come from?" And "This is going to take a while, you have any coffee?" When she knew he was staying, she broke. It came as a great sigh, followed by tears, and then she asked him to sit.

The professional in Bray felt a surge of excitement. The man in him burned.

🔔

The sun hung orange on the western horizon and cast rich, long shadows. Ginger avoided the twilight shadows and sat at the end of her pier, her feet dangling inches from the water. Chad was at play in the backyard with divisions of small lead soldiers—lots of explosions and bodies and armory flying in the air.

She heard the hollow growl of Win's boat several minutes before it rounded the point and headed her way. She could have left the pier and gone inside, but she didn't.

"The hint too subtle for you?" she said coolly as he drifted up after killing the engine.

"I came to make amends—to apologize," he said, grabbing the pier behind her and coming to a stop.

"I accept. I don't want to fight anymore."

Chad introduced air power. His imitation of a plane being blown out of the air was uncanny.

"Me neither. Can I stay for a minute?"

"My gun's inside if that's what you're asking."

Win laughed and stepped from the boat to sit beside her. "The reason you wanted me to help find Bryce's killer was that you thought there was a spiritual battle going on."

"You thought that. I just thought Christians were getting a bad rap."

"This afternoon was part of the battle. The guy with the pointy tail is trying to split us up and drive me off."

"Was it the guy with a pointy tail who acted like a jerk this afternoon?"

Win let it slide, then said, "It must be tough raising a son on your own."

Ginger turned her eyes on him, eyes that weren't sure how to react. She was still angry, still hurt, her pride still bruised, and yet his tone was one of understanding and a willingness to listen. She had longed for such a tone. She'd heard it so seldom in her life.

She threw a glance Chad's way. "Any minute now he'll come over and ask me about tanks and air cover."

Win smiled. "How do you answer?"

"I tell him air covers everything—including tanks. But those are the easy questions—and it's not the questions—it's the getting involved."

"How so?"

"Loving your kid is getting involved."

"Involved how?"

Ginger eyed him again. Was he interested? Faking? No, his eyes said he was interested. "Knowing who he is and what's best for him," she explained. "What he likes and dislikes. It's being a part of his life. And since I've never been a boy, sometimes I come up short. I'm not as involved as I should be—I'm too much a spectator or a referee and not in the game enough."

Win watched her watch Chad. The love was real—something in the eyes, in the line of the mouth, in the slight cock of the head. Chad was something precious to her. There was also a longing in her eyes. A longing that she could be more to him than she was. Win saw it all.

"My mom loved me like that," he confided.

"You miss her," she said sympathetically.

Win nodded but said nothing.

"You were mad today," Ginger said.

"Not at you."

"Grogan?"

"I've never hurt someone like that before—and I've never been hurt like that. I'm really not a fighter . . . "

"A lover then."

"Not much of either."

And they both laughed gently.

When they were silent again for several seconds, Win said, "I *was* mad—angry."

"If not me or Grogan, who?"

"That neighbor of yours put her finger on it."

"Betty?"

"Jesus loves like you love."

"No. Much better."

Win conceded her point with a nod. "He's involved—he knows us, takes care of us. Does Chad ever get mad at you?"

"Do fish swim—boats float?"

"What if he got really mad? What if he was pushed to some kind of a limit and got really mad? Maybe he was scared or felt an injustice was done—maybe by you and he got angry."

Ginger took the question seriously and after looking deeply into Win's eyes to see what might be behind the question, she turned toward the lake. The sun was still peeking over the horizon, the shadows were long.

"He got that angry once. I can't remember what it was about—I guess it didn't matter."

"What'd you do?"

"I started to get angry back—then I just let him go. He ranted and raved for a while and then when it was all out, we talked. It worked out okay."

"The first day at Sugar Steeple I saw a guy with a four- or five-year-old son. The son caused quite a scene, hit his father, kicked him I think. The father just hugged him until the tantrum was over." Win paused. "I wasn't sure about that then. The kid hit his father. Part of me thought the kid should have been disciplined right there on the spot. My dad would have done that. But after today . . . "

"What are you getting at?"

"I'm mad at God—Betty was right."

Ginger's brows twisted. "That's a little dangerous, isn't it? I mean lightning and everything?"

"This morning Maggie Selkirk and I . . . "

Shocked, Ginger turned a full face toward him.

"We didn't do anything. But I was that close. I mean that close. She put a move on me." Win softened. "Well, it wasn't all her fault. I did my share of moving. But I'm a vulnerable guy that way. There haven't been that many . . . uh . . . women in my life, and suddenly this one was all over me. She was married, a non-Christian, and I was a pastor—an assistant pastor." He took a deep breath. "I wanted her. Boy, did I want her. And what's more amazing, she wanted me."

"Understandable," Ginger said.

Surprised, Win lost a beat. But then he continued. "God let this happen. God let it all happen. And I got mad . . . and I'm still mad, I guess. This morning with you it was like all that anger—like a valve was being released and the steam was coming out and I didn't have control of it. When I had Grogan's hand—that steam made me want to crush it.

"God gave me a father—a Christian. But he wasn't the father I wanted. And God took my mother. He never brought me a woman, a Christian woman who wanted me and who I could want. Never. I was mad, and I guess I'm still mad." He chuckled at the irony. "Mad at God. Imagine. It's like kicking the boulder you ran into. That's juvenile. 'God works all things to the good of those who love him, those called according to his purpose.' I know that in my head."

Ginger looked down and saw that her hand was resting on his. She wasn't sure when she'd moved it, but she gave his hand a little squeeze.

"Are his arms around you?" she asked gently.

"I hope so. I need them to be."

Ginger nodded. "He took my husband—a non-Christian drunk. But at least he was a husband." She took her hand away. "I made a pie—apple."

"Got some decaf and a little vanilla ice cream? You got a microwave to heat it up?"

"Hills Brothers' French Roast Decaf, Ben and Jerry's Vanilla Bean, and a Sears microwave—I got it all."

"Indeed you do," he said, his eyes clearly stating that he meant more than what she'd just described.

Bray reached for the phone. He'd already done so three times before but had pulled his hand back each time. This time he got it to his ear and punched in Pamela Wisdom's number. He knew it by heart having gone over it at least fifty times since eating his frozen Swiss steak dinner.

"Hello," she answered.

At the sound of her voice, his breath caught. "Hi," Bray managed.

"Bray? I'm glad you called. I was trying to come up with a fun way to spend my break."

"Fun? Me?"

"Sure." He could feel the smile over the phone. "So, what happened in your life today?"

"Not much," he said. But it had been much. He was worn out from all that'd happened, both physically and emotionally. He took a chance and told her, "I made some progress on a case."

"Really? Great!" Her happiness for him sounded genuine. "What kind of progress?"

"It's a big budget crime we're dealing with," he said. "Bigger than the prize seems to warrant."

"Organized?"

"Not disorganized."

"You don't sound excited," she said, concern coming over the receiver. "If you made progress you should feel excited."

"Excitement is a luxury—there's too much disappointment in the job to get excited."

Even though she didn't reply he could hear the understanding warmth. "There are times when I feel the same way. I worked for a month on a bride doll and when I was stringing the arms, legs, and head to the body, the elastic broke and the head flew off and shattered on the floor. It isn't life and death, but it is disappointing."

"I imagine it would be."

"But that didn't stop me from being excited about the bride doll I strung just before."

Bray said nothing. He wanted to. He felt like something should be said, but he couldn't put a finger on it. Like the excitement he wished he could feel, it lay mute and covered, unreachable. "You like movies or something?" Bray heard himself ask.

"Some. You like movies?"

"The last one I saw was *Rambo*."

"Harrison Ford has a new one out."

"Who?"

Pamela laughed. "You do like movies."

Suddenly the line crackled. An efficient, cold female voice. "Emergency break in," it said.

Bray growled, "What?"

"Please hang up and await an emergency call," the operator said.

"From who?"

"I guess we'll talk about movies later," he heard Pamela say.

"I don't want to . . . who's breaking in?"

"They'll call in a minute, sir," the operator said efficiently.

"Talk to you later, Bray. Call me."

Bray wanted to reach into the receiver and push it back up to those wonderfully full lips. Not more than a second after he hung up the phone rang.

He wanted to shout into the phone, blow the eardrums on the other end of it into the caller's brain. But he didn't. "Hello," he said.

"I just saw your report," the voice was Breed's, a voice he now truly despised.

"And you couldn't wait a few minutes?" Bray groaned in weary defeat.

"You ain't got a few minutes," Breed growled.

Bray prepared to have even more potential excitement wrung from him.

# Chapter 14

Bray's Danish lay half-eaten, but he'd tasted none of it. His coffee remained untouched, and when he finally took a sip it was tepid. More gruff than usual, he called Marge to refill it. She brought him another cup. "You're upset," she stated and cranked a hip over to the right, pressing a wrinkled hand on it.

"Maybe it's time to be a security guard in some old folks' home in Florida."

"Blue-haired wimps," Marge croaked. "All of 'em."

He glanced at a short headline in the newspaper folded by his coffee. "Maybe I ought to get in on this." He stabbed a finger at the story. The Drug Enforcement Agency had bagged a medium-sized shipment of cocaine coming down Lake Champlain from Canada. "I got a buddy over there. And he owes me."

"That debt'll get you in a body bag," Marge pointed out dryly. "Is it Breed again?"

"Last night I was talking to a lady friend . . . and he broke in."

"I thought I was your only lady friend."

"We made some progress on a case—and, believe it or not, I hope I'm wrong."

"About what?" someone asked.

Bray and Marge turned to see Win standing there. He smiled his tentative smile and slid into the booth opposite Bray. "Coffee, Marge," he said. "I'll have my own Danish this morning—cheese."

The interlude over, Marge nodded stiffly. A moment later both were set in front of Win, who tore the Danish in two and set the largest piece in front of Bray. "You look like someone's got a firm grip on your intestines."

Bray's hands went up and waved him quiet. "No time for that. Talk to me."

Win sipped his coffee and leaned back. "Why do I think you want more than just a report?"

"Ah!" Bray exclaimed, "Again you saw the obvious."

"What do you want?"

"Your theory on this thing," Bray stated. "Why do you think the guy who's squeezing the candy man isn't the killer? And be convincing."

Win studied Bray for several seconds. Bray usually had a face belonging on Mount Rushmore, incapable of emotion. Now, even though his expression was still granite, his eyes betrayed his anxiety. *There's so much of my dad in it. Why do I like him so?* "It's a spiritual crime," Win finally said. "I'm convinced of that more than ever."

Bray didn't like the answer, but only asked, "What's that mean?"

Win searched for words, and he suddenly pictured the tower, felt the unearthly presence there, heard the argument between himself and Ginger, saw Maggie's eyes, felt the tug of seduction. "It's spiritually motivated. The killer killed for spiritual reasons."

"Why do you think that?" Bray probed, a curious hope underlying his tone.

Win took another, much longer sip of coffee. Another moment to study Bray. How much would Bray understand? How much did Win understand himself? Yesterday afternoon he'd faced the battleground—himself. And he recognized the combatants—himself and Satan. Bray was trying so hard to understand, yet he never would—maybe not "never," but certainly not now. Win would have to go slowly with him.

"Well, put yourself in the killer's shoes," he began. "If, as your theory goes, you're driven by the fear that Bryce might expose you, how would you silence Bryce?" Win asked.

"You tell me."

"There's all kinds of ways to kill someone so no one would ever find him. You could stage an accident—he could fall off a cliff, get chopped up by a propeller blade, or just get nailed by a hit and run. Or he could have been killed and put in a cement overcoat and dropped in the middle of the lake. Suddenly Bryce would just be gone. Nobody would care. The police would never be notified. It'd just be assumed the pressure got to be too much for him and he left. And he could have gone anywhere. Even if a relative asked about him the last thing people would suspect is murder—they'd just tell the caller he'd gotten fed up with the criticism and left."

Win let it all sink in. Then he continued. "But that's not the way it happened. Bryce was killed at the church, in the bell tower, no less. It could be argued that the killer didn't care whether Bryce's body was found, or if the death looked like an accident—the killer just wanted Bryce dead and the church at two A.M. was as good a place as any.

"Why not kill him in his office?" he continued. "Maybe he didn't want the body discovered right away. So he lured him to the tower, killed him there—but he *didn't* kill him there. He only rendered him unconscious. Then, rather than leaving him up there to be found days, maybe weeks later, he laboriously—and I mean laboriously—threaded that limp body through that 'eye-of-a-needle' window to have him land below in plain view and, of course, maybe survive."

Bray injected, "He probably thought he was dead—anyway, he knew the fall would kill him if he wasn't and the snow would foul up the time of death."

"The cold in the tower would have done the same thing," Win retorted, "and in the tower the body might not have been found for days."

"Under the snow it might have been hidden 'til spring," Bray fired back. He had the frustrated look of someone who truly wanted to believe but couldn't bring himself to. "Where does the spiritual part come in? You've described a queer set of circumstances, but most murders are surrounded by queer circumstances."

Win took another long drink of coffee and eyed the Danish. The time had come to tell it all, yet he knew how it was going to be received.

"There's more," Win warned.

"I'm ready."

"I'm not so sure."

"Try me."

Win nodded. "Bryce probably came to know the Lord—was saved—about three months before the murder."

Win heard a faint, sarcastic "Hallelujah!" under Bray's breath.

"Sugar Steeple seems to be a dying church—not in numbers, but in its gospel impact on the congregation and the surrounding community. Maybe God wanted to give them one last chance, or let them hang themselves—who knows. For whatever reason he brought Bryce in, maybe as a last hope. Of course, Satan didn't want Bryce to succeed."

"Of course," Bray said, the sarcasm remaining.

"I think Bryce was beginning to make an impact. Satan couldn't allow that, and, obviously, God decided not to intervene."

"Obviously."

"He allowed Satan to twist the mind of one of the congregation—I don't know who—and that someone killed Bryce." Again Win allowed the words to hang in the air for a moment before he continued. "The murder has a lot of symbolism in it. I'm not sure what they all mean, but symbols are ways of communicating."

"Communicating? With who? Between who? Certainly the killer's not saying something to the police."

"No. But the way it was done suggests symbols. I've done a lot of Bible study, and the scriptures are fulfilled with symbols. I've got a sixth sense for them."

"A fine talent, I'm sure."

"Before this is over I'll be able to tell you what they mean. Now I only have suspicions, so I'll wait."

"Thank you," Bray said with profound gratitude. "But if this killer used symbolism wouldn't he have to understand it?"

Win nodded. "Probably."

"To understand the symbols, would he have to know the spiritual language—like you do? Wouldn't he have to be one of you, then—a Christian?"

"Probably," Win acknowledged with an edge of reluctance.

"I thought Christians weren't supposed to murder people and stuff them through little holes three stories up."

Win nodded again. "I'm not so happy about that part of it, but there is precedent. In the Old Testament King David was a murderer—an adulterer—but his heart belonged to God."

"But he killed to get the guy's wife—a nonspiritual objective to use your terms."

"How'd you know that?" Win allowed some hope to seep into his tone.

"Everybody knows that," Bray stated.

"It all happened as part of the spiritual warfare. Satan will do what he can to make things tough on God's people. It's just his way of making it tough on the Lord. I think he thinks he can win. But, of course, he won't."

"Of course."

"But he'll keep trying."

"I know I would."

Win leaned forward, ignoring Bray's sarcasm—actually he found some of it funny, and part of him was suppressing a laugh while he struggled to change his tone to one that indicated his painful fairness. "The problem with my theory . . . "

"There's only one?"

" . . . is that there are very few Christians at Sugar Steeple and none who had access to the keys. I suppose Satan could have just compelled the murderer to do symbolic things."

"The devil made him do it."

"Yeah, right. Exactly. But if the murderer did them without knowing what he was doing that would put him in some kind of mindless trance, and I don't think that would happen."

"It certainly does stretch credibility."

"All of it makes for an interesting puzzle, doesn't it?" Win leaned back. "But I guess that's why they call it a mystery."

"Any more?" Bray asked, a tight smile on his lips.

"Yeah," Win said, reluctant to explain the next part. "Then I come along."

Now it was Bray who leaned back, his arms draped across the back of the booth. "Something's happened to you?"

"Satan wants me gone—he wants me discredited and alone. And he nearly succeeded."

Bray's brows knit. "How?"

Win shrank back. He'd gone this far, why not further? And yet to continue meant revealing what he preferred left buried.

"Come on, I haven't got all day."

A deep breath. "Maggie tried to seduce me."

"Selkirk?" Bray obviously corked a laugh. "You?"

"It almost worked. Then he—"

"He meaning Satan?"

"Yeah, right. He nearly drove a wedge between Ginger and me. She's my only Christian friend here, and she's tied to the only real Christian friend I have in the world. Turning us against one another would have isolated me. And succumbing to Maggie would have destroyed any ministry I would have hoped to have. He was close—very close." Win locked eyes with Bray. "But I'm still around. And I know he's at work. I'm spiritually stronger."

"A veritable Schwarzenegger of spirituality, I'll bet," Bray said with a mix of sarcasm and weariness. "But now that you have thwarted the devil, what happens next?" he asked with surprising sobriety.

"I don't know—but I've thought about it. I guess whatever it is I'll have to rely on the Lord to take care of me."

"Like he took care of Bryce?" Bray didn't wait for an answer. Instead he rubbed something from the corner of his eye. "You're no help to me, Win. No help at all."

"I guess I didn't expect you to believe it."

"Oh, I believe the facts—the conclusions leave me panting somewhere behind. I need a *reasonable* alternative theory. Grogan's making me look like a schmuck. He's got Breed's ear and in Breed's mind he's the one on top of this case. I was hoping you'd have something Grogan couldn't possibly predict. I guess you've got that, all right. It's just too weird. As it turns out the official theory's panning out. We now know there's a definite conspiracy going on against Peter Sweet—a high-priced one. And murders are often the result of high-priced conspiracies."

"What do you have?"

"A guy was paid to scare Sweet again by driving a car into a store next to his. A woman who works for the driver was paid to distract me when it happened. Big bucks—ten thousand each."

"Who paid them?"

"They never met him. All by phone. A disguised voice. The money was deposited in their accounts electronically leaving no trace. Home computers can do almost anything." Bray finished his coffee and raised the empty cup so Marge could see. A moment later it was refilled.

"You arresting them?"

"No. Whoever paid them needs to think he got away with it."

"So the stakeout continues."

"We'll be more discreet next time," he said. "We have phone taps on these two just in case they do know who the guy is and try to contact him. We have taps on Sweet's phone. We have a stakeout on the second story of the arcade across the street from the candy store and one on Sweet's home."

"The extortionist sounds inventive. He'll know there's surveillance."

"We're hoping he'll think we quit."

Win leaned forward. He suddenly felt a deep concern for Bray and communicated it with caring eyes and a furled brow. "Why aren't you excited? You're getting close."

Bray took a sip of coffee. "I wish this was scotch," he said, stalling. "I want you to win this horse race," he said but shook his head gravely. "But the more I hear from you the more I'm convinced that you've got a screw loose."

Win smiled as warmly and as understandingly as his inexperience would allow. "I guess we'll see," he said. "Any idea what your guy wants that's worth that kind of money?"

Bray shook his head. "No, it could be anything—a grudge, maybe he wants them to move, any number of things. They're all unimportant. What we know is someone's very serious, and very serious people sometimes kill people who are onto them. Bryce was onto him."

Win suddenly remembered something and reached into his jacket pocket and took out a folded 8 1/2 by 11 poster. He unfolded it and handed it to Bray. "I almost forgot. I found this tacked to a telephone pole near my home."

Bray scanned it. It was a small poster announcing the arrival of a Christian evangelist named Mel Flowers.

"So?"

"Remember Bryce's calendar? 'Flowers' appeared all over it. We thought he was buying flowers."

"He was seeing this guy?"

"Could be. Flowers is speaking on the islands tonight. We'll see if he remembers Bryce."

"What if he does?"

"Then we'll get some information." Win took the handbill back, refolded it, and stuffed it back in his pocket. He got up to leave.

"Before you go," Bray stopped him. "Know any movies out that a woman might like?"

Win kept his smile to himself. "A couple—there's a Disney family movie."

"Disney? Anything else?"

"Ask her what she'd like to see."

"I just thought you might know of something."

"You're taking someone out? Who?"

"Thinking about it," Bray said weakly. "A friend of Diane's—my wife—who died."

Win nodded with a knowing purse of his lips. "Just pick something that doesn't offend her. Movies nowadays can do that pretty easily."

"Not offend. I'll remember that." He gave Win a rare smile. "Thanks. Call me later when you know something."

"Right. Later."

Bray watched Win disappear out the door. After a moment, he said to himself, "I'll have to go easy with her—I hope she goes easy with me." Then his eyes went to the tabletop and rested there for a moment. He thought of those first dates with Diane. He could take her to any movie. He used to like them. He hadn't gone for a long time.

Bray sat for a few more minutes, then got to his feet and left. He had a murderer to catch.


Actually Win hadn't found Flowers's poster nailed to the telephone pole. Ginger had on her way to the station. He first heard her call from the end of his boat dock. It was about 6:30 and he'd been up since six. He'd found that the end of the dock made a good place for morning prayers, and he was in the middle of one when he heard her call. "Where are you?"

Raising his head, he turned as she came through the back door. There was purpose in her step. But her gun was still in its holster so her purpose didn't worry him too much.

She showed him the poster, and when he didn't make the connection right away, Ginger pointed it out. "Flowers. On Bryce's Day-timer. Maybe he was seeing this guy."

"I'll go see him this afternoon."

"Good," she said hiding other feelings with a manufactured enthusiasm. "I saw that, and I knew you'd want to follow up on it."

"This afternoon," he reaffirmed, taking a long, loud slurp of coffee.

"I guess I'd better be heading to work," she said, starting to back up, a certain reluctance in her movement. "Roll call's at seven."

"Don't want to miss that."

"Sure don't," she said, taking another step backward. "So I'd better be going." But she quickly turned back. "I wanted to thank you for yesterday."

"You thank people for yelling at you?"

"No. For listening to me—and caring about what I say. Thanks for that."

"I guess that goes for me too," he said, a serious sheepishness creeping in.

"Why?"

"Because you listened to me too."

"Yeah," she countered, "but I didn't care."

"Ah," Win replied, with a knowing sweep of his brows.

"If you wait until three when I get off I'll go with you."

"Where?"

"To see Flowers."

"I only let people who care about what I say ride with me."

"Then maybe I could meet you there," she returned, with mock indignation.

He brought the coffee mug to his lips and eyed her over the cup. "I'll see you at Judy's at three. We'll go in my car from there. You cops drive too fast."

They smiled awkwardly at one another for a long moment, and for the first time in a very long time for both of them, they felt safe in the company of another.

Now as Win drove up to the church, hoping Maggie wasn't there to find out what happened to him yesterday, he tucked the pleasant memories of the morning away and prepared for what lay ahead. Working beneath the eye of the tower.

He'd spent a lot of energy thinking about that tower since yesterday. Was the presence his imagination? After all, a man had been murdered there, and it was spooky as all get-out, and when the wind slithered over and through the openings it

186    WILLIAM KRITLOW

sounded like ghosts were on the march. It was small and enclosed and high up. Had he been hysterical?

Yet he knew it didn't matter. Even if Satan or one or a number of his horde hadn't taken up residence in the tower, Satan or one or a number of his horde was at work on the one who had been there—manipulating, lying, keeping him off balance, pushing his buttons at just the right moment. He suddenly thought of the painting—how vulnerable he'd felt after getting that painting and how close he'd felt to Maggie. Satan had even used his memory of his mother against him. Praise God that Jesus had provided the escape route, and praise God, he'd taken it.

But there was still the war.

He'd been placed in charge of a youth program, and today he would begin putting it together.

Then at three, he'd go see Flowers.

By eleven he had spoken to only answering machines, so he left a lot of messages and by noon he was bored out of his skull. After a long walk through the maples at the edge of the meadow and along the sharp cliff behind the church, he decided to study his Bible for the rest of the afternoon. As a consequence, he didn't pull his '54 Chevy up to Judy's Restaurant until 3:10.

Ginger didn't pull up until 3:15, so he was still able to rib her about being late. But it was a good-natured ribbing, tempered by the fact that he had never seen her look so beautiful. Though she looked crisp and fresh in jeans and blue blouse, it wasn't her clothes, it was her sweet smile and light expression. She was always beautiful, but now there was a softness, a gentle sparkle in her eyes. And it all came together when she stepped from her Blazer and actually looked glad to see him.

The afternoon was cool. Billowing clouds sailed in on growing breezes from the north. Their tops blossomed angel white while their underbellies darkened as the afternoon wore on.

Mel Flowers had set up his "Christ Is Here!" revival tent

just off Highway 2 north of Sugar Steeple on the outskirts of Minerva, a hamlet of just a grocery store, gas station, and fruit stand.

Camped near the edge of the highway, the tent's brilliant red and white stripes screamed to passers-by and with the upper left corner a scattered cluster of stars blazing in a patch of blue, the tent formed a huge American flag. A large sign was draped above the entrance: "Christ Is Here—You Be Too!!" In smaller letters, "Mel Flowers, Revival Tonight."

Although he'd been at the seminary a long time and attended with men from all over the country, some saved in revival tents like this one, Win had never heard of Mel Flowers. Had he, he would have taken little stock in him. He believed most traveling evangelists to be little more than charlatans and their messages only loosely related to Scripture. Corralling him this early meant he wouldn't have to listen to his message.

Win parked near the tent entrance. He noticed a man in his early forties step from the tent's dark interior, a large hand-some grin sprawled across his face while he waited for them. "Nice car. Wonderful car," he said enthusiastically. "I had one as a teen. Loved it. Ran it without oil once. I wasn't the smartest kid in the world." The man laughed and extended his hand warmly and introduced himself. "Mel Flowers," he said with a grand mix of grace and enthusiasm. Win found it impossible not to like him.

"Win Brady." Win shook the man's hand. "This is Ginger Glasgow."

"Lovely lady," Mel said smiling broadly. "We don't start for a few hours. Seven-thirty. You're welcome to stay, of course. Join me in prayer, if you'd like—spend a little time with our Lord."

"We don't mean to interrupt," Win began, "but if we could have a moment."

Mel nodded, his smile still intact. "I hope I haven't done anything wrong. I arranged for this place nearly a year ago. I hope everything's in order."

"I'm not from the authorities. I'm here about something else."

"Well, then, come inside. If there's one thing I have it's plenty of room to sit."

He did. Although large from the outside, the tent was immense from the inside. With the side flaps rolled up, a cool breeze wafted through, stirring the scent of pine from the thick, spongy mat of wood shavings on the floor. Nearly three hundred wooden and metal chairs were set up to face a raised stage draped with another banner proclaiming, "Jesus—My Life—Make Him Yours." They sat in three of the chairs.

"I don't see anyone else," Ginger noted. "You set this up yourself?"

Flowers smiled. "I borrow the chairs from local churches. A few of the teens helped me set up. I contract for the flooring, the tent, and the podium. There's only me. The hat's seldom full. I have someone coming to help seat people in a little while—a wonderful Christian woman. She comes early, and we pray together." Mel turned one of the chairs around to face them. "Now, how can I help you?"

Win wasted no time. "Did you know a young man named Dan Bryce?"

"Danny? Why yes? I tried to call him today, but I must have caught the church closed. No one answered."

The call must have come while Win was on his long walk. "How did you know him?"

"What's wrong? Is he okay?"

Win took a reluctant breath. "Dan Bryce was murdered— just before Christmas."

"Murdered?" Shocked, Mel's eyes rolled up and his head followed them away. Hands rose to his eyes and, although he shielded them, no doubt tears were forced back. Finally his hands came down, and the iron in him came to the surface. "Our hearts must always be ready," the evangelist muttered. Then, "Murdered? How?"

"At the church."

"The church? Was it random?"

"No. It looks like someone in the church."

Ginger added, "Or someone he knew."

Flowers instantly took a defensive posture and eyed Ginger with brows twisted in deep incredulity. "Are you suggesting that I. . . ?"

"When did you last see him?" Win took up the questioning again.

"About two weeks before Christmas." Mel got to his feet and stepped to the tent's open perimeter. A blaze of sunlight caught the side of the man and he looked lost. "I winter in Florida," Mel said, still peering into the light. "I love New England, particularly Vermont. But it gets too cold in the winter for a tent." His voice shuddered as he put a cap on his grief.

"Tell me about Danny," Win asked.

He turned back. "There's a bit to tell." He stepped back to the chair. "The Lord used Danny mightily in my ministry."

"Really? How?"

"I was about to give it all up. I run a three-state circuit in New England. I start in Vermont, head over to New Hampshire, then to Maine and back to Vermont. A couple of months in each. I love what I do. If I didn't preach to people I'd probably shove sticks in the ground and preach to the sticks. But last year was tough. The first time through Vermont was sparse, New Hampshire was a big disappointment, and Maine was as big a failure as I've lived through. At least half the nights no one showed up. The other half only two or three would come. My biggest night was ten people. In over six months the Lord saved no one." Mel paused. "I'd been in Vermont for nearly a month. It was late September. The kids were back in school, vacations were over, the nights were warming with Indian summer—attendance usually increases. It hadn't. I would have done better with the sticks. I remember I looked out at the five people in this sea of chairs and decided that when my Bible closed that night, my tent would also close. Forever.

"Danny Bryce was one of the five. When I came to the end of the sermon I nearly skipped the invitation. I just couldn't take another five minutes of rejection. But I didn't skip it. After only a few seconds Dan stepped forward. He was saved that night. He came back to the trailer with me, and we spent the night talking." Mel was alive again. "That boy turned defeat into victory for me—that quickly. I've been in a tent ministry for almost ten years. That boy's conversion was worth every heartbreak."

His arm made a broad sweep, and they followed it with their eyes. The tent was large but worn, the chairs numerous, but empty—very empty. "They won't be much fuller tonight. Have you ever heard of me?"

"No, I haven't," Win admitted.

"How about you, lovely lady?"

"I wish I had."

"I'm here every year. These islands aren't that big, yet few people who live here have heard of me. Tonight there'll be a few. Only a few. But I persisted. I work all winter in Florida to earn enough money to come back. I believe in John six, forty-four, 'No one can come to me unless the Father draws him.' That night the Lord drew Dan. I'm an alcoholic. I've been off the sauce for almost fifteen years and that night, in the middle of my message, I was thinking about getting back on. The Lord used Dan Bryce . . . Murdered. My dear, dear brother. Are you friends of Danny?"

Ginger smiled. "You might say that."

"What did you talk about that night?" Win asked.

"He started crying. He talked about how my message had convicted him, how he'd graduated from seminary, was an assistant pastor at a church near here, but only now did he really want to know Christ."

Win saw the man's mind travel back to that moment.

"He came often to see you. Why?" Win asked.

"For counsel," Flowers said. "Imagine me counseling a pastor."

"What did he need counsel about?"

"His church. Suddenly he learned what salvation meant,

and just as suddenly saw that his church, the church he was responsible for, was full of unsaved people—people on their way to hell. We talked for long hours about what he should do."

"What advice did you give him?" Ginger asked, her tone wonderfully gentle.

"Go slow. Get to know his flock." Flowers rose again, this time he leaned against the tent pole. "You generally earn the right to minister to the unsaved. Oh, sometimes the Lord'll give you the words to make an impact on a stranger. But more often than not, the unsaved will only listen to a friend they trust."

"A strange thing for a traveling evangelist to say," Win said, a hint of challenge in his voice.

"Perhaps. I spread the gospel and plant seeds. People like Danny lead, reap, and plant the gospel deep in the hearts of their people. I told him to get to know his people, to pray for them in specific ways, and to love them. And, most of all, he had to be willing to take lots of time doing it."

Ginger asked, "What did he find out about them?"

Mel Flowers straightened, his eyes firm, a little suspicious, "Before we go further, who are you people? You're asking questions I'm not sure I should answer."

Win glanced at Ginger. She took the lead. "I'm with the police," and with an official flip, her badge appeared from her back pocket. "Win's working with us. He now has Dan's job at Sugar Steeple Church. We're trying to find out who killed Dan Bryce."

Mel nodded, his expression more trusting. "We never mentioned names, but we talked about what he found. We discussed the people, the sins, the relationships. Then I'd play God and suggest how he deal with them. One thing for sure, that church is in sore need of the gospel."

"Was there anything he learned that might lead someone to kill him?" Win asked.

"A husband might kill his wife for not making the bed. In this sinful world anything could be the basis for murder. And what he found . . . well, there was an affair or two, a husband who'd used his wife as a prostitute on occasion, that kind of thing."

"In that little church?" Ginger registered surprise. "How'd he find all that out?"

"Talking. Listening. Some conjecture. Pictures he'd see at a home, inferences when they'd answer a question. He seemed to have a gift, a sixth sense about people. A few people actually opened up to him—really opened up. " Mel went on, "But with most people he didn't have to hear much, and he was able to understand them pretty well." Talking about Dan helped him confront his grief. "I was hoping to see him tonight. I stayed into winter last year because of him. I finally felt truly useful to the Lord. But I'm basically a warm-blooded sort, and around Christmas I decided to go. Maybe if I'd been here . . ."

"You would have just mourned him earlier," Ginger said.

"Did he ever feel frightened for his life?" Win asked.

"Only for that church, never for his life. I honestly believe that even if someone pointed a gun at his head he'd have felt more frightened for the gunman's soul than for his own life. He was that kind of a Christian. But to answer your question— no. He never felt threatened. Or, if he did, he never mentioned it to me."

"Did he have family?" Win asked, an interrogator's tone.

Mel straightened. "You know, I don't know," he said, surprise all over his face. "I thought I knew everything about him, and I never knew about family. The basics." He shook his head disbelievingly. "No wonder God keeps handing me empty tents."

"Could it be that he didn't have family?" Ginger asked. "If he didn't mention it . . . "

"He only talked about the church. Only the church."

Win said nothing for a moment, then, "Can you think of anything else that might help us?"

"No," Mel said thoughtfully. "Are you leaving? You sound like a real brother in Christ. You know we start at seven-thirty. Come back—listen. Give me some pointers. I can always use pointers. God knows. We usually have coffee afterward."

"I wouldn't mind coming back," Ginger said, focusing on Win, daring him to disagree.

Win didn't want to return. No matter how sincere the leader, he was still mistrustful of this breed of Christianity. "We need to be going."

"Chad could use this," Ginger said to Win, increasing the pressure.

"Your son?" Mel asked.

"A handful. He's ten."

"We can use Jesus at any age, can't we?" Mel said with perfect understanding. But then he became grave. "Just a parting thought," he said to Win. "I loved him. He was the most exciting convert I'd ever had. Literally drank the Scriptures. It's hard for me to say this, but I wouldn't look for his killer. The Lord knows who did it and why. We should be praying for the murderer's eternal soul. Finding him brings him to the world's justice. We need to pray he never knows God's. We need to pray that God's mercy might prevail."

Win nodded vaguely. "The Lord's into justice," he said. "And there's justice to be done here. Maybe the Lord's going to work through Ginger and me to make it happen." Win extended a hand. Before Mel could shake it they heard the grind of tires on the meadow rock.

"I guess we'd better be going," Ginger said. "Someone's coming." They shook hands.

Flowers eyed his watch. "My helper. She's another reason I probably wouldn't have given up that night. She's helped me for the past eight years. It was she who brought Danny that night."

Sandy Sweet, Peter Sweet's beautiful wife, stepped from the car. When she saw Win she smiled. "Hello. I wouldn't have expected to see you here."

"We've come to give Reverend Flowers some support," Win injected hastily, a wary eye on Mel.

Sandy nodded but turned quickly to Flowers, "Reverend Flowers, I need to talk to you."

Mel placed a loving hand on her shoulder and said, "I'm

sure these people won't mind if we excuse ourselves for a moment."

"We were just leaving anyway," Win said.

"I may be back," Ginger told him, a defiant glance toward Win.

"Good, bring your son," said Mel, and he and Sandy drifted toward the stage, Sandy talking agitatedly, Mel listening.

Win sat behind the wheel but didn't turn the key. He stared at the tent, but he wasn't seeing it. Ginger spoke first. "I like him. I like what he's doing."

"Bryce was a Christian."

"It's what you suspected."

"Now that I know, though, it's different. Different." The words were inadequate. They conveyed only meanings they had conveyed before and no matter what word he found it seemed clichéd. It was as if he needed a whole new vocabulary to express it. *Brother* seemed the most appropriate. There were others: *kinship, bond, tie.* But when all was said and done, *brothers in Christ* seemed by far the most appropriate. For all his depth of feeling, though, all he could say was: "It makes a difference. Brothers to the same father with the same mission."

"I'm bringing Chad back tonight," Ginger stated flatly.

As it turned out she couldn't find Chad when it came time to leave, and she didn't want to leave the house with him outside somewhere. So she just made microwave popcorn and settled in to watch some bad television.

When the bowl was half empty she heard Win's boat growling around the point. With the sun just an amber glow and dusk graying the lake and turning distant trees to charcoal, Win glided to the dock, killed the engine, and tied the boat off.

"You smelled the popcorn that far off?" Ginger called to him from the back porch.

"I saw your light—you didn't go?"

She offered the bowl of popcorn. He took a handful and threw a couple of kernels in his mouth.

"Chad disappeared on me," she admitted.

"I'm sorry. I know you wanted to go." Win glanced about the graying countryside. "Want me to try to find him?"

"He'll be back when he's ready. Want a Coke?"

"Let's stay outside. I need the air."

Win parked himself on one of the lawn chairs. Normally Ginger would have protested in some way. She didn't really care where they sat, but she usually wanted to be consulted. But she could tell something was bothering Win. She returned a moment later with two cans of Coke and sat beside him.

"Your flowers are pretty—a nice garden."

"I work at it," she said, scanning it. She did love her garden. There was something steady and predictable about it. Plant a seed, work it, and it grows. She wished life could be that way.

Win popped the top. "I love Coke and popcorn," he said, the child in him appearing for an instant. He took a sip of Coke after a handful of popcorn. "A Coke, popcorn, and the lake . . . "

"Right," she said impatiently, "now, what's biting you?"

Win didn't answer right away. He finally said, "I've been thinking about Bryce. I sat at the end of my pier thinking about him. Didn't see much of the sunset."

"And what were you thinking about Bryce?"

"I was an only child," Win said as he rolled the white puff of popcorn between thumb and forefinger, methodically crushing it.

"Me too. So what?"

"Even when my mother was still alive there were long periods of time when I'd be alone. You said love meant being involved. I played alone a lot—no one involved with me. Cowboys and Indians, race car driver—in the backyard, on the sand dunes for hours. While I played, I dreamed of a brother to play with. To talk things over with. Sometimes I'd write a brother into the scripts I'd be acting out." He brushed the crushed popcorn away. "Bryce was a brother." He paused, so many things falling into focus. "My brother," he stated as if it were the ultimate truth.

"Theoretically."

"More than theoretically. I'm sitting in his chair. Meeting the same people he met. I have the same responsibilities. Serve the same God from the same book. We have the same father."

"You take things to extremes sometimes."

Win nodded. "But it's the way I'm beginning to feel. And it goes further than that. This newly found brother of mine was killed to prevent a revival."

"Who'd kill him for that? Unsaved people don't even know about revivals."

"Satan knows."

"Satan?" She nodded broadly and said, "When you stalk a crook you stalk a pip. Don't you think you're having delusions of grandeur here?"

Win found a smile. "Maybe." He popped a few kernels in his mouth and downed the last of his Coke.

"You going to make a citizen's arrest on Satan?"

"If I decided to, I bet I know where I'd find him."

That caught Ginger's attention. "Now where might that be?"

"Someday I'll have to show you."

"You're not going to tell me?"

He thought of the tower. The belfry nailed closed. The bells hanging silent. The presence.

That's when Chad appeared from the side of the house. "Howdy doody, everyone," he called to them.

"Where have you been?" Ginger scolded. "I told you to be home in time to leave. Over an hour ago."

"You said seven-fifteen. That's what my watch says now." And he pushed his watch in front of her eye. It said 7:17. Just as it would had he reset it two minutes ago.

"Now you have your watch lying for you."

"How can a watch lie?"

"If you just set it. Why would it be an hour off?"

He shrugged remorselessly and grabbed a handful of popcorn.

"Go in the house and get ready for bed."

"But it's still early—not even seven-thirty yet."

"Get ready for bed," his mother insisted.

After a dismal groan, the boy retired to the house.

"He's a real handful," she said to Chad's back.

"Can you imagine the handful we are to God? I still haven't apologized to him for the other night."

She turned back to Win and for an instant let her eyes fill with him. "He's like that father you saw at church. Sometimes he spanks, and sometimes he loves us into submission. There are times when I wish I could actually feel his arms around me. I feel so alone sometimes. More than sometimes."

Win stood and reached a hand down to her. "Get up a second."

"Why?" she looked up at him. "What are you going to do?"

"Hug you."

"What if I don't want to be hugged?"

"You just said you did."

"By God. Not you."

"Get up. We'll pretend."

She hesitated, then with a smiling sigh of resignation she took his hand.

The hug was everything she wanted. He wrapped muscular arms around her and drew her close. She felt the firmness of his chest and the warmth of his cheek against her neck. She pressed warm palms against his back and pulled him closer. And then she felt a gentle kiss on her neck. An involuntary tear formed in the corner of her eye and rolled down her cheek, then another and she pulled away.

"You okay?" she heard him ask.

"It's been a long time," she managed.

He wrapped arms around her again and kissed her lightly on her forehead. "I'll call you tomorrow."

"If you want—" and then she said something that surprised her. "And you'd better want."

Happily, he didn't argue.

Win tried to reach Bray for almost an hour. He wanted to talk. Actually he wanted to do anything besides sit. Tides of restlessness broke over him, and no matter where he sat it didn't matter. He tried the dock for ten minutes, then the living room with the radio, but that lasted only a few minutes. Finally, after calling Bray for the eighth time, he got into his car. He remembered Bray mentioning a place called Archie's.

The hole-in-the-wall restaurant was all but deserted and dark, but the small side room had a couple of windows that glowed dimly yellow. Just as Win figured, Bray's Sciroco sat outside.

But Bray wasn't alone. A woman sat at the corner table across from him. She looked familiar—oh, yes, Maybell's funeral. Win smiled. In a way he'd brought them together when he'd told Bray about her. Both were casually dressed, and they had already completed dinner. They now sipped their wine speaking softly to each other as he approached the table.

"Hi," Win said and two pair of eyes came up. Neither looked particularly glad to see him.

"Phones don't work anymore? Can't I have some privacy?" Bray asked, openly hostile. "Oh, I think you've met Pamela Wisdom. A friend of my late wife's."

"And a friend of yours," she injected, a gentle hand reaching over and patting his.

"Nice to see you again," Win greeted, trying to sound as if he actually belonged there.

Bray smiled warmly at the hand, then its owner. Then steel eyes came up to Win's again. "What do you want?"

"A minute."

"This better be good." Bray scowled and got to his feet.

The bar was dimly lit, and they found a table off to the side. After waving the bartender away, Bray demanded, "Okay, your nickel."

Now that he had hunted Bray down, Win wasn't sure what

he wanted to say. The fact that his suspicions about Bryce had been confirmed wouldn't matter to Bray, yet that was the only thing he'd learned today that mattered to Win at all.

Finally he managed. "I met with Flowers today."

"The guy Bryce saw so often. What'd you learn?"

"Bryce wasn't in fear for his life at all."

"Ignorance is bliss."

"He never mentioned names—but there were some people in the church with some embarrassing secrets—there was some prostitution going on, for example."

"Why am I not surprised? Any idea who these people are?"

"I'll keep an ear to the ground." He wanted to cry out that Bryce had been saved. That God had brought him in and that Satan had knocked him off to stop his ministry. But none of that would matter to Bray, so he continued by saying, "Sandy Sweet showed up. She helps Flowers out. She looked troubled."

"I can imagine. Yesterday Peter Sweet deliberately slammed his hand through the top of a glass display case. Right after that car took out the store next to his. Blood all over the store. He nearly bled to death. He's still in the hospital. I got guys watching both him and the store. She just go to Flowers to talk?"

"I think so."

"You got any more?"

Tentatively, feeling more uncertain, Win said, "I'm more convinced than ever that this is a spiritual crime."

"Think what you want," Bray said impatiently. "Nothing's changed my mind. I know you've committed your whole life to the concept, but like it or not, there *is* no spiritual. No astrology, no palm reading, no tea leaf reading, no reading goat's entrails. There are no ghosts, no goblins, no devil, and no God. There's only me and Breed and Grogan and, tonight at least, that pretty lady out there. And I can't believe it, but she likes me." He glanced back toward the dining room. "Why would a pretty girl like her go for me?"

With Bray's repudiation of everything Win held dear ringing in his ears, Win wanted to say, "Because she's getting old and you're still breathing," but he didn't. He said, "Because she sees the real you."

"And what's that?"

Win paused, smiled, and replied, "Don't push it. I'll call you when I have something else." He left.

Win hadn't been dreaming. There'd been no noise. Nothing. But he found himself awake at 3:00 A.M. The night was impenetrably black, and outside the lake was still, not even lapping at the shore. The humidity felt like summer, and a bead of sweat popped on his forehead, meandering down his temple onto the pillow. But it hadn't been the heat that woke him.

It had been Sandy Sweet.

She'd been troubled. Her husband was being hounded by a maniac and was now in the hospital, a result of what subconsciously could have been an attempted suicide.

And Win had done nothing. He'd offered no support, no encouragement.

It could be argued that Sandy hadn't come to him, or to Worlly, to discuss her trauma. But what *she* did didn't matter. He was her pastor—like Bryce had been—and he'd done nothing. He'd call her in the morning.

*Like Bryce had been.* The thought repeated itself several times before he fell back to sleep. *Like Bryce had been.* If he persisted in doing things like ministering to Sandy Sweet, would he end up like Bryce?

# Chapter 15

**W**in rolled out of bed at seven, had his shower, read his Bible, had a few minutes of prayer, and was ready to take on the day at about eight. On his way out to the car he remembered his pledge to call Sandy.

When no one answered at her house, a number he'd gotten from the church directory, he called the hospital and asked for Sweet's room.

A couple of rings then a woman's voice answered. "Hello."

"Sandy Sweet?"

"Yes."

"This is Win Brady, from church," he said. "It was good to see you yesterday at Flowers'. I heard about your husband's accident, and I wanted to call and see if there was anything I could do."

A pulse of hesitation. "Thank you for your concern. We seem to be doing okay—for the moment."

"When will he be coming home?"

"This afternoon. He's regained most of his strength and should be able to cope at home."

"How about work?"

Another, longer, hesitation. "Why do you ask?"

"Owning a business and being laid up can be tough."

Another hesitation. Win sensed something wrong. Of course—his questions had made her suspicious. Did she think he was the maniac? On the phone he could be anyone. "I'll be going in for a couple days," she finally offered.

"Well, I just wanted to offer what support I could. I'd like to send some flowers."

"We have all the flowers we need," she said flatly. "Your prayers would be nice."

"Well, then, prayers it is."

"Thank you. I'll see you Sunday."

"Yes, you will."

The phone clicked.

He had thought of Sandy as being outgoing. Not so now. Her insides probably resembled macramé.

Sandy Sweet hung up the phone and turned to her husband. His eyes roamed the ceiling, the window, and the fields beyond. He was still angry. The same anger that had propelled his fist through the glass was still gnawing at his stomach and heart. He'd said only a few words to her that morning, and fewer still last night in the hospital. What he did say was tangled in angry knots.

Knots tied from tendrils of fear. Peter was terrified.

Peter lived his life terrified. But that was Peter. She had prayed for him—for his salvation, for his life to calm, for his fears to subside. The Lord had delayed answering those prayers. Quite the contrary, now Peter was even more terrified, and more angry.

"Can I get you anything?" she asked in a soothing voice.

He remained silent, his head turned to the window. The hospital was built on the edge of a pasture, and Holsteins wandered aimlessly, their black and white against the green. A peaceful scene lost to Peter.

"I'm going to open the store as usual today. I'll close up at two and come to get you."

He nodded vacantly.

"I love you, Peter," she said, standing at the door. "It doesn't matter what happens to us as long as we love each other. The Lord will take care of us." The words came automatically—too automatically. She was beginning to doubt them, and that frightened her.

"I'll see you at two," he said flatly.

"Everything will be all right, Peter. Everything."

"I'll see you at two," he said again. She was being dismissed. It hurt. But that's the way he got when he worried.

"Okay."

In the parking lot, she sat in her car for a moment. Before starting the engine she glanced down at a single red rose that lay across the passenger seat. She didn't know why she'd kept it. Maybe there was just nowhere to toss it. Although beautiful, it was the most depressing red rose she'd ever seen. Upstairs, lying in his white hospital bed, Peter had been surrounded by flowers. People from church, their suppliers, friends had all sent them. They'd all been addressed to Peter—all but one.

This rose had come individually in a golden box—with no card.

She'd been a loving, faithful wife for nearly ten years. Having come to know Christ soon after their marriage, she'd prayed every day for her husband. He'd responded by making her the object of his scorn. Through all of it, though, she'd remained a good Christian wife.

But now the rose lay there. No note, yet it spoke ever so eloquently—of betrayal.

It had to be from someone in a love relationship with her husband, someone unable to write her feelings, someone resorting to an anonymous rose to proclaim her love in Peter's hour of suffering.

The moment she saw it among the other flowers, Sandy had snatched it away.

The only person she'd felt comfortable talking to was Mel Flowers. "Hang tough," he'd said. "The rose could mean anything. It may not have even been for him. It could have been misdirected. And even if it does mean what you think it does, someone could be holding a torch for him whom he doesn't even know. No matter what, though, you have to talk to him. Sometime you have to talk to him."

Hang tough. It wasn't for him. And if it was . . .

She would hang tough. But her resolve didn't dissolve the knot strangling her stomach. "Oh, Lord, please."

Talk to him? She could hardly look at him.

She picked up the rose, and a thorn dug into her finger. She nearly let it go, but she didn't. Her grip tightened and the sting became pain and the pain oozed red. She shoved the bleeding finger in her mouth. Removing it, she watched the blood bead and prayed, "Lord, you are in control, aren't you?"

She picked the rose up again, more carefully this time, and stepped out of the car. She placed the flower beneath the front, driver's side tire, got back into the car, and backed over it.

Stuffed with the unknown, oozing with cheese and freckled with mushroom, the omelette lay there steaming. Chad frowned. "I hate eggs," he protested.

After talking to Sandy Sweet, Win had found himself punching in Ginger's number. After a few words between them she offered to come over for breakfast. Now the three of them sat at the kitchen table.

"Looks great," Ginger exclaimed. "What's in here?"

"Bacon, ham, cheese—anything with cholesterol. I sensed my level was falling." Win smiled, cutting it in half and dishing half of it onto another plate.

"What about me?" Chad asked.

"You don't like eggs?"

"No, but I gotta eat something."

"What about pancakes?" Win offered. "I can whip up a batch quick enough."

"Pancakes work."

"He'll eat what you put in front of him."

"If I can give him what he wants . . . "

"Let him give me what I want, Mom."

His omelette was a little cool by the time he set the pancakes down in front of Chad, but he didn't care and soon they were all finished and the dishes were in the sink. "You work at all today?" Win asked Ginger.

"Tomorrow afternoon—traffic. When we were talking to Flowers yesterday I kind of liked that detective role."

"Mom, I'm going outside." Chad was already to the back door.

"Don't drown," Ginger called to his back. She turned back to Win. "He likes you."

"He likes pancakes," Win said as he prepared the water and started washing the dishes.

"He likes pancakes too," she stated. "But we can talk about him later. What do you think of me?"

"Huh?"

"All you men do that. When you want time, you say 'huh.' You know what I asked."

"Huh?"

"Stop that. It's a legitimate question, and I deserve an answer."

Win wiped his hands on a towel and leaned against the counter. "It may deserve an answer, but I'm not sure what the answer is."

"How many answers are there?" Ginger still sat at the table, but now she leaned far forward, balancing on her elbows.

"There are a bunch of answers."

"Pick the most appropriate one."

"Come on, Ginger."

"Don't 'Come on, Ginger' me," she persisted. "What do you *think* of me? Do you like me, only tolerate me? Do you think I'm nice, average, a floozy? What do you think of me?"

"What prompted . . . ?"

"I want to know." She fell back into her chair. "I have to admit I didn't think much of you when we first met—you seemed a little like a wimp. But things changed."

"How?"

"No. Not yet. You have to tell me what you feel for me first."

"Why should I take all the chances?"

"Because that's a man's job."

Win hesitated. She looked so cute, so expectant, so vulnerable, and yet so strong. She could be hurt but not destroyed. He wanted to do neither. "There have been so few women in my life. There's probably a lot of things I feel for you that ought to remain a mystery."

Her lower lip shot out in a disappointed pout.

It worked. "I like you," he blurted. "What do you want from me?"

"I want to know if we have a chance. I'm starting to think about you a lot. Like in the middle of the night. And I don't want to waste valuable time thinking about some guy who's going to be gone in a few months with a handshake and a 'Glad to know you.' Do you think there's something going on here?"

"Yeah." He nodded thoughtfully. "Something's going on here. We're having breakfast together—an omelette for crying out loud. I don't make omelettes for just anyone. Sure, there's something going on here. Of course, I'm so inexperienced I haven't the slightest idea what. "

She smiled and took a nibble from a triangle of dry toast he'd made but forgotten to butter.

"What do you think about me when you think about me in the middle of the night?" Win asked.

"Usually I picture you in that car bed and laugh."

🔔

With the weather turning warm, a cool crispness that rode the lake breeze made everything fresh. It drew people to the lake, to their boats, to the ferry. Dressed in spring's raggedness, the students emerged from their dorms in droves. Everyone wanted an ice cream or popcorn or something else from the candy store. Working alone, Sandy could barely handle it.

She was thankful. Not for the money but that her mind was occupied. The moment there was a lull she saw the flower. Red, brilliant, lush—the shape of a heart. All the hearts . . . her husband's that longed for another woman, the woman's who longed for her husband's, and Sandy's, the one that was breaking.

"Hang tough." Mel Flowers's voice echoed in the back of her brain—a naive, childlike tenor that gave sound advice.

He was right.

Maybe the rose *had* been sent to someone else and delivered with Peter's by mistake. Or it could have been that the card wishing him a speedy recovery had been misplaced. It could have been any number of things.

But she knew it wasn't.

Peter had abused her any number of ways, an affair would just top it off. . . .

But something nagged at her. She was a Christian wife with a duty to Christ . . . and to her husband. She was to think the best, not the worst.

Yet for her heart to heed the Lord's admonition, it meant swimming against a powerful current, one that drove her to a sea of depression. Fortunately, when she found herself carried in that direction, the bell atop the door would tinkle and customers came in to distract her.

By midafternoon her torment had dulled, and by evening she'd convinced herself that Peter loved her in spite of the way he treated her. And even if he didn't love her, she was there to pray him into the kingdom. Her personal feelings would have to wait.

But such a resolve injected lead into her heart.

Win and Ginger took in a midafternoon movie. Chad was invited but didn't want to go, even though they'd chosen the movie primarily for him. Looking a little cowed, Chad sauntered out the front door. Betty called him a greeting on her way to her car, but he didn't acknowledge her.

Win and Ginger returned two hours later to the minute. While Ginger scanned the refrigerator looking for something that might make dinner, Win stepped idly to the French doors in back. "Oh, my goodness." Win gasped.

"What?"

"You're not going to like this."

Ginger's garden usually had a wonderfully peaceful quality to it. It was jammed with life and colors—marigolds, camellias, crocuses, and a vibrant shock of roses in the corner—there was nothing more pleasurable than having an early morning cup of coffee there.

Now it looked like war had broken out in it. The roses were bent as if something had rolled over them, the fence they clung to was pushed back and several slats were gone. Some roses were broken off at the stalk. The other plants were either broken or ripped out.

"Oh, no. Who could have . . . ?" Ginger was near tears. "My roses . . . "

Win pushed open the doors and stepped out into the wreckage. He knelt beside a camellia bush, a major branch split off and lying in the dirt. "It's either random vandalism, or someone was mad."

"Chad?"

"What's he think about us?"

"So you admit there's an 'us'?"

"What's he think?"

Ginger shrugged. She'd worked her way to the family of roses and bent to examine the splintered stump. "He's difficult—but this is mean. I've worked a lot of hours on the garden. I love this garden."

That's when Chad's voice called from inside the house. A moment later he stood in the doorway. The moment he saw the garden, his face twisted in surprise. Both Win and Ginger wondered simultaneously if his expression was genuine. "What happened?"

"You don't know?" Ginger asked, making little effort to disguise her doubts.

"No. Who do you think . . . ?"

"You don't know?" Ginger pressed.

"Should I?" Chad remained in the doorway, almost as if he were afraid to step into the garden. "You think I did this?"

"Frankly, I don't know what to think," Ginger's frustration mingled with deep perplexity.

"Well, I didn't do it," Chad insisted. He turned to Win. "I bet you think I did it too."

Win smiled. After all, it wasn't his garden, and it wasn't his kid. He could afford to be introspective. And a little clever. "I haven't decided yet. Of course, the Lord knows who did it."

"Then why don't you go ask him!" Chad retorted snottily.

"I think I will. If I spend some time investigating, he'll probably tell me. A clue here, a footprint there."

"My mom's the cop, not you," Chad fired angrily.

"Maybe I've got a little of the Sherlock Holmes in me too. While you and your mom go in the house, I'll do some investigating."

"What kind of investigating?"

"I'll look around. This is soft dirt. There's probably a footprint or two. That way we'll know for sure. It'll be like a police investigation."

Ginger's eyes lit. "Now that makes sense. That way there won't be any suspicion. And we'll give you the benefit of the doubt. If there's no proof, we'll assume you're innocent. It'll be like the real world."

"But I could have walked around out there any time," Chad said, a little worried.

"Oh, I'm sure the footprints will be clear enough," Win said.

Ginger ushered her son back into the house.

"Mom, you're supposed to trust your children."

"Where is that written? Come on, let's gather dinner together while Win does his thing."

Chad had little interest in dinner. Although he did gather dinner things from the pantry for Ginger, he did it halfheartedly, with one eye always canted toward the backyard.

Win gave him a lot to stare at. He moved both slowly and methodically, inching down one fence then another. He made a great show of each discovery, each mental analysis, and each discard. Where he had the opportunity to make something right, he replanted or straightened or put a plant back where it had been. Then, after what to Chad seemed forever, Win stopped short, knelt, pushed some debris aside and straightened. Chad's heart stopped as he saw Win turn and call out, "Chad, can I see one of your shoes—the left one?"

Chad eyed his mother, who was already looking at him.

"Do you want to tell us anything?" she asked more gently than was usual even for her. She'd taken on some of Win's calm about the incident, and she rather liked it.

"People's tennis shoes are mostly alike," he said, head slightly bowed, a slight tremble in his lips.

"Mostly, I guess," Ginger replied.

That's when he bolted. Ginger caught a quick glimpse of his face just before his feet started churning toward the front door. It was panic, but that wasn't all. Stamped on the wide eyes and frightened mouth was a hint of sadness. It was the sadness that caused her to run after him and call to him from the front door, "Come back, Chad. It'll be okay."

But Chad had already disappeared down the street and between a couple of cottages.

Win came quickly. He got there in time to see Ginger turning and closing the front door behind her.

"He took his shoes with him," she said to him.

"I'm not sure I did the right thing, but I didn't find anything out there."

"Ah," she said knowingly. "A trick. Well, it sorta worked. He's either guilty or honestly believes all shoes are the same." She looked at Win and placed searching hands on both his arms. "I think I need one of those hugs again."

Win wrapped his arms around her, keeping his muddy hands from her back, though he wanted to use them to pull her to him. She tucked her face near his neck and rested her head on his shoulder. "You're right out of seminary, for crying out loud. Why do I feel so safe here?"

He didn't answer. He drew his wrist gently over her hair and nuzzled her with his chin.

"You don't know anything about life yet. You've got a whole world of mistakes to make yet. Why do I want to make them with you?"

He nuzzled her again and kissed her hair. It felt right. He, too, felt safe.

He pulled away. "Should we go looking for him?"

"He'll be back," she said with the confidence of a mother who'd been through this before. "You like jazz?"

"Don't know."

"Let's just sit. I know a good jazz station. We can have dinner later. I just want to sit for a while."

Chad came back in about an hour. They agreed that he'd help put things right again. They'd all put the garden right —Ginger, Chad, and Win.

Later, back at his cottage Win had a revelation that bathed him in uneasiness. In his mind's eye he saw the garden again— torn apart with a savage recklessness—like an animal might have done. He was reasonably sure Chad had done it. But he knew who'd put him up to it, who'd whispered in his ear telling him it was a good idea, who'd brought him to that pinnacle of anger where he had to do something destructive. Satan had attacked again, and they'd weathered it. But it was a probing skirmish. Satan was just letting him know he was still around, biding his time. Had he toyed with Bryce this way before he lowered the boom? Was the boom already poised over Win?

Night stakeouts were like watching grass grow. Walter "Beer" Schlitz, hated them. This one was the worst. He sat in a second-story window watching the candy store across the street. In the few hours he'd been there nothing in the store had moved. His only diversion was in taking his binoculars and scanning the neighborhood on the hill. Although the houses were all dark, there had been some interesting activities in the back of a station wagon up there. But that seemed to have died down. He was bored out of his skull.

At 1:45, however, he thought he saw something move in the store's large front windows. The impression was fleeting, spectral, and when he turned his binoculars on it he saw nothing. He peered into the black interior for several minutes, but there was still nothing.

He heard a man shout in the distance. There was a light on in the house where the station wagon had been parked. A man stood in the illuminated doorway and angrily screamed at the car. He could only make out a word or two—"daughter" was prominent. Beer grinned. He was driven to laughter when a girl, holding her clothes to shield her front, her backside naked, scurried around to the back of the house. The man in the doorway stormed toward the car. The driver was standing, looking over the top of the car, shouting defiantly back.

"Get out of there, fool," Beer muttered to the distant boy. "You're gonna get killed."

The father was at him now. He stood at the front of the car, arm outstretched, shaking a fist at the boy. Another light in the house went on as did a light in the house next door. A neighbor shouted for them to be quiet while the boy screamed back. That was it. The father leaped on top of him.

Beer called for a patrol car to break it up. Putting the mike down he eyed the battle. The father was killing the kid. "Ain't love grand?" Beer sighed.

He watched the fracas for another few minutes until the patrol car arrived. And then he watched it some more in the hope the blue on duty would call the girl out. He wanted another look at her. But he didn't, and after a half-hour things died down and he was bored again.

"Is that the phone?" Peter groaned, the digital alarm glaring 2:13 A.M.

"Huh?" Sandy shook off the drug of sleep. The phone whined next to her ear again. Sandy had brought Peter home from the hospital at two in the afternoon, and he had planted himself in bed ever since. After sleeping all day, Peter had been awake for some time, so the phone call was no interruption. But it was to Sandy. Reaching a feeble hand in its direction, she found the receiver and pressed it to her ear. "Hello."

"Mrs. Sweet?"

"Who's this?"

"This is your security service."

"At the store?" Sandy was slowly gaining consciousness.

"Who is it?" Peter was on his elbows.

"The security service," Sandy told Peter.

"Oh, what now?"

"What now?" Sandy asked the phone.

"Your silent alarm went off at 1:43. We got there at 1:50 and found nothing. We think there was a short or something. Or maybe we scared them off. But we wanted to report it."

"What is it? What are they saying?" Peter leaned on her, his ear near hers.

"The alarm went off. They think it was a short."

"Give me that." He grabbed the receiver. "What happened?"

"As I told your wife, the alarm went off, and it took us about five minutes to get there . . ."

"Five minutes! The world could come to an end in five minutes. Your contract says . . ."

"Ten minutes, sir. There was nothing there. We went through the place and found nothing out of place. We think it was a short."

"A short?" Peter bawled into the phone. "What kind of equipment do you have? A short?"

"Sometimes these things happen. They're very delicate devices."

"Right . . . delicate." He hung up and handed his wife the receiver. "A bunch of dolts."

"I'm sure . . ."

"What are you sure of? I have people trying to drive cars into my store and now a delicate instrument says someone's been in there. They probably planted a bomb."

"Then call the police."

"Do you think so? Would they . . ."

"They might."

Peter was silent for a moment. "Would you call them?"

"I guess," Sandy said flatly, still hurt by the rose's legacy.

After a curt request for her name, address, and phone number, the officer on the other end of the line seemed to listen. "It's probably like your security people said, just a short, lady. It happens all the time," the desk sergeant said.

"But my husband's been the target of a number of attacks."

"Attacks?"

"Well, not really attacks. Close calls."

"Close calls? What kind of close calls?"

"Well . . ." Her brain recited them and she immediately felt silly. Somehow hoaxes about ground glass, exploding gas mains, and a car acting as a misdirected missile all sounded a little far-fetched. "That doesn't matter. We have reason to believe that someone is trying to hurt my husband. We want the police to check our business for a bomb."

"A bomb?" She heard a snicker on the other end of the line.

"Yes, a bomb."

"Do you know what it takes to check for a bomb? There's dogs, bomb squads, equipment—lots of equipment. We come when there's a reasonable suspicion but . . ."

"My husband . . ."

"Lady, if anything's out of the ordinary in there, call us. I don't want you to think we're not sympathetic, but we need more than an alarm going off."

"Well," she felt defeated, "thank you." She hung up and faced Peter.

"No hounds?"

"No hounds."

Peter nodded. "What time is it?"

She eyed the digital clock on the night table next to her. It was 2:35.

"I'm going to check things out. I won't sleep until I do. If there is a bomb it's probably set to go off during the day."

"What if it's set to go off when you go in?"

"The security people would have found it." Peter slid out of bed. "I'll be back in an hour."

"You want me to come along?" Sandy said.

"No, get some sleep."

"Right," she said, and turned her back.

Normally she'd have fawned all over him to help, now she showed him her back. "What's wrong?"

"Nothing," she said, her face buried in her pillow.

"Something's wrong. You're angry about something. Sweet little you is upset."

"Don't push it. I'm tired and I'm not in the mood."

"I got a bomb in my store and you're actin' weird."

Peter slipped into a pair of jeans and a T-shirt.

The deserted city streets, wet from a light rain, glistened with reflected street lights as he drove to the store. Sound seemed exaggerated as his car door squealed open and his footsteps echoed on the pavement. His bandaged wrist throbbed uncomfortably from driving.

He left the door standing open as he stepped in.

No matter what his security people said, his assailant had been there. That person had lurked in these shadows, had breathed that air, all for a reason. What reason?

In the next several minutes, his arm pulsing, Peter searched every inch of the place. For the second time that week, Peter moved about quickly and efficiently.

He searched the back room, painfully moving boxes about. He found nothing. Then he scanned all the shelves, then the drawers. Nothing.

Wait a minute.

Something caught his eye in the drawer nearest the cash register. He reopened it.

In its deep recesses a shape appeared, a shape he knew but which was foreign to his store. A pistol—short barreled with a polished wooden handle. It had not been there before.

Peter gingerly reached for it and felt the heavy, cold steel first on his trembling fingertips, then in the palm of his hand. He'd never owned a gun. His father and mother hated guns and wouldn't allow them in the house. Now he held one in the palm of his hand. He rolled the cold steel from palm to fingertips. He allowed the weight to settle in and his hand mold around it. He rubbed his thumb on the hammer and felt the strong resistance as he pulled it back. But he retracted it only a fraction of the way then gently replaced it. His forefinger found the trigger and he imagined pulling it. He imagined the resounding explosion and the bullet smashing into a dark, shadowy figure. To his surprise he wasn't afraid of the weapon. In fact, a rush of courage coursed through him—an incredible rush. *Let whoever put this here come again.* He'd give the present back, one bullet at a time.

He finally had the protection he needed.

Elated, he pushed the weapon far back into that same drawer. As he closed it, his heart caught. He heard footsteps on the pavement outside. He looked up to see a rumpled figure standing in the doorway.

"Mr. Sweet, anything wrong?"

"Wrong?" Peter straightened. "You're a cop."

"Bray Sanderson." He nodded his introduction. "After the car hit the building next door we've been watching this place. What are you doing here?"

"Couldn't sleep. I remembered something. I'm leaving now."

"Ah." Bray Sanderson said. "Are you sure everything's okay?"

"Everything's fine—fine."

The rumpled cop pushed a two-finger salute his way and, after giving the inside of the store a quick scan, left.

# Chapter 16

"Bray?"

Through the curtain of sleep, the receiver near his ear, Bray heard Grogan's disquieting voice. "What time is it?"

"Good cops never sleep," Grogan reminded him.

"Then you must be calling from a coma."

Grogan groaned a laugh. "Good one."

The curtain was open wide now. He rubbed his eyes and glanced at the ancient alarm clock—6:30. "It's early. You must have a big club to hit me with this time."

"Schlitz says your boy visited the candy store last night. Sweet told you all was well?"

"He couldn't sleep."

"Did you check the desk sergeant's call sheet?"

"No." Bray straightened. Here it comes.

"Sandy Sweet called at two-twenty-three A.M. Wanted our guys to go out there and check for a bomb."

"Bomb? Why'd she think that?"

"Their silent alarm went off at one-forty-three A.M."

"What did the security people find?"

"Nothing. They got there in five minutes and found nothing. They explained it to the Sweets as a short in the system."

"Just a sec." Bray rubbed his chin, covered the receiver, and took it away from his ear.

Sweet was paranoid. That accounted for him checking up on the security people. When he'd checked things out he'd find no bomb. But his paranoia wouldn't let him think the store was clear. He'd think the bomb was still there, he just missed it. But when he saw Sweet at the store he wasn't nervous—he looked excited. Why excited? Something didn't add up. Lifting the receiver back to his ear he said, "What do you think?"

"Me? This is your case."

"You admit that, do you?"

"I think Sweet's been contacted. That's why he didn't talk to you about the bomb. He'd have been all over you for a search team if he still thought the bomb was there somewhere."

Bray's mind raced. If Sweet had been contacted he may have been many things: angry, frightened, frustrated, worried—but excited? "Could be," he said dryly. "I'll check it out from here. You did a great job. You'll make a good detective someday."

"You should have checked the desk sheet."

"I sure should have. You've really taught me a great deal. Talk to you later." He hung up.

He dialed the stakeout. "Beer? You awake?"

"Yeah, why?"

"Grogan called you."

"About twenty minutes ago. The guy's a hound."

"You didn't tell me anyone had been in that place before Sweet this morning."

"You mean those security people. He mentioned that. They must have gone through the back."

"Security people check all the doors."

"Grogan said something about a silent alarm." He emphasized the word *silent*.

"A short in the system. Their security company checked the place out."

Beer went silent. "A domestic disturbance on the hill drew my attention away. I called a patrol car it got so bad."

"People went through the door, Beer. You missed people going through the door."

"I guess. But this gal was naked, Bray—buck naked. And it was an awfully long night." Beer sounded apologetic. "There was something else." He paused a moment to collect the memory. "I just remembered." He hesitated as he shuffled the facts in the proper order. "About one-forty-five I saw something move inside the store. When I didn't see it again I thought I hadn't seen anything at all."

"What was it?"

"I don't know. Movement. Maybe a streetlight reflected on something . . . an arm flexing . . . who knows? Maybe the alarm wasn't a short."

"Why didn't you write it down?"

"A sparkling little bottom bounding across a street knocked it out of my head."

Bray sighed. "You're a cop, Schlitz. I'm disappointed."

There was silence on the other end of the phone. "Sorry, Bray." Beer was sincere.

Sincerity always worked with Bray.

"No harm done. Did you tell Grogan this?"

"No. I just remembered. Just now."

It was refreshing to know something Grogan didn't. He wasn't sure where this fact would lead, but it had to lead somewhere Grogan hadn't yet been. That in itself was a trip worth taking. "Anything else?"

"No."

"Okay. Talk to you later." Bray hung up. Someone had been in the store. Maybe he'd left a note—or something else—that Sweet had found. What in heaven's name, though, could make Sweet excited?

It was 6:45. The Sweets were probably still in bed. After a quick cup of old, microwaved coffee and an equally quick shower, Bray dressed and made his way over there. At 7:36 he pushed the doorbell.

Seeing Sandy Sweet was always a pleasure. Willowy, graciously soft features, eyes that warmed the coldest heart, she only had to stand there and occasionally speak to make meeting her a treat. She looked a bit like Diane, especially the moment she answered the door—no makeup, hair slightly mussed, lips casually pale—yet the beauty that was at her core radiated even in a rumpled robe.

Bray flashed his ID. "Bray Sanderson, Burlington police."

"Did someone break into the store?" she asked, face immediately concerned.

"Not sure, Mrs. Sweet. I'd like to see your husband."

"He's been up most of the night. You're aware that our alarm went off."

"I saw him down there. Something I'd like to check with him. Won't take a second."

Sandy smiled. Yes, just like Diane. Diane wasn't as beautiful. But there were moments—a smile, a caress of light or shadow, a particular brush of her hair—when she went beyond beauty to angelic. Pamela was prettier, but not angelic—not like Diane. But Diane was gone. "Come on in. There's coffee brewing. Pour yourself some and I'll get Peter."

Peter took his time. Bray was on his second cup when he came in. The excitement was gone, replaced by a persistent irritability.

"I'm not sure I can take seeing you twice in a twenty-four-hour period."

"I wanted to check something out with you." Bray took out a small notebook. He'd jotted a few questions on it.

"What?" Peter asked flatly.

"You've been the object of someone's vendetta. Correct?"

"Yes."

Bray shook his head, "These 'attacks,' if you will, have been a bit indirect—a bit like terrorism. Sound 'bout right?"

"Terrorism's a good description."

"Last night you were called about a silent alarm going off at the store—about one-forty-five. That right?"

"You going someplace with this?"

"You went there to search for a bomb or something the intruder left, if there was an intruder. Right?"

"They said it was a short. I wanted to be sure."

"You didn't find a bomb. In fact, when I saw you there, you said everything was okay. You actually sounded excited." Bray allowed his words to sink in and the inconsistency bubble to the surface.

To his surprise, Sandy Sweet fired a hurt, confused, furious eye at her husband. *That doesn't fit,* Bray thought.

"Why did you seem excited?" Bray asked the question, glancing at each of them in turn.

Sandy's rage became increasingly confused and swallowed up. Peter's expression remained cold, irritated and—something else, something that surprised Bray. It was courage, maybe a hint of rebellion. Peter Sweet's posture was straight, his eyes bright and determined. He'd found something in that store, something that excited him last night and gave him a shot of courage today.

Finally Peter responded, "I wasn't excited. I was glad I hadn't found anything. When you showed up I was glad you were a cop and not someone who was going to kill me. I suppose I could have looked excited."

"Did you find anything in your search that wasn't there before?"

Peter hesitated. He was a poor liar. "No. Nothing."

Bray glanced at Sandy. She'd been hurt. Her hands rubbed together fiercely.

"Are you sure?"

"Why wouldn't I be sure?" Peter straightened even further. "Now, my wife needs to get ready for church, and I need to get ready for the store. I've decided to go in this morning."

"You have?" His plans were a surprise to Sandy. Eyes wide, mouth slightly open, she seemed more surprised than the news warranted. Anything unusual must be extremely worrisome to her.

Bray thought for a moment. *The only thing that gets that kind of rise from a wife is an affair.* Was Peter being hounded by an irate husband? Had she just found out?

"I'll be in touch," he said. "Mrs. Sweet." He nodded her way, but she was glaring at Peter. Bray left.

Chuck Hunt woke to distant, muffled singing. He brushed a fallen leaf from his bristled cheek and slapped away something crawling across his forehead. Another slap at an unknown intruder, this one near his ear, and he began to work the sleep from raw eyes. The singing persisted, and he eased himself to a sitting position against the maple tree. He picked an ant from the back of his dirt-encrusted hand then shook the thick, crystalline dew from the thin blanket he'd stolen off a clothesline the day before.

He moved to stand and came in contact with a thousand aches—knees, feet, ribs, arms. Attacked by the lumps and valleys of his earthen mattress, his body groaned as he stretched and retrieved from his pocket a half-smoked cigarette and a matchbook with only a couple of matches left. He lit up. The smoke was wonderful—magnificent—soothing. A king couldn't have felt better.

Content—except for a gnawing hunger—he could now concentrate on the singing. He'd been a singer once—guitar and Pete Seeger music. He'd traded the guitar for a bottle of Ripple on a night he could no longer remember. The congregation in that little white church was booming away. Chuck grunted and eyed the sea of cars. Church people rarely lock their cars. That gnawing hunger could be satisfied by something in one of them.

He rolled the blanket, tied each end with some string from his jeans pocket, and slung it over his shoulder. He'd not eaten since yesterday morning and then again a day before that. Somewhere in those cars was something he could turn into food. He knew it.

Chuck made his way to a Chevy furthest from the road. Unlocked, it yielded nothing but a couple of magazines. The next two were foreign and locked, but the one after that was open. He scanned the front seat quickly, then the back. Behind the driver's seat, tucked underneath, was a Polaroid camera. Just a cheap one, but maybe worth something somewhere. He grabbed it and shoved it into his coat pocket.

The next was locked, the one after that unlocked but, like the rest, gave up nothing but paper.

Chuck had been hungry before—very hungry—but after spending this past winter living in frigid barns and rescue missions he'd hoped things would be better. He was getting discouraged—a whole parking area full of unlocked cars and everyone a neatnik.

After a couple of seconds to scan for another likely candidate, he straightened and smiled broadly. A large black stretch limo was parked near the front of the church. Being out there in front of God and everyone there was a risk. The rewards, however, might be large: television, stereo, a bar. Of course, it was probably locked.

His heart leaped into his mouth when he found it open.

Although nothing was lying out, he immediately saw a number of possibilities, pockets, cabinets, and a refrigerator. The pockets contained a book and a couple of maps, the cabinets were empty, but the refrigerator—ah, the refrigerator—held a package of Twinkies and two diet Cokes. Ravenously he tore the cellophane, stuffed a whole one into his mouth, rewrapped the other, and pushed it into his pocket next to the camera. He hated diet drinks—the aftertaste—but beggars can't be . . . He downed one without tasting it and left the other. A protest.

Then he leaned back and let it all settle. He looked around, and his hand came to rest on a control panel sprinkled with buttons and toggle switches. He pushed one of the buttons. Nothing happened—then another and another. Suddenly an electric hum buzzed about his head—a chessboard unfolded from the side door. The board lit with the silhouetted chess pieces scattered about. A game was in progress. "I could live for a year on what that cost," Chuck mumbled, shaking his head.

He leaned back. The comfortable leather seats creaked around him. He saw a phone next to the refrigerator and smiled at it. There were people he could call—people back home, people who wondered where he was, people who worried. The buttons looked confusing. Too confusing, and he felt relieved.

He heard voices, chattering, laughing. He shrank back, then peeked through the window. People were filing from the church.

Ooops.

He ducked and slid from the car, closing the door softly. Stooping, gliding from car to car, he headed for the trees but then realized that he was missing an opportunity. He casually strolled between the cars toward the emerging congregation. He asked an older couple if they could spare him a buck or two. They ignored him.

The second couple eyed him up and down but remained mute.

The third and fourth told him he should get a job. He ignored *them*.

His fifth opportunity was a knot of people. They talked animatedly as he approached them. "You guys have anything you can give me? I haven't eaten in over a day."

"I got a buck," one man offered. He stuck a hand in his pocket and brought out a couple. He pushed both into Chuck's outstretched hand.

"Thanks," Chuck said. Two bucks would get him a beer with breakfast.

Someone called from the steps. "Hey!"

Chuck turned, squinted in the sun. A tall, wire hard, nail of a man stood there. "Huh?" he said back.

"Stop bothering people. If you have a need, you'll have to speak to our deacons."

"I ain't no bother. I'm just askin'. . ."

"We have rules."

Chuck eyed the nail—a nail with bug eyes. Two bucks and Twinkies weren't much, but he didn't want trouble. He finally nodded and walked toward the road. He knew a small grocery store about a mile up the road. He ate the other Twinkie on the way.

He'd been by this store a hundred times. Sometimes he'd gone in and looked around. Sometimes he just stood outside. Each time he marveled at the riot of colorful, ancient promotional stickers on the door and windows: Nehi Root beer, Marlboro cigarettes, and hundreds of others. He'd stand and admire them and imagine the time when they all were new. This time, however, he didn't hesitate but stepped quickly inside. A roundish woman in her mid-forties sat on a tall stool behind the counter. Her hair was mussed, her lips pale without lipstick. She smiled pleasantly. He smiled tentatively back.

"You got some money this time?" the woman asked.

"Some."

"Before you go on that spending spree, want a cup of coffee?" Although she remained expressionless, her voice sounded warm and caring, "I just made a pot."

"Really?" Chuck perked. "Any sugar?"

"Sweet'N Low."

"No real sugar?"

She laughed softly. "I'll see what I can do."

She poured a Styrofoam cup of coffee and meticulously searched the shelves. Finding a packet of real sugar, she broke it and allowed the contents to dribble into the black. She handed it to Chuck who took a long, appreciative drink.

"It's great," he said, catching sight of a pack of cigarettes on the far edge of the counter.

She smiled. "They're filters."

"Everything's filters nowadays. Can't never get a real smoke."

She shook one from the pack and he took it. After she lit it for him he took a long, satisfying drag. The smoke, not tainted by someone's old ashes, felt wonderfully filling. He expelled the smoke as a lover might.

"That's wonderful. Really wonderful." He sighed.

"How much you got?"

"Two bucks. There's a church not far from here. I caught

them on the way out," he admitted, taking more coffee, more smoke.

"It's a wonder you got anything out of them hypocrites."

"Hypocrites. Right." He slurped another long drink. The liquid burned his tongue, but the sting didn't squelch its magnificence. "I'm going to buy some food."

"Two bucks won't get you much. Add another buck to it. Three won't go far either, but it'll go further than two."

"Really?" Thrilled, Chuck nearly choked on his next drag. "Warm up?"

"Sure." Chuck pushed the cup excitedly at her.

Refilling it quickly, she was about to ask him his name when the phone rang. "Hello."

On the other end a husky voice whispered, "May I speak to the man with the bedroll?"

Her brows furled. "You're kidding."

"May I, please?"

"Uh, sure." She pushed the receiver at Chuck. "It's for you."

"For me?"

"For you."

Now it was Chuck who furled his brows deeply, with massive uncertainty. After setting the cup down on the counter, extinguishing the cigarette, and placing the precious butt in his pocket, he cleared his throat, and pressed the receiver cautiously to his ear. "Hello."

"Go outside to the telephone pole. There's a rock beside it. Pick up what's under the rock and come back to the phone. I'll hang on."

"Is this a joke?"

"Do it, please."

Chuck nodded at the phone. "Right." He set the receiver next to the coffee and shrugged at the woman. "He wants me to do something."

Chuck found the rock. About six inches across, surrounded by new grass, it looked like it hadn't been moved in years. He lifted it easily. Underneath amid the hard shell bugs and white worms that twisted spasmodically in the harsh sunlight was half of a hundred dollar bill. Shocked, excited, frightened, Chuck looked all around and saw nothing but a vacant lot, weeds, and a scattering of houses with the lake's great expanse beyond. He picked it up, shook a spider from it, and stepped quickly back inside. The door slapped behind him. The receiver pressed to his ear, he whispered, "I found it."

"Want the other half?"

"Well, yeah." He felt the crisp paper, rubbed it, wadded it. "What do I gotta do?"

The woman at the counter watched curiously as the bum became solemn and nodded gravely after several intense interludes. He seemed to be getting instructions. Finally the guy, his expression still like a cemetery, said okay and handed her the receiver.

"What did he want?"

"I can't say. He wouldn't let me say."

"Who's gonna know? What did he tell you to do?"

"Who's gonna know? He's gonna know. How do you suppose he knew I was here?"

"Prob'ly saw you come in."

"Well, I got half a hundred here and I want the other half. I ain't takin' no chances."

"Here, finish yer coffee." She pushed the cup his way.

But he ignored it and headed for the shelves of merchandise. "Whatcha lookin' for?"

"A light bulb."

"The end of the next aisle."

He grabbed a box containing two and brought them to the counter. His gravity had been replaced by a huge, anxious smile. "This is very strange, you know." The woman lit a cigarette of her own and took a quick, nervous puff.

"It's gonna get stranger," Chuck said and handed her two dollars.

She gave him thirty-one cents change and slipped the box in a bag. "Where are you off to now?"

"Can't say. Nope. Can't say. But tonight I'm going to be sleeping indoors."

"Listen, people don't give hundred dollar bills away for nothing. Whatever you've been told to do might sound innocent, but be real careful."

"Oh, it ain't innocent. But it ain't all that bad neither."

"Well, you just take care."

"Right," he said, but he said it with a laugh.

At thirty-four Chuck had been on the road nearly twenty years. His mother died when he was eight, and his father, an unsteady man who masked his unsteadiness with booze, raised him until the county split them up when Chuck was twelve. His father had left him alone once too often and a neighbor had complained. As a ward of the court, he was planted in foster homes. When he'd run away and got caught, the county orphanages took him.

At fifteen he'd run away and it took. He was on his own. Thirty hit him like a bolt—he had nothing, was likely to have nothing. He'd made a vow to become something. But, like his father, he forgot about his nothingness and the pesky vow, when sipping from the stale mouth of a bottle. Maybe this was his chance. Maybe this job would bring more jobs, and a roof, and a place to settle down. Maybe it was the first step to the good life.

Chuck stood in front of the arcade in Burlington, bells and bleeps assaulting his ears.

Only moments before he'd been anxious to get it over with, now he stood wondering how he was going to screw it up.

He'd screwed up everything that ever mattered to him. His father had told him, "You're nothin' but a screwup—a liar and a screwup. If only you'd been smart you might get away with it. But you're not. You're stupid too."

Here he was, thirty-four and a screw-up. But there was a C-note at stake here. He'd have to risk it.

After a deep, calming breath, he opened the bag and took the two light bulbs out of their box. He dropped them loose back into the bag, rolled the top, and slapped the bag against the side of the building. The bulbs popped and shattered. Unrolling the top, he took the metal out and tossed it away. Then he slammed the bag again and the glass broke into even finer pieces.

He took another deep, anxious breath and eyed the candy store across the street.

The time had come.

He waited for a couple of cars to glide by before he crossed the street. The single customer in the store faced a woman who stooped over barrels of ice cream.

"Can I help you?" a man's voice asked.

It came from the popcorn. Chuck hadn't seen him and a question from that direction caught him off guard. "Uh, yeah . . . I'm just looking."

The man looked doubtful. "Well, when you're ready."

He was ready. But the guy stood too close.

Chuck turned and surveyed the candy on the shelf that stretched across the back wall while out of the corner of his eye he watched the guy. He didn't move. Just when Chuck was about to give up, another customer came in and diverted the guy's attention. "Peanut clusters? Right over here." He moved away from the popcorn.

Seizing the opportunity, Chuck unrolled the top of the bag and grabbed it by the bottom. With a single flick of the wrist, he threw the glass into the popcorn and, even as the shards clattered on the stainless steel, he threw himself through the door. Gratefully outside, he dodged a car and scrambled toward the opposite side of the street.

From behind he heard a frantic storm of words. Most he didn't understand but the last few. . . "Peter? Where'd you get that? . . . You can't . . . Peter!" An explosion. A fiery spike drove savagely into Chuck's shoulder. The force spun him around and slammed him to the pavement. Lying on his back, his shoulder inflamed, burning lava coursing through his bones, he stared up at the man from the candy store, the barrel of a gun shaking only inches from his skull.

"You miserable . . ." The man's face was contorted in an incredible rage. "Who. . . ?"

"Man, please, don't shoot. Please . . ."

"Who put you . . ."

"Please." Chuck forced back tears. He was going to die. He knew it. All his chances were used up.

"I'm going to split your head like a melon." The man spit on him as he spoke, the barrel a tunnel to eternity.

"Peter . . . don't!" He heard the woman screaming.

Another voice, more distant. "Sweet. Don't. It's murder."

Chuck couldn't just lie there. Legs churning, he reached around, his shoulder blade painfully in action, squirming away, the gun stalking him.

He heard the gun cock and a siren, and he felt something in his coat pocket—the camera. Had he been thinking rationally Chuck would have thrown the camera at the man. It was heavy, and the impact would have given him a moment to escape.

But he didn't throw it. He brought it up with his good hand and pushed the button. The flash startled the candyman and the gun barrel flinched. The picture fell on Chuck's chest, and he pushed the button again. The flash—the flinching barrel—more shouts—siren—and then the gun fired, again, and his shoulder erupted in blood as fire blazed through nerves and bone.

"Peter . . . Peter . . . Oh no."

The beautiful woman grabbed the man by the shoulders and pulled him back. Then there were two blue-clad cops, one slapping handcuffs on the guy with the gun.

The other knelt beside him, and a guy in a rumpled London Fog stood peering down. He said, "Hang on, we got the paramedics coming."

"She's beautiful," Chuck heard his own faint voice saying, his throat volcanic.

"Easy . . . don't move . . . the medics are on the way."

# Chapter 17

"How is he?" Peter asked Sandy, his voice bound up in defeat.

They were in the visitor's area. The size of a living room, divided by a floor-to-ceiling steel mesh that sliced the table at which they sat, Peter sat on the jail side. Sandy had a right to be angry. He'd overreacted. He'd done more than that. In a single, violent, nonretrievable moment, he'd changed their lives. But she wasn't angry. Like the room, she seemed cool, rigidly unperturbable—distant. He would have rather seen her angry. The steel mesh not only divided them physically; it cut them emotionally.

"His shoulder's shattered. He's thankful he's alive."

Peter's eyes dropped to his hands. They fidgeted frantically, "I did it this time, didn't I?"

Sandy's eyes were ice. "Yes, you did." Her heart realized that any coolness was too much. Peter was still her husband, and he was in very deep trouble. But she couldn't help it.

"I'm going to jail for a while," Peter said, eyes still cast downward.

"Just what whoever it is wanted. I don't know why he's doing this, but he knew you'd use that gun. Why didn't you tell me about it?" She leaned back. "No matter now, I guess. We got a good lawyer. You've been under a lot of stress . . ."

"But I did it, Sandy. I shot that man." Eyes still looking down, his voice shaking. "I wanted to kill him."

"Want to see how you looked?"

"Huh?"

"Here, look at these." She held up the two Polaroids the transient had taken.

Peter's heart stopped. The gun barrel was only inches from the lens, his face blurred, but there was no mistaking the hate stamped on it.

He pulled back and whispered shamefully, "I can't look."

"I couldn't believe it when I saw you grab that gun." Her eyes washed over him like a nor'easter. "Then you ran outside yelling. All I could see was your back. I could see you leaning over him. I prayed and I prayed . . ."

"No prayers will help now. No apologies. Nothing will help." Peter dropped his head in his hands. "How can you ever forgive me?"

She couldn't.

It took root in her heart like a bitter herb. The rose and now the gun. She could forgive his momentary insanity, no matter how violent. She could forgive his insults and his rudeness— but his infidelity? He'd met his lover that night, the alarm had gone off, and she'd given him the gun. She'd convinced him to use it. He deserved to be sitting behind steel. Sandy only wished the other woman could be sitting there with him.

"Your attorney will be here in an hour or so. He's working on bail."

Peter looked up at her, his eyes bruised with guilt, his breathing caught on hooks of shame. "You can't forgive me, can you?"

She glanced away and surveyed her heart. She felt a profound mixture of regret, pity, and sorrow. But forgiveness? No.

"I have things to do," she finally said.

"I'm sorry, Sandy. I'm so, so sorry." His fingers gripped the cage.

"I'll be back later."

She turned her back on him and left.

Bray Sanderson wasn't sure what to expect as he entered his third hour in the gray room watching the front of the candy store. Sweet blasting the bum, however, was a definite surprise. "You'd better question the bum," Breed commanded.

"I plan to."

"Does Sweet have any idea why this is happening?"

"None."

"You should have searched that store," Grogan said.

"Why would they want him in jail?" Breed finally asked what they all wondered.

"I guess it doesn't matter. Your theory's still intact," Bray offered. "Bryce could still have been just the first casualty."

"Right," Grogan said.

"I'll question the bum when he's able," Bray said, and Breed waved an approving hand.


Bray stood at the foot of the hospital bed as the young nurse checked the intravenous drip rate. Finding it satisfactory she turned to the detective. "He's all yours."

"Right." Chuck grinned with brown teeth. "I'm all yours."

The detective stepped to the side of the bed. "You dumped glass in the man's popcorn."

"I did that. Yes, I did."

"Why?"

"A prank."

"No one put you up to it?"

"I hate candy stores. My dad had one, and he spent every minute of his time in it. I hate them."

"I don't believe you."

"It was a prank. A mischief I'll pay dearly for. The doctor says I'm going to have pain for a long time."

Bray nodded. "We found half a hundred dollar bill on you."

"You took that." The statement was an accusation. "It was my good luck piece."

"It was new."

"A new good luck piece." Chuck smiled and said, "I want

it back too. I want to tape it to the other end I got right here."
He reached under his pillow and pulled out the matching half.

Bray pushed an inquisitive face at him. "That wasn't on you earlier."

"You just didn't look hard enough."

Bray groaned angrily. His quarry had been there and gone—undetected. This guy must be *The Shadow*. "The guy who paid you the other half tell you you'd be shot for the effort?"

"It was a prank."

"Right." There was little else to say. If the bum didn't want to talk there was little he could do to make him. "If you decide to cooperate, call me." Bray left and found Win standing in the hallway.

Win asked, "Do you think the extortionist has accomplished what he set out to do?"

"He put a gun in the store and gave Sweet someone to use it on. He knows Sweet pretty well and having him in jail benefits him. I think his wife believes he's having an affair. Maybe a jealous husband's had the perfect revenge. It seems, though, that he's done all he can to Sweet. Maybe he'll get away with it—maybe both Bryce and Sweet will go unavenged."

Win said nothing, but inside he saw the battle continuing. Sandy Sweet was one of the only Christians left at the church that he knew about. Satan had launched another seemingly successful attack.

"So close," Bray exclaimed, swearing. It made him feel better and he turned to Win. "I'm going for a drink. Want one?"

"No, thanks," Win said. "What are you going to do after your drink?"

Bray laughed and shook his head. "I'll figure that out while I'm having it."

They parted.


When Sandy had returned home, a stack of sympathetic messages stumbled awkwardly from the answering machine, and in the last half-hour at least ten people from church had called. Each person began with sincere expressions of sympathy and shock, then turned quickly to his or her real purpose: finding out what happened. Only Maggie Selkirk seemed honestly in tune with Sandy's confusion and torment. Maggie revealed that she understood how brutal husbands could be and after saying something incoherent about her own, she cried unashamedly.

Now Sandy felt very alone.

The sun had fled behind a hedge of gray clouds and although a moment before a hint of crimson bolted across the indefinite horizon, the sunset had quickly faded to an enveloping dreariness. Within easy reach of the kitchen light, she remained in darkness, believing it her friend. Light brought definition, darkness obscurity. She'd had too much definition for the day. Like the sun, she preferred to bury herself in black. But with black came loneliness—loneliness like she'd never known—never. She'd come from a big family, grown up on a farm in Connecticut, brothers and sisters seemed to outnumber the chickens. She could remember longing for a moment to herself—just a moment's reverie to ponder some great thought, or scratch herself in some forbidden place.

Now her moment had come, and she hated it. But being alone was only a small part of her torment. She also felt distant from her Savior, her Comforter. She felt straightjacketed—unable to cry.

She knew why. Anger was her straightjacket. Anger bottled up her tears, dulled her feelings, and drove a wedge between her and Jesus. More than anger—rage. It seemed both unfair and just. Her husband not only faced years in jail, but was also the object of her rage. He and his lover. Did Sandy know her? Was she a friend? How long had it been going on?

She now knew how Peter could slam his fist through glass. She felt like doing the same—but not to glass. She wanted to place their faces nose to nose and slam her fist through both . . .

The doorbell rang.

Sandy dreaded answering. But when she did, the woman lighted by the dim porch light looked familiar . . . Oh yes, Sandy had seen her at Flowers's tent.

"Ginger Glasgow," the woman greeted, extending her hand with a warm smile.

"Yes," Sandy said.

"I don't know if you remember me. I'm a friend of Win Brady's. He's trying to lend your husband a little support, and he thought you could use some too. I volunteered. How you doing?"

"I'm fine."

"You don't look fine. Can I come in?"

"I really would rather . . ."

"No you wouldn't," Ginger stated flatly but gently. "We're sisters in the Lord. I've come to help."

"I don't feel like a sister in the Lord."

"That's normal from time to time. Lord knows I haven't lately." Her persistent smile and friendly, eager eyes broke through Sandy's thinly constructed crust, and she moved from the door.

Sandy said, "I know you're sincere. Everyone is sincere. But for the life of me I don't know how you can help."

"First, I can get some light in here." She set her purse down on a chair, flipped a switch near the door and a corner floor lamp lit. Then she turned on a table lamp near the center of the room. "How's your husband? Peter, isn't it?"

"Yes. Peter. He's not good. He's defeated—he's defeated himself."

Ginger nodded. "How about you?"

"I really don't want to talk about it."

Ginger nodded again. This was a new role for her, and she wasn't sure of the words or the actions. Her Uncle Joel was so much better at it. He'd visited an injured friend of hers once and immediately set the woman at ease, and when he left everything was better. Ginger decided to keep busy. "Can I make you anything?" she asked. "Coffee, tea? Maybe get you a Coke?"

"That's my line."

"No, it's mine. I love to putter around in the kitchen. Let me make you some coffee or tea, or something cold while you relax for a moment."

"Relax?"

"Yes, relax." There was a touch of firmness. "You've had a shock. We all have 'em from time to time. Mine came a few years ago when my husband was killed. Relax and let the Lord work. You've got a right to be upset. Your husband made a mistake that will change both your lives . . . you might be a little angry at him."

Sandy gnawed her lower lip.

Ginger's brows climbed. "Or maybe you're *really* angry at him. I know that feeling." She'd struck a nerve. "Sit. I'll make us some coffee and we can talk."

Sandy knew it was time to talk, time to bring it all out into the open, and this woman had earned the right to hear. But she couldn't let someone else be the hostess in her own home. "I'll help."

"Okay. Maybe busy hands'll help." The kitchen was just off the living room, and they both moved toward it.

Sandy felt something therapeutic about moving around with purpose, even if the purpose was just making tea. "I tried to pray earlier," she finally said, the flame yellow-tipped beneath the kettle. "I've never not been able to pray before."

Ginger suddenly remembered the night a policeman she worked with brought her the news about her husband's death. She hadn't been able to pray then, either. The rage was too great.

"Would you like to pray now?" Ginger asked. The words felt as foreign to her as any words she'd ever spoken. And yet they felt right.

"I think I'd like that."

There in the kitchen, both leaning against the counter, the two women prayed. Ginger felt obligated to start and she began feebly. But when she finally fell silent she'd prayed for comfort and understanding and strength—safe things, she thought, but also things she needed. Things she longed for. Sandy picked it up. The words came more easily to her now, and she prayed for Peter's soul and for her anger, and although she didn't specifically say what caused her anger, her anger was considerable.

As if on cue, the moment they said their collective amens, the doorbell chimed.

"Want me to get it?" Ginger asked.

"No. My job." Revived a little, Sandy crossed quickly to the front door. To her surprise Martin Sorrell stood there.

Hunched slightly, a posture that went a little further than shyness, he spoke in a cramped whisper, "I hope I'm not disturbing you."

"No, no. Of course, not, Mr. Sorrell," she greeted. "You're just in time for tea."

Sandy noticed Sorrell glance over her shoulder and instantly register worry. Sandy turned to see Ginger stepping from the kitchen.

"I can't come in," Sorrell said, glancing anxiously at Ginger again. Then he asked, "May I speak to you privately?"

Sandy found Sorrell an enigma. All that money and all the power that naturally accompanied it and yet he was so debilitatingly shy. She couldn't refuse him. "Perhaps we can talk on the porch."

Sorrell nodded, eyes darting toward her, then away. She led him to a wicker sofa on the porch and they sat.

"I wanted to tell you how sorry I was to hear about your husband."

She nodded. "Thank you."

"It's such a shame. You are such a wonderful woman to have such a husband."

She cocked her head, not sure how to reply. She agreed with him, and she was ashamed that she did.

"He will be in jail a long time," he said.

"It looks that way." The evening sounds were thick—a powerboat on the distant lake, dogs barking, frogs. Peter wouldn't hear these sounds in a jail cell.

"Too long for a wonderful woman like you to wait."

Sandy's mind returned to the conversation. "But I will wait," she said, almost realizing it for the first time. Her commitment had been there lurking in the shadows, but saying it brought it out in the open—made it real.

She heard Sorrell speaking again and she refocused. He'd changed. His subdued, defeated expression was now uncharacteristically alive. "I have a lot of money. It can set you free . . ."

"From Peter? But I'm his wife."

"But you can't love him."

"On days like today it's tough. But I do love him. I have to love him."

"But you can't! I've seen the way he's treated you. And now this."

"I'm his wife," she said resolutely, beginning to resent Sorrell. She was Peter's wife. And no matter what he'd done . . .

Sorrell suddenly moved away, his face flushed with the agony of disbelief. "You can't love him. I love you. I love you more than I can ever tell you."

"Mr. Sorrell. Please. Of course, I'm flattered . . ."

"I've loved you from a distance for so long . . . you're so precious, so beautiful. Then someone ridiculed me because I didn't act. He said I should take the things I wanted . . . like the chess king. I wanted you. You can't love that man. He doesn't love you. He treats you like dirt. Didn't I show you that? When he was threatened he pushed you away. I would never push you away." He paused, his eyes alive, bloodless lips trembling. "I sent you my heart."

Sandy could scarcely believe what she was hearing. "Your what?"

"I sent you my rose. I have never sent a woman a flower before. I spent months cultivating it. I nurtured it, fed it. It was my heart. I gave you my heart."

"*You* sent *me* the rose?" Now she understood. "You sent me the flower?"

"It was precious to me. Just as you are."

"You did all this to Peter? How could you?"

"I showed you what he was—a frightened child, selfish, not worthy of someone like . . ." He uncoiled to his feet, eyes flaring. "Do you know who I've become indebted to for you? Do you know how powerful they are? I've risked everything

240    WILLIAM KRITLOW

for you." Rage blistered his eyes, and for an instant he looked like he might strike her. But just as suddenly he became aware that Ginger now stood at the door and would overhear. He went mute. Finally, after a horribly long moment when the fire within him made a sputtering transformation to fear, he said, "I must go. Yes, I must. Please, no tea. I have to go."

He stumbled from the porch, ran awkwardly to his limousine, and fell into the backseat. The limo sped away.

"He sent me the flower," she muttered disbelievingly to Ginger. "He did all that to Peter."

"Sorrell?" Ginger automatically grabbed for her purse to pull out her Glock, but after a few quick steps toward the disappearing limo, she stopped. Sorrell wouldn't go anywhere and Sandy needed her now.

"Oh, my Lord, I've been such a fool," Sandy was saying. "Such a fool." Tears broke, hands cupped over her mouth. "Peter . . . I have to go to Peter." Sandy ran to her car, threw herself behind the steering wheel, and slammed the door. Seconds later, tires squealed from the driveway, toward town.

Win was just turning onto her street as Sandy barreled by. Ginger still stood on the porch.

"I'm surprised you're not writing her a ticket," Win said as he stepped from the old Chevy.

"It was Martin Sorrell. He's the one who did this to Peter."

"Sorrell? You're kidding."

"He wanted Sandy."

"I'd better call Sanderson. Where's she off to?"

"Her husband. Something about a rose or something."

Win glanced back at the road. Sandy had long since disappeared. "I guess that happens when you marry a beautiful woman." Then he smiled back at Ginger. "I guess I'll get used to it one day."

"Fat chance."

Peter Sweet sat caged in steel. He thought it a fitting place for him—angrily scrawled walls, a wire mesh bed and a thin, uncompromising mattress, a stainless steel sink and toilet. This would be his life from now on—as it should be.

With his face buried in his hands, the bed upon which he sat groaned as he breathed. It groaned so loudly that he hardly became aware of a voice talking to him. "I saw your name on the rap sheet," it said. Looking up he saw Mel Flowers standing there, a guard beside him.

Over the years Sandy had dragged him to several of Flowers's shows. Peter had gone and returned angry. He wasn't angry now.

"Can we talk?" Mel asked—then to the guard, "Can I talk to him?"

"Anyone you want," the guard said.

Heavily weary, Peter's eyes burned as he looked up. Mel smiled. "The administrator here's a Christian. He attended my service today and invited me over." Mel kept talking as the guard unlocked the cell door. "I understand you lost it today." He stepped inside as the door closed behind him.

"I did. I really did." Peter's heart groaned each word.

"Tell me about it."

"I've lost Sandy," Peter rubbed his eyes and pushed a fist feebly into his palm, "lost everything. She is everything."

"How did you lose Sandy?"

"I've treated her so badly." A tear bled down his cheek. "I've been thinking about her." He sniffled the tear away. "All the time . . . I've yelled at her. Pushed her away. Hated her. I love her . . . oh, I love her." All his energy propelled his hand in a broad circle. "And now this. This is where I belong. It's all my fault. Everything is my fault. I deserve to be locked up—alone."

Mel placed a warm, encouraging hand on Peter's shoulder. His other hand carried an ancient book. "I've done a lot of thinking about this too. You know? In a cell. In darkness. Alone."

"Huh?"

"We're all criminals, Peter. All of us. Praise God for his grace—to his people. Praise God." Mel saw a sudden longing in Peter's eyes.

"I deserve this. I deserve . . ."

"We all do, Peter. All of us. Even the best of us." Mel stepped to the corner of the small room, eyes surveying it. "We all fell in Adam. We're all criminals. We're all against God, deserving a cell like this, alone. We all deserve hell. But Christ came to save his people from all that, and through him we have the Lord's forgiveness. And if God forgives us, who cares about anyone else? With forgiveness, there's restoration." Mel thumbed quickly through the worn pages of his Bible. Mel read Isaiah 1:18 to him. "Do you know what that means to you, Peter?"

"Forgiveness—I've never been forgiven anything." His face fell into open palms. Then it rose. "I killed my dad's dog. My dad went hunting for the weekend. He left his car home, and I took it. I was fifteen—didn't even have my learner's permit yet, and when I came home I hit his dog. When he got home he nearly killed me. He wouldn't talk to me for a month, maybe two months. I don't deserve forgiveness. It's my fault. Losing Sandy. Hurting that guy. All of it. My fault." He sniffled and seemed to be lost in his past and reliving his present.

Mel thumbed calmly to another page, then read Acts 4:8–12 to him, reading the last verse twice. "And that?"

"Jesus." The name slipped from trembling lips and hung in the air between them. Tears joined it. "Jesus?" A budding revelation as if the precious name now returned to the trembling heart. Through growing tears, he whispered, "Forgiveness? I'm not sure what it means."

"It means it's okay. In Jesus you are loved. You have a Father in heaven who loves you more than any dog—more than anything you've ever done. He nailed his son to a cross for you. There's no greater love than that. No greater love. He's your salvation. There is no other."

Peter said nothing for a long time. After several tortured moments, he began to weep, unashamedly, with his whole body. "I've lost her."

"Then it's time to find Christ, isn't it, Peter?"

"He's real, isn't he?" The words came through the groanings

of his heart, the tremors of all his life. "I know he's real. Sandy was right . . . oh, Sandy, please."

"Would you like to pray? Would you like to come to Christ, Peter?"

"I have to come. I have to. Oh, Lord, please, Lord, I need you so. Please, forgive me, Lord, please."

"Humble yourself before the Lord. Oh, Lord, accept my brother."

Peter fell to his knees. He didn't feel the rock hardness of the floor, he didn't feel the tortured tears, he only felt his hands clasp and his head bow deeply. "What do I pray?"

"What's in your heart? Pray it, Peter. Say it all."

Peter jerked spasmodically. He breathed in tortured gasps and finally words emerged. "Oh, God, please forgive me. I've done wrong. I'm all those things I think I am, and I need you so. Lord, please, Jesus, please."

The words faded.

Peter lifted his head. "I need Sandy. I need to talk to her."

Mel smiled warmly down at Peter, tears trickled from the corner of his eye. "Jesus is sweet." He whispered and took Peter's hand and helped him to his feet. Then he hugged him, tightly.

"I feel all put together. I feel right." Peter glanced at the guard who, having witnessed the drama, stood dumbfounded at the bars.

Mel searched his jacket pocket and took out a small Bible. "Peter, take this. It's a New Testament. Start with John and never stop. I'll get you a complete Bible as soon as I can. In the meantime, I'll find Sandy. We'll get her here."

Heart soaring with the eagles, Mel didn't have to go far. As he emerged from the cell block, Sandy came through the front door.

The desk sergeant curtly pointed out that visiting hours were over, Mel made a quick call to the administrator, and soon Peter was brought, heart pounding, to the visitor's area. The moment the guard unlocked the door he pushed it open. Breath caught in his throat, eyes swelling with tears, he ran to the table, pushed yearning hands against the mesh and felt the warmth and longing of the hands that waited for him there. The mesh melted away as their fingers entwined. Lips, moistened by tears, searched each other out amid the steel. Pressed there, their hearts knit in a longing far stronger than the steel that separated them. They kissed and kissed again, their tears becoming a single rush of joy and hope.

"I want to tear this down." Peter moaned.

Lips still pressed against his, Sandy whispered, "It doesn't matter. I've never been closer."

"I love you so." Peter pulled back, sniffling, that he might see his wife, see her, in many ways, for the first time.

Before he could speak, though, tears brushed back, Sandy said, "I've been such a fool, Peter. Such a fool."

"None of that matters. Nothing matters anymore. Sandy, I know him. I know Christ."

Sandy's heart caught as it took a moment to understand, then it bloomed, filling her heart with a joy greater than she could have ever prayed for. Hopeful, forgiving tears became immensely grateful as an uncertain mouth opened in a wide smile. "You do?" she squealed. "Oh, Peter. I've been praying for so long. Praise the Lord." She pressed her hands to his again and wove her fingers in his again.

"I love you," Peter whispered, pressing his lips to hers again.

"How . . . did it happen?"

"Mel came to see me," Peter said. "I know Jesus is mine and I'm his. I'm behind bars, facing jail, and I'm at peace.  Oh, Sandy, I've been such a horrible husband . . ."

She straightened, joyous eyes became serious. "I doubted you. Forgive me."

"Forgive you? Forgive me." And then he pulled further away, wiped his eyes with the palms of his hands, and brushed his nose on his sleeve. "Can you believe all this? What are we going to do?"

"It doesn't matter. The Lord will work it all out."

For the first time in his life, Peter knew that would be true.

"Sorrell?" Bray nearly spit. "Why'd it have to be him?"

Win and Ginger had caught up with him at Archie's, and Ginger quickly told him everything. When she finished Bray stared at her for a long moment, then he took another drink and frowned. "When you gonna get some Chivas?" he whined at the bartender. "This stuff's turpentine." The bartender shrugged without interest. Bray turned to Ginger, then to Win. "People with money have powerful friends."

"People who blow up gas mains and plant guns. They probably recruited the fake news people and the bum."

"Maybe. Sorrell comes from old money. Maybe they laundered a little. Maybe they did some favors." Another drink, another frown. "Sorrell's going to be tough to prosecute." Then he smiled. "But it's going to be worth it."

"It seems a remark from John Selkirk started all this. He ridiculed Sorrell. Said he was spineless. Said he let too many things stand in his way. Said he ought to take what he wanted. He decided to take Sandy Sweet."

"I try that with Pamela she'd drop a mold on my foot." Then a thought struck. "Did this happen before or after Bryce's death?"

"Don't know. Bill Simms heard the confrontation between Sorrell and Selkirk, and he wasn't sure. It was about the same time. Sorrell came to the dealership to get his limo fixed after an accident."

Bray pushed a frustrated hand over his eyes. "It was after." This time he finished the scotch. "The night of the murder the chauffeur took the limo without permission, slammed it into a tree, and skipped town. We never found him."

He called to the bartender, "Beer this time." When a mug was safely in his grasp, he said, "We thought for a moment that he might be involved, but there was no connection at all. I guess there's no connection here, either. You were right." For an instant he sounded depressed, but then grinned broadly. "Grogan was wrong. Grogan is wrong. I've been shinnying up the wrong pole, and I've never been happier about it. It's going to make prosecuting the bozo even more fun."

Win weighed telling Bray the next part. He decided he would. "Something else happened today."

"I'll bite. What?"

"Peter Sweet accepted Christ in his jail cell."

Bray didn't reply at first. He took a long sip and stared at a dim light reflected in the dust-smudged mirror behind the bar. "Is that supposed to mean something to me?" he finally asked.

"I hope someday it does," Win said.

"I know you do." Though his eyes were distant, he seemed to be listening. "Jail can turn people crazy. Seen it lotsa times."

"I've seen 'crazy.' Peter isn't crazy. In fact, he may be sane for the first time in his life."

"You know what crazy is. Crazy is when you go to your favorite bar for a drink and to relax and you get caught up in a senseless philosophical discussion. That's crazy. I know you mean well, Win. But you're taking your victory too far. One more of you guys in this world won't make much difference one way or the other. The only thing that matters is that we haven't found our murderer and we're back to square one."

"We're a little further along than that." Then he asked, "Danish in the morning?"

"No. I need some time to think. You signed on to help find a murderer, and so far you've done a poor job of it." He ordered another beer. "I also got a millionaire to nail."

Mellow from the alcohol, Bray eased into his recliner and closed his eyes. Time slipped by. Had he slept? The phone was ringing. He reached out a hand and answered it.

"Sanderson?"

"Yeah, right."

"This is Grogan. I hear you got Sorrell."

"Yeah."

"Sorrell's untouchable."

Bray was fully awake now. "Sorrell's what?"

"You heard me. It's a shame it didn't solve your murder. I thought your theory had merit. Gotta go."

"Grogan . . . "

But he'd hung up.

Bray held the receiver for several minutes. Untouchable? Nobody's untouchable. He punched another number. His voice clouded in sleep, Breed answered.

"Breed, Bray. I need to talk."

"Mornings were made for talk."

"This can't wait."

Bray heard a long resolute sigh and a few groans as Breed sat up, "Okay, shoot."

"I want to prosecute Sorrell."

"We'll talk about it in the morning. It's nearly two."

Two? Bray must have slept. "I want to prosecute."

Breed was firm. "In the morning."

"Grogan called. He said Sorrell's untouchable. What's that supposed to mean?"

Breed seemed to soften. "We'll talk in the morning. This is too much to talk about now."

"What makes him untouchable?"

"Powerful friends who have other powerful friends who collect favors and make threats. That makes him untouchable."

"I want to prosecute."

"Bray, lay off. This is real life. We're all big boys."

Bray felt a surge of feeling—betrayal, anger, defeat—but mostly betrayal. Finally he said flatly, "I got a murderer to find." He slammed the receiver down and, until dawn, assessed many things—many important things.

# Chapter 18

The tower bells at Sugar Steeple Church rang loudly for the first time in twelve years at 7:30 A.M. Monday morning. Even when they were being rung regularly, they'd seldom been rung with such energy and purpose.

Win rang them.

He'd started thinking about ringing them at five in the morning. Dawn was just a notion on the eastern horizon when his eyes popped open. The instant they did he felt the undeniable rush of a warrior.

And he knew why.

The battle was raging around him: at Ginger's with Chad, at the Sweets' where there'd been both victory and a sort of defeat, in the church, at an evangelist's tent, between Maggie and himself. And, of course, with Bryce. Win himself might be the next casualty. It was time to attack, time to jump in with both feet, strike a blow, and where Bryce was concerned, be an avenger of blood. It would take a bold, irretrievable act. An act that drew a line in the sand and dared the guy with the pointy tail to cross it.

As he lay in bed he came to the conclusion that the line in the sand would be drawn by the sound of bells.

He found a hammer in his garage and tossed it into the backseat of the Chevy and drove to church. He got there at seven. Unlocking the tower, he flipped on the naked bulb and quickly negotiated the first flight of stairs. He was about to do the same to the second, when a feeling of dread hit him squarely in the face.

What would they say? The police might haul him away for disturbing the peace. Worly would surely fire him. Though the magic checkbook would keep him going for a while, his father would probably cut him off if he lost the one job he had been able to get. If the police did haul him off, his ministry would be ruined because he'd have a record. No church would hire him after that and any hope for serving the Lord would be dashed. All because of one reckless morning when he didn't think things through.

*Stop. Think about what you're doing, Win. You're throwing a lot away . . .*

Win did stop, mid-stride, his foot poised above the second step after the landing.

*I've never taken a path I knew was dangerous.*

*And what'll it prove? That you know how to ring bells? Any fool can ring a bell. It takes a special intelligence to know when not to, when treading softly is the best approach, when quiet persuasion is the best witness. That's when the great truly become great. Flying off the handle like this is just another indication of how you're better off in a library looking up important facts so that others more in tune with the church environment can use them and spread seeds for Christ.*

Win stepped back to the landing and began to turn back.

No.

The voice was small at first but then became louder.

No.

"Satan, you're doing it again," Win muttered, spinning back and looking up the staircase toward the door above. "You're lying . . . and it's time you heard the truth ringing in your ears."

Once he was in the room, he hefted himself on a stud support and swung the hammer at the slats that had enclosed the bells for so long. The weathered wood instantly splintered with each blow, raining back on him and the grass below. He shifted places with each window, and after only a few minutes, the bright morning flooded in.

Now the rope. It was wrapped around the thick beams from which the bells were suspended. He reached up and fell short. Then he found a foothold a little higher and reached again. Still short. Finally, more out of desperation than any plan, he tossed the hammer at the rope. The hammer neatly clipped it, and the rope unraveled to the floor while the hammer rico-cheted off a belfry sill and fell harmlessly to the side.

Win peered out the narrow window. The morning traffic was beginning to form on Highway 2.

*Do you really want to do this? Think of the embarrassment. And people are only going to see it as a nuisance. You'll be gone, and they won't even remember.*

"Stuff a sock in it!" Win called to the walls and he grabbed the rope. Then, with all his considerable strength, he pulled it. He couldn't believe how loud it was. Boldly rich, the sound resonated in his head and chest, attacked his ears and the base of his skull. They were too loud, yet too loud was what he wanted. He pulled it again and again, and it rang again and again. Soon his brain ached. He didn't stop until his head could take it no more. And when silence returned, he knew the line had been drawn in the sand—deep.

When he finally stumbled down from the tower, his ear buzzed and his head split and the phone was ringing persist-ently in Worlly's office. Feeling the elation of victory, Win answered it. Worlly was on the other end of the line. When he heard Win's voice he came unglued.

After a restless night, Sandy woke to the bells. She'd heard and loved them as a child, and hearing them again gave her the feeling that all would be well today. As it turned out, it was.

She got word from the public defender's office that Peter could be released on bail. But, due to the violence of his crime, the bail was stiff, $200,000. Though their contribution to the bail bond would be only $20,000, that was more than they had.

To her joy, as soon as Steve Taylor heard, he hurried over and wrote her a check for the full amount. Sandy cried grate-fully and hugged him warmly. "You wonderful man," she managed through her tears and hugged him again.

After he left, Sandy called Ginger. Ginger's support the day before had made her special. Sandy told her the good news. "He'll be coming home today."

"That's wonderful. Is your place unlocked?"

"My house?"

"Yes. Monday's my day off this week. Actually thought about sleeping late, but something woke me—bells or something. Anyway, I thought I'd freshen things up—make it nice for Peter when he gets home."

"Really?" A warm ember glowed inside. "I can't believe you're . . . well, thank you. That's a wonderful offer."

"Good. I feel useful already."

Forty-five minutes after he'd called Win, Pastor Worly stormed into the church. Hearing his footsteps, Win decided it was best to meet him head-on. Win's headache had dulled and his ears still rang just a bit. But he was ready.

"What possessed you to do that?" Worly fired at him when Win appeared before his desk.

"I guess I was excited."

"You would have to be. That tower looks like a hurricane hit it, and I've been getting calls ever since demanding an explanation. And now I demand one from you."

Win had one. It didn't go into all the reasons he'd done it, but it was partially the truth. "I was celebrating. Peter Sweet came to know the Lord yesterday afternoon. That's cause for a bell ringing if I ever heard it."

"Don't tell me you subscribe to that nonsense."

"What nonsense?"

"The notion that God does not forgive us all is a devil's doctrine, Mr. Brady. Christ died for all. God forgives all. Christ is in all. Our job is only to point that out. The only salvation is salvation from talk such as this." Worly spoke firmly.

Win couldn't nod, that would be agreement. He couldn't smile, that would be assenting. He couldn't argue, that would be futile. He finally said, "A friend tells me that Peter's made bail and should be on his way home shortly."

"That's not my immediate problem," Worly said dryly.

"That would be me. Right?"

"Very perceptive. Those bells had been silent for many years. I don't know how long. And it's been our intention for them to remain so. I want you to clean up the mess you made, tie up the bells, and board up the windows again. Youthful exuberance is an excuse once. Never a second time. Is that clear?"

"Very," said Win. Of course, he had no intention of silencing the bells too soon. Ringing them had been a blow for Christ, and silencing them would be a blow against Christ. Win couldn't do that. Something mischievous inside him, though, prevented him from saying so. He wanted the victory to linger, and leaving things as they were for a while would do that.

"Then you'll get started right away."

"I'll start gathering up the materials. It would be nice to do a nice job."

"Good."

As Win left and heard Worlly on the phone apologizing to Charlie Briggs, he had the impish feeling he was playing a game of cat and mouse. Just how long could he delay repairing the belfry?

He grinned as he made his way back down the hall to his office. But then he sobered. He had the uncomfortable feeling Jesus wouldn't play this game. Maybe he'd ring them again tomorrow morning. Just one more slap at Satan's face.

Back in his office he poured himself a cup of coffee and was about to take his first sip when the exhilaration of what he'd done broke over him anew. The only thing that could possibly make this moment better was to feel the wind off the lake, smell the sweetness of it, and sense its wonder and beauty. He deserved rest and recuperation—R&R—from the battle. He deserved a walk through the woods and along the cliff in back where the wind off the lake lived. He decided to take it.

The meadow grass, deep and green, speckled with yellow dandelions, brushed against his legs as he walked to the maple grove and then to the cliff's edge. He stood there for a moment savoring the morning breeze.

The sky blue of the lake was melting into the blue of the sky. Several white-capped sailboats snuck between the swells, and a distant ferry eased away toward New York.

Restless energy directed his feet north, and he skirted the edge of the cliff toward a road he'd seen his first day that led down to the beach below.

Voices.

He cocked an ear. With no wind to churn the waves the voices drifted up to him. A woman's angry tone. A man answering. It was impossible to decipher words, but the emotions were clear enough.

Silently he moved along the cliff to another vantage point. A Ford Probe. Bill Simms. Now he recognized the other voice—Maggie.

He stepped gingerly along the crest to see if he was right. There was Maggie's Taurus.

"How could hearing something like that make any difference?" Maggie pleaded loudly, her voice dropping at erratic intervals when she realized how loud she'd become. "They're just bells—you hear 'em every Christmas at the malls. What about doorbells? You don't suddenly change your whole life when you press a doorbell!"

"Depends on the doorbell," Bill countered. "Listen, you know how I feel about you, but when I heard the bells this morning what little conscience I have got the better of me. It's time we stopped this."

"But you can't," she pleaded, as if her whole life were in the balance. "You just can't walk out on me like this."

"It's not right, Maggie. I'm no prude, but it's just not right. And the bells . . . my dad fought like mad to keep the bells. My dad would kill me if he knew what I've been doing."

Maggie's reply was too soft to hear, a gentle cooing. Bill's, too, dropped below what Win could understand. He moved closer and saw that Maggie had prevailed. The two were leaning against the rocks locked in an embrace. Finally they separated. He saw Maggie keep her arms around Bill's neck, her hands clasped. "You don't want to lose that, do you?" she said.

"Now that my self-respect's gone it's all I have left," he said, unclasping her hands and pulling away from the rock. He moved toward his car. "I'm already an hour late for work."

"I'll make sure you're paid for it."

Bill smiled sheepishly back at her. "Maybe I already have been."

Maggie all but melted. Win saw her knees buckle slightly, and she literally had to fight to maintain her footing. "I love you, Bill."

"I'll call you," Bill said and he climbed into the Probe, fired it up, and sprayed gravel as he sped toward the highway.

Maggie leaned dreamily against the boulder. Suddenly she heard a "whoop" and the sound of rocks and dirt dislodging above and cascading down the cliff. She also heard the yelp of someone bounding down with it. She turned in time to see Win do a bottom-bounce off the boulder above her, then tumble sidelong to the not-so-sandy beach. Her instinct was to run to him and try to help. But she fought that instinct and instead stood over him while he rubbed the bump on the back of his skull and the bruise at the base of his backbone.

"Ooooo," he groaned. The groans stopped when he looked up and saw her gazing down at him. "Hi." He grinned.

"You pig," she spat, her anger like a flare. "You were listening. How dare you listen to private conversations."

Still aching from his fall and trying to buy time, Win struggled to a sitting position, his long legs finally arranged in front of him. "I was walking and happened on your conversation."

"You were spying on us."

"Maggie, you've got a problem. You know you do."

Maggie didn't like that. Her chest puffed up, her eyes bugged, and she looked like an eruption was due any second. "How dare you judge me?"

"Maggie, I'm your pastor."

"You rang those bells this morning, didn't you? Only you would ring those bells."

"They're only bells, and I rang them for three, maybe four minutes. You people act like I killed somebody."

"I need Bill. I need what he gives me," Maggie stated. There was no plea for understanding, no apology or repentance. It was a fact, angrily stated. "If there's a God in heaven, why does he put me in a place where I need Bill?" Her head cocked, and her manner became softer. "I needed you for a day or two. But you made a choice. Now I need Bill more than ever."

"What if John finds out?"

"He wouldn't care."

"Sometimes men care, but they don't show it."

"What do you know? I could make love to Bill in the front room during the evening news, and John wouldn't care."

"Sometimes marriages seem that way . . . "

"Marriage? You know something about marriage?" She waved a hand. The argument was over. "There's nothing between you and me. There might have been but there isn't now." She took a couple of steps toward her car. "I've got to go."

Win got to his feet, legs and arms bruised, but there was no time to nurse them. "Maggie, you're right about my level of experience. But it doesn't take experience to tell you that Christ can be your refuge. He's there for us when everything else seems broken."

Without responding, Maggie forced a smile and said, "I'm leaving." A minute later her Taurus sped up the dirt road, leaving Win brushing the dirt from his pants and nursing his bruises up the road on his way back to the church.

The rest of the day was boring, except for his decision to seal his fate by ringing the bells the next morning. Win went home and watched the sunset by himself from his backyard. Turning back to the house Win was suddenly confronted by a dark, shadowy figure. Had he been standing his full height, the man would have been tall, nearly statuesque. But he stood with a weak slump, almost as if he'd just risen from a sick bed. The figure didn't speak but stood as if waiting for Win to speak first, his face hidden in darkness, outlined by the house lights behind him.

"Who's there?" Win asked cautiously.

"You know my wife," the figure said.

"Who's that?"

"Maggie Selkirk."

"John?"

The figure rubbed his eyes wearily as if he'd just regained consciousness after a long, deep sleep. *A tough day at the dealership,* Win thought.

"I heard the bells this morning," John said, his voice thin, almost lost.

"They sounded great, didn't they?"

"I haven't heard them in twelve years. A long time. It's like they woke me up."

"In what way?" Win asked. He wanted to get this ghostly apparition into the light. Everything seemed spooky in the shadows.

"Those are God's bells. Ringing for the Lord."

Win felt a spark ignite within him. Was John really saying this? He remembered the photograph of John actually driving the nails that closed the bells up. Had hearing the bells rekindled his faith? Was the Lord really going to bless the ringing of the bells by bringing back a sheep to the fold? It seemed too much to hope for.

"They were ringing for the Lord, yes. I was ringing them for the Lord. Come into the house and we'll talk about it."

"It's been so long," John said, his voice distant, almost dreamy.

"Do you want to come back?" Win pressed, taking a step or two toward John. John took a step back.

"I am back," John corrected, his face still darkened and his expression made indiscernible by the light behind him.

"Would you like to recommit your life to Christ? We can do that inside."

"Recommit? It's been so long." John turned toward the house. The backyard light must have been too bright for him, he covered his eyes as if protecting them from a bright sun. "I need to go back. Thank you for ringing the bells."

Win suddenly believed it important to see John's face—see his eyes as he spoke about his newly rekindled faith. He again suggested, "Don't you want to talk inside?" Win took another step, and John backed up again.

His face still in shadows, John straightened, suddenly startled. "I need to go," he said, his voice suddenly anxious.

Feeling like a fisherman with the fish pulling away, Win said, "No, stay. It's important we talk."

"Don't mention this to Maggie," John said. He then turned and walked hurriedly to the side gate. He disappeared beyond it.

Standing there suddenly feeling all alone, Win whispered to the darkness, "Ginger'll love this one."

# Chapter 19

Obviously preoccupied, Bray tore a piece of his half-eaten Danish, dropped it on his plate, then took a long swallow of his second cup of coffee. He ate the piece, finished the cup, and called for a refill. When Marge had poured it he eyed Win tensely. Win had told him all about John Selkirk's visit—how he found the visit strange, how it ended on an anxious note, yet how he had no reason to doubt the man's Christianity.

Bray had nodded absent-mindedly. Finally he spoke. "I'm going to leave the department for a while."

"A leave of absence or something?"

"Something like that," he said.

"Why?"

"Things have happened."

"Connected with Sorrell?"

"Partially," he said flatly. "I need to get away for a while. I was up most of the night talkin' to Breed. Then I called a friend who works for the DEA. He's been after me for years to turn my knowledge of the lake into something important."

"What knowledge of the lake? You're a landlubber."

"Who's a landlubber? I know this lake. Well enough, anyway."

"What are you going to do?"

"Drugs are flowing down the lake from Canada. I'm officially on a special detail working with DEA."

"What about Bryce's murder?"

Bray's eyes dropped sheepishly then came up again. "Breed's closing it. He's going with the transient theory and putting it inactive." He rubbed the side of his nose and continued, "Actually he's tired of it and doesn't see it going anywhere."

"Then I'm fired."

"From this job anyway."

"No more coffee and Danish," Win stated, noting the anxiety in his friend's eyes. "You okay with this?"

"I got some things to work out. I'm a good cop—I want to do good-cop things."

"We going to see each other now and then?" Win asked.

"Buy drugs and you'll see me."

"Couldn't I just call?"

"That's another alternative."

"What happened that caused all this?" Win asked.

"They're not going to prosecute Sorrell."

"Why?"

"They got reasons."

"Good reasons?"

"Reasons I can't stomach."

Win paused, a charge of frustration rifling through him. "Well," he said, "at any rate, I'll keep working . . . "

"Keep me posted. I realize I'm not supposed to think so, but since the Sorrell thing worked out the way it did, I've come to think you might be on to something."

"Ah, a breakthrough." Win laughed gently.

"My arteries go rock hard when I think about telling Pamela."

"Sounds serious."

"For me it is. Being alone stinks, but women are funny. They can run hot and cold. Right now she's running warmish. But I'm not much of a catch—and running up and down the lake getting shot at makes me less of one. I don't know how she'll take it."

"Everything will turn out fine," Win said with a huge smile.

"Is that it?"

"I hope you find Christ out there. Without him there are no real words of encouragement."

There was no smart comeback. Only a smile laced with friendship and appreciation. Then a wave and Bray was gone.

Win looked over to Marge. "Want more coffee?" she asked, walking his way.

He nodded.

Marge poured the coffee and while she did she said, "I hear you're the bell man."

"Guilty."

"Do it again. We can use the business."

"I'd planned on ringing them this morning, but I overslept."

"They're giving you a hard time, I bet."

"How'd you know?"

"This wouldn't be Grand Isle if they didn't."

She returned to her place behind the counter while Win thought about his evening visitor, the one brought by the bells. John Selkirk. Should he go see him? If John did want to recommit himself, even if he was experiencing some reluctance, wouldn't he be glad for a visit? Or should he wait and possibly lose him? But he couldn't lose him. If the Lord wanted John to return to the fold, John would return. He decided to wait for John to contact him again.

What would John's recommitting himself to Christ mean to Maggie? *Everything,* Win decided. Maggie would have everything she wanted. Everything.

That night Win was sitting on his pier. He missed Ginger and was so lost in thought about her and a possible future with her that he didn't hear the buzz of a small outboard approaching. He only heard it when the buzz stopped and the hull of the twelve-footer bumped the wooden pilings, jolting him from his thoughts. He looked down to see Chad looking up.

"I don't think your mom wants you out after dark."

"I know the lake well enough."

"From what I've seen that's like saying I know a wildcat well enough. Knowing doesn't protect you from it."

"I don't need protecting."

Win smiled at the foolishness of the statement and the futility of convincing Chad that it was foolish. "So what can I do for you?"

"I just came by to tell you that I don't like you."

"You could have phoned that news," Win told him, undisturbed.

"And that if you marry my mom I'd make your life a living hell. I mean it."

"I'm sure you do. I'd do things differently though."

"How?"

"I'd try to love you the best I could."

"Your best won't be good enough," Chad said, his voice hard as nails. "A living hell. And I can do it."

"I believe you can," Win affirmed over the engine's buzz. "You're remarkably bright for your age. I've not heard Bogart imitations that good in kids twice your age. It's a shame you're not using that to make things better for yourself."

Win would have chuckled, but it was possible that Chad would one day be in a position to make good on his threat.

It was a strange moment for Martin Sorrell. He'd never felt like a prisoner before. He'd experienced humiliation, befuddlement. He'd been misunderstood, condemned through no fault of his own. But he'd always been free to leave. His father had always given him that option—to just leave.

He had always been afraid to exercise the option, but it had always been there. Even when he was exiled to the island, he could come and go as he pleased. Of course, he didn't please to that often. But at least he could leave if he wanted to.

No longer. The debt he owed to whom he owed it . . .

They had taken over.

The moment when he realized it was after an early dinner when he stepped out of his inn out onto the back veranda, a lush grassy area that sloped to the lake. One of them, the one who'd rigged the gas main and who'd been the television news cameraman, stopped on his way out. He grabbed Sorrell by the biceps. "Where you going?" he'd asked as if he had the right and the power to stop him.

"Just for some air," Sorrell said. The man actually looked like he might refuse him passage from his own home. He didn't.

That's why, when the young man eased up in the aluminum boat and asked him for a couple of bucks for gas for his outboard, Sorrell gave it to him.

"It's late," Sorrell warned as he plucked a five-dollar bill from his sleek leather wallet. "And it looks like some weather coming up."

"What do I care?" Chad Glasgow fired back, grabbing the money.

Sorrell watched the youngster as he gunned the engine and headed toward a filling station nearby. In spite of his age, the kid was free on that lake. Of course, if he stayed out on it, the wind growing like it was, he probably wouldn't be free all that much longer. But he was free now, and Sorrell envied him that.

"How long you stayin' out there?" came a voice from the distant doorway, the clear implication being that he'd stayed out long enough.

The Taurus rolled down Win's gravel drive and parked. It was about nine and a wind was coming up. Waves began to crash against the rocky beaches. Maggie opened the car door and instantly felt her hair being whipped by the wind. Normally she would have quickly closed the door and salvaged her hairdo. Not now. There was no point. She liked the wind; in a way, she wished it would sweep her away with it, flying hair and all.

A call from the front door startled her. She greeted Win, "Hi."

"Hi, yourself," he returned the greeting. "I saw your headlights. Thought I'd come out and see who it was."

"It's only me. And you don't have to worry. I just want to talk. I know it's late but . . . "

"Talk's fine anytime," Win said, holding the door open against the wind and waiting for her to enter.

"Worlly's still upset about the bells. He's actually sounded a few of us out about asking you to leave."

"And?"

"Believe it or not, Jim Marks and Bill Simms came to your defense. And Sandy Sweet told me how caring you've been. That made it too tight a vote to force you out. You've made headway at lil' ole Sugar Steeple Community Church. It's about time someone nice stayed around. Dan left far too abruptly. Your staying will be the first time that something I want actually happens. I count very little there. I guess I don't count much anywhere, but certainly not there."

"You count here," Win said, and he received the shy little smile he'd hoped for. An emotional flag went up. He liked those shy smiles far too much.

"So, what's on your mind?"

Had John finally talked to her? Was it now time for the thank-yous for ringing the bells and drawing him back to the Lord?

As it turned out—no. "I really appreciate how you've helped Sandy," she commented, fidgeting uncomfortably with her fingers. "Maybe you can do the same for me."

*Here it comes,* Win thought and he leaned forward attentively. "I'll give it a shot."

After a "here goes" breath, she said, "You showed Sandy and Peter real compassion—real love. I need a strong dose of that kind of love too."

Win nodded understandingly. "We all do—and lots of it. But sometimes *my* tank runs low—like I'm running on empty."

He must have said the right thing, for now she leaned forward, ready to tell it all. Casting self-conscious eyes at the fire, she said, "You know about my affair with Bill," she admitted, feeling a wave of relief break over her when she said it in plain English—no more innuendo. "The other day on the beach . . . "

"I know."

"When I met John he didn't pay much attention to me at first. He was pretty committed to church things, and I was going to Sugar Steeple just because my girlfriend was going. He was nice and everything . . . " she melted a bit. "Really nice."

"He must have paid attention to you at some time."

"He did. We ended up in a group that went out for a soda and ended up talking for a while. I think I fell in love with him that night. He was so warm and such a gentleman."

She looked so much the child. Win's heart went out to her. "Go on," he said encouragingly.

"You promised compassion. Right?"

"Right."

Maggie nodded and went on, "Well . . . when I was fifteen I ran away from home. I suppose I could blame it on strict parents or bad friends, but I can't. I just wanted to see the world, and I was stupid enough to think I knew the best way to do it. I went to Boston and after being there just a couple of nights I got cold and real hungry."

She eyed him appraisingly; satisfied, she continued, "I hooked up with this woman who took me in and before I knew it . . . I was a prostitute." She eyed Win again for his reaction. But there was none. It was as if she'd revealed she'd had eggs for breakfast. "I was a prostitute for nearly a year. It was horrible. I see all these movies where prostitutes have hearts of gold and being a prostitute's all fun and games."

"It's rough," Win affirmed, as if he knew.

"I was beaten up at least a dozen times. I saw a man killed right in front of me. I saw another girl slashed and disfigured."

"Sounds like the Lord protected you."

"And I ran fast. After a week I wanted out, but it took me

a year to get the courage. I escaped to a halfway house, a Christian one, and after I left I got a job. A girl where I worked was going to church, so I went with her." Her eyes searched the flames. But, after a while, she looked up at Win.

"When John and I started talking about marriage I never felt so happy. Never. Marrying John was a dream come true. It sounds trite, but it was. He was so much gentler, so much more loving than any other guy had ever been to me that I thought I'd died and gone to heaven. *And* he was going to be rich. Everything seemed wonderful. I even broke down one night and told him about my past.

"Then he took over the dealership and stopped going to church. But to me he was still wonderful. So wonderful that I even overlooked some of the not so great things—the mood swings, times when he'd just disappear for a day or so at a time. The business was so much pressure—so many things you have no control over—the economy, the product, the workers. There were times when he'd be loving and other times when he'd explode. But the loving times seemed to make the explosions bearable.

"About a year after he got the dealership there was this client—a guy who wanted to buy a fleet, a couple hundred cars. John came home in a snit, more than a snit, he was angry—almost desperate—said he was having trouble with the negotiations, and he wanted me to be nice to the guy one evening. I thought he just wanted me to be *nice*, friendly, boost his ego a little. The guy nearly raped me. His hands were everywhere, and when I told John about it he got mad at me for resisting.

"My heart broke—I can't describe it any other way. I could feel it split in two. This was my husband, the man who was supposed to protect me." Her eyes remained fixed on the flames in the fireplace.

"I can remember when he proposed. It was a night girls dream about. It'd been wonderful—dinners out, romantic evenings on the lake, champagne for no reason at all.

"One day we were on his boat. He liked to speed around,

slap off the waves. He liked nothing better than to spin around and slam over his own wake. It was exciting. Finally on the way in we saw a small beach, one we'd never seen before. It was late afternoon and a little cool. We laid a blanket down and snuggled for a little while. That's when he asked me. Suddenly the slamming around was over and I was gliding safely into port. No more bumps and bruises. John was going to take care of me—forever. And then, after only a little while all that safety was gone . . . worse. The dreams were gone too . . . I did anything he wanted after that. I became a prostitute all over again."

"Why?"

"Why?" She began to cry. She wiped her nose on her sleeve. "Because he wanted me to. He was my husband, and if he wanted a whore for a wife he was going to have a whore for a wife." She sniffled and her eyes narrowed, "But I'd also be someone else's whore—Bill's. I would have been yours, too, if you'd have had me." She brushed away her tears, dabbed her eyes, and finally stopped crying.

"That was more than revenge. The first couple of years with him had been heaven. He worked long hours, but when he'd come home we'd have a couple of drinks and snuggle down in front of a fire or in the summer, on the porch. We lived on the lake then and sometimes at night we'd take the boat out.

"And then, suddenly it was gone. He wanted it to be the same. He'd come home and want his snuggle time, or he'd want his time on the lake, or he'd want me . . . just me and raw, unadulterated sex. But things had changed. I was a prostitute now, and he was no better than my pimp.

"I could have divorced him. But there's no better revenge than an affair. And anyway, if I did divorce the creep I'd probably just end up with another loser. At least this loser is a known quantity."

"Have you talked to John recently?" Win asked, hoping he'd find some reason to forsake his promise to John and tell her about his visit.

"We don't talk much. I bet we haven't been in the same room together in over a month."

Win felt his heart leaden. John had broken through his guilt to visit him the previous night. Had his guilt re-enveloped him? Or had that visit just been a dream? Surely it had really happened. Win toyed with the idea of telling her everything but then remembered his promise and said, "Are you happy with your life now?"

"No. But anywhere else I go might be worse than where I am now."

"There's somewhere that's guaranteed to be better."

She looked up but didn't respond. "I liked Dan Bryce so much." Win's question reminded her of similar questions Bryce had asked. "When he was unconscious and being shoved out that little window I was committing adultery. Nice gal, eh?"

"Did Dan know about your relationships?"

"Everything. Those last three months you could tell Dan anything, and he'd listen. He was young and his advice was a little naive, but he cared. I told him everything. He even confronted Bill. I'd told him not to, but he said that the Bible said he had to . . . "

"Matthew eighteen."

"Right." She recognized the reference. "He mentioned that. Bill came unglued. I didn't tell John. John never knew, still doesn't know."

"But you just said you were out until two A.M. the night Dan was murdered. He'd certainly know."

"Separate rooms. We'd have separate houses if I had anything to say about it."

"Did Dan tell you about Jesus?"

"Every day."

"What do you think about Jesus?"

"I'm not sure. I wasn't sure then, and I'm not sure now."

"What isn't clear?"

"I guess I just don't buy it yet. If he's God then I'd better sign up pretty quick. But if he's not, then you guys are just a little nuts."

"More than a little," Win smiled. "Do we seem nuts?

"Listen, Win, I need your understanding. I need a hug or something. I came to talk, not to be converted. I need to be pumped up so that I can get back in the ring and do a couple more rounds."

"You need Jesus."

She stopped and leaned far back in her chair and finished off the coffee. Setting the mug down, she stared at the blackened fireplace. "I need a husband who loves me. I'm tired of revenge. I'm tired of trying to hurt people whether they've hurt me or not. I guess I'm a fighter who doesn't want to fight anymore."

He wanted so much to tell her that she might already have that sort of husband. Even if he had resubmerged himself, he could always come back to the surface. For a moment last night, he seemed so sincere. He simply asked, "What are you going to do?"

"I've decided to leave John. Not divorce him just yet. I love him . . . or rather I love what he used to be."

"Why did John leave the church?" Win asked. Maybe if he knew more, John's action would seem less strange.

She cocked her head. It seemed like a strange question. "Are you going to try to get John back into church? Dan tried—and failed. You're gonna fail too."

"Maybe. The way you describe John, it seems like he was a committed Christian at one time—when you first knew him—and then he just turned away. Why? Was he offended by something?"

"No. He inherited the dealership and never went back to church again."

"Too busy?"

"I don't know. He just never went back. More than that. He became hostile—angry. John had trained all his life to take that dealership. His uncle encouraged him. That relationship between John and his uncle—love-hate if ever there was one. John trained with him, did anything he wanted—but down inside he hated him. I'm not sure why, but it would come out sometimes. John never talked about it, but I knew it was there.

"Sometimes I think there was some revenge in John's wanting the dealership—he wanted everything his uncle had—his house, everything. But John was basically honest, hard working, business smart. The other nephew, Walt, was the opposite—he was a crook. Once did some jail time for theft. John wanted the dealership more than anything else in the world. It was his dream. And he was a great one for wanting something without working for it.

"When his uncle died, John took over," Maggie went on. "And everything changed. He didn't need church anymore—he actually said he hated church—he could run the race without it. Maybe the business grew because of it . . . "

"It certainly allowed him to use you."

She nodded gravely. "He never missed religion as far as I could tell. He filled his life with things—like all those old weapons he's collected—swords and things."

"Maybe he'll come back one day," Win offered, very interested in how she might react.

"That'll be the day cows fly."

Before he could answer the telephone rang.

"I'd better be going."

"No, stay. I'll get whoever it is to call back." He stepped to the kitchen and answered the phone. "Hello . . . Oh, Ginger, hi. Maggie Selkirk's here and I was wondering if I could . . . well, he came by here a while ago." There was a long moment. "Now don't worry. He's not stupid. With the wind coming up he's probably moored somewhere." He clapped a hand over the receiver. "My friend's ten year old is out on the lake and there's some weather coming in. Or at least she thinks he's out there. I need to go help."

Suddenly a gust of wind hammered at the back door and the lake, illuminated by lights from the house, glowed as hostile waves began to form.

Maggie walked to the door. "Looks like a storm's coming,"

she said, concern in her voice. "Sometimes the weather stays like this and just worries us. Sometimes the storms grow pretty fast. Bill has a boat. He and Jim Marks go fishing sometimes. He'll help look."

Win pressed the receiver to his ear and spoke to Ginger. "We'll get a couple more boats to help. I'm sure all will be fine. See you in a minute." He hung up then scribbled Ginger's phone number on a piece of paper. "Have Bill call her, and we'll coordinate the search."

Then he suddenly thought of someone else he should call. "Mel Flowers? Win Brady. We may need your support tonight—"

Leaving Maggie dialing the phone, Win threw open the back door and headed down the walkway toward the boathouse. The wind slapped at him. There'd been a moon earlier, but clouds had been moving in all evening and now they were piled high. With no hesitation, he climbed into the Bayliner, fired it up, and as the engine throbbed he eased it onto the lake.

The lake instantly took control. Swells caused him to rise and dip, and though the violence of the storm hadn't arrived yet, he could see that it was on its way. Not used to being tossed around like this, he quickly remembered old seafaring movies and pointed the nose into the swells and eased the throttle forward. Seconds later, as the Bayliner slapped and plowed through the peaks, as cold spray clawed at him when the wind caught it and spit it at him, he took back control. He roared toward Ginger's.

Just as he made the turn around the point, out on the blackened horizon, a slash of lightning ripped a jagged seam from sky to earth. An explosion of thunder detonated—a sudden, nerve-shattering slap at the heart.

Win tied the Bayliner off and gave Ginger a reassuring, albeit quick, hug. "Maggie called Bill Simms—"

"I just got off the phone with him. He and a friend from Sugar Steeple are going to look on the mainland side. They said they'd see if they could get some others to help."

Another flash of lightning ripped a white gash in the black horizon—again the ear-splitting thunder. "This is horrible," Ginger gasped.

"I'll take the boat on the island side."

"But you're no better on the lake than he is," she exclaimed. "You've only had that thing a week. We'll end up having to rescue you."

Win headed back toward his boat. "I'll stay out of trouble. He's probably close by."

"We need more help. I'll call Bray. He'll know what to do. But in the meantime, you be careful," she cried at him, the wind a steady whine now. Even in the short time since Win had arrived, the wind had intensified. It now sent tight fists to flail at them. The water reacted angrily, forming white, frothy fists of its own and battering the shore. The trees became instantly restless, the limbs clawing and screaming as Win leaped into the boat, threw off the line, and fired it up. With a grave expression, he eased the bobbing craft away from the dock.

Ginger yelled, "Be careful! I don't want to lose you so soon after I found you."

Win blew her a kiss and pulled out into rough water.

# Chapter 20

It took Win some time to find the switch to the Bay-liner's searchlight. But when he did, it did a job. A solid white beam tunneled through the darkness.

Although Win couldn't see them, he knew the clouds were piled high, a lid on the darkness. The only relief came from lights that studded and partially defined the shore. But playing the reckless adventurer, Chad would likely avoid the lights.

The wind grew, buffeting the small craft and inciting a swarm of waves against it. Another flash of lightning ripped the sky to the south and west. Several seconds later bombs detonated in the clouds.

No rain yet.

Win found a prayer on his lips—more instinctive than deliberate—a few words asking deliverance for Chad and himself. He felt close to the Lord when he prayed it. Nothing changed at the amen, but he felt a little more courageous facing what lay ahead.

After a couple hundred yards Win slowed, eased the craft toward shore, and scanned it. The searchlight was brilliant, although darkness diffused and swallowed much of it. After sweeping the small cove twice, he saw no boats around.

Win pulled the boat a little further north, idled about twenty yards offshore and scanned the trees, rocks, and beaches—fighting brutal waves and currents as he did.

Inside her house, after leaving a message for Bray, Ginger paced. She could never remember pacing before. She always thought pacing was a theatrical thing, something characters did on stage when screaming unintelligible phrases seemed inappropriate. Leaving a message for Bray while her son might be drowning in a boiling lake was itself a seemingly hopeless act and only added to her anxiety. Ginger knew in her head that God was taking care of her. But somehow that message wasn't getting to her heart or her emotions. She was terrified.

She could lose her son and Win Brady on the same night. Her chest was a knot, her breathing erratic. She could understand the terror she felt for her son's safety, but she'd only known Win for little more than a week. Yet she found the thought of never seeing him again terrifying as well. And, as terrified as she was, there was nothing she could do. It was completely out of her control. That didn't calm her a bit. She paced, rubbed her hands, and massaged her temples. But after she realized that she'd paced from kitchen to front door, wrung her hands, and massaged her temples exactly three times in succession, she knew she had to break the cycle. Reaching the front door a fourth time, she grabbed the knob. Maybe she could do something outside.

But when she opened the door she found Mel Flowers standing there. Sandy Sweet stood beside him. Both wore grave expressions that changed to warm understanding the moment she stood before them.

"Miss Glasgow?" Mel greeted

"Reverend Flowers, I didn't expect . . . "

"Mr. Brady called," Mel stated warmly.

"And Mel called me," Sandy injected.

"He said something about your son being on the lake," Mel continued.

"Win's out there looking for him now. There's at least one other boat helping. I've called a policeman friend, but he's out. I wish I had more friends."

"It's time for me to return your kindness," Sandy said sweetly. "Coffee? Tea?"

"Strong coffee," Ginger prompted.

"And Miss Glasgow and I will go into the other room and

say a prayer. God's in control of this thing, and we need to tell him that we trust him."

At that moment, Win Brady was thinking how nice it would be back at Ginger's. For the last half-hour he'd been plowing through the rising, indignant surf staying about fifty to one hundred yards offshore for a while, then moving in to search. Battered by waves and wind, he had found it increasingly difficult to hold the beam of light steady long enough to determine anything. Often he'd scan the shoreline several times before he concluded there were no aluminum fishing boats either in the surf or hidden on the shore.

He had a couple of close calls. Rocks studded the shoreline, and more than once he'd been scrutinizing the bobbing, lighted areas and lost track of the rocks. Twice he gunned the engine just as the currents were about to slam him into them. But this was Ginger's boy and, as the search wore on, Win was beginning to understand how motivating that fact was to him.

Having just spent a particularly grueling time in a larger cove, Win decided it was time to head to deeper water and take a look at a small island he'd seen a while back. Planting himself in his seat, he spun the wheel. The Bayliner responded and swung around toward the island.

Suddenly Win was confronted by a huge, surf-battered boulder. Partially hidden by writhing waves, it had been invisible in the blackness. Reacting, he spun the wheel to starboard. The Bayliner reacted, but not fast enough. The bow swung, but the stern slammed into the rock. The hull squealed like a wounded animal, then screamed as its flesh was violently torn. Win pushed the throttle as far as it would go. The engine screamed and the bow leaped high then slapped, jarring him, but within seconds he was out of danger.

Until he sensed his feet sloshing in water.

The stern sat low in the water, a steady stream coming in through the hull.

"Great," he sighed, "I'm sinking."

Feeling surprisingly calm, he backed off on the throttle, spun the wheel toward shore, then hit the throttle again. Initially the boat had good speed, but then it slowed as the stern filled with more water. When the water reached the engine, it sputtered, caught again doggedly, went another twenty or thirty yards, then sputtered again. Then died.

Fortunately he wasn't far from shore. He rode the sinking boat until its hull dragged the bottom. When it did, Win grabbed a tie rope, jumped into the surf, and waded ashore. Dragging the boat as far as he could, he tied it up to a nearby tree.

Wet to the skin and defeated, Win made it to a nearby road, and after he finally figured out where he was, he started walking toward Ginger's.

Ginger gasped when she saw Win standing at the door. His sandy hair was in his eyes, his clothes were soaked, but worse, he looked horribly dragged out, beaten. "I didn't find him."

"What happened?"

"I hit a rock. Tore the boat up. It's tied up in some cove up the way. The storm'll beat it to a pulp before morning."

"Are you okay?"

"Maybe I need a boating lesson or two."

Sandy brought him a towel and as Win dabbed his face dry there was a knock at the backdoor. Bray Sanderson, a yellow rain slicker melted around his face, opened it cautiously. "You okay?" he called in to Ginger.

"No," she replied, "Chad's still out in that storm."

"I notified police dispatch. They'll have their eye out on shore. I called a few of the off-duty guys with boats. A couple are out there right now looking around. But I got the real remedy tied up at your dock."

"Really?" Ginger brightened. "What?" She stepped to the back window. At the end of her short dock, a sleek speedboat bobbed in the waves. "Where'd you get that?"

"From drug-busting friends and associates," Bray announced, then eyed Win. "Come on."

Ginger cringed, turning to face Win. "I don't know about this."

Win's brows dipped. "What?"

"I nearly lost you once tonight," she said, turning to Bray. "And you know about as much about boats as he does."

"A mere perception, beautiful lady," he said, sounding more alive than she'd ever seen him. "It's fast, Ginger. We can look in a lot of places real fast."

"But a wave could catch you and flip you like a pancake."

Bray placed a reassuring hand on her shoulder. "Nothin's gonna catch us in that thing. Least of all a wave."

Bill Simms and Jim Marks were on the opposite side of the island from Win and Bray. Bill was at the controls, it being his boat, and he guided it deftly through the raging swells.

On dry land, Jim lived cautiously; on the lake, however, he exhibited an uncharacteristic animation. Tonight was no exception, and Bill was grateful. Not only because he was a far better fishing companion than a fellow trustee, but Bill also knew that tonight he'd need Jim's energy.

In the distance the lightning danced—tangled threads of fire dangled for an instant then disappeared, thunder rumbled, its elephant walk closing in. "I can never get over the lightning," Jim mused.

"When the brunt of the storm hits I want to be by a fireplace somewhere." Bill grabbed the radio mike. "Win Brady's out there somewhere. Let's see if we can raise him."

To Bill's surprise, they heard Win's voice a few moments later. "You wouldn't believe what I'm in out here," the assistant pastor said.

"It better be seaworthy. In about an hour that storm's gonna hit. What we got now are just the preliminaries. The main bout's gonna be something."

"Have you seen anything?"

"No, but we haven't covered that much ground either. Keep in touch."

"We will."


Bray's speedboat clipped the tops off the waves as it knocked along. He and Win were battered and partially blinded by the rain, but that didn't slow Bray down. Strapped into the seat, he kept a rigid hand on the throttle and eyes riveted ahead.

"Isn't this great?" he laughed. "Those DEA guys have great toys."

Win felt each slap and was nursing a tongue bite when he said, "I'm not as thrilled about this as you are. Do we know where we're going?"

"How well does Chad know the lake?" Bray asked.

"He's on it all the time," Win said. "He probably knows at least the immediate area pretty well."

"Diane and I used to spend a lot of time on the lake," he said. "I haven't been able to get Pamela out on it yet. Anyway, we found some caves, once. The kind a kid would like to play in."

"Where?"

"Don't remember for sure," he said. A brilliant flash tore the sky in front of them. Thunder slapped. "I don't like that stuff. Fries people."

Feeling the hair on his arm bristle, Win said to himself, "He'd probably like a cave. One with bats."

Then his ears perked. Voices scratched over the radio.

"Bray? You there?"

Bray acknowledged the voice.

"We just found a couple of people on Tory Island who saw the kid about two hours ago. Said he was headed east."

"Good," Bray said into the mike. "Keep at it. Out." He placed the mike on the cradle.

"Did you hear that? East from Tory Island."

"Two hours ago and estimated by people worried about getting off an island," Bray said. "It could have been four hours ago and east could be any direction."

Win frowned, then leaned back in the chair.

"Don't worry," Bray said, "we'll find your kid—probably at a friend's house."

Win understood the emphasis on "your kid," and he understood the implication. And now that he was trailing that kid over a dangerous lake likely to get more dangerous, the thought that Chad might someday be his responsibility scared him. Yet Ginger and Chad came as a package.

Oh, well, he'd cross that bridge when he came to it.

Bill Simms and Jim Marks had been searching for more than an hour, and they were tired. When they found a cove protected by a horseshoe of high cliffs and realized the storm's fury was locked outside of it, they decided to take a few minutes there.

Ginger was on her third cup of coffee. She could feel the caffeine working on her brain, and she longed to feel calm again. She prayed. Was God really with Chad out there?

"Reverend Flowers," she said, "Chad doesn't believe. If he dies out there he'll go to hell."

Flowers looked away from the back window where he'd been standing, watching the rain and the boiling lake beyond. "God uses times like these to bring his children to him," he said. "Don't worry, Ginger, God loves you."

"I can't remember what being loved is like . . . but I'm not sure it's like this."

"When this is over, you'll see God's hand in it," Flowers said as gently as he knew how.

Her house perched on the crest of a tall hill, Maggie Selkirk had a panoramic view of the lake. On a clear day she could see forever. On a night like this, she saw more than she wanted.

The prelude to the storm was already furious. It buffeted her windows, made the trees in the yard creak and groan, and flailed the front lawn. Maggie stood at the floor-to-ceiling windows knowing that Bill was out there. She tried not to care. But she did.

"Quite a storm," John said as he came in from his library.

"They're looking for a little boy lost on the lake."

"The kid is fish bait," John stated coolly.

"Bill Simms is out there looking for him."

"Simms? Why?" John showed interest.

"He's just helping."

John's eyes registered surprise, as if he'd become aware of something important. Then he nodded. Stepping over to the window beside her, he said, "He's a good mechanic." Something in his tone caused her to look up at him. It was concern— far more grave than she expected. "I hope he'll be okay—he's a good mechanic."

Maggie's brows dipped sharply. "I hope so too. He's a friend."

John smiled uneasily and went back to the library.

Bill and Jim noticed a large, white Victorian home nestled on a low meadow that skirted the inlet. After a few minutes the front door to the cottage opened casting out a broad wash of light. A girl about twelve years old, wrapped tightly in rain gear, made her way to a small dock not far from them. "Are you guys looking for the boy?" she called.

"Have you seen him?" Bill called back.

"No, but I have some coffee for you." She waved a thermos. "My mom thought you'd like some."

Neither could believe the kindness, and Bill sent the boat growling to the dock. Tying up, they took the thermos, poured some into the lid, and each took a sip in turn.

"Thank you," Jim said and smiled broadly. "This is great."

The girl was pleased. After they got her name, Jessi Radzinski, and address (Jim wanted to send a thank-you note), they finished the coffee, returned the thermos, thanked her again, and pulled out to the middle of the bay.

Simms eyed Marks. "It's been more than ten minutes."

"You sure?"

"Very."

Jim peered through the opening in the rocks to the storm beyond, "It's not safe out there, you know."

"If it's not for us, it's really not safe for the kid," Bill groaned resolutely.

After a furtive glance at the cottage, they eased their craft toward the open lake.

The sky above was black. The rain's intensity remained constant. The whole world seemed in a vise, caught between a violent earth and a falling, violent sky.

As they glided toward the mouth of the inlet, the lake became increasingly agitated. "I'm not looking forward to this." Bill said, his knuckles white as he held the wheel.

A salvo of thunder went off like a cannonade. Detonating just overhead, the sound fell like an axe to the skull. Overcome by instinct, Jim ducked. When the moment passed he looked up to see Bill's surprised face. "Like 'Nam," he explained, sheepish eyes darting away.

"You were in Vietnam?"

Jim only nodded.

It was a surprising revelation. Jim Marks didn't seem like someone who'd lived through a war. Or maybe it was the war that had shaped him.

Closing in on the opening to the cove, the boat began to thrash more violently.

Bill aimed it toward the center of the inlet and gunned it.


"There!" Bray thrust a finger into the rain and throttled back. The engine became a cavernous grumble, the boat no longer jetting across the waves, tossed unmercifully in the surf. "I think I see them," Bray announced.

Win leaned forward, squinting, trying to penetrate the blackness. "What? The caves?"

"Let's throw some light on the subject," Bray said and

flipped a switch on the control panel. A sudden ray of intense white flooded the cliff in front of them.

"Impressive," Win said.

These cliffs were ragged and stacked high with rusty earth and boulders. The lake frothed angrily at their feet, boiling with sharp indignation against an adversary that would not be moved.

The beam did little to illuminate the caves, but it did highlight every detail on the cliff's face.

Win straightened. Something had moved. "Shine it over there." His arm went up to the right of the caves.

Bray saw immediately and directed the beam where Win pointed.

"It's a man," Win cried.

Sure enough, someone was plastered against the face of the cliff, hands clinging to rocks above, feet planted on a ledge below. But he wasn't stranded there. He was climbing down. When the light hit him his face turned toward them. Startled, his face blistered by the brilliance, he looked like he wanted to shield his eyes with his hand, but had he let go he would have fallen.

"Can we talk to him?" Win asked anxiously.

Bray grabbed something that looked a little like a bullhorn and pressed it to his lips. "You on the cliff—can you hear me? If you can, wait a second then just talk to us normally." Then he grabbed another bullhorn thing and handed it to Win. "Point it at him."

Win did, though the boat bobbing around made it a challenge.

Suddenly, a blast of lightning, the sound of an intense rip, and a tree atop the cliff exploded in flames, fragments of fire cascaded down the rocks. The man on the cliff attempted to melt into the rock as flaming debris cascaded only a few yards from him. "Did you ever have an idea just go bad on you?" they heard the man say.

Bray shouted through the bullhorn, "What are you doing up there?"

"Trying to be a hero," the man said through the back of the device.

"How?" Bray fired back.

"There's a kid down there—"

Bray and Win stiffened. "Where?"

"Down there," the climber managed, pointing with a strained nod of the head. "Maybe still alive—last time I heard him was a while ago—I think I've gone as far as I can go."

"Where is he?"

"In a hole. I heard him screaming. Thought I could climb down—bad decision."

"Can you climb back up?" Bray called out.

"Up's easy—down's tough," came the reply.

"Then start climbing. We'll take care of the kid." Bray knew instantly that "taking care" of the kid was going to be no picnic. He eased the throttle forward, and the powerful engine growled in response. They moved closer to shore.

"Hole? Do you know what he's talking about?" Win cried over the engine, wind, and pounding surf.

"The boulders along the edge are in all sorts of weird formations. He probably . . . " Suddenly he pointed toward a string of irregularly shaped boulders that looked like a jaw of bad teeth. "His boat!" Bray shouted and pointed.

An aluminum boat like the one Chad had "borrowed" lay wedged between two of the more formidable looking bicuspids. "He's got to be over there somewhere," Win shouted back.

"I'll get as close as I can. See if there's a helicopter available."

"In this weather?"

"Call 'em."

Win did, and the police command center said they'd have one in the air, if anyone would fly it, as soon as they could.

"Pass the amplifier along the rocks there. Maybe it'll pick up something."

To their surprise, it did. A boy's cries for help—frantic, strangled by a raw throat.

Bray pushed the boat closer but had to pull it back when the lake grabbed them and nearly propelled them to a rocky spike. "I can't get much closer. Any more and they'll be out here rescuing us."

Win eyed him with a grim resolve.

"Don't even think it," Bray argued. "You'll be beaten to death out there, and the kid will still be in trouble."

Win only smiled as he slipped out of his wet tennis shoes and rain gear. "A man's gotta do what the Lord gives 'im." And without a moment's hesitation he leaped into the surf.

Those long nights on the exercise equipment now mattered. The instant he hit the angry water and its cold wrath closed around him, he called upon those hours of training. But even though he stroked and kicked powerfully, the angry lake tossed him around like a stick, carrying him toward the boulders as if it had every intention of plastering him all over them. But he couldn't think about that. He thought only of the Lord and Chad. He prayed with every stroke. God had to be in control because Win knew *he* wasn't.

Suddenly he was there. At the rocks, at those teeth, the waves slamming him against them, then pulling him out to slam him again. Each time he hit with another part of his body. His shoulder first, his side next, then his feet. Each time he'd attempt a foothold, or try to grab something, and each time he came to the same conclusion. There were no footholds, and there was nothing to grab. Like teeth, the boulders had been battered clean and smooth.

He tried to work himself to a different place and was beginning to make some headway when a huge swell lifted him up. He could feel himself at the mercy of the wave, could feel its overwhelming power, more powerful than any that had come before it. This was it. Battling for breath, his sides and ribs aching with bruises and lack of oxygen, he knew when he hit the rocks this time, they'd have to fish him from the lake piece by piece.

The wave came down and he came with it. The world turned to stone, and the water washed away from him and the rain battered him again. Eyes open, he saw that he had been deposited in a wedge between two boulders. He was about to survey his cuts and bruises when he heard Chad's unamplified cry for the first time, over to his left. But as it echoed off the rocks, it was hard to pinpoint where he was.

Since standing would be too dangerous, he began to crawl in the general direction, working bruised knees and hands over the rocks. "Chad? That you?" he cried, his ribs aching with the effort. "Chad?"

"Win? It's you? Really?" Hoarse, but now charged with excitement, Chad cried out, "Help me. Please help me. The water's coming in, and I can't climb out."

"On the way," Win called back.

He crawled faster, dodging powerful waves that battered the wall of boulders. The easiest going was on the inside of the "jaw" where he was able to stand and run occasionally. Finally, reaching the hole, Win peered in. About five feet across, its smooth walls were formed by several tall boulders. The boulders probably protected it from the lake outside, except in weather like this when the lake went wild. Now they failed. At the bottom, standing in chest-high water, was Chad, his terrified face staring up at Win's.

As that moment, a huge wave broke over the top and a stream of water cascaded into the hole. The water level rose only a few inches at a time, but the times were getting close enough together that Chad only had a short while left. Win needed to act quickly.

"Enjoy your ride on the lake?" he called down.

"I can't get out of here."

"Well, we'll just see about that," Win said. Lying beside the hole, Win reached down, but they both saw immediately that that was futile. Even when Chad worked his way up the side as far as he could, a couple of feet separated their hands.

There was only one alternative and when the next wave broke over the top and sent an unusually large stream into the hole, pushing the level near Chad's chin, Win slid down into the hole beside him. His added bulk pushed the water level over Chad's head, but the boy bobbed quickly to the surface and pressed his nose to Win's chest.

"Now we're both stuck," Chad stated.

"Climb on my shoulders."

"Really?"

"Here, put your foot in my hands."

Chad looked immediately both grateful and overwhelmed. Another wave came and although the stream of water wasn't as formidable as the last, it pushed the level up another couple of inches. "What about you?" Chad asked.

"We'll cross that bridge when we come to it. Get on my shoulders," Win insisted.

Obedient, but still frightened, Chad planted his foot in Win's cupped hands, then felt an immense relief when he found himself sitting piggy-back on Win's shoulders.

"Stand up," Win cried.

Holding Win's hands for balance, Chad stood on the strong shoulders.

"I can't just leave you here," Chad cried down.

"Bray's in a powerboat just offshore. Tell him what's happening—anyway, I think I can shinny up these rocks. I should be all right."

Chad let go of Win's hands and threw his own at a jagged handhold. A moment later he stood on the rocks, safe.

Another wave pounded the rocks, and another stream of water emptied into Win's little pool. The water was up to his shoulders. Now he wished he had his rubber-soled shoes; in his bare feet, the slippery rocks gave him little traction.

He pushed a foot against one boulder, then the other against another boulder, but when he put weight on the first in order to step up, his foot slipped back to the narrow base of the pool. He tried it again, then again, each time, after one or two steps, he was back where he started. When he told Chad that he'd shinny out, he knew it was a long shot. He didn't realize how long it was. And now another stream of water poured in. The water was up to his chin.

Once it was over his head, how long could he dog-paddle? Maybe five or ten minutes. *Lord, any suggestions?*

Chad climbed as quickly as he could to a wedge between the boulders. Immediately buffeted by crashing waves, he ducked a few times to keep from being washed back, but after a moment to rest, he saw the boat. Knowing he couldn't possibly be seen where he was, he took a chance and balanced himself higher up and started waving and shouting.

Bray saw him immediately and grabbed the bullhorn. "Where's Brady?" he yelled, aiming the amplifier for Chad's reply.

"He's in the hole. He lifted me out, but now he's stuck."

"Great," Bray groaned. "Would a rope help?"

"Sure—a ladder's better."

"Don't have a ladder—got a rope, though. Step out of the way."

Chad ducked behind the rocks. A moment later a projectile flew overhead, a rope unraveling behind it. The projectile turned out to be a claw-like thing that slapped the rocks behind him, and fell only a few feet away. He leaped to his feet. "I got it," he cried.

He saw Bray release his end of the rope. "Pull it toward you then lower the rope to him. Wedge the claw between the rocks," he shouted.

Chad only nodded. He grabbed the claw end and laboriously dragged in the rope. When he had what seemed like a hundred pounds of wet line over his shoulder, he ran back to the hole.

Win was in critical shape. He was leaping to grab a mouthful of air before disappearing again below the water, which was already to his forehead.

Working fast, Chad anchored the claw between boulders and threw the line into the hole. It hit Win right on the head. Chad saw a face come up, then hands grab the line, then a huge expression of relief as Win began pulling himself to safety.

Bray had never examined his feelings for Win before. The guy had just come on the scene and spouted a few nonsensical religious statements. Yet Bray had sensed a safety with Win. He could say anything to the young man without worrying about it getting to the wrong ears or being used against him. Bray suddenly realized that Win was a buddy. Bray had had few buddies in his life. Now his buddy could be dying less than twenty yards from him with no one to help but a snot-nosed brat. Bray felt useless and defeated.

But when Win rose above the rocks and stood with Chad, waving, all of those feelings evaporated. Bray started shouting joyously. Greatly relieved, he tied a couple of life jackets on a rope, loaded the projectile in the mortar, and blasted it across. Then, he told them to hang on to the rope, and he reeled them both through the pounding surf back to the boat.

Chad, now truly safe for the first time in hours, fell into the boat and looked up at Win. "Thanks," he said, his eyes revealing that there was far more he wanted to say, but couldn't.

"You're welcome." Win smiled.

Bray was already on the boat's cellular phone. Although the signal was weak, he heard the cheers from Ginger's when he told her the boy was safe. Ginger's reply came over loudly. "Put Chad on. . . Oh, Chad, talk to me so that I can really believe it."

Though exhausted, Chad managed to sound truly grateful. "I'm fine. Win saved my life—he saved my life!"

Win wrapped an arm around the boy and gave him a quick hug. All seemed completely well. Through his joy and relief, Win heard Bray call to the man on the cliff. He looked up to see that he had arrived at the top safely. "We'll get you when we can," Bray told him. But at that instant their attention was drawn to the radio.

A static ridden, frantic voice grated over the frequency. "Mayday, Mayday," it barked. "It's Jim Marks. We're in deep weeds here."

When Bill and Jim had steered into the inlet, the violence of the lake had released them almost gently. But as they'd returned to open water, that same violence wrenched them from the calm with a tortured quake. Bill had been at the wheel, and the shock threw him back. Had he not grabbed the handle of the storage locker, he'd have been thrown overboard. But for an instant, the boat was without a helmsman, long enough for the lake to take charge. Within a heartbeat they were headed for the rocks.

Jim dove for the controls and gunned the engine, but it didn't respond. Perhaps water had gotten in, perhaps he'd throttled it too quickly and the engine had flooded. There was no time to figure it out.

"What's going on?" Bill shouted to Jim.

"Boat's broke!" Jim fired back with a strange calm.

Bill grabbed the controls again, but the boat was now only a few yards from the rocks. Just as it looked like they were going toward them, they were caught in a backwash and driven further away. For an instant they thought they were clear. Bill throttled the engine, this time more slowly. But it still wouldn't respond. "There's something wrong," he shouted to Jim.

Jim didn't reply, but grabbed the radio mike. "Mayday, Mayday. It's Jim Marks. We're in deep weeds here."

A voice scratched back. "Where are you?"

"Not sure. At the mouth of an inlet on the eastern shore."

"We need more than that."

"The . . . what's their names? Radzinski's."

"Radzinskis. Big house—white."

"Right. Gotta go. The rocks are getting close."

They were. Very close.

"Get that engine going," Jim said.

"It's going fine; it's just not responding."

The rocks loomed inches away, and a moment later they plowed into them. Their hearts lodged in their throats as they heard a rasping scrape, a yawning tear, and felt the boat shudder and quake, pressed between the relentless waves and the obstinate boulders.

Jim stated, "We have to climb these rocks. There's no hope out there." He cast a chin toward the boiling lake.

He was right. They wouldn't last a minute in the water.

Whatever they did they had to do it quickly. Hungry waves washed over the bow, and the stern had already been swallowed to the water line, while the boat's midsection was gnawed by the rocks.

But there were no footholds. Waves kept the boat strapped to the boulders and had turned the boulders to glass.

Jim took charge. He cupped his hands below his waist. "I'll heft you up. When you get there, grab my hand."

Relieved, Bill didn't wait to reply. He planted a foot in Jim's hand and felt a muscular heave. Propelled up the side of the rock, waves crashing around him, he reached out and felt his body spread across the boulder's face. He immediately began to slip. He grabbed at everything but found nothing. He slipped further, waves slashing around him like warring machetes.

Then he stopped. His Topsiders had caught on a razor thin ledge.

Jim called up to him, "Hurry up. It's getting wet down here."

But Bill couldn't move. If he moved his feet he'd lose his foothold. And there was nothing to keep him from sliding into the surf.

He called back carefully, afraid to move his lips, "I can't. I can't move."

A wave poured over him, and the force of it dragged him further down.

Suddenly he became aware that he had company. Jim was plastered against the rock beside him. How he got there Bill didn't know, but he was there, and the waves now washed over both of them. Jim didn't hesitate. Filling his lungs with strength, he scrambled up.

"How'd you do that?"

"I'm spider man."

"Well, don't leave me here."

"Grab a piece of rock. Then hold on and pull."

Bill grabbed and slapped at the rock, each time he tried desperately to find a crag, or fissure, or something—anything.

Having heard the Mayday, Bray cried to the others, "Buckle up." Then he eased the powerboat around in the direction of the cove with the large, white house. The Radzinskis had had a prowler one night and Bray knew just where it was. Win strapped Chad in the front seat, the safest, and himself on the bench in back, just in time. The instant his buckle snapped shut, Bray gunned the engine.

Another wave enveloped Bill. It closed over his head and nearly drowned him. Coughing, he threw his hand out above him, grabbing at whatever he found.

This time he felt something. His fingers took hold of a rocky rib and to his elation he pulled himself up. He reached again, nothing, but the second time there was a crag. Feet scrambling, he pulled himself up again.

Another wave.

It pulled him back, but after a moment's frustration and the horrific realization that delay meant death, he reached out blindly again—and again. He found a crag and pulled, then another handhold, then a foothold.

"Keep going," Jim called down. "It's only a little further."

The next struggle was a little easier—the waves weaker, the rock less worn. After a few minutes he crawled up next to Jim, who sat in the palm of a boulder.

"I'm still alive," Bill groaned. "I can't believe it." Although the rain still pelted him, he felt safe. He looked up to the summit. "We gotta get up there," he finally said.

Jim waved a weary hand, his chest heaving, and bawled over the thunderous sound of the waves, "You work with your hands all day long. You're in pretty good shape. I'm not. My legs are rubber."

"Do you think someone's coming to rescue us?"

"Sure," Jim panted. "You heard 'im. The Radzinskis are famous."

"They shoulda been here by now. I'm going up. I'll get to the Radzinskis' house and get some help."

"Vietnam taught me to stay where I'm safe. I'm safe. I'm stayin'."

"I'm going up." Bill was definite. He got to his feet.

"Stay here, man. Give the people some time."

Bill cast his eyes to the summit, swallowed hard, and shouted, "I'll get us some coffee."

The climb went easier than he expected. Although he slipped a couple of times, nothing kept him from reaching the summit. When he did he heard the growl of a speedboat and saw the lights. He ran to the eastern cliff and began calling and waving.

On the speedboat, Bray knew he was close and throttled back. That's when they all heard someone calling. Bray, Win, and Chad looked to the top of the cliff. None of them would ever forget what he saw.

A sudden tear of lightning blazed white and ragged. Like a serpent's electrified tongue it reached down from the boiling mound of black clouds toward Bill. Horror-struck, Bray, Win, and Chad watched the explosion of fire and sparks. Though it was all over in a split second, the image was seared into their brains—the figure of a man, twisted, frozen in the agony of death grotesquely silhouetted against a white ball of flame.

Chad's expression turned to stone cold horror. He instantly tore off his seat belt and dove into Win's arms, burying his face in Win's chest.

# Chapter 21

Except for their brief encounter the night before, Maggie couldn't remember the last time she and John had been in the same room. Just before 6:00 A.M. she pushed a blueberry muffin in the microwave for breakfast, then flipped on the small television anchored below the cupboard near the sink. The first few minutes the news was just background noise as she fumbled with the muffin again, prepared coffee, and tried to find a crock of butter in a hopelessly jammed refrigerator. But then she heard Bill Simms's name. When she straightened, the news cut to a wet correspondent on a cliff overlooking the still very restless lake.

The mike pressed to his lips, mournful eyes staring at the camera, he said, "Bill Simms had just spent at least three hours searching for young Chad Glasgow, who was lost on the lake last night. He and his partner, Jim Marks, navigated through a treacherous storm. After taking a quick break in an inlet not far from here, they resumed their search. They made their way cautiously . . ." and the voice droned on. The moment the newsman began she knew Bill was dead, and now the voice made it true.

She wasn't sure how she felt—perhaps just numb.

Bill.

Dead.

Dear Bill. So alive . . .

"Simms died?" John's voice came from behind.

She turned to him but was suddenly struck dumb. John was riveted to the television and did not acknowledge her even when she began to weep.

The commentator's voice cut in, ". . . through the narrow

passage and out to the lake. But the storm was too strong. It drove them onto the rocks. This is Bill's companion in the boat, Jim Marks. Jim, please tell us about those last few minutes."

Jim looked tired. "The boat was driven onto the rocks. I gave Bill a foot up, and he made his way to safety. I jumped and did the same. We were okay. The lake was pretty rough, but we were okay. Then he decided he wanted to get help. I decided to stay put."

"Did you know there was danger from lightning?" the newsman asked.

John made a sound like a gasp then clucked thoughtfully a few times.

"We had just beat the lake," Jim continued. "It was touch and go for a while. I guess we just didn't think about anything else. Sure, everyone knows about lightning. But we didn't think about it. I sure didn't. I was just glad to have my feet planted on land again."

The newsman turned to the camera and reported, "A tragic end to a hero's life. Bill Simms. Selflessly giving that last full measure of devotion that a young boy, Chad Glasgow, might be found. As luck would have it, the Glasgow boy was found just before Bill Simms's death."

The anchorwoman came back on, and Maggie sank against the counter, tears falling like the rain on the windows outside.

John said it again, "Lightning."

Maggie's tears were unashamed, her sniffling spasmodic. She grabbed a paper towel from the roll and blew her nose loudly and defiantly.

"Incredible," John mumbled. "It's done . . ." He started toward the sliding back door and then turned back. "You're crying."

She sniffled and hiccuped. As she tried to find words she hiccuped again. "I . . . uh . . . knew him from church," she finally said, thankful it sounded so true.

"Bill Simms . . ." he repeated, his voice strangely tense, a current rifling through it. "I know," John said to his wife. "I know it all." His eyes remained fixed on her for a long moment until she replied:

"I guess there's nothing to know anymore, is there?"

"Maybe," he said, his arctic eyes on her for another heart-beat. "It's happened, and now I'll be home late." He threw a grave smile her way then closed the front door behind him, leaving her with a chill cork-screwing up her spine. Something was going on—but she didn't want to know what.

After a wild and joyful reunion with his mother and a warm bath Chad fell into bed. But he woke up screaming at about two in the morning and didn't go back to sleep again until after three. When Win returned at about seven, Ginger was already up, her hair in her eyes, her eyes red from lack of sleep. But when Win stepped through the door after a soft knock, she dropped everything and ran to him. As she wrapped longing arms around his neck, she began sobbing.

He rubbed her back and she nuzzled his neck, and before long the tears became soft sniffles. "Thank you," she said, wiping her nose with a tissue.

"You get any sleep?"

"Seeing Bill Simms die made quite an impression on Chad. He woke up in the night screaming."

"I felt like screaming a few times myself," Win stated. "I bet Maggie's upset. She and Bill were . . . well . . . good friends."

"Chad's feeling pretty wretched about what he did. He's genuinely upset."

"It would have been a good time to mention Jesus."

"I calmed him down so he could get some sleep."

They heard a small voice came from the hall. "Maybe you could tell me about Jesus now, Mr. Brady?"

Win and Ginger turned to see Chad standing there, his shoulders slumped, his eyes ringed in red. Win had never seen a more hopeless looking ten year old.

"Well, okay," Win began and about fifteen minutes later,

amid tears and self-recrimination, Chad Glasgow came to know that he was in need of a savior and who that Savior was. Chad Glasgow became Win Brady's first convert.

"You saved my life twice," Chad finally said at the end of his prayer.

"Oh, Chad. I love you so much," Ginger exclaimed, scooping Chad up in her arms and hugging him until his eyes bulged.

Win smiled and gave him a hug of his own. "After a night like last night, I should think your mom would keep you home from school, just to recuperate."

Ginger nodded. "I think she would."

"Then what say we have breakfast out?" Win suggested. "Sort of like a family. Now that you're my new brother in Christ, and your mom's my sister."

"What say," Chad began, "we start talking wife in Christ."

"Chad," Ginger admonished. "We've only known each other for about ten days."

"He saved my life, Mom. He jumped into a hole and nearly drowned himself for me. I want him to be part of our family."

Win couldn't help but backpedal, "It's been a very emotional time for all of us. It's easy to get caught up in things . . ."

Ginger nodded, suddenly more detached. "That's true. That's very true. We both need a little more time. More time to know if what we feel is real." She looked directly into his blue gray eyes. "You do feel something for me, don't you?"

"Does a duck quack?"

"But it's not a zoological question."

"No, but there's some animal in it somewhere," Win said. "Rest very assured I feel something, a great something. But it's too early to talk marriage." Then to change the subject, "Listen, I lost my boat last night. I drove by the cove where I'd tied it up and it was gone. It's probably at the bottom of the lake right now. What say we take the day off and go boat shopping again."

It was a wonderful day. They ate breakfast at Judy's, found a larger, more expensive boat before lunch, made the decision to buy it over hamburgers, then Win wrote the magic check at about two in the afternoon. They all had a big laugh about the magic checkbook and by four-fifteen they were flicking frozen yogurt at one another in a nearby park. At five-thirty they were having a large pizza and at seven they were back at Ginger's.

And at 8:30, the three of them were sitting on the dock, the angry-tiger lake of the night before a purring kitten tonight. They sat silently together, none of them eager for the night to end. Win sat in the middle, Ginger holding his right hand, Chad his left. He thought back to two weeks ago at the seminary, with his two settings—Einstein and who? Daffy Duck—no— what was the other setting? Goofy, that's right, Goofy.

They heard a boat approaching. Over the glistening obsidian surface of the lake plowed Bray's powerboat, Bray at the helm. "You guys have a good day?" Bray asked.

"Great, actually," Ginger offered, giving Win's hand a squeeze.

Bray smiled at Win. "I was proud of you last night," he said as sincerely as he knew how. "I'm the one who should have jumped in, but I didn't. You did what needed to be done. I was proud that I knew you. Proud to call you a friend."

"Really?" Win said, his heart swelling in his chest. "I hope we'll be able to work together again."

"Well, wish me luck," Bray asked.

"Why?"

"I'm going to see Pamela."

"What are you going to do with her?" Win asked.

"I don't know. But she and I have to have a talk. I think I'm in love."

Win laughed happily. "All right! There's blood still pumping through those old veins."

Win felt an immense satisfaction for Bray. He knew his loneliness and had hoped for him to find someone who'd end it. Now only if Bray would come to know the Lord . . .

Win smiled. "I saw the look in her eye the other night at the restaurant. I don't think you have anything to worry about."

"Really? Her eyes?"

"Both of 'em."

Bray smiled. "Well, I'll see you later."

After Bray had glided away, Ginger said, "He's right, you know."

"About what?"

"You did do something to be proud of last night. I'm proud of you too."

Win took his reward in the form of a kiss and then got to his feet. "I'm about ready to fall over. I think I'm going to head home."

Ginger frowned. "Really? I was hoping we could sit inside and listen to jazz or something. Chad was just going to bed, weren't you, son?"

Chad groaned, but Win was having a tough time keeping his eyes open, so he kissed Ginger good-bye and headed home.

Barely getting there before his eyes slammed shut, he fell into the '57 Corvette and a moment later he was asleep. But a few hours later he woke to the phone ringing. Win slapped at the phone and finally answered it.

"Reverend Brady?"

The voice sounded familiar, but he couldn't place it through the haze. "It's me," the voice said.

"Uh, who?"

"John Selkirk." He had that same apologetic sound that he had the other night.

"Yeah, right," Win managed. "I'm sorry, I was asleep. Rough night last night. It's good to hear from you. What's up?"

"I've been hearing about Bill Simms all day. He was a friend of Maggie's."

"Of all of us," Win said, wondering where this was going.

"Life is so fragile," came the voice, so distant, ethereal. "We're not promised tomorrow, are we?"

"Sometimes the next hour's a bit iffy." Win yawned and eased himself up against the headboard.

"Bill has made Jesus real to me again."

"I thought he was real to you the other night."

"I have been teetering on the edge. Bill's death . . . " John paused. Win heard a deep, quivering breath as if driven by an unfathomable emotion, so deep that tears would be inappropriately shallow. "Bill's death toppled me to Jesus' side. I need to talk to you tonight."

"I'm still not recovered from last night. Can I meet you for breakfast in the morning? A little more prayer wouldn't do you any harm."

"I need you tonight. There's so much inside me—I've been so evil—I feel so guilty. I need to begin healing or there may not be a tomorrow for me. I've treated the woman who's loved me so badly—so very badly."

"Just tell her how you feel," Win said wearily, still hoping to delay the inevitable. "She's waiting to hear it."

"I need you—now." John insisted. He did sound on the edge.

Win pushed a hand over his face and yawned again. "Where are you?"

"At the church. In the back. I'm calling from the car phone. It's quiet here."

"Usually is about this time," Win agreed, eying the clock as he swung into a sitting position. It was 1:30 A.M. "I'll be there in a few minutes. Collect your thoughts."

"And prayers."

"Sure, prayers." Win got to his feet, climbed back into his clothes, and dragged himself out to his Chevy and drove to the church.

Driving past the bell tower, he continued on to the rear of the church and parked near the grove of trees where he expected to find John's car. It wasn't there. He got out of his car and walked closer to the trees. "John, you out here?"

In the dim glow from a nearly full moon, he noticed a white paper nailed to a tree. Stepping over to it, he found a page from the Bible. Printed on it in black marker was: "Hang on—be right back." In the dim moonlight, Win noticed a few verses on the page—the story Jesus told about the shepherd leaving the ninety-nine sheep to search for the one that was lost. Win smiled. *Appropriate.*

That's when the earth beneath his feet came up, wrapped around him, and lifted him unceremoniously into the air. Suddenly he was hanging eight feet off the ground—suspended in a net, twisted and bobbing, his feet pulled into an unnatural stance, his face mashed against the crisscrossed cords. "Oh, no," he groaned, his nose poking through the mesh.

"Like the pun?" came a voice he knew from down below. "'Hang on?' You hanging on up there?"

"John," Win said, the energy to speak causing him to spin and swing. "I can't believe it. When you slip back, you really . . . you seemed so sincere the other night." Still swinging and spinning, Win had difficulty focusing on the dark form standing beneath him. The moonlight helped—it reflected off a bald spot on John's crown then it caught his upturned face and his look of shame.

"It was a moment of extreme weakness," he said, then quickly turned away presenting the bald spot again.

"You're going to kill me."

John shook his head but looked up again, his eyes dark, shadowy holes. "I have to," he said. Win hoped he heard just a hint of regret.

"Have to?"

"Have to," he stated again. This time the regret ran through his words in deep furrows.

"Did you kill Bryce?"

The moonlit face came up again. Then a hesitation filled with thoughts and calculations. "A terrible night, that one," he said. "I was beyond angry—out of control. I don't get that way anymore."

"What happened?" Win asked, trying to keep him talking. While he was talking he wasn't killing.

"Bryce pushed me—wouldn't let me alone. Like all you people. What's buried is buried. What's forgotten is better left that way. But you people have to dig it all up again. Wave it in front of our faces. Anything buried a long time stinks. But Bryce paid. And you'll pay too. But his was a long time in coming, it was a slow boil inside me. When it got white hot, killing him was the only release."

"Why'd you push him through the window?"

Athletic shoulders shrugged. "There's a lot about that night I'm not sure of. I even tacked up a page from the Bible like I did with you." He slammed a fist into his hand. "I even chose a particular page, certain verses—the devil tempting Christ—"

"Jump off and I'll give you all of what you see," Win paraphrased.

"I helped him jump—it just seemed like the thing to do."

"Symbolic," Win said softly.

"And then I tore out of there. Forced Sorrell's chauffeur off the road. What was he doing out there at two A.M.? I couldn't believe it when that rich numbskull brought the car in for repairs a couple days later. I handled it okay for a while, but then seeing the car brought it all back. That was the second time I lost control. I vowed not to again."

"Don't you think you're losing control tonight?" Win asked him.

The face came up. "No—I'm *in* control. Killing you is just something I gotta do. I've done a lot of things I just had to do. This'll just join the long string."

"You don't seem angry now."

"I'm not—particularly. I should be. Those bells you rang stirred up the dust again. Just like Bryce did. I hate those bells, but I didn't get angry when I heard them. No, not angry."

"Then why kill me?"

"I made a deal—at least I think I made a deal," John said. He laughed distantly, tragically as if he'd made a poor, tragic joke.

"Deal?"

"No handshake or anything," John said, the bald spot moving toward a nearby tree and leaning against it. Then he shrugged as if stating the obvious. "No hands . . . I don't mind telling you I'm just a little scared."

"Scared? I'd be terrified. Killing two of God's ministers can't sit well with him."

The face came up white in the moonlight again—an expression as deep as a grave. "No I'm scared that if I don't kill you, they'll find out about Bryce."

"From me?"

"Maybe," John said. "The idea came soon after you did. I'd be sitting in my office alone, or in a sales meeting, or out to lunch with one of my fleet customers and suddenly I'd feel uncomfortable—like I was being watched. Afraid. I'd feel the hammer slamming against Bryce's skull, and I'd know that someone would find out any minute—the phone would ring and I'd be on my way to jail—disgraced. Found out. I hate that feeling. I'd shake it off in a little while. But only until it happened again. Then you rang the bells." His voice trailed away and Win heard him sigh a couple of times. "That was worse than Bryce ever was. I hate those bells—hate what they do to me."

"Jesus?"

An angry finger came up, blazing eyes behind it. "Don't mention that name to me!" Then the eyes immediately softened. "It makes me weak. I say and do weak things—like my visit to you the other night."

"And after I had a couple drinks at home it came to me—I had to kill you too. You were breaking me down again, and I can't afford to be broken down. Weakness could kill me. But the more I planned—the more I knew I couldn't do it. I'd killed Bryce in anger. I couldn't kill you coldly. And so I just got drunk." A jeering face came up. "You ever get drunk, preacherman?"

"No."

"After a bunch of booze that night, what I saw and heard was through a thick—very thick—fog."

"What things?"

"Weird things. Very weird things. Things that seemed to make a deal with me."

"Deal?"

"I guess. The next morning with my head splitting it all seemed like a dream—sometimes comical, sometimes frightening. I remember a question though. 'Who do you hate?' I remember it as if someone really asked it. Like a voice."

"Your answer?"

"Simms. I remember saying his name out loud. He was having an affair with Maggie. I tried to tell myself I didn't care, but I did. I even followed him some nights. Parked out there in the trees and watched them."

Win remembered the car door slamming the night that he, too, had heard Maggie and Bill.

"I hated him. So I answered 'Simms.' And then he, or it, said, 'Okay, Simms for Brady.' I would get Simms in exchange for you."

"Me?"

"And if I didn't carry out my part of the bargain, the police would find out about Bryce. It—whatever it was—would make sure of that. I woke up knowing the deal was real and yet it all had to be a dream—a nightmare, a booze-induced horror show. I tried to forget it—but couldn't."

"Then Bill was struck by lightning," Win stated.

John took several steps toward the church, hesitated at the edge of the trees, then turned back to him. "It had to be lightning. He couldn't have died from a bad hangnail or terminal bunion. There's something supernatural about lightning."

"Who's your deal's with?"

The face stared up to Win, but John said nothing. There was nothing to say. His dark, shadowy eyes said it all. It was immensely disconcerting to owe something to someone who tosses bolts of lightning at folks.

"So you think killing me will appease this—person?" Win asked.

John remained at the edge of the trees for a long moment, and the longer he stood there, the more his hands seemed to take on lives of their own. They leaped from his pockets to his chin, then they rubbed the side of his nose and remained cupped there. "It's probably just the start," he said. Taking a couple of steps toward Win, his eyes became deeply resolute. "I'm sure you got prayers you want to say. You'd better say them now."

While John Selkirk waited for Win to talk to his God, a set of ten-year-old eyes popped open. Chad glanced at the digital clock near his bed. 2 A.M.

He was wide awake. But more than awake, he was excited. He knew Jesus. He knew God—the real God, a specific God, the only specific God. He'd never even thought much about God before. He had always been something to battle against because his mother was always pushing God down his throat.

Not now—never again.

Chad never knew such excitement. He wanted to tell someone about it—not just someone, a lot of someones.

It was 2 A.M. but that didn't matter. He knew what he wanted to do. He grinned as wide a grin as his face allowed, leaped from bed, dressed, and headed for the garage. A moment later, the top rung hooked over his bicycle seat, he pedaled down the road dragging his dead father's long painter's ladder behind him.

Win's prayer was not so much a prayer as it was a frantic plea mixed with several abrupt detours into panic. Until John suggested he pray, Win thought he might still talk John out of it. But that hope had been crushed. Escape? No. The net was too strong to tear through and too tightly drawn to climb out of. And even if he were able to climb out, the drop would probably break his leg. In the final analysis, there was no way out.

He was going to die. He should be dwelling on great spiritual thoughts right now—about soon being with Jesus, about being a forthright witness for Christ up to the end, about crying to heaven to forgive his murderer as Christ had done. He felt profoundly guilty for hardly thinking about them at all. He had but one thought: *I'm going to die and I don't want to.* Strangely enough, he found the idea of not seeing Ginger again the most disagreeable part of it all.

"How does it feel to make a pact with Satan?" he heard himself saying, the sound of his voice surprising him.

The face came up but said nothing.

"What happened back then?" Win continued. "You believed. You were a good Christian kid. What happened?"

"Talk's over," the deadpan said.

Win watched as the bald spot moved over to a nearby tree. From behind it John pulled out a long, Excaliber-like sword—ornate, doubled-edged. "It's no Ginsu, but it'll do. It's part of my collection—eleventh-century Saxon."

He swung the blade and the brilliant edges glistened.

Win swallowed hard. "Would you have thought back then—before you boarded up the bells—that one day you'd be hooked up with Satan?"

No reaction. The sword swung again.

"You know, where there's a Satan, there's a God. You can't have one without the other."

The sword swung again. But with a beat of hesitation.

"All these years you've told yourself he didn't exist. Isn't that it? It's not just that you're making deals with the bad guy—but you're dealing against the good guy—a very powerful good guy. You're dealing against God. That's what drives you nuts, isn't it? You can't deny Jesus anymore."

The sword came up jabbing at Win. "I told you not to mention that name. Never mention that name." A jab punctuated each word. One punctured his leg. Warm blood oozed down his ankle.

"Cutting me won't change anything. You're all over the wall at church. You loved Jesus."

John's face came up, this time twisted in rage. "I did work for him. I did ring those bells—I spent Saturdays polishing 'em.

I went to all the meetings. Did meals on wheels. I did it all. And then he nails me."

"Who?"

"Every morning I read the Bible. Memorized verses. I agonized over the crucifixion. I did all the things good little Christians were supposed to do. And then he pays me back. The only thing I ever wanted was that dealership. From my cradle I wanted it."

"You got it. God gave it to you."

"God didn't give me anything. No one has. I earned it all—and what I didn't earn I took. I worked for my uncle. I worked every job—nights, days, weekends. He told me he'd leave the dealership to me in his will—even showed it to me. In those days I had two commitments—the dealership and church. My uncle and Jesus—there I said it. I prayed for that dealership night and day. On my stinking knees I prayed for it."

"You got the dealership."

"I stole the dealership."

"Whoa," Win whispered, startled. "Stole it? You throw it in the back of a pickup and take off with it or something?"

John fell against a tree, the sword point in the ground before him, his hands folded over the grip. "When he actually died I found a newer will. This one left everything to my cousin. A felon. It seems my uncle liked felons better than Christians— and since I was a Christian . . .

"God nailed me. He took the only dream I'd ever had and flushed it. Me and my uncle finally had something in common. We'd both had it with organized religion. So I took charge of my life and hid the newer will. I should have burned it. I ended up losing track of it and was so afraid of its being found that I burned my house down."

"Sometimes the Lord . . ."

"I don't want to hear it," John exploded, on his feet again, the point of the sword swinging at Win. "I buried that one long ago. Digging it up's only given me one more reason to kill you."

"But Jesus is real, you loved him once."

But the sword was up now. Like a pitcher in a windup, John swung the heavy steel weapon over his head. During the second sweep, his eyes came up to Win, again like a pitcher preparing to deliver the goods.

But the moment his eyes came up and locked on Win's—the tower bells began to ring.

Loudly, triumphantly—resounding hope, the sound reaching into the trees, bounding from limb to limb. And as the bells tolled, Win saw John's eyes suddenly shift, his face turn toward the tower, his shoulders drop and with them the sword. Showing only his back to Win, he planted the point of the sword in the earth and stood erect listening to the bells.

Suddenly his knees caved. Steadying himself with his hand, he sank to the ground.

Win could not see John's face, but he heard John cry, "Can't you leave me be? My life's my life. Can't you just leave me be?"

The words echoed off the trees, cut through the clattering limbs, were swallowed by the night.

"No, he can't," Win said.

John turned to him, his face streaming with tears.

"You're his, John, and he's calling you back."

"I don't need him—I've done it on my own. No one's ever helped me—no one . . ." but his head dropped to his hands and his voice crumbled to tears. Win wanted to wrap loving arms around John, to give him encouragement. But for one thing, he was hanging ten feet away. This was a moment between a prodigal and his father—no one else.

The bells had stopped. Now there was silence even from John below—the dark figure hunched now as if brooding. Win dared not breathe for fear of interrupting. His life seemed to depend on it.

Picking up the sword again, John stood. "The fun's only starting for you," he said, and he hefted the sword up, the point in Win's direction.

Win cringed as he saw the edge of the sword glisten in the moonlight as John took position. Whatever had happened in the last few minutes hadn't changed anything. "Get ready," John told him.

Win braced himself for his last moment as John swung the sword. Eyes closed, Win heard the violent swish and felt the net tug as the sharp edge cut the rope that held him. Suddenly the net dropped out from beneath him, and he fell the eight feet to the hard, but welcome ground. Relieved beyond words, he watched as John flicked his wrist and the top of the net fell open. Win was now looking at an outstretched hand.

He took the hand and was helped to his feet. But John didn't wait for talk, sword still in hand, he turned toward the church and began steady steps toward it. Afraid to speak, Win just followed a safe distance behind. When John reached the church's front door, he pulled a key from his pocket and opened it, then he stepped inside.

"Win!" came a call from above.

Win spun on his heels and saw Chad standing at the small window waving, his ladder still standing beside the tower. Win couldn't believe what he was seeing, but there was no time or energy to question it. He merely called back, "Good ringing. You don't know how good."

"I just had to celebrate and tell someone—I got a headache."

"It'll pass. See you in a minute. I'll unlock the inside for you. You'd kill yourself climbing from that window."

"Be right down," Chad said and disappeared inside.

With the church doors closed behind him he realized that John wasn't in sight. Hearing a voice coming from Worlly's office, he headed there to find John just hanging up. He glanced up as Win entered. "I just called Maggie," he said calmly, but with a touch of sadness. "I told her to meet us at the police station."

Then he turned his back to Win and studied the wall of books for a moment. Seemingly satisfied, he turned back.

"The one thing I'll never understand is why he didn't wake me up before I killed Bryce. . . . " Suddenly tears. They welled and broke so profoundly that John needed to steady himself on the edge of the desk. Win went to his side and held his arm thinking that he might be on the verge of collapse. But John was a strong man and after a moment, he brushed the tears away and recomposed himself. "Thank you," he said, taking a deep breath. "Come on. I've got some sins to pay for."

Win led John into the hallway and immediately heard Chad banging on the tower door. "Oops! Forgot," said Win. He ran quickly to the door and let Chad out. The moment the ten year old broke into the hallway, Pastor Worlly burst through the church front doors. "What's going on around here?" he called. "Who was ringing those bells? Who did it?" Seeing Win, he shouted, "I told you to board those bells up!" Then he saw John and Chad. He glanced curiously at the boy, but eyed John with great surprise. "John, is that you?"

"Yes. It's been a long time."

"What's going on around here? . . ."

"You'll hear all about it in the morning," Win told him. "We have to get going."

"But who rang the bells?"

"I did," Chad said without guilt.

"You? Why? Do you have any idea the trouble you caused?"

Win stepped protectively between Chad and Worlly. "He saved my life, Pastor Worlly."

"We must go now," John interrupted. "Watch the morning papers. I'm sure you'll read an explanation for all this in there." He turned to Win and Chad. "We need to hurry. Maggie'll be worried." He remained behind for a moment. When Chad and Win were out of earshot, John said to Worlly, "Don't be too hard on the boy. He saved my life too."

# Chapter 22

Normally John would have been arraigned in the morning, but after Win explained everything to Bray, Bray decided to avoid a media show and hustled a friendly judge out of bed. The judge looked over the affidavit and denied John's guilty plea and entered, over John's protest, a plea of not guilty. Since no bail was set for a capital crime, John was remanded to the psychiatric ward at Burlington General Hospital for preliminary psychiatric tests. After they were complete, he was to be held for trial at the North East Correctional Center on Ferrell Street. Except for his brief plea protest, John was quiet and orderly during the whole proceeding. Maggie never showed up.

"He's not crazy," Win protested to Bray as they walked out.

"He'll be more comfortable there than at North East. And he's got to undergo a brain exam anyway."

Only after seeing John cuffed and carted off in an ambulance, police cars fore and aft, did Win and Bray have a chance to talk. But Bray didn't want to talk. "I'm mad," Bray said coldly. "I did my job in there because I wanted to rub Breed's face in it—show him that whether the case was closed or not my plans work. And as far as he's concerned—" he poked a firm finger into Win's chest, "—all this worked according to my plan."

"Why're you mad? You are the one who brought me into this. In a way it was your plan . . . "

"It's got nothing to do with that, and I don't want to talk about it. If I never see you and your kind again it'll be too soon." He left Win standing in the Winooski Street station lobby while he walked back to his office.

At 8:30, after he'd only been in bed a few hours, Win heard

a banging on his front door. A moment later he felt a heavy weight bouncing on his chest. Eyes popping open, he saw Chad's knees inches from his chin, a huge smile on his face. "The papers call you a hero," Chad announced. "You risked death."

"No more than I am right now."

Ginger appeared at the bedroom door. She looked beautiful and smiled broadly. "John Selkirk? You fought him off and brought him in? Maybe you're not such a Pooh Bear after all."

"Is that what they said?" Win maneuvered himself to a sitting position.

"Something like that," Ginger said. "I'm proud of you. And the little guy too. Not that I want him to go around ringing bells at two in the morning.

"There's another reason I'm here," Ginger continued. "Maggie called."

"She was supposed to meet John at the station but she didn't come."

"She's apprehensive—scared, actually. Wants you there when she talks to him."

"Now?"

"Get dressed. She's on her way to the hospital—probably there already."

Where the day before Sugar Steeple Church was mourning Bill Simms's death, the news about John Selkirk allowed them a collective sigh of relief. When interviewed, Worly said it best, "Now we can return to what we are. We, as God's people, are vindicated. It was not one of our own who did that horrible crime."

Maggie sat in the waiting room with an old *Time* magazine, vacant eyes scanning the pages as Win, Ginger, and Chad stepped from the elevator. "You look horrible," Maggie said to him.

"Rough night," he replied.

Bray came down the hallway. "Oh, you're here. He's not my usual murderer. I can't shut him up. He's telling me everything. What he says is confirmed by all the evidence. He's still upset about the forced 'not guilty' plea. Why can't you people be so good *before* you commit crimes?"

"So he did kill Dan?" Maggie said, her voice soft, but iron with anger.

"He did," Win said, turning to her. "Not to minimize what John did, but Dan's in heaven now—better off than any of us. But John sent him there. John's done a lot of things he regrets now. One of them is the way he treated you. I know you want me there when you talk to him, but you needn't worry. You'll like what he has to say."

Maggie's expression remained stone for several heartbeats, and then her head cocked questioningly. "Really?"

She hesitated, but then got slowly to her feet. "I've been hurt a lot, and I don't want to be hurt again."

"You won't be," Win told her, and he wrapped one arm around her and gave her a loving pat on the back. She stepped haltingly down the hallway.

Bray watched her for a second, then turned to Win. "I've got all I need. See you later."

"Wait a minute," Win said. "Let's go down to the cafeteria and get a Danish and cup of coffee and talk."

"I'm not sure I want to have a cup of coffee," Bray said coolly.

"Sure you do. We're friends. You're one of the first I ever had. If I've offended you I want to un-offend you."

Bray eyed him for a long moment, twisting his lips in thought. Finally, "Okay, but just coffee. The way they make Danish here makes me puke."

Ginger winced. "Great image."

They found a table near the corner of the cafeteria, and a few minutes later Win set coffees in front of three of them and a Coke in front of Chad.

"I want to go first," Ginger said, turning to Bray. "If you're mad you could take a while."

"I'll be mad for the rest of my life. A couple more minutes won't matter."

"Good. Are you suggesting that a guy who was a Christian through his teens and most of his college days got mad at God, turned away, and forced his wife to become a sort of prostitute?

"Then to keep from being found out, he kills Bryce, then nearly kills you, but is brought back to Christ when he hears church bells ringing? Is that what you want me to believe?" Ginger asked, brows cocked to emphasize her incredulity. "I think he's working a con. He's decided he can't get away with it and figured he'd get a lighter sentence if he cooperated. And he'd get your help if he said he was a returning prodigal. That's what I think."

Win shrugged. "I can't look into his heart. But let's look at the big picture—Satan was winning at Sugar Steeple. He had negated their witness and turned most, if not all the leadership, away from Christ. Then Bryce comes along. Jesus plucks him out of Satan's grasp, then Satan watches him make headway with Maybell Winowski and Maggie, and be an encouragement to Sandy Sweet and others." He paused. "Satan decides to destroy him. He probably tries to ruin his ministry like he tried with me, but when that fails, he twists John's mind in knots and has John do the dirty deed.

"But, to my way of thinking there's an even higher purpose to Satan's act. Satan was telling Christ to back off—that this church was his. In a way, Bryce's being pushed from a great height was like Satan finally doing the same to Christ. After all, in that church, Bryce was Christ—symbolically."

Ginger frowned, obviously not accepting all of Win's arguments. "But how could John abuse his wife like that?" she asked distastefully. "That was despicable."

"Very," affirmed Win. "The first rule in denying God's existence is to avoid morality like the plague. He made Maggie no better than a prostitute because he had to. Or at least he thought he did and unless you acknowledge a higher moral authority—God—there's no reason not to treat people that way. He needed the sale, and I guess the guy liked his wife."

Win hesitated. He had more to say, and he had to dig deeply within himself to find it. He went on. "In this war we're a lot of things—battleground, army, weapons, ammunition, sometimes fodder—but whatever we are—we're God's beloved children. He's big enough to withstand all our faults and sins, and he loves us through them."

Ginger detected a tear in the corner of his eye and she placed a warm hand on his.

"He's even big enough for our anger—our rage at him—he loves us through that, too. Even as big a rage as John had—or I have." He reached into his jacket pocket and pulled out the magic checkbook. "Of course, Satan uses our anger, especially our anger at God. He maneuvers us into doing things we know are wrong—things we rationalize away. But God loves us through all that—helps us rise above it." He tossed the checkbook on the table. "I don't think I'm going to be using this any more."

"Are you sure?" Ginger asked, giving his hand an encouraging squeeze.

Bray was finished listening. He leaned forward and clapped impatient hands on the table. "A bunch of hocus-pocus," he said flatly. "People kill for a lot of reasons, and you religious people can fit God and Satan into every one of them. But now it's my turn."

"Okay, shoot," Win said.

"Don't tempt me. It's about Pamela Wisdom."

"What about her?"

He pulled back in his chair. "You people have reached in and gouged out my heart. And I don't like it."

"How?" Win asked, surprised.

"Pamela Wisdom is infected with religion—caught it from that Flowers guy and now says that we can't be serious about each other—that it wouldn't be right for her. That she's certainly willing to convert me but nothing else." Bray's expression twisted in real disdain. "That burns me up. You guys are like Jonestown or that wacko in Waco—Koresh."

Win leaned back. "Pamela?"

"It's true," Ginger told him. "Sandy was telling me."

"That's great." Win smiled.

"It's not great at all," Bray barked. "I care for that woman. She's the best thing that's come into my life since I lost Diane, and now she's thrown me out with the trash. I'm supposed to be your friend, and you're treating me like an enemy."

Win gnawed his lower lip for a moment. Then he leaned forward and clasped his hands around his Styrofoam cup. "You're not going to like this," he said, having trouble looking Bray in the eye. "But she's right."

"It's something I've learned," Ginger said softly, slipping an arm inside Win's and giving him another squeeze.

"Well, it's teaching me something too." Bray pushed the chair back from the table and stood. With eyes that spoke loudly of the storm raging inside—of anger and betrayal, of being deserted—he said, "I'm glad you got your man. See you around."

"Bray, it's not like that . . . "

But Win was speaking to his back. Win felt his arm being squeezed again, but it didn't change the fact that he might have just lost the only buddy he had ever had.

The damper on his mood of triumph only lasted a moment. Suddenly Maggie appeared at the cafeteria door, her eyes huge as her smile. Unable to contain herself, she called out for all to hear, "You were right. He loves me. He loves me!"

# Chapter 23

**W**in's attitude about Chad's ringing the bells was the last straw for Worlly, who quickly asked for Win's resignation. At first Win thought about fighting it, but changed his mind when the workmen showed up to re-enclose the belfry. For the rest of the day Win heard the sawing and the nails being driven in place and before he left that afternoon the bells had been closed down once again. He bid Pastor Worlton good-bye and decided to see if Mel needed any help building what he had decided the day before would be his new church. Mel welcomed Win with open arms, and the rest of the week was spent on the phone letting the locals know a new church was beginning.

Maggie was busy too. After she'd spoken to John in the hospital, she never left his side. Even when he was transferred to North East, she came whenever visiting hours permitted. Her smile seemed a permanent fixture. John, too, improved. There was still long moments of self-condemnation and guilt, but as time passed, and Mel's visits became more frequent, John became increasingly cheerful. Each day he and Maggie seemed more in love. On Friday, Mel returned from a visit to John and told Win, "Maggie's in."

"She's saved?"

"John spoke with her this morning before I got there. What a God, what a wonderful God! She leaped into my arms the moment I stepped through the gate. Even the police guard was moved."

Maggie didn't go to church that Sunday morning, but chose to spend the morning with John.

Sunday revival services were different from any Mel had ever held before. Although he was still in his tent, this church was permanent. Along with a few others, the core group attended: Sandy and Peter Sweet, Win, Ginger and Chad, and Pamela Wisdom, whom Ginger liked right off. Pamela surprised Mel that morning before the service with a beautifully crafted porcelain cross for the altar. Mel nearly broke down.

After church, they all gathered for coffee.

Ginger immediately took Pamela aside and told her how Bray had reacted to Pam's dumping him.

"I didn't dump him. It was the hardest thing I ever did. I like the old coot, and I'm praying for him. Oh, please, pray for him too. He's such a grump sometimes, but he's so lonely. And I like him so much."

After a while Pamela decided to leave but returned just a moment later. With eyes wide and fixed on Peter, she told them all, "I just heard on the radio that the guy you shot has dropped the charges."

"Why?"

"Didn't say. But he phoned Channel Two and told them. Said he couldn't send a family man like you to jail."

"There's more to it than that," Win said, his detective's antennae up. "Sorrell engineered that whole thing, and I bet he doesn't want the attention. He probably paid the guy off. My guess is that before long, all charges will be dropped—Sorrell doesn't want the notoriety."

Then Chad piped up. "Well, we caught the murderer and he's doing okay. Mr. Sweet's in good shape now. There's just one more thing left."

"And what's that?" Ginger asked her son.

"It's whether you and Win are going to get married."

Ginger's jaw dropped and Win's formed a broad grin.

And the others in the room just laughed and patted the ten year old good-naturedly on the back. "Well," he went on, "it seemed like the right question to ask."

"But it's not you who asks it," Ginger told her son.

"I figured I'd just help Win along, that's all," Chad said.

Sensing it was time to take charge, Win said seriously, "I

don't think I'm saying something wrong when I tell you that your mom and I care for each other. But we've only known each other for a couple of weeks. I can be very obnoxious sometimes . . . "

"So can I," Ginger inserted quickly.

"And we need time to get to know one another."

"What's to know?" Chad asked.

"A lot," Ginger said, almost too eagerly for Win's taste.

"Well, I don't know if there's *a lot*," Win said.

"Sure there is," Ginger told him, still with an underlying anxiety.

"Well, we'll talk about this later."

"Oh, will we? I don't want to get married . . ." Ginger tossed back.

Mel intervened. "Now, now, you two," he said gently, the smile never leaving his lips. "What say we take a little walk."

Both sets of eyes stared up at the intruder and for an instant some in the tent thought that they might refuse, but Win nodded and then Ginger nodded, and they both got up from the folding chairs.

"I want to come too," Chad announced, but Sandy Sweet took his hand.

"This is their time," Sandy said.

The revival tent was located on one of the narrow parts of the islands and the back of it pushed up against the shore. Summer was on the way, and the day was bright and hummed of bees and the breezes off the lake. Mel walked between them. "How are you two doing?"

"I'm scared," Ginger said, the fear evident in her voice.

"Of what?" Mel asked as they walked to the shore.

"Of making a wrong decision. I made one before, and it hurt—I've made lots of them before, and they all hurt."

"And you, Win?" Mel asked.

"During my hanging-in-the-net experience waiting for my sword-in-the-side experience, I decided that I love Ginger."

"Tell her that."

Win did, as sincerely and joyously as he knew how.

Ginger immediately burst into tears and fell into Win's arms. "I'm so scared," she repeated.

Mel placed a hand on her shoulder and said some things about choosing spouses, about all things working together for good. Neither she nor Win was listening though. They both knew they just needed to wait—that in time they'd know.

They did. About two months later while on a Saturday afternoon outing they stopped in at the Ben and Jerry's Ice Cream Factory, a little east of Burlington on the road to Stowe.

Perched atop a small hill, Ben and Jerry's was the favorite of locals and tourists alike. In a field on the lower terrace several black and white Holsteins lazed about, while tagged on the side of a cluster of white buildings was the factory's most popular feature, a patio where visitors sat and devoured the large ice cream cones bought at the end of a long, friendly line.

Ice cream in hand, they found a table and sat, Ginger with her Cherry Garcia and Win with his vanilla. "Don't look at me that way, I like vanilla," he said.

"I was thinking," Win started, ice cream dripping down his chin and a dollop of it at the tip of his nose.

"Wipe yourself," Ginger said.

"What?"

"You've got ice cream all over you."

"That's why the vanilla. It doesn't show." After his face was clean again: "I was thinking."

"You already said that. You're always thinking. That's what Mel likes best about you—you're creative."

"Right—but I don't want to talk about Mel."

"My uncle Joel called today. He still wants to come up, but he's in the middle of planning for next fall. Asked again when you're going back to the seminary. He wants to examine your settings."

"My settings? Oh, the Einstein and Goofy settings."

"I told him you had a lot more settings now, but I think I

shocked him a little." She took a large bite of Cherry Garcia. "I think I'm addicted to this stuff."

"What shocked him?"

"I told him that he couldn't examine your settings until after I did—and believe me—" her brows flapped seductively. "I plan to do just that!"

Win swallowed hard. "That's sort of what I wanted to talk about."

"Yes?"

"I want to ask you something."

"Yes."

"Yes, what?"

"Yes, I'll marry you."

"You will? Just like that?"

"It's dripping on your hand."

"Huh?"

"The ice cream. It's dripping on your hand. Men sure do make a mess. I guess I'll have to get used to that again."

"You'll marry me. You really will?"

"Sure. How else am I going to get setting-examining rights? Anyway, I know enough about you, and I can live with your faults."

"My faults? What faults?"

"You have faults—big ones. But I love you anyway."

"Well, so do you."

"They're nothing like yours, though." She smiled and placed a hand on his. "But I love all of you—strengths, weaknesses, all of it. Everything but that Corvette bed."

"What about the bed?"

"It's a Corvette. If I'm going to sleep in your bed, you're going to have to trade it in for a Lincoln."

Win laughed. "Deal."

They finished their ice cream, Ginger planning the wedding, Win wondering whether he'd be able to find a bed with wide, audacious white walls.

# About the Author

Bill Kritlow was born in Gary, Indiana, and moved to northern California when he was nine. He now resides in southern California with his wife, Patricia. They have three daughters and five grandchildren. Bill is also a deacon at his church.

After spending twenty years in large-scale computing, Bill recently changed occupations so that he could spend most of the day writing—his first love. His hobbies include writing, golf, writing, traveling, and taking long walks to think about writing. *Crimson Snow* follows Bill's first book, *Driving Lessons*.

*An excerpt from Book Two in the Lake Champlain Mysteries, coming in Winter 1996:*

*Bray Sanderson, now on temporary assignment with the DEA, is part of a plan to intercept a large shipment of cocaine coming down Lake Champlain from Canada. The shipment appears to be on board a number of speedboats using the lake excursion party boat, the St. Albans, as a shield. The interception is successful. But in the battle that ensues, Bray is wounded and one of the drug boats catches fire, and, with throttle stuck, is heading for the party boat and all those aboard.*

Kritlow, William        (paper)
(1) Crimson Snow

## DATE DUE

| | | | |
|---|---|---|---|
| MAR 2 7 2001 | | | |
| JUN 0 5 2001 | | | |
| JUL 2 4 2001 | | | |
| | | | |
| | | | |
| | | | |
| | | | |
| | | | |
| | | | |
| | | | |
| | | | |
| | | | |
| | | | |

**SOMERSET COUNTY LIBRARY**

6022 Glades Pike

Somerset, PA 15501

(814) 445-5907


10 cents per day

overdue fines

DEMCO